THE WORST KIND OF EVIL

AN ELI COLT NOVEL

BOOK ONE

WILL MARLER

Join My Legacy Readers Club

Will Marler's Legacy Readers Club members get free books and unique items to accompany the novels.

Members are always the first to hear about Will's new book launches and publications.

At the end of the book there is more information on how you can sign up.

PART ONE

BACHA BAZI

fghanistan 2014

From the front seat of the refitted Chevy pickup, Sergeant Eli Colt of the 3rd Battalion, 75th Ranger Regiment, scanned the cluster of mud-brick buildings that made up the Afghan village. Ragged boys kicked a patched soccer ball across a dusty field, their bare feet kicking up little puffs of dirt. Two women, draped in faded hijabs, worked at a communal well. It was a scene Eli had witnessed countless times on patrol. Quiet, mundane, almost peaceful.

Until the boy appeared.

Eli's grip on his M4 tightened as a uniformed officer stepped out of the local police station with the teenager in tow. The boy's bright yellow blouse and flowing silk pants fluttered in the dry breeze. His face, painted with rouge and kohl, bore an unnatural sheen that made Eli's stomach churn. But it wasn't just the outfit that made Eli pause—it was the boy himself. How did he get to this village 250 kilometers from Kandahar Airfield? And why was he dressed like a girl?

"Slow down," Eli ordered the driver to ensure it was the same boy. The same boy who'd sold DVDs from a makeshift booth inside the base every Friday. The same boy who'd taken to baseball like a natural when Eli pulled out his ball and glove. The same boy who reminded Eli of his younger brother Jacob when he and Eli were kids.

The pickup slowed. Sweat dribbled down Eli's spine. His scalp itched under his tactical helmet.

"What's going on, Sergeant?" Lieutenant Reginald Hendricks from J2X, an intelligence unit, looked up from a map he and his Afghan interpreter were studying in the back. Hendricks was to meet with Malik Rahmani, a powerful warlord and informant, to learn what happened to millions of missing US dollars earmarked for a reliable power plant.

"I know that kid. His name is Aziz." A sudden unease tightened Eli's jaw. "Stop the car, Corporal."

The pickup stopped in front of the police station. Eli's eyes locked with Aziz's, whose frightened expression begged for help. But help from what?

"*Bacha bazi*," said the Afghan interpreter, his words just above a whisper.

Eli turned in his seat. "Bacha bazi?"

The interpreter's pitiful gaze stayed on Aziz. "A blasphemous centuries-old tradition. The Taliban outlawed it years ago."

"What is it?" Eli asked.

"Child slavery," the interpreter said like he'd chewed on something disgusting. "Men abusing young boys."

Blood thumped in Eli's eardrums. "That's insane." He grabbed his M4. "Let me have a talk with this policeman."

"Don't move, Sergeant," Hendricks said. "We're here to provide these people electricity, not to get bogged down into whatever this bacha bazi is."

"Didn't you hear your terp? It's pedophilia."

"And the man in uniform is the local police commander.

It's not our concern, Sergeant." Hendricks waved ahead. "Drive on, Corporal."

The pickup jerked forward. Aziz walked with the police commander, his eyes wide and framed with terror. Eli's mind locked onto that expression as their vehicle traversed the uneven terrain.

Eli's memory of Aziz in Kandahar carried the pop of a baseball hitting leather. An unexpected bond had broken through their cultural and language barriers when they found common ground in a simple game of catch. It was more than a distraction. Amid the unpredictability of war, those moments with Aziz became Eli's sanctuary, reminding him of a time he used to spend with his kid brother—a time he'd never experienced with his dad.

————

In a dimly lit room in the home of Malik Rahmani, the air was heavy with the scent of harsh tobacco and strong tea. Eli sat across from the warlord and informant, his boots planted firmly on the dusty floor, his M4 slung across his chest. Rahmani, a middle-aged man with piercing black eyes that likely carried untold horrors, spoke in a low, measured tone. Hendricks, seated beside Eli, leaned forward with practiced ease, nodding at Rahmani's every word as the interpreter translated their conversation.

Eli barely listened. His mind kept drifting back to the village. To Aziz. To the painted face and pleading eyes.

Rahmani gestured broadly, speaking with the confidence of a man who held power in a land where power was fleeting. The interpreter relayed his words. Something about local officials. Corruption. Missing funds. A party. Hendricks responded with measured diplomacy, his voice calm, controlled.

Eli tapped his finger against the edge of the table, his foot jiggling beneath it. The smell of tobacco turned his stomach.

"Focus, Sergeant," Hendricks muttered without looking at him.

Eli forced himself to still, his hand clenching into a fist beneath the table. "What about the party he mentioned?" Eli asked, cutting into the conversation.

The interpreter paused, glancing at Rahmani before speaking. "He says it's a gathering of local leaders. Important men."

"Bacha bazi," Rahmani added with a casual shrug, the term rolling off his tongue like it was nothing.

"What kind of men attend these... parties?" Eli asked in a low growl.

The interpreter hesitated. Rahmani leaned back, his dark eyes locking onto Eli's. "Men who hold power," the interpreter translated. "Men who make things happen."

"Good," Hendricks said as he straightened. "Tell him to go to this party and get answers." He turned to Eli. "Focus on the mission, Sergeant."

Eli clenched his teeth but said nothing.

———

After their meeting with Rahmani the next day, Eli and his security team rattled through the village in their pickup with Hendricks and his terp, the main road dissolving into dirt and dust. Hendricks had declared the mission a success. At the previous night's party, Rahmani had learned what government officials were responsible for stealing the funds. But the triumph didn't do much to ease Eli's disdain for his failure concerning Aziz. With the Army having no jurisdiction over the Afghan population, Eli couldn't bring charges against the men responsible for the crime. And once Hendricks had learned where to recover the power plant funds, he'd arranged for his immediate departure from the forward operating base.

The vehicle jolted as it skirted a crowded alley, and Eli caught sight of a gathering of men. Something about their hushed voices, the urgency in their movements, made his gut twist.

"Stop the truck," Eli barked.

The corporal hit the brakes. Eli was out before the vehicle had fully stopped. He pushed his way through the growing crowd, shoving men aside until he reached the center of the circle.

In the middle of the ring lay Aziz—face up, eyes open, neck sliced—a clean crimson line that connected the edges of his jawbone.

The buzzing of flies and the smell of blood twisted Eli's insides. He dropped to one knee. His fingers hovering above the boy's lifeless form. His throat tightened, but no sound came.

Hendricks' voice cut through the haze. "Get back in the truck, Sergeant. We're done here."

The weight of Eli's inaction pressed down on him like a leaden stone. He'd seen the evil, felt its shadow, and done nothing. Because it wasn't the mission. Because it wasn't his place.

Because he'd followed orders instead of doing what was right.

The painted face and empty eyes of the boy he couldn't save burned into Eli's memory. Pain shot through his gut. Guilt throbbed in his chest, heavy and hard. He'd seen an evil that threatened the life of his young friend and did nothing. And because he did nothing, Aziz lay amid the squalor of an Afghan alley.

Dead.

ONE

*E*ight years later.

Loud voices streamed through the open porthole over the pounding rain, over his crew mate's snoring, over the ship's humming diesel engines. And despite fifteen hours of pulling wrenches and changing gaskets, thirteen-year-old Cedro woke from a deep sleep.

He pressed his hands against the oil-stained mattress and craned his head to the porthole and the voices above deck—Riley barking orders to his minions and his minions barking back. Not the first time the security force argued over his porthole at this time of night. And it could only mean one thing. The same thing.

Another girl was dead.

Zoe?

How many girls had disappeared since he'd come aboard six months ago? Three? Would Zoe make four?

Kids came and went on *Leviathan*. Cedro boarded the ancient yacht at a marina in Miami, hoping to escape homelessness and find purpose for living. Zoe arrived on a smaller yacht not far from their current location in the Rigolets, hands bound with blue cord and led like a dog by a man with curly brown hair and a trimmed beard.

From the moment she'd arrived, Zoe showed an attitude, refusing to satisfy Commodore's every need. But an attitude didn't stand a chance against the psychotic Commodore, the devil-man that ruled this ship. Not a chance in hell.

Cedro liked Zoe. Liked her almond-shaped eyes. Liked how she smiled at him in the galley. Liked how she took no guff from Riley or any of the ship's officer who hounded her. But unlike Cedro, Zoe's survival skills were poor. She went too far, going off on Commodore. And on this ship, that could get you killed.

Hopefully, the commotion wasn't about Zoe. And tomorrow morning she'd show for breakfast.

But Riley and his minions were shouting about something.

Careful not to wake his crew mate, Cedro snuck out of his quarters, past the engine room, then up the stairway to the main deck. Cold rain pelted his head and shoulders. A shiver shot into his bones. Darkness gave way to flashes of lightning like a strobe light at a Miami dance club.

He turned the corner and through the downpour, he saw Zoe's naked body. Her head covered in plastic, her eyes open but without focus, her feet bound with the same blue rope that bound her hands when she'd arrived, attaching her to the leaky intake manifold he'd changed yesterday.

Below her hip, a raised red blister in the shape of an anchor overlaid with the letters CMRE. The same image on the flag that waved above *Leviathan's* pilot house.

"*Madre de Dios,*" he cried and took a step back. His throat tightened and ached. His body got really cold.

Four girls. Dead.

Another lightning strike. Another thunder boom. Another chill blasted his bones. But this chill struck him deep.

Struck him with fear. Fear that rattled every muscle, every tendon, every bone in his body. He'd been scared for the six months he'd been on board, but tonight Zoe's death seared into his brain as the last warning. Get off the ship, or he, too, would die.

"Hey, you," Riley screamed from the ship's bow.

Cedro had been spotted.

The redheaded chief of security rushed from the wheelhouse, leaning into the wind, shielding his eyes with his forearm.

Cedro stumbled backward, tripped over a metal cleat, regained his balance, sprinted aft to the stern. Funny how under pressure, the nautical terms came to him. He'd struggled for months learning the terms, but now he could recite them like a midshipman.

The vessel pitched from starboard to port, black waves banged against the old wooden hull.

"There's no place to run, boy," Riley yelled. "Make me stay out in this weather any longer and I'll feed you to the fish."

Cedro streaked to the stern and pressed himself against the railing. No lights, no land, no other vessels waited for him if he jumped. Just the dark water of the Louisiana Rigolets.

He could swim—but could he make it to shore? And if he could, where would he go then? New Orleans?

Riley kept coming—forcing Cedro to decide. Stay, and most likely die from a beating. Or leap into these lonely waters and drown alone.

He jumped onto the stern's railing, flung himself, and hit the cold water with violent force. Pushed away by the ship's propulsion, he flapped arms and legs to stay afloat, straining to see through eyes blurred by brackish water and warm tears.

The ship's yellow lights glowed from its gunwale, berths, and staterooms. Commodore, clad in brilliant white, appeared with binoculars at the railing near his cabin. Bright searchlights from the upper deck flooded the waters until they found Cedro. Commodore pointed and offered a pitiless wave. Cedro's head slipped below the surface, and the dark waters pulled him down, down, down.

Two

Soaked to the skin from the pouring rain, fifteen-year-old Tara Colt entered her modest New Orleans home to Rick's ranting—again. And again, a glass of whiskey swished in his pudgy fingers spilling on his thick thigh.

He wobbled toward her. "When I s-say, in before dark, I mean, in 'fore dark." His voice stammered through his walrus-like mustache with a half-bottle slur.

She rushed upstairs to her bedroom. "Where's Mom?" Her tone offered no respect.

"Don't you worry 'bout your mother. This is 'tween me and you. I told you to be in 'fore dark, and you're two hours late."

"You're not my dad. You can't tell me what to do."

Rick tried to follow her but stumbled on the first step. "I'm the man of this house, and I will not be d'respected."

His thick tongue made Tara giggle. "You're no man, Rick. You're a freeloader. Do Mom a favor and take a hike."

"Get down here, you little—"

Tara slammed her bedroom door. She hated Rick acting

like her dad. She hated his voice, hated his face, hated his Jabba the Hutt belly.

She slipped out of her damp shorts and tee-shirt and into her robe, sprawled over her duvet and scrolled down her phone. Zoe hadn't answered any of Tara's texts. Missing school for three weeks didn't send up any flares but not responding to her texts was unusual.

Tara longed to tell her the latest about Andre. How he'd driven her around town in his shiny Escalade, taken her to restaurants, and bought her a beautiful silver necklace. Not many high school sophomores had a rich older boyfriend.

Andre had also promised to teach Tara about modeling and making money so she could get away from this house. He said he'd take her to New York and buy her a ton of new clothes. They'd fly on a private jet, stay at the Plaza, eat at expensive restaurants, and take in a show. What a blast it would be to walk on Andre's arm down Broadway, her obscenely expensive dress shimmering.

Here at home, Rick wanted to move them all to Nebraska. He'd found work at an ethanol plant and asked Mom to go with him, and Mom had agreed. He'd probably lose his job after ten minutes, and Tara would be stuck in some Podunk town until she was eighteen.

She glanced at the photos on her dresser, a memorial to happier times. Mom and Dad together. Grandma and Grandpa. Tara at her fourth birthday party laughing on her Uncle Eli's lap. Memories on her dresser. Happiness that didn't exist anymore.

Why'd Dad have to join the Army? Why'd he have to die during that dumb training exercise?

Downstairs, glass shattered. The warmup to Rick and Mom's nightly theater. Mom screaming obscenities. Rick countering with some version of, "If she were my daughter..."

Would this ever stop? Not likely. Would she ever get rid of Rick? Probably not.

Escaping to her laptop and typing New York into the search engine, she scrolled through images of the iconic skyline, the Statue of Liberty, and the Brooklyn Bridge. She pulled up the Plaza Hotel website. Then on to Broadway. Neon lights, Times Square, playbill banners—*Hamilton. West Side Story. Moulin Rouge*. Fireworks exploded in her belly.

She clutched her new necklace. No way she was going to Nebraska. She'd run away with Andre instead.

THREE

Eli Colt listened to Tim McGraw sing "Country Girl" over his Jeep satellite radio. The early September sky peeked between the tall pines that hugged the sides of Valley Road in Central Mississippi.

He enjoyed his peaceful drive into town each morning. But today, he sang along with Tim, his mind free from all concerns, engaging in mental daydreaming of his upcoming Labor Day weekend in Nashville with the hottest girl in the county, Gina Barrow.

His life had changed since leaving the Army and arriving in Solace. The daily grind of dodging IEDs and tracking armed criminals had transformed into the monotonous life of a small-town cop. Not that he was complaining. His life expectancy had increased by at least two decades, and he slept better despite the nightmares.

"Eli, you there?" Linda's drawl crackled over the radio, ignoring all protocols. Linda Manning was the police dispatcher, town gossip, and consummate busybody, known for using the radio to spread rumors as much as dispatching police officers to calls. So, when the *Solace Register* wanted a scoop on anything related to the police, they called Linda, not the chief.

Eli pressed the send button to his handheld rover. "Copy Dispatch, what's up? Over."

"I heard you and Gina have a romantic weekend planned. Nashville. Sweet."

Was Linda really interrupting his idyllic morning drive to talk about his love life? "No banter on the radio. I'll be in the office after breakfast if you want to discuss my personal life. Over."

"I'm afraid breakfast will have to wait. We got a call from Clancy's Mini Mart. A robbery." Linda's tone took on a no-nonsense formality.

Eli's pulse jumped at something more serious than teenagers tagging the I-20 overpass. "Copy. Anybody hurt? Over."

"Not sure. Clancy caught the thief and has him locked in his storage room."

"What was stolen? Over."

"Let me see. Two bananas, a can of potted meat, a loaf of bread."

Eli exhaled air and all hope of a real crime in Solace. "Linda. That's shoplifting, not robbery. Send a patrol car. Over."

"They're all out on the interstate with their radar guns. We missed last month's quota, you know. Chief wants you to handle it."

Eli scowled, peeved for having to put off his breakfast for some kid stealing a snack before school. "Okay. I'll see you when I bring him in. Over."

"Nope. You'll be bringing him to County. Juvenile detention," Linda said.

Eli couldn't believe the uselessness of this task. Sure, Solace was small with few major crimes, but he was a detective. "Get in touch with the boy's parents. I'm surprised Clancy called us in the first place. Over."

"Kids not from here. Clancy's never seen him before."

"Where's he from? Over."

"Kid ain't talking. Clancy says he's kind of grungy. Looks like he's been on the road for days."

"How old? Over."

"Thirteen or fourteen. I bet he's from Jackson. From what I hear, they got parents who lock their kids in attics."

He inhaled—long, slow, deep. He's not a detective. He's a babysitter. "I'm on my way. And Linda..."

"Yeah."

"Don't spread this around town."

Linda laughed as if what Eli said was a joke. "Gotta get the chief his coffee. Have fun."

This was the price Eli paid for a peaceful life away from war and hard-edged perps. Going to a local convenience store to pick up a subject so dangerous the owner could lock him up.

What did he expect as the lone detective in Solace, Mississippi, population 13,517? But tomorrow night, he'd be at the Grand Ole Opry, tapping his toes to classic country with Gina, the girl he'd marry next spring.

Ten minutes later, he arrived at the store, he and his sarcasm ready to arrest the notorious thirteen or fourteen-year-old criminal and protect Solace's good citizens from harm.

Clancy, the proprietor, leaned against the cinder block building with a carton of milk in his hand, his thin frame hunched, his thin hair disheveled, his thin lips pressed tight against the butt of a lit cigarette.

Eli lowered his brow and glared at Clancy. "You called about the crime of the century?"

Clancy pushed off the wall, dropped his cigarette into his

milk, and ignored the sarcasm. "You took your time? I've been waiting almost an hour."

Eli didn't like Clancy. Nobody liked Clancy. He was one of those people a town put up with but didn't exactly know why. "I got the call ten minutes ago."

Clancy spit and flared yellow teeth. "You tell the chief if he weren't so dang busy writing speeding tickets to law-abiding citizens, maybe he could be catching real criminals."

"Tell him yourself. There's a city council meeting every month. Chief's there to hear citizen complaints." Eli pulled the glass door open and felt Clancy hurrying behind.

Inside the store, Clancy stuffed the carton into an over-filled trash bin, pulled a can of Skoal from his pocket, and lined his lower gums with dip.

Eli walked past dozens of cigarette cartons crammed behind the cashier counter and between stacked cases of beer to the back of the store.

Several complaints had been registered against Clancy for selling beer and tobacco to underage teens. Eli hoped to find a transgression he could pin on Clancy and arrest him instead of the kid. That would save Eli a trip to county and get him to Polly's Pancakes before they changed to their lunch menu.

At the back of the store, Eli stopped, crossed his arms, and waited for Clancy to catch up. "Where's this hardened criminal?"

"In here." Clancy led Eli past restrooms that reeked of urine, unlocked a corner storage room, and turned on the light.

Inside, a spindle-thin teenage boy in a tattered shirt three sizes too big cowered against beer cases like a feral cat found in the corner of a garden shed. His hair was like matted fur, his right eye wide as a four-lane highway, his left eye a swollen slit as narrow as a footpath and dark as ash.

Eli squeezed his fists into sledgehammers. He turned on

Clancy like a bobcat on a squirrel. "You hit him?" His tone was fighting mad.

Clancy gave ground and jabbed a finger at the boy. "He tried to run."

"I should arrest you for child abuse." Eli's voice raged like a three-alarm fire.

Clancy splayed open fingers over his chest. "Arrest me? I was protecting my business. This punk was stealing from me."

Eli felt the vein in his neck pulsing. "What'd he take?" he asked, even though Linda had filled him in.

"Huh? Oh...uh...he ate two bananas right in the back of my store. Plus a loaf of bread and a can of potted meat got damaged when I caught up to him."

"How much?" Eli reached for his wallet.

Clancy pulled at his ear. "What?"

"How much for the bananas, the bread, the potted meat?"

"Uh..." Clancy rubbed his chin like simple math was a problem. "Uh...Two-forty-nine for the bread, two-seventy-five for the can of meat, and fifty cents apiece for the bananas. Plus tax."

Eli handed over a five and two singles. "That should cover it. If you want to press charges, follow me to county."

"County. That's twenty miles."

Eli gave his best I-don't-give-a-flip stare. "You coming?"

"My wife won't be here for another two or three hours. I'll come then."

Eli shook his head. "That doesn't work for me."

Clancy flailed his arms like bat wings in slow motion. "You just can't let him go."

"I'm not. I'm going to take the poor kid to the hospital and ask if child protective services wants to press charges against the guy who hit him. Which would be you."

With a face red as boiled crawfish, Clancy stomped back to

the entrance and pulled open the door. "Just get him out of here and make sure I don't see him again."

Eli let the boy exit the store, then paused to press his face within inches of Clancy's. "You still selling beer and tobacco to minors?"

Clancy squinted so tight only his pupils flared. "Get away from me."

"You make money selling booze and smokes to underaged kids, yet you can't toss this one a break? I'm gonna lock you up one of these days, Clancy. Count on it." Eli's phone vibrated in his pocket. He pulled it out. New Orleans area code. But he couldn't place the number. Probably some telemarketer selling extended warranties for used automobiles.

———

With the boy in the passenger seat, Eli sped his Jeep ten miles per hour over the speed limit to catch breakfast. The boy yawned and stretched his arms. His hands extended beyond his sleeves to reveal dark ligature marks from a cord, a rope, or something else to bind his wrists.

Eli's shoulders tensed, sending waves of fury to the tips of his fingers. He should drive back to Clancy's and pistol-whip the idiot. But after catching another glance, the boy's wounds weren't recent.

"You must be hungry," Eli said. "I bet those bananas didn't fill you."

The kid lifted his head but said nothing.

"I was on my way to eat when they called me about you. You want to join me for breakfast?"

The kid stayed silent, but his tongue glossed his upper lip.

Eli chose to lay on the delicious. "I'm gonna have the gut-buster. That's three fried eggs, a heaping of creamy corn grits, savory sausage, and salty ham, a stack of pancakes with apple butter and cane syrup sweeter than LeAnn Rimes."

The kid's good eye widened like a sail catching a gust of wind.

"What's your name?" Eli asked.

"Ce-Cedro." His voice rose an octave between syllables.

"Cedro, huh." Hispanic name but no Hispanic accent. Kid's a Latino, but from where? He didn't appear to be Mexican or South American. More Cuban like Eli's lance corporal in Kandahar. "I'm Eli. So, you want to grab some grub?"

Cedro didn't answer, but his stomach growled.

Polly's Pancakes and Food Emporium had a stone façade of browns and black, with its name stretched above in bright red letters. Eli parked near the entrance and led Cedro inside to the end of the counter, pointed at a giant chalkboard where the menu was written in block print. "Order what you like."

Cedro climbed up on the chrome stool, staring at the selections.

As always, Zeke, the forty-something owner and cook, wore checkered pants, a full-length apron, and a rag draped over his shoulder. He bounced more than walked and had the ever-present pot of coffee in his ebony hand. "Morning, Eli. Who's your friend?"

Eli loved Zeke's exuberance as much as he did his food. Eli had eaten at Polly's almost every day since he'd arrived six years ago. "Cedro, this is Zeke. Zeke, meet Cedro."

"Hello, Cedro." Zeke studied the boy's face, and his brow crinkled. "Man, that's some shiner. Who gave you that, Connor McGregor?"

Eli didn't hesitate. "Clancy."

Zeke's lips curled. "Moses's sandals, what for?"

Eli decided to stick to ordering, hoping to dispel his

friend's obvious fury. "I'll have some of that coffee. How about you Cedro? You want something to drink?"

Cedro dropped his chin to his chest. "Coke."

"And what about breakfast? Food ain't bad," Eli winked at Zeke. "Like I said on the drive over, I'm having the gut-buster."

Zeke poured Eli's coffee. "We're out of grits."

"Out? You can't be out. I've been craving your grits all morning. Why didn't you save me a serving?"

"Didn't know you was coming. Have the country potatoes."

Eli slapped his heart. "How could you not know? I come here every morning, and every morning I have grits."

Zeke pulled the rag off his shoulder and wiped the counter. "Not this morning, you won't. No grits"

"And I thought we were friends, Zeke. You've ruined my day." Eli sipped his coffee.

"Don't blame me. Should have got here earlier." Zeke said.

Cedro choked on a chuckle. And if eyes could laugh, his did.

Eli struggled not to smile. "Oh, you think that's funny, do you?"

Cedro flashed teeth that hadn't seen a dentist in years.

Zeke leaned into the counter. "Well, what are you going to have, Cedro? Bacon and eggs? Pancakes? Biscuits and gravy? I got some good sausage too."

"But he ain't got no grits." Eli scowled over his steaming coffee.

Cedro's head bobbled like a buoy in rough seas.

"All of it?" asked Zeke.

The boy's eye brightened.

"There you go, Zeke," Eli said. "Give the boy the works. I'll take my gut-buster breakfast—with country potatoes."

Zeke tapped his knuckles on the counter. "You got it." He caught Eli's attention and nodded toward the register.

Eli followed Zeke to the far end of the counter.

Zeke's face wilted. "Did you see those rope burns on Cedro's wrists?"

"Yep."

"That boy's been restrained."

"Yeah, I thought it might have been Clancy. But those marks aren't fresh."

"And there's something else." Zeke lowered his voice to whisper status.

"What's that?"

"That kid's been tortured. I know the look. And this is torture over months if not years. Somebody's been working that kid over."

"Yeah. You're probably right." A flashback of Eli's nightmare from Shurandam paid him a visit. "Give Cedro anything he wants."

"Plan to." Zeke breathed in deeply. "And it's on the house. I know where this kid's been, and he ain't seen much kindness."

Zeke's rough childhood was known by the entire community bouncing between shelters and foster homes from Louisiana to Mississippi. Until the Andersons, a kind couple outside of Solace fostered, then adopted him when he was twelve.

"I swear..." Zeke stared out the window. "If Clancy comes in here, he might leave with more than one of those knots under his eye."

Eli stroked his forehead. "How often does Clancy come in here?"

"Never. But I can dream, can't I?" Zeke left to fill coffee cups throughout the diner.

Zeke returned, set the pot on the burner, and emptied the

grind basket into the trash bin. "What are you going to do with Cedro?"

"Take him to the hospital."

"And then?"

Eli internally struggled with Linda's instructions. "Child protection services?"

"No, no, and hell no." The pitch in Zeke's tone elevated. "Please, don't put him in the system, man. You know what'll happen."

"I do. He'll likely run and be back on the streets. But I don't have other options."

Zeke filled the basket with fresh coffee grinds and slid it into the housing. "Instead of the hospital, take him to Doc Leena. She'll treat him right and won't report she's got him right away. I'll take him to the Andersons. I just need time to contact them."

"Can I do that?" Eli mumbled.

Zeke leaned over the counter. His face uncomfortably close, his eyes filled with concern. "Sure, you can. The Andersons are registered foster parents. They'll treat Cedro right."

"You should know." Eli looked back at Cedro, who sucked Coke through a straw. "They're still licensed, you're sure?"

"Sure, I'm sure. They fostering a couple of kids now, and they got plenty of room."

Eli knew this scenario wasn't anywhere close to protocol, but he trusted Zeke. And Cedro...he deserved a break. "Okay. I'll take him to Doc Leena. Can you pick him up there?"

Zeke patted Eli's back. "Absolutely. You doing the right thing."

After breakfast, Eli and Cedro jumped into the Jeep and headed for the doctor's office. Eli's phone vibrated. The same area code, the same number, and Eli had the same question. Who would be calling him from New Orleans, his hometown? He hadn't been back there in seven years.

FOUR

Eli and Cedro entered Doc Leena's clinic. Pale blue walls, magazines tucked in a wooden rack, and a receptionist as old as Methuselah greeted them.

"May I help you," she blared as someone hard of hearing.

"We're here to see Doc Leena," Eli spoke to meet her volume.

With blue-veined hands as wrinkled as crumpled paper, she handed him forms on a clipboard. "Grab a seat, hon. She'll be right with you."

Eli sat Cedro in one of the few remaining chairs and leaned against the wall beside him. A morning talk show on a small television attracted little attention in the near-full waiting room.

Eli read a canvas that hung next to the TV.

"For God so loved the world that he gave his one and only Son, that whoever believes in him shall not perish but have eternal life. John 3:16."

This famous scripture was as familiar in Solace as a

welcome mat at a front door. And like a welcome mat, it produced the same indifference in Eli.

And why shouldn't it? Where was God in the Afghan desert or when his brother died at Fort Benning? Or when Eli's parents said they wanted nothing more to do with him? He had his fill of religion, having attended parochial schools from kindergarten through high school. He felt no need for faith in an unconcerned god who'd cared little for him while growing up and less now.

A polished woman opened a door and stepped out. She appeared in her late sixties, wearing a white lab coat over a green pantsuit. She walked right to Cedro, bent down, and spoke to him. "Do you like jelly donuts?"

Cedro looked at Eli as if to ask permission.

Eli smiled. "Cedro liked to empty the pantry in Zeke's kitchen. But I bet he saved room for a donut."

The woman turned to Eli and held out her hand. "I'm Doc Leena, and we got a dozen still warm in the back."

Eli accepted her hand and shook it.

Cedro grinned and walked to the open door.

Doc Leena kept her eyes on Cedro but lowered her voice. "Zeke called. Seems my intervention might be needed ASAP. I'll let you guys jump the line."

Eli had seen Doc Leena around town, but they never had a conversation.

"Zeke says good things about you, detective," she said.

Eli felt his face blush. "He said good things about you, too."

Doc Leena led them to an examination room more modern than the waiting area. She patted a paper-lined table. "Let's see what's going on with you, young man."

This time, Cedro jumped up on the table without seeking permission, probably with donuts fresh on his mind.

After taking Cedro's temperature and blood pressure, Doc

Leena weighed him on a scale and measured his height, noting all information inside a manilla file. Eli suspected the boy, because of malnourishment and abuse, was well below the physical development for his age.

Next, Doc Leena inspected Cedro's black eye, and her neck tensed, showing tight cords. "I may have to pay Mr. Clancy a visit real soon."

Eli was beginning to like Doc Leena—a lot.

"Now, let's look at these wrists." She peeled back Cedro's sleeves and examined the marked skin. "Has somebody tied you up, Cedro, say about two weeks ago?"

Cedro said nothing. He pushed the sleeves down. His cheek twitched as if his fear followed him like a shadow, darkening every corner of his world.

Doc Leena opened a door different from the one they entered. "This is my office, detective. Make yourself at home while Cedro and I have a brief chat."

Eli entered the room, which was more home-like than professional. She had everything arranged in meticulous order, much like a first sergeant. Her desk was dark wood, the chairs maroon leather. A few manilla files were stacked neatly on the desktop beside an ancient computer monitor.

Dozens of framed photos sat on the shelves of a credenza. Most were of Doc Leena and a man about ten years older—on vacation, at restaurants, with friends. In a large gold frame, the couple stood outside this building, both in white lab coats, both about thirty years younger, and both with enthusiastic grins. The photo was dated October 16, 1990.

Two board certificates for Dr. Leena Lemoine decorated a wall, one for pediatrics and one for internal medicine. Another wall had several more photos aligned in a montage—toddlers laughing, middle-grade kids on bikes. Teenagers with diplomas, beaming in cap and gowns. Young adults dropped off at college—fit men standing erect in military uniforms.

The door opened from the exam room, and Doc Leena entered alone. "Cedro's with my receptionist Mary trying to choose between jelly donuts and crème filled."

Eli pointed at the wall with the kids. "Seems like you've had a lot of practice with children. Are they patients?"

She walked to her desk and picked up a picture of her and the older man. "No, not patients. My late husband, Charles, and I fostered over eighty children in twenty years."

She glanced at the montage. "The Lord saw fit to close my womb, but these kids sure filled that void. But you didn't come here to go down memory lane with me, Detective. You came because you have concerns about Cedro."

"Yes, ma'am. How is he?"

"Physically, he's fine. The black eye and rope burns withstanding. But Cedro has psychological scars." She stared at the wall with all the photos as if she were pulling things out of her memory. "Cedro's been abused physically and emotionally and needs help."

"Yes, and that's why I brought him here."

"I specialize in medicine to heal the body." Doc Leena sat behind the desk. "But my life experience tells me that Cedro needs love."

Eli had no experience dealing with runaway teens or the foster system. "You realize Cedro is a runaway. He's not from here."

"Yes, and I do have experience with kids like Cedro." She pointed at the photos of her foster children. "But I'm alone now, and Charles has passed."

Eli witnessed the pain in Doc Leena's voice and offered the only words he knew. "I'm sorry for your loss."

"Thank you." Unshed tears filled her eyes. "But I'm so extremely grateful for our time together."

Wanting to change the subject, Eli asked, "Zeke said something about knowing a couple who are licensed foster parents who might take Cedro. Do you know them?"

"Yes. The Andersons. They have a farm off Old Mill Road. Good people. Patient people. They'd be perfect for Cedro."

Eli's mind raced back to the dancing boy in Shurandam. "It sounds like what Cedro needs is a miracle if you believe in that sort of thing."

Her facial features softened, as did her tone. She closed her eyes and tilted her head back. "As a matter of fact, detective, I do believe in miracles. You see, although Charles died three years ago, it wasn't his first time."

"First time for what?"

"Dying."

"Excuse me."

"Charles first died of a heart attack in 1995."

Suddenly, Eli worried that Doc Leena, despite her polished, refined appearance, struggled with mental illness or the onset of dementia. "I'm sorry. What did you say?"

Doc Leena's eyes lit with an inner glow. "You don't believe me, do you?"

Eli's shifted his weight, not sure how to respond. "I'm not sure what you're telling me."

"Let me start from the beginning," Doc Leena leaned back in her chair. Her tone became reverent, almost mystical. "When Charles was forty, he was driving back from a conference with a colleague when he felt chest pains. They stopped near Hattiesburg, and he called me. I told him to get to a hospital, but he felt he could make it home because the pains were minor."

"That's a two-hour drive from here," Eli said.

"Exactly. And when Charles' symptoms worsened, they stopped at another colleague's clinic where he went into cardiac arrest."

Doc Leena stared out her window. "For an hour, his

colleagues administered over 4,000 chest compressions and tried thirteen electrical shocks. But his heart and lungs didn't respond."

Eli wanted to feel sympathetic, but he had difficulty understanding what Charles' story had to do with Cedro.

"They pronounced Charles dead less than ten minutes before I arrived."

"That must have been horrible."

"It was." Her face beamed. "But that night turned out to be the most wonderful time of my life."

"How?" he said with an confused edge.

"Because I pleaded with God, reminding Him I was only thirty." She let out a brief giggle. "And that He'd called Charles and I to foster dozens of children. I simply demanded a miracle." She smiled at her and Charles' picture as if he were still alive. "Then God breathed life into him. Charles' heart started beating again, and his lungs filled with air."

Eli didn't know what to make of her story. His religious understanding was developed in Catholic school catechism, where miracles were limited to biblical times or distant aberrations.

"God gave Charles and me another twenty-seven years together." She sighed so deeply it was as if the air stirred.

Eli still didn't know where to file this strange tale. But he was 100 percent sure Doc Leena believed what she said.

She placed the photo back on the desk, straightened in her chair, and resumed a professional air. "About half of Solace thinks I'm blessed. The other half thinks I'm crazier than a sack full of raccoons. But one thing nobody can deny. God used Charles and me to be useful parents to the children he gave us." A brightness filled her eyes. "Some of my boys are serving their country in the military. You're ex-military, aren't you, detective?"

Finally, a question he could answer. "Yes, ma'am. I was an

Army Ranger, then became an investigative officer for the Criminal Investigative Division."

She leaned in with a wise and knowing look. "And you were injured quite badly. If the local gossip is correct. You were almost killed."

"You must've talked to Linda Manning." Eli tried to make his tone light but failed.

"Just as God saved Charles, don't think He didn't spare you, detective." Her voice was certain. "The only question now is...why?"

"Why?"

"Why did God save you? For what purpose did He keep you alive?"

FIVE

ndre Badeau sipped coffee on the balcony of his New
Orleans penthouse, watching the muddy waters of
the Mississippi flowing fourteen floors below. He'd
devised a plan to find more girls—but not for long-term
projects. Once he got them to Vegas, they'd be Leon's problem, not his.

Badeau worked hard to be successful. At thirty, he'd
survived in the skin trade for almost a decade with plans to
expand. Selling sex provided him a prosperous lifestyle—a
riverfront condo, a fully loaded Escalade, a small fortune
stashed in Caribbean banks.

His life, by most indicators, shouted achievement. But he
wanted more, much more. He read somewhere that a business
not growing was dying, so he figured the risk of expansion by
trafficking girls to Vegas was a wise move. But it would take
careful planning. He dialed his nephew, Freddy.

"Yeah." Freddy's voice was rough and sluggish, like Charlie
Sheen's after a night on tiger blood.

"Wake up. I've got a job for you."

"Ahem. Wa-what?"

Badeau hated wasting time. Sure, Freddy had dropped out of high school two years ago to help Badeau find girls and boost his inventory, but he mentally cursed the kid.

Freddy coughed and choked right into the receiver. "Oh... okay. I'm up."

"That weed I gave you last week holding up?" Badeau said.

"Yeah. Ahem...but I'm running low. Some dudes I was with last night almost smoked me dry."

Badeau went inside and refilled his coffee. "You had a party?"

"Something like that," Freddy said.

Badeau had witnessed Freddy after a night high on booze, coke, or fentanyl patches and now imagined his nephew dragging his tail in his Mid-City shotgun rental—shirtless, dark hair disheveled, spittle running to his chin. But who was Badeau to judge? He'd been there a time or two when he was young and stupid. "I want you to throw another party. Tomorrow night."

"No can do, Unc. I'm low on scratch. You know what I mean?"

Badeau tried to relax at his breakfast table, watching a tugboat navigate a barge down the Mississippi. "Don't worry about that. I'll rent a couple of rooms. The same place we had that bachelor's party for the city comptroller, remember?"

"Yeah, in the Bywater," Freddy said.

"I'll take care of all expenses. Booze, dope, food." Badeau sipped his coffee slowly to let his words sink in. "But what I need from you is to fill the room."

"Cool," Freddy said, his voice clearer. "How many can I invite?"

"Get about twenty of your buddies from school. Popular, like your quarterback friend."

"Just dudes?" His voice sounded confused.

Badeau rolled his eyes at his nephew's slow mind. "I've got some girls in mind."

Something on Freddy's end clicked, followed by a bubbling sound and dry heaving. Freddy was firing up a bong.

Badeau struggled to temper his anger at Freddy for not taking his job seriously. "Four girls were hanging by themselves at the high school football game last week. I need those girls at the party."

More bubbles. More heaving. More irritation brewing inside Badeau.

"What girls you talking about?" Freddy snorted. "All girls hang out in cliques, you know. Except for those stragglers you taught me to look out for."

Badeau tapped his alligator boots on the marble-tiled floor. The girls he had in mind were perfect for making quick work on short notice. They had that look. That look of no direction and an inability to fit in. "These four girls were different. Withdrawn from the others. Like all they have is each other. Like nobody else—"

"Now, I know who you're talking about." Freddy's voice came alive. "Those girls at the concession stand."

"Those are the ones," Badeau said, pleased he finally got through to his nephew. "Who are they?"

"They a little strange. Live in a group home about five miles from school. They orphans, or something like that."

"Perfect." Badeau had worked that foster shelter before with success. He had one girl currently working for him. Another he recruited had got herself hooked on meth and became useless. But any girl from that shelter would serve his purpose. "I counted four of them. Can you get more?"

"Get more for what?"

Fury engulfed Badeau like a tidal flood. "For the party tonight, you hophead. Quit sucking on that bong and pay attention."

"So, you want some babes for the party, right?" Freddy's tone was uncertain.

"Correct." Rage remained in Badeau's tone.

"Sure. I can get all the babes you need." Freddy sounded unbothered by Badeau's outburst. "I'll fill your whole building if you want."

Badeau couldn't have that. Parents crying on the evening news because their daughter went missing could cause him problems with the police. Not even his mentor, Javier, and his political connections could protect Badeau from that publicity. "No, man. I need girls that come from that group home. How many can you get?"

"I don't know. I don't hang out with them girls, man. Like I said, they kind of weird."

Weird was good. Girls who disappear from a group home are classified as runaways. Happens every day. "Look, Freddy. I'll give you two C-notes for every girl from that home you bring, you dig?" Several seconds passed. Badeau turned his attention to the traffic crossing the Crescent City bridge.

"I gotta friend," Freddy said. "He used to date one of them babes, but he dumped her because she hooked up with another dude."

"Now you're thinking." Badeau's praises reminded him of training a dog. "Get him to help you if you want, and I'll get you all the crank or molly or ganja y'all can handle. If you come through, I've got some good rock here, too."

"Okay, let me make some calls, and I'll get back to you soon." As expected, Freddy sounded determined once he heard there'd be a payday.

An hour later, Freddy texted Badeau, saying he had five girls coming, maybe six. And he had his friend working on a couple more.

Badeau answered to stop at five. Any more might get the shelter to come looking.

Badeau typed a text to Leon in Vegas. "Ran into problems, can only do 5."

Leon responded with one word. "Thursday?"

Badeau sent him a thumbs-up.

The stakes were higher now. Taking on Leon as a customer would make Badeau's business more prosperous, but it did come with risk. If Badeau's plan worked, he would have the number of girls he needed on a bus by Wednesday. If he failed, Leon would lose Badeau's phone number and possibly work with a competitor. Badeau must get those five girls to Vegas, or his business would suffer and possibly die.

Once he got five girls on their way, he could fly to Vegas to ensure they arrived, collect his money, and try his luck at craps. Then back to New Orleans to find more girls for his New Orleans customers and to traffic to the city of sin.

He would diversify in a year or two, traffic girls to Atlanta and Miami, but with the increased revenue, he would need a place to park his cash. Javier Navarro had used his Bourbon Street club for decades and became the city's most powerful pimp. It was where Badeau was thrust into this business twenty years ago when he was ten.

He should go and talk to Javier. It'd been a while. He could get his perspective on his expansion and advice on dealing with Leon.

Some people were born to become doctors, others to be lawyers. Badeau had been born for this life of selling girls for sex. He worked hard to make the most of his unconventional history—like being prostituted to deviants as a minor. But today, he lived the high life by forcing others to do what he once did. Tomorrow would be determined in the next week.

Badeau's goals were sky-high. He would make a name for himself in this town. Money could do that. Javier had proved it. And it all started with getting five girls to Vegas.

He should start breakfast. He'd heard Tara stir in the guest room.

———

Morning sunlight shimmered through window sheers, waking Tara from a deep sleep. She shielded her eyes, blinked, then realized the room wasn't hers. She lifted her frame from the firm, comfy mattress and scanned her eyes across the strange room.

Her reflection in a mirror on the far wall sparked her memory. She'd left home late last night to meet Andre, who would change her life forever.

"Everything Has Changed" by Taylor Swift drifted through a central sound system. Tara stretched her arms and let out a satisfying yawn. She caught movement in the doorway, and the door swung open.

She yelped.

Andre, in high energy and a black apron, waved a spatula. "Good, you're up. Pancakes?"

She laughed a nervous laugh, nervous about having spent the night alone with a grown man. Then, her stomach howled. She missed dinner last night because of drunk Rick and her mental mother. Instead, she remained in her room and waited for them to pass out so she could escape.

Escape had proven easier than Tara tip-toeing past Mom and Rick still drinking at two in the morning. After they'd finally settled, Tara called Badeau to pick her up. She grabbed her bag and sneaked down the stairs to the foyer, past Mom's bedroom, past Rick snoring on the couch, past the front door for the very last time.

She skipped with excitement to the Escalade at the corner. Sure, she'd miss Mom and her home and her friends at school. But no way would she move to Nebraska—no way in hell.

Now, in Andre's gorgeous condo, she had no regrets. She entered the adjacent bathroom, peed, and fussed with her hair.

Why didn't she sleep with Andre last night? Sex was a mystery, but not really. Was it because she'd passed out once they got home from all the excitement? She wished she could talk to her best friend Zoe. What happened to that girl?

Wood floors cooled her bare feet as she walked out of the bedroom to the smells of butter and bacon and sweet syrup. She found Andre flipping a pancake in the kitchen. At home, she'd have to fix breakfast for herself—definitely the right decision.

"Sit." Badeau pointed his spatula at an elevated table near a full-length window. The Mississippi River snaked below. The sun glinted off its rolling ripples like scales. Down, way down, sat the Riverwalk Mall.

Tara and Zoe often traveled by streetcar to wander through the specialty stores. But she was through with that kids' stuff. From now on, she'd live like a Kardashian, just her and Badeau, in this riverfront luxury. Joy frothed like shaken soda in her belly, rising to her throat.

How awesome. How awesome. How freak-in awesome.

Andre placed a plate of pancakes dripping with butter in front of her. "Bacon's coming right up."

A choice of syrups lay on the table—maple, strawberry, apple cinnamon. Just like IHOP. Could life get any better than this? She cut into the small stack.

What awesomeness would happen next?

Six

Eli pushed open the double metal doors at the back of the century-old Solace Police Station. Doors dented from decades of abuse by brawlers and drunks and the occasional criminal. He snuck in the back, hoping to escape for the long weekend without explaining to Chief Palmer what he'd done with Cedro. Because sure as roast beef on Sunday, Clancy would have complained to the chief by now.

In Eli's office, he unclipped his Sig Sauer P225 and its holster at the small of his back and plopped it on his desk—a wooden door he'd found in the public works yard propped up by two knee-high file cabinets. He'd transformed his workspace from a holding cell, abandoned after the city built a detached detention center a decade earlier. Although not aesthetically pleasing, the room was practical for Eli's needs.

His office gave him quiet and privacy and plenty of room, not confining like the cubicles crammed into the squad room and under the snooping nose of Linda Manning.

Nothing was pressing on his office phone's voicemail, but on his computer monitor hung a sticky note with a disturbing message in Linda's handwriting.

Call Your Mother.

Mom? The New Orleans calls? If so, she hadn't been calling from her home number, a number Eli'd known his entire life. Maybe Dad finally caught up to the twenty-first century and got them cell phones. It'd been seven years since the custody battle between his parents and Julia over his niece, Tara. Eli crumpled the sticky note and tossed it toward the trash bin. It fell miserably short.

"Eli, you in there?" Linda blared over the desk phone's intercom.

He leaned back in his chair, stared at the phone, then finally hit the phone's speaker. "Yes, Linda. Just checking my messages."

"Chief wants you in his office, pronto."

"Any idea what he wants?"

"You. And right now." Her tone carried an air of authority.

Eli gave the phone a mock salute and ended the call. "On my way, Broom Hilda."

He strolled to the station's command center, finding Linda at her cubicle, her headset down at her shoulders, her blue uniform stretched to its limit over her matronly form. Her pale lips enveloping a powdered donut, red jelly oozing from her mouth to her chin, dangling briefly, then fell on her large thigh.

She grabbed a napkin and wiped her face and pants, leaving a crimson streak on her uniform. Then, without a hint of embarrassment, she motioned Eli to the chief's office. "He's waiting."

Palmer sat behind his desk. "Come on in, Eli. You ready for a romantic weekend in Nashville?"

Eli fell into a seat across from Palmer. "How'd you know about my weekend? Did Linda tell you?"

A grin swept across Palmer's face. "Nope. The mayor. Your future father-in-law and I had a budget meeting early this morning. Good news, he gave us a 10 percent boost in our budget for next year."

"No fooling," Eli said. Mayor Conner Barrow, the county's wealthiest citizen, was a stickler about the city budget. Eli's fiancée had more success prying substantial funds from her father for a shopping spree than the chief could to run the police department. "Maybe we can start on that crime lab we've been discussing."

Palmer shot him a thumbs up. "You're right. I've been thinking about the old Stevenson Pharmacy. The place has been vacant since the old man died ten years ago. His only surviving relative is his daughter, who lives in Jackson. She's itching to sell."

The chief, Eli's former captain in the Army, and Eli had been working to modernize the department since Palmer hired Eli as Solace's only detective."

"The old pharmacy sounds like an opportunity." Eli sat erect, ready to kick the elephant in the room. "But I'm sure you didn't call me to discuss Mayor Barrow's generosity. I'm guessing I'm here about my visit to Clancy's this morning."

The chief leaned back and swiveled in his chair. "The only time I hear from that old cuss is when he's complaining about something. If I could afford the overtime, I'd stake a patrol car outside his store every weekend to scare off his underage customers."

Eli let out a hearty chuckle. "I'd do that off the clock."

Palmer scratched his chin. "Maybe me, you, and a bottle of George Dickel can sit outside his place swapping war stories. I'm willing to bet we won't be out there an hour before that degenerate Clancy sells a six-pack to a sixteen-year-old. Then we could revoke his liquor license and get him out of my rapidly disappearing hair."

Chief Palmer was being cordial, but for how much longer?

"Where's the boy?" Palmer rested his elbows on the desk. "I called CPS. He's not there. You take him to the hospital?"

"I took him to eat at Polly's."

The chief wore a look of confusion. "Polly's Pancakes? Why?"

Eli relaxed back in his chair. "I missed breakfast, and he was hungry. Kid's as skinny as a split-rail post."

Palmer's eyebrows pinched together. "Cut the crap, Eli. Where's the kid now?"

"After breakfast, I took him to Doc Leena's because Clancy roughed him up. Then Zeke picked the boy up to bring him to a foster couple deep in the country."

Palmer rested his head on his right fist. "Look. We have rules that dictate how to handle this situation for the good of the child."

"Somebody bound the kid's wrists," Eli's words came out rushed and sharp. "And he may have been tortured." He paused and swallowed hard before continuing. "So, if we put Cedro back in the system, we may throw him back into the same fire that got him burned."

Palmer leaned back in his chair and clinched his hands over a modest belly bulge. "Tortured, huh?"

Eli piled on. "Probably. And Clancy gave him a good welt under his eye."

Palmer turned his attention out his office window to the city square and the quaint gazebo that had been there since the Civil War. "What a world we live in. The stuff you and I saw in the Middle East, and then we come home to this."

Eli followed Palmer's focus. Such a serene setting. Peaceful. Pleasant. This tranquility had attracted him to Solace. A place to escape evil. To get married, have children, raise a family on sprawling acres and rock a grandchild on his knee.

Not confronted with kids like Cedro or the singing boy in Afghanistan.

"What do you suggest I do about this?" Palmer asked Eli with pained eyes.

"Doc Leena tells me the county shelter is full. So, CPS won't make a big stink, especially over a holiday weekend."

Palmer chewed on a thumbnail. "CPS may stay quiet, but Clancy won't. He's already making noise. Want's you fired. Did you really threaten to arrest him for child abuse?"

Eli let a grin creep across his face. "I did. I thought he was going to wet himself."

Palmer's face flashed brighter than neon. "I would've paid to see that."

"Oh, and Clancy wants me to tell you that you spend too much time writing law-abiding citizens speeding tickets instead of solving real crimes."

Palmer pinched his chin with his thumb and forefinger. "What crimes? The kid?"

"Yep."

The chief sat straight. "He's got a point. We bagged seven-speed demons on the interstate this morning. Clocked a plastic surgeon from Jackson going over ninety. That's a couple of grand in our coffers." Palmer flashed a satisfied smile.

"That should make the mayor happy."

"Yep. He's the one who set the quota."

Hoping to avoid further reprimand, Eli stood to leave.

Palmer held up his hand. "I'll give you the long weekend. But come Tuesday, if I get a call from CPS, you'll have to bring the kid in."

————

Eli followed the young hostess across the restaurant's rustic wood floor to a corner table near a window that extended from the baseboard to the ceiling. Thankfully, Gina had chosen the Harvest Grill, only a short walk across the city square from the police station, for lunch.

Gina sat with Princess Kate grace in a floral summer dress, sipping white wine from a long-stem glass, her eyes raking over him through long mascaraed lashes. Her beauty stimulated his senses—her short dark hair, her flawless skin, her full lips, and her dark, sensual eyes. Eli stooped to kiss her, catching a whiff of her flowery aroma that would stay with him long after lunch.

Inside the Harvest Grill, the weekend had started. Wine and beer and cocktails flowed freely on service trays held over servers' heads, stopping at every table. A young man dressed in black materialized. "What would you like to drink, sir?"

"Sweet tea," Eli said with a grateful smile.

Gina gave Eli a glassy stare. "Oh, come now. It's our weekend. Have a beer, at least."

Eli tapped his watch. "Can't. I'm on the clock."

Gina crunched her eyebrows downward. "It's Friday before a three-day weekend. Everyone in Solace is leaving work early, even Daddy and your precious Chief Palmer."

Outside the window proved Gina right. The town square bustled with people anticipating the long weekend. Some would head off to the popular beaches in Gulf Shores. Others would spend the time at their fishing camps. Many stayed home to enjoy a backyard barbecue with family and friends.

Eli unfolded his napkin and placed it on his lap. "I wouldn't let Palmer hear you call him precious. He's hard-tack Army brass, that one."

Gina flaunted a seductive grin. "I can be hard tack too. And as you know, I like to get my way." She reached across the table and caressed his hand. "What's wrong? You look depressed."

"Just a weird morning."

Their server reappeared with his tea and took their food order. Gina opted for her standard green salad with oil and vinegar.

Eli chose a burger with fries.

Gina parted her lips. "So, what happened this morning?"

Eli surveyed the restaurant as if looking for an answer. "I don't know. I get the strange feeling my past is sneaking up on me."

"What are you talking about?"

"My mother left me a message at work."

"Your mother? Good Lord. How long has it been?"

"Not since that legal squabble my parents had with my sister-in-law."

Gina's gaze grew distant. "Legal trouble?"

Eli's heart sank into his gut. He rarely spoke about his former life and never with Gina. And thankfully, outside his Army citations, she'd never questioned him about his life before her. "My parents tried to take my niece from my brother's widow."

"That's horrible, sweetheart." Gina waved at someone behind Eli and smiled. "How long ago?"

"The summer before you and I met."

She displayed her empty wine glass to their server. "Did your parents succeed?"

It suddenly seemed odd to Eli that Gina didn't know the answer to her question, considering they would be married soon. The legal battle had sent Eli into a woeful state for months. "No, they didn't win, thank goodness. But I was a character witness for my sister-in-law to help her keep my niece."

Gina watched the server fill her glass with little emotion. "How'd your parents react to that?"

"Not well, I'm afraid." A familiar panic rushed through

him. He raised his hand to his chest. "As I said, I haven't spoken to them since."

"And now your mother is calling you?" Gina giggled.

Her reaction surprised Eli. Did she not hear what he was saying? With the suddenness of a tornado, the message on the sticky note, "Call your mother," screamed at him from his office across the square. And then, Cedro and the dancing boy from Shurandam flashed behind Eli's eyes. He struggled to breathe.

Gina snapped her finger for the waiter. "Where's our food?"

Eli's heart pounded like a jackhammer. His armpits moistened. His vision got hazy, like looking through obscure glass. "Excuse me." He stood and wobbled slightly. "I'll be right back." He staggered to the men's room.

"Eli," Gina called after him. "Are you alright?"

He weaved his way through the crowded dining room to the lavatory. He ran cold water into the basin and doused his face. He breathed deeply and exhaled slowly as the Army therapist had instructed him. Then, he closed his eyes to slow his thoughts down.

He reminded himself of this weekend and the fun he and Gina would have. He preferred these mental exercises to medication. But why was his PTSD rearing its spiteful head now? He hadn't had an attack for over a year.

The server pushed through the men's room door. "Excuse me, Detective Colt. Miss Gina wants to know if you're alright?"

Was he? His past seemed determined to upset him—first, Cedro. Then, the mysterious call from Mom.

Forget about Afghanistan. Forget about Mom and Dad. Forget about his sister-in-law and niece. Forget about New Orleans and focus on the future. Gina and Solace were his life now, and he would live happily ever after in his storybook future. "Yes, I'm fine. Lead the way."

Eli followed the server to his table. "Sorry, darling. Something from work has my stomach in knots."

Gina touched his arm with her long fingers displaying impeccably manicured nails. "Is it that business at Clancy's this morning? Something about a ragamuffin?" Her tone became less alarmed.

Eli gulped more of his tea. "Don't tell me Linda called you?"

Their server appeared with their food and placed the plates on the table.

"Not Linda. Daddy," Gina said. "According to him, Clancy called his office and was hotter than Cajun gumbo."

His PTSD exercises had his heart rate back to normal, and he breathed more freely. "Yeah. That dust-up with Clancy this morning kind of set me off."

"What'd you do with the boy?"

"Left him with Zeke. He has a soft spot for kids in trouble."

"Considering his past, I can understand why."

Eli crunched on a salty fry.

"But please don't let your foul mood ruin our weekend." Gina stabbed a fork into a tomato slice. "I've been looking forward to our trip all week."

But could Eli enjoy the weekend with his mother's attempts to reach him? Why did Mom want to talk to him now?

After lunch, Eli walked Gina to her convertible BMW parked in the restaurant's loading dock. "You're lucky you didn't get a ticket," he said.

"They wouldn't dare. My father's the mayor." She kissed him. "And my fiancé is a high-ranking police detective and war hero. They know a ticket wouldn't make it to the courthouse."

The feel of her body eased his torment. "I don't know. Your father sets the ticket quotas."

"You let me worry about Daddy. You worry about us leaving tomorrow on time."

Eli opened her door. Gina folded her long legs behind the wheel and gave him a wink before speeding down Main Street.

Eli's phone vibrated. The number from New Orleans. He should answer. Mom was the last person he wanted to talk while enjoying his weekend in Nashville.

SEVEN

Eli answered the call in the loading dock outside the Harvest Grill.

"Hello, is this Eli?" A woman's voice but not Mom's.

His mind raced through his mental Rolodex. Few contacts in New Orleans remained. "This is Detective Eli Colt. Who's calling?"

"Eli?" The voice sounded tired but familiar.

Could it be his sister-in-law after all this time? "Julia?"

"Yes. It's been a while." Julia's voice trembled.

A sudden coldness swept over him. It'd been seven years since he'd last talked to Julia. Eleven years since his brother, Jacob, died during a training jump at Fort Benning. Jacob's death had sent Julia into a dark place—a place she may still inhabit.

"I'm sorry. I know this is unexpected. The last time we spoke..." Julia's breathing became erratic. "I wasn't at my best."

A vibration in Eli's chest jumped to his throat. "That's putting it mildly. How did you get this number?"

"Your mother."

When did Julia and his mother start talking? And who gave his number to Mom?

"Please." Her voice choked on the word. "You must help me. She's gone, and I don't know where to turn."

"Who's gone?"

"Tara," Julia said. "My baby has disappeared."

Eli's heart sank as the news of his niece's disappearance hit him—a new fear in the air—one he'd never felt before. "Disappeared? What do you mean, disappeared?" His voice quivered, not wanting to believe what he'd just heard.

"She's...gone." Her tone was manic. "I don't know where she is. I don't know—"

"Okay. Calm down." Eli struggled to manage his own emotions. "Start from the beginning."

A soft, slow whine, almost like a whistle, followed, increasing in volume and intensity, then transformed into a series of wistful sobs.

"Julia. Please. Listen to me." His tone was more challenging than he intended. "I can't help you if you don't tell me what's happened."

Her cries slowed, and she cleared her throat, then spoke somewhat in control. "Last night, Tara didn't come down for dinner. Just stayed in her room, which isn't unusual. I checked on her at about eleven, and she was on her computer. I said good night, but when I peeked into her bedroom this morning, she wasn't there. No note, no call, no text." Julia paused and took a deep breath. "I've called the school. I texted her friends. No one knows anything. Please. I feel so hopeless. So desperate. What do I do?"

"Did you call the police?"

"Of course." Her voice rose in volume and outrage. "They sent two officers who asked a few questions and left after saying a detective would get in touch. But, so far, nobody's called. You're a detective. Please help me find my baby girl."

Memories flashed—Eli's childhood. His brother Jacob. Four-year-old Tara on Eli's knee.

"Eli, are you there?" Julia said.

"I'm just...thinking. I'm going out of town in the morning."

"Eli, please." Her sobbing returned. "Tara's only fifteen."

He stopped at a park bench and sat. "Okay. Is anything missing from Tara's room?"

"Yes. Some clothes, toiletries. Her laptop. Her phone."

Eli glanced at his watch. Fifteen hours since Julia last saw Tara. "Go on."

"We watched television until late. Tara was angry and spent the entire night in her room."

"Who's we?" Eli asked.

"Excuse me."

"You said, 'We watched TV?' If Tara was upstairs, then who's *we*?" His voice had a twinge of judgment.

"Rick." Eli barely heard the man's name. "He's my boyfriend."

"Does Rick have a last name?"

"Bresnick."

Eli made a mental note to run a background check.

"Oh, Eli, what do I-I-I do?" Her voice wavered.

Weighted with pity, he struggled to respond. If anyone deserved a pass for their negative reaction toward him after his brother's death, it was Julia.

"Are you coming?" Julia said.

"To New Orleans? I'm not sure. Let me call you back later, and I'll let you know." Eli hung up and saved Julia's number to his contacts.

How would Gina react to losing her Nashville weekend if he hightailed it to New Orleans to look for his niece, Tara?

———

Eli's world slowed down with the news that Tara had vanished. He moved through the town square, his feet heavy, each step dragging until he reached the station. He returned to his office and collapsed behind his desk. Every corner and crevice whispered Tara's name.

His gaze found the sticky note crumpled on the floor. The message screamed.

Call Your Mother.

Did he dare? The wounds inflicted by Jacob's death and his father's condemnation remained raw. Dad said he never wanted to see Eli again. And with Mom submissive to his father, she hadn't spoken to Eli in years. So why was she calling now? Was it about Tara?

Eli gritted his teeth and picked up the receiver. He tapped the 504-area code, then slammed the receiver down.

What if his father answered? What would that conversation be like? Had his disappointment in Eli softened? Had the years healed the loss of Jacob?

Julia implied she and Mom were talking. Was that why Mom called? Perhaps Tara got mad at Julia or this Rick and ran to her grandparents. But Mom wouldn't call him. Surely, she'd call Julia. No, Mom's call meant something else.

He stared at the phone, then at the crumpled note. His reluctance morphed into gumshoe curiosity. He grabbed the receiver. His fingers flirted with the keypad, touching, then pulling back. Finally, he dialed the number of his childhood home.

"Hello." The woman's voice hadn't changed.

"Mom."

A silence lasted several moments, like the first person to break it would lose.

She spoke. "I've been trying to reach you since yesterday." No warmth in her tone. No hint she missed him. No, how have you been since we broke all contact with you seven years ago?

"I just got your message this morning." There was a hard edge to his words.

"And here it is, almost two in the afternoon." Things hadn't changed. Same condescending tone. Same demand to be available whenever one of his parents called.

"Did you want something, or is this a social call?" He spiked his response with sarcasm.

Silence, tension, and bad blood fizzled across the airwaves.

"Tara. You remember your niece, don't you," she finally said. "Your brother's daughter has gone missing. I thought you might care."

Heat simmered in his arteries. "Julia already told me. Is there anything else?"

"Oh. I didn't—"

"Look, I've got work to do," he said between teeth clenched tighter than vice grips on a stripped bolt.

"So, are you coming?" she asked.

"Are you asking?" he countered.

His mother took a long ten seconds to reply. "Yes, I'm asking."

"We'll see." Eli ended the call.

EIGHT

Eli entered the near-empty Miss Polly's Pancakes. Only an elderly couple sat having coffee in a booth near the entrance.

Zeke, a dish rag draped over his shoulder, scraped the grill with a steel spatula. "If you're here for dinner. We still out of grits."

"I'm not here to eat. Had a big lunch at the Harvest Grill."

"Hmm." Zeke scowled and sprayed industrial cleaner on the stove. Its noxious smell replaced the baked bread and charred meat aromas.

"Cedro's squared away?" Eli strolled to the counter.

"He's at the Andersons. They'll treat him right, I guarantee." Zeke pulled the rag from his shoulder and wiped where he'd sprayed. "So, what brings you here if you're not having dinner?"

"I need to run something by you." Eli pointed to the rear of the restaurant. "Can we talk?"

Zeke grabbed two cups and a coffee pot, leading Eli to a booth in the far corner. "What's up?"

"Clancy made a stink about the boy." Eli slid across the vinyl seat.

Zeke filled their cups and sat across from Eli. "That Clancy's a piece of work. Don't matter how you handle him. Hit him, hug him, harass him. He gonna come after you either way. That's why nobody will work for him except his mousy wife. And I heard she's about fed up."

Eli lifted his mug but stopped short of sipping his coffee. "Clancy's wife's leaving him?"

Zeke rolled his shoulders in a who-cares shrug. "That's what they say."

"How come everybody knows what's happening in this town except me?" Eli sipped the warm brew.

"What's wrong? Those crack detective skills failing you?" Zeke sat back and sipped from his mug. "What you need is a reliable CI."

Eli chuckled at Zeke suggesting a confidential informant. "What do you know about CIs?"

"Someone who'll tell you what's happening around town." Zeke kept his mug just below his lips as if hiding behind it.

"And you want to keep me abreast?"

"Why not? But my information don't come cheap." Zeke rubbed his thumb across his fingers.

Eli commenced to enjoy the lighter side of his day. "Not likely happening. All police discretionary funds are designated to the new crime lab. And besides, Solace doesn't pay informants."

"See. That's why you don't know the goings-on in town." Zeke scratched the top of his balding head. "You could pay me out of your pocket."

"Don't you know I'm poor?" Eli took another long sip.

Zeke lifted a confident chin. "Get the money from Gina. She's loaded."

"That's her money, not mine."

"Come springtime, though…" Zeke tapped the table with his knuckles. "You'll be married and in high cotton."

"More like polyester. Ever heard of a prenup?"

Zeke's head jerked back. "Gina had you sign a prenup?"

"Not her. Her dad."

Zeke nodded, his lower lip jetting out. "That's how the rich stay in mansions and Mercedes. They keep the cash in the family." He set his mug down. "Barrow owns half the county. Don't you have your camper parked on his land?"

"I do."

"For free?"

Eli did not disclose that he paid rent to park his Airstream on Barrow land.

Zeke crossed his arms and stiffened. "That's cold. Barrow is making money off everybody in this town."

"So." Eli tapped the edge of his cup for more coffee. "Back to Cedro? How do we keep CPS from picking him up?"

Zeke obliged and poured. "If CPS wants him, they'll get him. But I wouldn't worry about it. The social workers are overwhelmed with kids who need homes. They ain't gonna come looking for Cedro unless they have to."

"Which brings us back to Clancy." Eli blew the steam from the top of his cup.

"Exactly," Zeke said. "He ain't the kind to let this go. But the Andersons live way out in the country and pretty much off the grid."

"So, you're thinking of this as a long-term solution?"

"Not just me. The Andersons, too."

"And Cedro?"

"Good bed to sleep in, good food to eat, good people to love on him. He'll be like a hog on a thousand acres of slop." Zeke looked at the counter and the dessert case. "You want some pie? It ain't gonna move over the weekend with nobody in town."

"Sure, you got apple?"

"Rutabaga."

Eli scrunched his nose. "Isn't that a yankee dish?"

"It is. But I like it okay."

"No thanks." Eli said. "I don't like turnips."

Zeke ignored Eli's refusal, stepped to the counter, and returned with two forks, two plates, and three-quarters of a pie. "Have some. It's delicious, and it's free."

The pie was unwelcome, but the news about Cedro gave Eli a warm thrum of satisfaction. Much better than the frigid ice that sloshed through his veins when he talked to Julia and his mom. "Look, I may be leaving town for a few days."

Zeke scanned his empty restaurant. "Who ain't? You're going to Nashville with the future Mrs. Colt, right?"

"I'm not sure."

Zeke's eyes widened into a blank stare. "Don't tell me you getting cold feet about marrying Princess Gina?"

"No. This is about my niece in New Orleans."

Zeke cut two slices and put them on the plates. "I almost forgot you got family there."

"Seems she ran away from home last night."

"How'd you find out?" Zeke dug his fork into his pie.

"Got off the phone with my sister-in-law, Julia, after lunch." Eli pushed his plate to the side. "She told me Tara's laptop, suitcase, and some of her clothes left with her."

"Her mama got any idea where she went?"

"Nope. And Julia's all torn up. Wants me to go to New Orleans to find Tara."

Zeke shook his head. "That's heavy, bro. What's Gina say?"

"You're the first person I've told. Gina doesn't know much about my past."

"Ain't she gonna find out when you go to New Orleans?"

"If I go."

Zeke's eyes widened as if Bigfoot entered his diner. "You're the girl's uncle. You gotta go."

Eli's fists tensed, and his throat tightened. "I barely know her. Or her mom." His tone bit hard. "I haven't seen them in seven years, not since Tara was eight, and only a few times before that."

If looks could kill, Zeke would have sent Eli to the morgue. "Makes no difference. You're her uncle. She's your blood."

"I know." Eli's voice cracked. "But it's complicated. I still grieve for Jacob, my brother. And then my parents blamed me for his death." Eli drummed his fingers on the table and let out a sigh. "So, if I go back, I'll have to deal with all that. My situation with my family is pretty messed up."

"You want to talk about messed-up families?" Zeke swallowed hard. "Yours don't hold a Roman candle to the crap I went through. I never knew my daddy, don't know if he's dead or alive. And as for my mama, she kissed the end of a crack pipe more times than she ever did me. If it weren't for the Andersons, God bless their souls, they'd have buried me in a three-by-six box or a six-by-eight cell long ago."

Compared to Zeke, Eli understood his childhood was like going to Disney World without the long drive. He probably should be grateful to have family who reached out. And he did have a long weekend. And the skills. But he didn't look forward to telling Gina he would screw up her Nashville plans.

Zeke squinted his eyes and tilted his head. "Why they point the finger at you for killing your brother? I thought you said he died in a training accident."

"He did. But my dad blames me because I joined the Army instead of attending law school."

"Are you sure?" Zeke grimaced, and his gaze grew cloudier.

"That seems a bit of a stretch. How did you're joining the Army cause your brother's death."

"I told you. Complicated. And a long story."

"I'm all ears." Zeke returned to his pie.

"So, ever since I was a kid, Dad wanted me to be a lawyer like him. He had it all planned. When I was fifteen and my friends were getting Xboxes and Nintendos for Christmas. I received a collection of books—*The Paper Chase, QB VII, Anatomy of a Murder,* and *Law School Confidential.*"

Zeke scrunched his nose like he smelled something foul. "Books for Christmas. Man, that's really brutal."

Eli sensed sarcasm in Zeke's tone, but he went on. "And Dad demanded book reports. Wasn't long before I decided I would never practice law."

Zeke leaned back in his chair. "Lawyers are crazy. Huh?"

Eli admitted the story sounded ridiculous but kept on going. "When I bailed on the law, dear ole Dad handed the books to my little brother, Jacob, who, anxious to please him, accepted the challenge and never missed a report. Then Jacob attacked the law books in our father's study and continued the assault throughout high school. When Jacob graduated from Loyola, Dad bought him a bigger book collection after Jacob's acceptance into Tulane Law School."

Zeke rubbed his temples. "So, how did your brother go from law school to getting killed training for the Army?"

"Again. Complicated." Eli tried a piece of rutabaga pie, which surprisingly didn't taste that bad. He hadn't talked this freely about family since Jacob died. But the calls, his past resurfacing, and sitting across from Zeke had him feel like sharing. "I was wounded in battle, and Jacob got a bug up his craw about patriotism and honor and serving Uncle Sam. So, with a wife and a four-year-old daughter, he chucks law school to follow me, his big brother, into war."

Zeke's face wore an expression heavy with concern. An

expression Eli hadn't seen on anyone who knew the story—his parents, his commanding officer, his Army therapist at Brooke Army Hospital in San Antonio.

Zeke laid his arms on the table, palms up. "Man, so your dad gets wound up that Jacob's leaving the law and blames you."

"Exactly. I pleaded with Jacob to stay in school. He was a natural advocate, not a warrior. But once a Colt decides to do something..." Sadness fell over Eli. A heavy gloom crept into his consciousness. "Jacob died at Fort Benning during jump training. And his death left his wife without a husband, his daughter without a father, and me without a relationship with my mom or dad."

Zeke leaned across the table. His expression was serious yet sympathetic. "Man, it's not complicated now. You got to go find that girl."

Eli suddenly wanted to drink something stronger than coffee. "I wouldn't recognize Tara if I saw her. She's a stranger to me."

"That's why God made cameras. C'mon Eli, she's family."

"So are my parents, and they're the last people in the world I want to see."

Zeke stood and peered down at Eli like a father would a son. "That's blood under the bridge. You're wiser now. Your niece—she needs you to find her."

"I don't know."

Zeke pressed his fists on the table. "Let me tell you from someone who ran away when he was ten. Nobody will look for her. Not desperately, anyways. It doesn't matter what your mama or daddy did to you. What Julia did. Tara deserves you to go looking. She do anything to you?"

"No," Eli whispered the word more to himself than to Zeke.

"Your sister-in-law, she got someone else in her family who'll look for Tara?"

"No. Julia's an only child, and her parents won't help. After Jacob died, her parents flew in from Boston on the morning of Jacob's funeral and left the same night. They didn't stay to support Julia or take her and their grandchild back to Massachusetts. They left Julia and Tara to deal with Jacob's death alone."

"So did you," Zeke said.

Zeke's comment caused Eli more pain than the shrapnel that got him a purple heart. "You're right. I was a coward. In a lot of ways, I still am."

"You don't have to be, now. Go to New Orleans and find your niece."

The image of a little Tara sitting on his lap escaped a tiny fissure in his mind. Eli had been on leave. Tara's fourth birthday. She was giggling and squirming. Eli was smiling and happy. "You're right, Zeke. Blood under the bridge."

Now, to face Gina.

———

The evening breeze outside Bethaven, the Barrow estate, and Gina's home chilled Eli's bare arms to signal an early hint of autumn. And his arrival at the two-hundred-year-old plantation signaled a shift in Eli's weekend plans. He walked to the old manor, its massive white columns, its winding antebellum stairway, and its Old South balcony with wrought iron railing and French doors. He pushed the doorbell to trigger a melodious chime.

Pete, the Barrow's modern-day butler, a tall, thin, elderly black man dressed formally in coat and tie, answered the door. He'd worked for the Barrows since his father retired from the post when Pete was a young man. "Good evening, Mr. Colt. You here to see Miss Gina."

Eli smiled at the good-natured man. "I am. Unexpected, I'm afraid. Can you let Miss Gina know I'm here?"

Pete bowed. "You set yourself in the parlor, and I'll go see if she's finished her supper."

Eli often wondered how many butlers were still left in Mississippi. He thought Pete's position was one of many ways the Barrows held on to the past.

White-paneled wainscoting and paisley-patterned wallpaper welcomed Eli into the parlor. A mural of the antebellum Bethaven, when cotton was king, encompassed an entire wall. Opulent. Ominous. Alluring.

Pressing Eli to join its nineteenth-century grandeur, Gina wanted to make the old mansion their home after the wedding. Eli resisted, but he couldn't ask her to live in his Airstream trailer parked in the middle of nowhere.

"What a pleasant surprise," Mayor Connor Barrow said from the doorway, dressed in a green polo and starched khakis, an unlit cigar in his left hand. "What brings you out this late? I thought you and Gina weren't off to Nashville until morning."

"Sorry for the unannounced visit, Mr. Mayor. I just dropped by to see Gina."

Mayor Barrow strolled into the room to an old-world globe resting in a four-columned walnut stanchion. He pulled the North Pole and lifted the Northern Hemisphere on hinges to reveal crystal decanters surrounded by matching glasses—a bar in a globe.

The mayor held up a bottle. "Brandy?"

"No, thank you, sir. I'm driving."

Barrow poured three fingers of the amber-tinted liquid into a short-stemmed goblet. "You don't need to impress me, Eli. You're practically family."

Eli raised a hand. "All the same, sir. I'd rather not."

Barrow left the globe open, stepped to a gold-trimmed Victorian armchair, and motioned to the couch across from him. "I'm glad you came by tonight. With our many civic duties, you and I rarely talk outside City Hall and the police station."

Eli sat erect on the old sofa, his chest as tight as piano wire. It was true he and Gina's father didn't do the obligatory chit-chat between father and prospective son-in-law. But Eli understood if he disappointed Gina, he'd disappoint her father too. And disappointing Conner Barrow in Solace, Chief Palmer once told Eli, was not a wise proposition.

Conner Barrow sipped his brandy. "Mrs. Barrow and I are excited for you and Gina. We're thrilled our daughter is with such a standup fellow like yourself. An ambitious law officer can do this family well."

Ambitious? Eli wasn't ambitious. If he were, he would've parlayed his extensive policing experience to land a detective position in a large city like Atlanta or Memphis.

Barrow set his drink on an end table. "We both feel you and Gina are a perfect fit."

Eli shifted on the sofa and struggled to relax. "I appreciate you and Mrs. Barrow's confidence in me, sir. Gina is everything to me. I'm a lucky man."

"Luckier than you think. Someday..." The mayor waved his hand around the room like a real estate agent, the imposing mural in full view behind him. "This will be yours."

"Well, sir. I'm just a policeman. Not sure if I'm cut out to manage such a great place like this." Truth be told, Eli wanted a simpler life than Bethaven offered. But Gina was Connor Barrow's legacy, which made Eli Connor Barrow's legacy too.

"That's where you're wrong, son." Barrow inspected his cigar as if he considered lighting it. "When you become a part of this family, you become a part of Bethaven, and Bethaven becomes a part of you."

The mansion in the mural seemed to nod its approval.

Gina entered the room. "Why, look who's here. Who would have guessed?" She bent over from behind the couch to plant her lips on Eli's cheek. "You're not home packing?"

The kiss rushed warmth through Eli like a fever. "There's something we need to discuss."

Gina strolled to the open globe and poured herself a drink. "Is everything okay?"

Connor Barrow lifted himself from his chair. "If you'll excuse me. I'll give you two some privacy. Eli, good to see you." He offered his hand and a wink. "Take care of my little girl in Nashville."

Eli stood, shook the mayor's hand, and watched as he left the room, closing the double doors behind him.

Gina took her father's seat. "So, what's so important that you couldn't wait to tell me in the morning?"

"It's about our trip." Eli cleared his throat. "Something's come up."

Gina looked away with a frustrated headshake.

Eli swallowed against a dry tongue. "I've heard from my brother's widow today. My niece is missing."

"Niece?" Gina spoke the word like Tara's existence was a complete surprise. "When did she go missing?"

"Last night." Eli forced his hands to stay still. He worried Gina wasn't taking the news well. "According to her mother, it looks like Tara ran away."

"How old is she?"

Eli had to think. "Fifteen."

"A fifteen-year-old girl running away," Gina reacted to the news like the matter was trivial. "When I was her age, I snuck off to Meridian because Mommy and Daddy wouldn't let me go to Europe with them."

"How long were you gone?"

"Just the afternoon. I ran out of money."

Eli glanced at his watch. Gina's privileged bubble in Solace prevented her from understanding the seriousness of Tara's disappearance. "She's been gone almost twenty hours."

Gina inspected her nails. "Oh, I wouldn't worry about it. The girl's probably acting out."

"I can't go to Nashville this weekend, Gina. I'm afraid the situation is more serious than that."

Her eyes narrowed as thin as daggers sharp enough to penetrate Eli's resolve.

Sweat formed on the small of Eli's back and trickled down below his belt. "It's family. Surely you understand."

Gina's slender neck corded. "Aren't I family? Aren't we getting married in the spring?" Her words came out like a carbine spitting out bullets. She lifted her eyes to the sky-blue ceiling. "We've been seeing each other since you moved to Solace. I can't remember you once taking a trip back to your hometown to see your family. I do remember you telling me that your past is not worth talking about and to respect your privacy. I didn't press." She sighed heavily for emphasis.

Eli's stomach soured like warm buttermilk. "I was talking about my parents, not Tara. I'm going there to find her, not to see my mom or dad."

"So, you're going to rescue some teenage girl you haven't seen since when?"

Again, Eli had to think. "Since she was eight."

Gina took an audible intake of air. "That was seven years ago. We hadn't even met. You've lived another life since then, a life with me. So let those people take care of their own problems. They don't concern us."

"An hour ago, I would have agreed with you. I did agree with you." Eli straightened his shoulders and forced the words from his chest. "But I've come to myself, Gina. I have to go."

"From what you've shared with me, and that's very little." Gina's tone soothed to a sympathetic tenor. "Your family has caused you nothing but grief. You haven't mentioned any of them more than a handful of times in my presence. And when you do, you get as quiet as a convent. I don't want to see you hurting, sweetheart."

Eli wanted to argue, but what Gina said was true. If he went to New Orleans, he'd open himself up to an emotional smorgasbord with his little episode at lunch seem like a starter on the menu.

Gina downed her brandy. "Don't you get it? I'm your family. Mommy is your family. Daddy is your family. Practically all of Solace is your family. Not those people in New Orleans who cause you nothing but pain."

It would be easy for Eli to tell his mother and Julia to hire a private investigator. But Zeke was right. What did Tara do that would cause Eli not to look for her? "This isn't about my parents. Or my brother's widow, or me. This is about an innocent young girl who happens to be my niece. And she could be in serious danger."

"Why you?" Gina said like a jab to his forehead.

Eli didn't stagger. "Because I have the skills to find her."

Gina rose from the couch with Southern grace and ambled back to the globe for more brandy. "Very well. If you feel you must go, then go. But don't think I'm staying in Solace with most of the town away for the weekend."

Eli became nauseous. He hadn't thought about what Gina might do this weekend without him. He searched for a warning from her sensual dark eyes. His throat quivered. And not for the first time. Loving Gina came with a cost—men gaped at her, flirted with her, and tossed provocative innuendos to her. Men with more money, more influence, and more prospects than Eli hoped to have.

"You could come with me," he said. "You once told me you haven't been to Commander's Palace since high school."

Like a high-stakes gambler, Gina's expression offered no tell. "I had my heart set on Nashville. I planned this weekend down to the minute." She sipped her second brandy and returned to her seat.

"I know. I'm sorry. I wish I could go. I swear."

Gina sat on the couch like a pampered Scarlett O'Hara at Twelve Oaks.

And Eli, more like a love-struck suitor, not the larger-than-life Rhett Butler pleaded, "Come with me."

"Well, it's late." She set her glass next to her father's on the end table. "You need to get to your glorified tent and start packing. If not for Nashville, then for New Orleans, I guess." She popped up from her seat and left the room as abruptly as she entered.

Soon after, Pete appeared to show Eli to the door.

NINE

Soaked in sweat and shaken by the recurring nightmare that plagued him since Afghanistan, Eli sat up in bed. His hell had found him in the stillness of his Airstream parked in the wilderness six miles outside Solace.

The same dream, the same boy dancing, the same music playing, the same men watching with their same hungry eyes. And the same guilt he bore every time the nightmare terrorized. Mercifully, he woke. His phone showed 3:30 a.m.—two more hours before the alarm.

A gentle wind whooshed against the trailer's metal exterior. The calming hoot, hoot, hooting of an owl helped slow his heart rate. He slid out of bed and splashed his face with water in the sink two steps away. He needn't dwell on what evil does to children. That happened in Afghanistan. Not here.

Stripping off his damp boxers, he pulled on his GO ARMY tee shirt, PT shorts, running shoes and loaded the coffee pot for after his ten-mile run.

His Hokas ground against the gravel road for five hundred yards, then he hit the highway. Although his pace started slow, his mind raced like Usain Bolt sprinting to win gold at the Olympics.

Admitting there was comfort in Solace and probably distress awaiting him in his hometown of New Orleans, he debated his decision to return. He struggled to rationalize his risking happiness for a niece he barely knew. But he kept hearing Zeke's lecture like an annoying jingle. "You're her uncle. She's your blood." By the end of his run, he acknowledged the mission. Going to New Orleans was the right thing to do.

Although upsetting Gina typically upset him, something deep down, deeper than Eli could determine, left him confident with his decision and not overwhelmed with regret at disappointing Gina. He made a mental note to call her from the road to ease any friction between them.

Back in his camper, he studied his watch and scowled at his run time, thirty seconds a mile slower than when he'd left the Army.

He showered, poured his coffee, packed his duffel bag, and fended off bad family memories—the parents he'd disappointed, the sister-in-law he'd abandoned.

Taking a last gulp from his cup, he poured the remaining coffee from the pot into his Yeti, flung his bag over his shoulder, and stepped outside. A mist accompanied the faint light of dawn, immersing him in the calming sounds of a Mississippi morning—birds singing, the cascade of water over rocks in a nearby stream—Solace.

Invading this serenity, the faint sound of tires grinding over gravel. Headlights rounded the curve like probing eyes, hell-bent on catching him.

Gina's BMW.

She parked parallel to the Airstream and opened her door. Then, unfolding her long legs adorned in frayed jeans, she emerged from behind the wheel, striding in ankle boots like a fashion model parading on a runway. She stopped and planted her backside on the left rear fender of her car, her mouth slightly upturned at the corners, her provocative eyes penetrating deep into his.

Clearly, she planned to spend the weekend with him, but was it to be Nashville or New Orleans? Romance or finding Tara? On her terms or his? This surprise arrival had him searching for a clue.

Although Eli had settled his mind on this matter during his long run, Gina's presence attacked his willpower, like a spell from some witch in an ancient myth. She aimed at his weakness—his attraction to her.

His throat thickened, making it difficult to speak. "Didn't expect to see you this morning. Especially this early."

Gina crossed one thin ankle over the other. "I planned a trip. We were to leave at daybreak, remember?"

Eli tossed his bag in his Jeep. "That was to Nashville. I told you. Things have changed."

"They don't have to. You could just put your bags in here." She stepped away from her Beamer, pressed its fob, and the trunk opened. "There's plenty of room." She stood, palm lifted, like Vanna White on *Wheel of Fortune*.

Why was he sacrificing his wonderful weekend with this woman for a place that had caused him so much grief? "I'm sorry. I must do this. I know it sounds crazy, but I won't be able to live with myself if I don't go."

"Well, then." She left her car and stepped toward his Jeep. "Be a dear and grab my bags."

"Excuse me?"

Without pause or the slightest turn of her head, she pulled the handle on the Jeep's passenger door. "If little Tara needs saving, let's go save her." She climbed in as if going to New Orleans was her idea all along.

He loaded her bags and slid behind the wheel, unsure of

what just happened. He shot her a side-eyed glance and caught her smiling. Gina was taking control of the weekend, albeit in New Orleans and not Nashville.

What did this mean?

Eli made a mental tally of the weekend's possibilities, him finding Tara quickly and he and Gina enjoying the Big Easy. Or him not finding Tara and Gina pressing him to abandon the hunt. "So, you're coming with me? To New Orleans?"

Gina waved her hand as if repulsing an annoying fly. "Yes. Like with everything else, you need me on this ill-advised trip. Although I disapprove and can't seem to make you see that dependable forest beyond the dangerous trees, I've decided to help you. I've booked us a room at the Four Seasons and made reservations for dinner tonight."

"The Four Seasons?"

"You're not going to tow that aluminum bucket, are you?" She thumbed back at his Airstream.

"And where's dinner?"

"Commander's Palace. Where else?"

The weekend just got more complicated. How would Eli find Tara and keep Gina entertained?

PART TWO

TEN

Eli drove west on Interstate 10, crossing over the Industrial Canal heading into New Orleans. The Jeep's tires ka-thumped over each plate of the bridge's construction. At the crest of the bridge—the only significant elevation between the Mississippi state line and New Orleans —the city's skyline lay against blue skies splattered with threatening clouds.

"It's a beautiful city from a distance." Gina adjusted her designer sunglasses. "And the closer you get, the more you appreciate its charm."

Eli had to agree. "More so than Nashville?"

"I love Nashville." Gina lowered the car's sun visor to apply a coat of lipstick. "But New Orleans is a nice getaway. And where else can you find such delectable food?"

Eli's insides curled at the sight of his hometown. He was born in New Orleans and raised in New Orleans, but he hadn't missed New Orleans since he'd left to join the Army.

Too much disappointment, too much pain, and too much remorse.

Twenty minutes later, the Four Seasons doorman in a

double-breasted jacket and top hat unloaded their luggage onto a brass cart.

At their room on the sixth floor, Eli tipped the bellman, plopped the bags on the stadium-size bed, and kissed Gina. "I'll be back in a few hours. I'll go talk to Julia, then to the police to learn what I can about Tara."

Gina stepped to the bathroom with a small bag. "Be back in time for dinner. We have reservations for 8:30, and you'll need to shower and change." Gina turned to face Eli with a frown as if she'd broken a nail. "You did pack nice clothes, didn't you?"

Eli hadn't planned for a fancy dinner weekend and didn't repack after Gina arrived at his trailer. "No. Sorry. I didn't."

"No worry," she said as if his negligent packing was an opportunity. "I'll do some shopping. Saks Fifth Avenue and Brooks Brothers are close by."

Eli was more likely to walk on Saturn than into either of those stores. But he was sure he would be wearing some of their finer selections come dinnertime. He hustled out of the room, his mind refocusing on his meeting with Julia, the first piece to the puzzle of finding Tara.

———

For Eli, it wasn't Bourbon Street or St. Louis Cathedral or the French Quarter, but St. Charles Avenue, with its hundred-year-old mansions and electric-powered streetcars, that caught the essence of the New Orleans appeal.

Jefferson Avenue, where his brother Jacob and Julia had purchased their first home, was almost as charming. Live oaks served as a natural veranda, their interlocking branches providing shade for the picturesque neighborhood. Jacob had moved his young family into the uptown community soon after Tara was born. He couldn't afford it, but Eli's father provided the down payment and co-signed the loan.

It was always a source of contention between Julia and Eli's father after Jacob had died. His dad tried to impose on her life like he did with Jacob and Eli. However, his father learned Julia valued her independence more than her father-in-law's support.

Eli edged to the curb across from Julia's house. His phone buzzed. He stupidly answered before learning who was calling.

"Hello." His mother's voice blared. "Eli? Hello. Son. Are you there?"

His neck muscles constricted. He sucked in a deep breath. "I'm here." The gravel in his throat could have filled a long driveway.

"Thank goodness you answered," his mother said. "I tried your office, but they said you were in Nashville."

"How'd you get this number?"

"A sweet lady was nice enough to give it to me. Her name was uh...Linda."

Eli pictured Linda on her headset with donut-white-powdered lips, gossiping with his mother. He clutched the steering wheel with trembling hands.

"So, you're in Nashville?" she asked.

Eli said nothing, not wanting to lie or have to see his parents if he confessed he was in New Orleans.

"Eli? Are you still there?"

He remained silent, determined to let this pregnant pause go full term.

"Eli. Hello."

He relented. "I'm here."

"Oh, my. I thought I'd lost you."

Eli was tempted to hang up, feign a dropped call, but a flicker of guilt floated inside his belly.

"We thought you'd be coming home son. For Tara's sake.

After all, she's all we have left of your brother." His mother's tone was thick with grief. "You can bring your fiancée."

How did she find out about Gina? Linda, of course. The last thing he wanted to do would be to discuss Gina with his mother.

"Why didn't you tell us you were getting married?" She complained as if protesting a grievous injustice.

"Because Dad said he wanted nothing to do with me, and you didn't say a word to the contrary." He enunciated each word.

"Oh son," his mother sighed. "That was seven years ago." Her voice was a mixture of disappointment and resignation.

"Funny how some things stay with you," he said with mocking irony.

"I know it's a lot to ask," she continued. "But we need you here to find Tara. You could bring Gina. That's your fiancée's name, right?" She paused for a beat. "I have to tell you, learning about Gina was quite the shock."

Eli wanted this call to end. He started his breathing exercises to relax.

Slow inhale. Slow exhale.

"Sorry, Mother. I've been busy." He knew the excuse was weak.

But his mother didn't seem to mind. She went on. "I'd like to meet Gina. Your father would, too."

At the mention of his father, any warmness Eli tried to flame turned to arctic cold.

"Could you come to New Orleans, Eli? Today. We'll pay for your airfare. Gina's, too. You could stay in your old room."

Eli didn't intend to visit his parents. But he hated lying. "We changed our plans. We're not in Nashville. We're in New Orleans, and I'm parked outside Julia's house right now."

Another silence, another Mexican standoff between Eli and his mom. But this time, in a rush to talk with Julia, Eli spoke first. "After I'm finished here, I'll go to the police and talk to the detective in charge of Tara's case."

"Yes...I see," his mother said. "Where are you staying?"

"Gina booked us a room at the Four Seasons. But I'll be busy all day looking into Tara's disappearance."

"What about dinner? I could make your favorite—seafood gumbo."

"Sorry, Mom. Gina made reservations for tonight." Eli massaged his forehead, trying to rub out an oncoming headache. "I'll call tomorrow. Fill you in on what I find out."

More silence. More discomfort. More fluttering in Eli's stomach.

"Yes, please call," his mother said. "I'll be back from Mass at eight."

Eli lifted his eyes. Julia stood in the doorway. "I gotta go. Julia's waiting."

———

Julia's house stood out in the uptown neighborhood with its neglected upkeep—its faded yellow exterior trimmed in dull white. Its brick walkway overrun with green mildew, its flower beds with wild weeds thriving.

Eli crossed the street and stepped into Julia's yard. Her once bright eyes were hooded, her good looks still present but a few years past their prime. "Thank you for coming so quickly."

A man with a muffin top sagging over faded jeans stood behind her. His walrus mustache flapped in and out with his labored breathing.

Eli focused his attention on Julia. "Have you heard anything about Tara since our last conversation?"

"No. But I called just about everyone in Tara's school directory. Nobody knows where she could've gone." Julia turned and touched her scruffy friend's shoulder. "This is Rick."

Eli offered his hand. "Hi, I'm Eli. Tara's uncle."

Rick shook hands with a weak, wet grip.

Julia, Rick, and Eli settled in the front room. Eli sat in a gold satin settee. Julia and Rick took the two matching chairs across a coffee table strewn with empty glasses, soda cans, and an open bag of chips—a far cry from Jacob's obsession with neatness.

Eli pulled his notepad from his back pocket. "Let's start by telling me everything, no matter how irrelevant you think it is."

"Well, I told you most of it on the phone, but there is one thing," Julia said. "It's probably nothing."

"Go on."

Rick coughed. "You want something to drink, Eli." Ever so slightly, the man overcompensated his consonants and vowels. Rick was working on a buzz early. "Coke? Coffee? Something a bit stronger?" He winked.

Eli declined with a brief head shake. "Too early for me."

Rick turned to Julia. "Honey?"

Julia looked at Eli, then to the floor. A blush swept across her cheeks and neck. "No."

She clearly wanted a drink but was embarrassed. Embarrassed because of Rick or embarrassed with herself?

Rick stood. "Well, I need a drink. It's been a stressful morning." He trudged down the hallway.

Eli's gaze followed Rick as he left the room. "You were saying? Something you hadn't mentioned?"

"It's just that a couple of her friends told me that for the past month or so, they saw Tara hanging with this guy after school."

"What guy?" How could Julia think this was not important? "Does he go to school with her? Does he have a name?"

"No, I don't think he goes to her school. I don't know his name. Her friends said he's older."

"How much older?"

"I don't know."

"You ever see her with a guy, older or otherwise?"

"No..." The word trailed like Julia was trying to remember. "Tara had some girlfriends that would come around, but she's mostly shy. No guys."

The sound of phlegm rattling in Rick's throat and the smell of Scotch announced his return. He entered, balancing a full glass of whiskey over ice. Rick took a generous sip. "I've been trying to lay down some rules for Tara, but she doesn't listen to me. She doesn't listen to either of us. Does what she wants."

Eli leaned back onto the sofa to make the atmosphere more comfortable. "How long have you been living here, Rick?" Eli asked the question not for an answer but a reaction —a baseline for when Rick told the truth or lied.

Rick got cozy in his chair, matching Eli's posture. "I don't know. About a year."

The Army's Criminal Investigative Division trained Eli in kinesics, the science of reading body movements and gestures as nonverbal communication. "And these rules you've been laying down. Did they cause any conflict, disagreements, or arguments with Tara?"

"Ah...no, not really." Rick's voice went up a notch, and he averted Eli's gaze. "We mostly got along."

Eli kept a stoic expression. "Define *mostly*."

"You know...I mean, there were challenges, sure. But for the most part... "Rick ran his fingers across his mustache, then rubbed his bristly chin. "We got along okay."

These stress signs told Eli the man was not being truthful. His pausing was classic for someone being deceptive and touching his face displayed evasiveness. But Eli knew kids, especially teenagers, rarely got along with their parents, let alone a mother's boyfriend, so the deception was not out of the ordinary.

But Eli was confident he had his baseline comparisons and was ready to ask his bombshell question. He leaned forward. "Rick, I'm going to ask a tough question, and I want to let you know I can tell if you're lying when you answer."

"Excuse me," Rick said.

"Did you take Tara away from this home?"

Rick's eyes froze open like he'd witnessed a killing. He leaned into Eli as well. "No, of course not."

"Did you kill Tara?"

"Who do you think you are, you son of a—"

"Eli." Julia's voice was loud. Her chin trembled. "What are you doing?"

"Sorry," Eli said with a crisp nod, satisfied he'd cleared Rick. "I had to ask."

Julia pressed her hand to her forehead, then touched Rick's arm. "Honey, why don't you take your drink to the kitchen? I want to talk to Eli alone."

Rick glared at Eli, his head tilted down, his mouth pinched. "Yeah, sure." Rick slunk down the hall.

Eli rested his forearms on his thighs. Rick may not have been directly responsible for Tara's disappearance, but he'd played a role in her wanting to leave. "How well do you know Rick?"

Julia's eyes grew as wide as mortar rounds. The thought of Rick being responsible never occurred to her. She looked down the hall like Rick might barge back in. "He has nothing to do with this," she whispered.

"I'm sorry I was a little rough on Rick. But I'm not only Tara's uncle, I'm also a cop. Those questions had a purpose, and now, I'm pretty confident Rick didn't have anything to do with her disappearance. Not directly, anyway."

Eli pressed his pen to his notebook. "What's Tara's phone number?"

Julia told him.

"Do you have a tracker on her phone?"

Julia fidgeted and pressed her knees together. "No."

Eli relaxed his shoulders and made eye contact with Julia. "I'll need the names of her friends with their addresses and phone numbers. Maybe you could let them know I'll be calling."

Julia stood. "Eli." Her voice quivered. A single tear rolled like clear syrup from her cheek to her chin. "You'll find her, won't you? Please tell me you'll find her."

Eli looked up at a mother, not just his sister-in-law, a mother who wanted reassurance. He couldn't give it to her. Maybe he didn't have enough information. Maybe the years had created too much distance between them. Or perhaps he was trying to hide his guilt of not being a better uncle and brother-in-law. He never made promises to victims' families and wouldn't make any now. He said what any other detective would say in this situation. "I'll need to see her room."

––––––––

Tara's bedroom would impress any drill sergeant. A taut bed cover with squared corners and every item in the room seemed to have its place. It took nine weeks of Army boot camp and six years in the service to drill this type of orderliness into Eli. Jacob had been organized for as long as Eli could remember, and it appeared he passed his neat freak gene to his only child.

Posters of pop stars and actors adorned the walls. Most were unfamiliar to Eli. But they hung in a sharp symmetry. So were Tara's photos on her dresser, her nightstand, and a montage on a cork board above her desk.

Several of the photos were of Tara and a girl her age. The

two contrasted in appearance. Tara had delicate features, blonde hair, light eyes. Her friend had dark hair, dark eyes, and a bi-racial complexion. They posed on a streetcar bench and arm-in-arm at the Audubon Zoo. And in front of a dull-painted door between peeling columns, Tara with two fingers raised behind her friend's head.

An inner glow had Eli smiling. He removed the photo from its frame to examine it closer and to hopefully connect with his estranged niece somehow. He tucked the image between his notepad pages. He'd ask Julia for the friend's name when he completed searching the room.

He went to Tara's nightstand. Inside the drawer lay one item. A picture of Eli and Jacob at Jacob's graduation from Loyola—Jacob in cap and gown, Eli in his pressed Army uniform. A fracture formed in Eli's chest. It stretched and grew until his heart ached from the strain. He shut the drawer but not the memory. Coming here, surrounded by remembrances, Eli couldn't help but miss Jacob. And Eli knew he had to find Tara—Jacob's only child.

Another glance and the room offered more. On Tara's dresser, among pictures of her with her father and mother and Tara's birthday celebrations arranged from age one to five, was another photo. As a young Army corporal, Eli sat on the downstairs settee with a flushed-cheeked four-year-old Tara laughing in his lap. The image pierced Eli like shrapnel once struck his body, but this time pricking Eli's heart.

He stroked the glass over the photo. The gap in his heart now a canyon. His lashes turned warm, then wet. If only he could go back to the time this picture was taken. With Jacob alive and in this house, a happy home.

But Eli refocused. This photo showed that Tara missed her father, who died way too early. Fathers are important to young girls. To adult brothers too.

The photo haunted Eli.

Eli should've filled the void Jacob's death left behind. As an uncle to Tara, he'd failed. Failed to the point that she'd deliberately run away.

Eli sensed a brutal enemy. A familiar enemy he'd once encountered in Afghanistan that hid in the shadows. An enemy that preyed on kids.

He gazed at the photo with sadness. "I'll find you, I promise." Eli said to the photo as if Tara could hear.

ELEVEN

li parked three blocks from the New Orleans Police Department on South Broad Street near City Hall. As an Army CID investigator, he'd dropped in on local authorities dozens of times, checking in to give a courtesy heads-up that he'd be working a case in their town. That's when he was in the military and part of the federal government. Now, he carried a badge from Solace, Mississippi, which carried the same weight outside his jurisdiction as a tin star found in a box of Cracker Jack's.

He pushed open the front doors, emptied his pockets on the security system's conveyor belt, walked through the scanner, showed his identification, and stopped at the information desk. "I'm here to talk to the detective in charge of Tara Colt's disappearance. I'm her uncle."

A uniformed officer handed him a visitors' pass and pointed to a bank of elevators. "Go to the second floor and check with the desk sergeant."

The desk sergeant escorted him through a near-empty squad room to the chief of detective's office.

Captain Leo Guidry, a fit man of about forty with a

ruddy complexion and pale eyes, sat behind a metal desk. He wore chinos, a short-sleeved button-down shirt, and a friendly expression. He glanced at Eli's badge and ID and motioned to a straight-back chair made for quick conversations. "Have a seat, Detective Colt." Guidry's accent was thick Cajun.

"You're lucky I'm here on a holiday weekend. My in-laws are in town, yeah?" He winked as if his secret was safe with Eli. "So, I took the opportunity to get some paperwork done." The captain held out Eli's badge. "Solace, Mississippi? I don't believe I've ever heard of it."

Eli nodded. "I don't expect you have. Small town. Small force."

"Well, I'm from Mamou, Louisiana." He pronounced the state Lew-zee-ana. "A city that counts pets and rag dolls for the population sign coming into town." Guidry handed Eli his ID. "Anyway, I hope you enjoy your stay in New Orleans and find it productive. If you need anything, I'm the guy to ask. I can't promise to be accommodating, but if it's within my power to help, I'll be happy to do it. So, with that out of the way, what brings you to New Orleans?"

Eli explained Tara's disappearance and that she'd been missing for nearly thirty-seven hours. "The girl's mother is upset and asked me to look into her daughter's disappearance."

Guidry scribbled on a legal pad. "And you're here to ensure we're doing our job, yeah?"

"Something like that."

Guidry clicked his keyboard and studied the computer screen. "Well, the case is in the system. Reggie's got it. Reggie Toussaint." He lifted his eyes from the screen to gaze at Eli. "You learn anything yet?"

"Nothing specific, but here's a photo." Eli pulled the picture of Tara and her friend from his notepad. "The girl making the hand gesture is my niece. According to my sister-in-law, the other girl's name is Zoe Prevost."

Guidry glanced at the photo and returned it to Eli. "You talk to Prevost's family?"

It was a fair question. Eli had considered driving to the Prevost house before coming to the police station. But that could have set the wrong tone for a solid work relationship. "No sir. I figured I should check in with you first."

Guidry nodded approvingly. "What's your niece's home like? Problems?"

"My brother died seven years ago, but his wife and daughter seem to have adjusted." Eli lied, unwilling to admit to his absence during Tara and Julia's time of need.

"More times than not, these kids run away because of an argument or problems at home. So, she's been gone, what...over thirty-six hours, you said." Guidry punched the keypad to his desk phone three times and picked up the receiver. "Reggie in?" He listened, hung up, and stood. "Follow me."

They walked through the squad room. Most desks were empty except for a few plain-clothes policemen scanning their computers or on their phones. Eli and Guidry turned a corner to find a pear-shaped detective, his back to them, sitting in his cubicle like a chubby bear stuffed in a small cage. On his desktop, two paper cups lay on a coffee-stained file next to a half-filled box of donut holes. Toussaint popped a pastry into his mouth with a hand the size of a catcher's mitt.

"Reggie." Guidry's greeting caused Toussaint to lurch in his seat. "This is Detective Eli Colt from Solace, Mississippi."

The hinges of Toussaint's chair sang as he turned toward Eli and Guidry. A catalog of women's photos filled his computer screen with the name of a dating site at the top. The man had watery eyes, a bulbous nose, and stringy hair two months past due for the barber.

Guidry fixed his eyes on the monitor. "Detective Colt's here about his niece who went missing yesterday."

Toussaint straightened and tapped the keyboard repeatedly until the website finally disappeared.

"You caught a case yesterday." Guidry glanced at his legal pad. "Tara Colt. Been missing since late yesterday."

Brushing sugar glaze from his chest, Toussaint spread a smear across his NOPD pullover. Red splotches crept across his cheeks. "Yeah. I looked over the file yesterday. Called the house a couple of hours ago, but nobody answered." Toussaint rubbed his thick double chin, displaying similar stress signs as Rick, Julia's boyfriend.

Eli didn't react to the lie. He'd been at Tara's home two hours ago, and there'd been no call.

"Well, this is the girl's uncle," Guidry said. "You keep him up to date."

"Hold on, cap." Toussaint put his glaze-crusted fingers on a stack of files. "My plate's brimming over with new cases, and I have more in open and unsolved."

Guidry gave the computer monitor a tight-eyed stare as if the dating site remained. "I expect you to keep Detective Colt up to speed with his niece's case." Guidry turned with a shake of his head and walked off. "And straighten your workspace."

"*Salaud*," Toussaint mumbled like a schoolboy caught cheating but not sorry for his sin. He shut his computer down and lifted his massive torso from the chair. "I'm going to grab a smoke." His tone was not pleasant.

Eli felt like spitting, disgusted with the detestable detective who caught Tara's case. Regardless, he followed him outside to a dumpster surrounded by cigarette butts.

"Been on the job since ninety-seven. Longer than him." Toussaint pointed his cigarette back toward the station, then struggled to light it due to a sudden gust of wind.

The man was a slob and unprofessional. But Eli needed to

tread carefully and keep his temper in check. No matter Eli's opinion of this slug, it would be better if Toussaint would work with and not against Eli.

"I'm not here to jam you, Detective." Eli made his tone sound friendlier than he felt. "How about I buy you lunch?"

Toussaint's shoulders loosened, and for the first time, he focused on Eli. "Now you're talking. Where'd you have in mind?"

"You choose."

Toussaint shot Eli an open-mouth smile, revealing the dark fillings in his back teeth. "I know a place."

———

Eli sat across from Toussaint at a dark wooden table under a Dixie Beer logo and a photo of The Parkway Tavern as it stood in 1965. Eli salted his cheese fries. Toussaint poured Tabasco over the roast beef on his po'boy sandwich.

"The place used to comp cops' meals back in the day," Toussaint said. "Now, you can't get so much as a free drink anywhere." He wiped gravy from his chin and took a large pull from his draft beer. "How do they take care of the police in, uh...where'd you say you from? Starkville?

"Solace," Eli said, thinking of Zeke and Polly's Pancakes. "Not bad. Small town, you know?"

Toussaint grunted and took a bite of his sandwich, chewing like a cow eating hay. "Man, times are a changing. I miss when men were men, and police were treated like royalty."

It wasn't hard for Eli to get the measure of the guy sitting across the table. After seeing Toussaint with his disheveled hair, obese frame, and cynical attitude, the detective was clearly in the waning years of his career and had no intention of working Tara's case with the commitment it deserved.

"So," Eli said. "How long have you been with NOPD?"

"Started back in the nineties. No Black Lives Matter, then, I tell ya. No defund the police, no homeless under the overpasses, no video phones waiting to end your career. That's when we would come to a pub like this, and they would roll out the red carpet. Today, you show a badge and hope they don't spit in your food." Toussaint studied his beer as if he should order another.

Eli regrettably agreed with Toussaint's complaint. He had friends and acquaintances who were cops in urban areas. It was getting tough for cops, especially those who worked in the larger cities. "Been in missing persons long?"

Toussaint leaned back from his sandwich and crossed his arms over a spot of gravy he spilled on his chest. "Why do you ask?" he said, his pale face flushed red.

A weight of regret settled on Eli for his unintentional slight. In the metropolitan police departments, missing persons served as a temporary post on the path to a gold shield and homicide. Rarely would a detective Toussaint's age find themselves still stuck in missing persons. "Just making conversation, that's all."

Toussaint returned to his beer. "So, what do you do in Somerville, fella?"

Eli forced a smile. "I'm just a small-town cop. Yesterday, I picked up a teenager for stealing bananas."

Toussaint lifted his chin and picked up his sandwich. "Being a cop in the big city ain't easy. missing persons is an important job, and I do it well. It's a good fit for me."

Eli nodded as if he agreed with this clueless idiot. "How many missing kids do you get in a year?"

"Plenty," Toussaint said, filling his lungs to their fullest. "Seems like an amber alert goes off every hour. I have a dozen files on my desk right now. And those are the recent ones. I got thirty or more open and unsolved."

"Is Tara Colt's file on your desk."

"It was reported, what...yesterday?"

"Yesterday morning."

"I talked to the girl's mom, of course." Toussaint rolled his shoulders, another tell of the same lie. "I'll get out to her house after the weekend. I'm leaving for my fishing camp this afternoon after my shift."

Eli thought back to Zeke, explaining how if Eli didn't look for Tara, nobody would. "Taking advantage of the long weekend?"

"Yep." Toussaint's jowls lifted with the corners of his mouth. "I'll be casting a line before dark."

Eli lifted his iced tea but hesitated before drinking. "So, you haven't looked into Tara Colt's case yet."

"Like-I-said." He emphasized every word. "I have over a dozen files on my desk, and the Colt girl is on the bottom. It was last in and will get the last look."

Eli's ears burned hot. He placed his hands under the table and pressed them against his jeans. How'd this guy get to be a policeman? He'd worked with many detectives close to retirement. They counted the days until they could put a golf club or fishing rod in their hands seven days a week. "Trust me. I understand. I'm a small-town cop now, but I used to work as an investigator for the Army. I worked with enough city detectives to know you got plenty on your plate."

Toussaint crammed the last of his sandwich into his mouth. "So, what's the fishing like where you come from?"

"Freshwater mainly." Eli was no fisherman. But he understood the local fishing from tall tales told by men during breakfast at Polly's. "Perch, catfish, bass. Nothing like around here."

The sloth detective welcomed the change in subject. He took another swig of his beer. "Here we got the best of both worlds. Freshwater in the lakes and inlets, and saltwater in the gulf. I got a camp not too far from here."

"Yeah? Go there much?"

"Not nearly enough. But I'll be living there after I pull the pin." He rubbed a napkin across his mouth. "Hey, I could take you out on my boat. So when exactly are you leaving town?"

There was an obvious purpose behind Toussaint's question. He wanted to know when Eli would leave town and cease to be a threat to Toussaint's lazy work ethic.

"My fiancée would rather we were in Nashville. We were supposed to go there for the weekend before I learned Tara had disappeared."

"Well, I wouldn't worry too much about your niece. She'll show up sooner or later, and we'll learn she had a blowout with her mom or dad."

It was clear to Eli that Toussaint lacked the passion for the job and possibly never had it. "Not her dad. My brother is dead."

Toussaint took another sip of his beer. "Whatever."

Instead of reaching across the table and breaking this jerk's nose, Eli remained polite, not wanting to alienate himself from the NOPD on his first day in town. "Mind if I poke around and see what I can learn while you're fishing? I'll share anything I learn."

Toussaint wiped his lips with his forearm and shot Eli a challenging stare. "I do. I don't take kindly to out-of-town cops poking around my city."

Eli eased back and opened his posture. "But I'm her uncle."

"Guidry said to keep you up to date, not give you carte blanche of this city. The only place that badge in your pocket works is in that hick town of yours." Toussaint waved to the waiter and pointed at his empty mug. "I catch you flashing your hardware around town, and I'll lock you up for obstruction of justice. You hear?"

Lifting his hands and showing Toussaint both palms, Eli slid his chair away from the table. "Hold on, detective. I just want my niece found. We're on the same team."

"Are we? You look like a hotshot to me. And believe me. I can spot a hotshot from a nautical mile." Toussaint's empty mug was replaced with a full one, and he chugged a third of it down. "Hotshot thinks he knows better than a seasoned detective," he mumbled.

"That's not me. I'm happy in my hick town running down kids smoking pot in their daddy's pickup. I just want to know everything is being done about my niece. I promised her mom."

Toussaint flipped a business card at Eli like a Vegas dealer. "Call me Tuesday, and I'll let you know where we stand." He sucked down the rest of his beer, stood, then motioned to the waiter. "Bring him the check."

Toussaint turned to leave as his phone chirped in his pocket. He stopped, looked at the screen, and answered. "What...huh...the Rigolets?" His eyes found Eli's. "How old?" He terminated the call and turned toward Eli.

Eli sensed something was breaking in Tara's case. "What is it?"

"How old did you say your niece is?"

"Fifteen. Why?"

"Girl about that age washed up near St. Tammany Parish. In the Rigolets." A satisfied grin spread on Toussaint's face. "I gotta get out there and see if I can close her file before the weekend."

TWELVE

Eli parked his Jeep facing the early afternoon sun that disappeared behind purple-tinged clouds over the Rigolets, a deep-water channel that connected Lake Pontchartrain with the Gulf of Mexico. Blue lights flickered through thick, damp air from three police cruisers parked among pickup trucks and aluminum trailers at a boat launch alongside Fort Pike. A young Eli had visited the nineteenth-century fortification on an eighth-grade field trip that included the nearby Chalmette Battle Grounds during their studies of the War of 1812.

Eli exited his Jeep to the stench of rotting flesh. His stomach roiled like the sea in a Cat 5 hurricane, but not because of the odor. He had experienced the sights, sounds, and smells of death in the Afghan desert and dozens of murder scenes. But he wasn't there to battle Islamic extremists. He was there to possibly identify Tara's body and make his nightmares more unbearable.

Eli grabbed his rucksack from the back seat and stepped to the outlying police tape that extended the length of a football field from the water's edge to a chain link fence that bordered

Fort Pike. He maneuvered for several yards around puddles and discarded beer cans. Bamboo stalks brushed against his blue jeans, and jagged-edged limestone tried to penetrate the thick soles of his boots.

A young, uniformed patrolwoman with bleary eyes, a sweaty forehead, and a name tag that read *Pierce* stood guard with a clipboard by an opening in the tape near the fence. "Name and badge." Her voice was shaky, her complexion pale, her eyelids fell low.

Pulling out his Solace police shield, Eli hoped she'd overlook his jurisdiction.

Pierce studied Eli's credentials, then put her hand on her chest and dry heaved. "What's that say?" she said shakily. "Solace?"

The girl's obvious distress from the smell had Eli reach inside his rucksack. "Yes. I'm here with Detective Toussaint." Eli produced a jar of vapor rub and waved a finger above his upper lip. "It helps with the smell."

Pierce wrote his name on the clipboard, then dipped her finger in the jelly and rubbed it under her nose. "Thanks." She handed him back the vapor rub, then looked back to the crime scene. "But I'll need to confirm you're working with Toussaint."

A barrel-chested man in his fifties with a creole complexion and a gold shield in his right hand arrived at the tape from the boat launch. He wore dark slacks, a white shirt, and a blue blazer. "Manny Mancuso. Homicide."

Wheeling away from Eli and Mancuso, Pierce dropped her hands to her knees and wretched.

Mancuso touched the girl's shoulder like a doting father. "You okay, officer?"

Pierce shuttered a gag. "I'm sorry sir."

"No need to be sorry," Mancuso said. "It's a tough odor to get used to, but you'll be fine. I'm going in, okay?"

She breathed through an open mouth. "Okay."

Mancuso came belly-to-belly with Eli. "You a reporter?"

Eli showed his badge. "No sir." He tilted his head toward the crime scene. "I'm here to see if that's my niece."

Mancuso opened Eli's credentials, pulled half glasses from his jacket, and placed them on his nose. "Solace, huh? Been through there on my way to Memphis. Nice quiet town."

"Yes sir."

Mancuso peered at the shoreline. "What makes you think she could be your niece?"

Eli massaged the back of his neck. "Tara disappeared last night. Detective Toussaint said the girl they found is about her age."

"Toussaint, huh?" Mancuso rubbed his close-cropped, silver hair. "You know Reggie?"

"Nope. Just met him today. He caught my niece's case."

Mancuso adjusted his glasses and glanced at Eli's identification again. Time seemed to slow, and Eli felt a prickling under his scalp. Finally, Mancuso patted Eli on the shoulder. "Okay son. Let's pray she's not your niece."

Eli and Mancuso moved about a hundred yards to the shoreline. Men and women clad in reflective yellow-green windbreakers, CSU (Crime Scene Unit) emblazoned on their backs, scoured the grounds, and flashed cameras. A grey-bearded man in a white hazmat, probably the medical examiner, hunched over a corpse by the water's edge.

Toussaint paced inside a fifteen-foot section around the body bordered by police tape, a phone pressed to his ear. A swirl of smoke trailed the lit cigarette he held between two fingers. Eli trod closer to the crime scene, stopping at the yellow blockade about ten yards from a girl's nude body. Her head turned away from Eli, making her impossible for him to identify.

The medical examiner reacted to Eli's presence and looked up. "How'd you get back here?"

"I'm with Mancuso. Here to identify the body if I can."

The medical examiner stood and stretched.

Toussaint stampeded toward Eli like a buffalo in an old western. "Didn't I warn you? If I caught you poking around my city, I'd—"

"Reggie." Mancuso boomed the name in a guttural roar. Toussaint stopped like a dog restrained by a short chain on its collar. Ashes spilled from his cigarette.

"You're trampling over my crime scene. What are you, a rookie?" Mancuso's voice was sharp and biting. "And you're smoking, leaving ash everywhere?"

"They've been over this area already," said Toussaint with a defiant expression.

"Doesn't matter." Mancuso paced the tape line, his nostrils red and flaring. "CSU is still working the area. You should know better."

Toussaint sneered and motioned at Eli. "What's he doing here? I told him to stay clear."

Mancuso drew a breath and released it before speaking. "He's here to identify the body if he can. Now get out of the perimeter."

Retreating under the tape, Toussaint muttered something inaudible.

"What do we have here, Charlie?" Mancuso asked the ME.

Charlie stepped away from the body. "Fourteen or fifteen-year-old female, naked as the day she was born."

"Can we come closer?" Mancuso asked.

Charlie removed his plastic gloves. "Sure, I'm finished with this section. But I'll need to get Toussaint's shoes for impressions. He paraded around here before we gave the okay."

Mancuso cupped his hand around his mouth to shout

something, then thought better. "I'll take care of it," Mancuso said to Charlie.

Eli slipped under the tape to approach the body, his heart striking his ribcage like a bell clapper. The young girl's corpse rested face-up on football-sized breakwater stones, open eyes staring past him. He pressed his hand to his forehead. It was Tara's friend, not Tara.

The choppy channel sloshed beside Zoe Prevost, then retreated to the inlet. A blue cord with a frayed end extended six feet from a knot tied at her ankles. Eli covered his eyes with a trembling hand.

"What's this above her left calf," Mancuso said.

Charlie answered without looking. "Burnt flesh."

Mancuso leaned in lower. "What is that? CRME and an anchor? Looks like some sort of logo."

"A brand," Eli said. "The girl was branded."

Charlie peered at Eli with a puzzled expression.

"This is what Mississippi calls a policeman. Meet Detective Eli Colt. Eli, this is Charlie Latimore, New Orleans' finest forensic pathologist."

"Pleasure," Charlie said. "I'd say the branding happened before the time of death. Maybe a week or two, judging by how far along it's healed. He pointed at the blue line. "She was in the water a few days before whatever she was tied to broke free."

Mancuso stepped to the other side of the body. "So you're calling it a homicide?"

"I am," Charlie said. "I'm calling it now."

"Well Detective Colt?" It was clear Mancuso didn't want to ask if it was Tara. "Take your time, son."

Eli pulled out his notepad and handed Mancuso the photo he'd taken from Tara's bedroom. "My niece is the girl holding two fingers over your victim's head. According to my sister-in-law, this girl's name is Zoe Prevost."

Mancuso studied the photograph, then the girl. Finally, he lowered his head in disgust or prayer. Eli couldn't tell. "Who found her?" Mancuso asked Charlie.

Charlie looked out into the channel. "A couple of fishermen coming in from the Gulf. The smell got their attention. Plus, buzzards were circling overhead."

Eli scanned the body for other trauma, and faint marks on her neck caught his attention. "You have a cause of death?"

Charlie's expression tightened as if he were frustrated. "Not yet. And I won't until I get her on the table."

"When will that be?" Mancuso asked.

Charlie lifted his eyes and fluttered his lips. "I'm thinking Wednesday or Thursday. Best I can do with the number of homicides we have on ice."

"So, off the record..." Mancuso raised his head. "What's your best guess as to the cause of death."

"The most obvious would be drowning," Charlie said. "See those tiny red splotches on her eyes and the purple ones on her neck and face? All point to asphyxiation." Charlie swatted his cheek. "Blasted mosquitoes. Can I take her and get out of this bug-infested marsh?"

"I don't think you'll find water in her lungs." Eli had found something Charlie had missed. "Those purple marks below the ear. They're linear. Something was around her neck."

"I ruled strangulation out," Charlie said. "The hyoid bone is still intact."

"She wasn't strangled." Eli leaned into the body. His eyes fixed on the girl's neck. "Something like a plastic bag was pulled over her head. Look at those faint marks above her Adam's apple. Connect them with those below her left ear, and you have a ring."

Mancuso bent closer. His knees popped. "He's right Charlie."

Charlie crouched over the homicide detective's shoulders and let out a disgusted sigh. "I must be ready for retirement. I can't believe I missed that."

"You're overworked." Mancuso stood with some effort and let out a slight moan. "You would have caught it during the autopsy. Besides, our friend here seems to have some detective skills." Mancuso led Eli outside the tape.

A knot formed in Eli's belly, anticipating the heave-ho by Mancuso. Eli joined the homicide detective out of Charlie's earshot.

"You surprised me, Colt," Mancuso said. "Don't tell me you learned your policing skills in Solace, Mississippi. Let me guess, military?"

Eli's muscles relaxed and the knot in his belly worked free. "Army. CID."

"Impressive. You got anything else you can share?"

Was Mancuso protecting his turf like Toussaint? His experience working with local authorities found them defensive about their cases. "Look, Detective Mancuso, I'm here to find my niece, not to impede on your or Detective Toussaint's investigation."

"Do you think Reggie and my cases are related?"

"Don't you?"

Mancuso's eyes brightened. "Hang tight for a minute. I need to talk to Charlie and the crime scene unit. Then you and me will have a chat."

———

A half hour later, the humid air over the Rigolets thickened to a drizzle, but Eli's patience waiting to chat with Mancuso had worn thin. He grabbed a rain slicker from his rucksack and his phone from his back pocket pulled the slicker over his shoulders and called Julia for Zoe Prevost's address.

"What does this mean?" Julia's tone bordered on frantic.

"It means nothing," Eli said with feigned confidence. "The two situations aren't related." He hated lying to Julia about what his instincts told him was true—whoever killed Zoe had some connection to Tara's disappearance.

Two men in hazmat suits peeled down to their waists, placed Zoe Prevost into a body bag, carried her to the boat launch, and placed her on a gurney to roll into a coroner's van. Eli thought Mancuso should've come talk to him by now, especially with an impending deluge of rain. But Mancuso remained on the scene and spoke with most of the members of the crime scene unit. Toussaint had disappeared when the first drops fell.

Eli used the time to call the Prevost girl's mother, who agreed to meet with him and Mancuso if he brought her two packs of Marlboro Lights. Then the drizzle turned to a sprinkle to a shower to a downpour, the drops popping on his rain gear in a succession of beats like a heavy metal drum roll.

Mancuso finally broke away and beckoned Eli to join him out of the rain in an unmarked cruiser. A chill from the storm crept through the sedan's doors and windows. Mancuso rummaged through the back seat from behind the wheel. "They didn't find a scrap of evidence within a fifty-yard range of the body. What does that tell us, Detective Colt?"

"That she died up channel north of here. But there's no telling how far her body traveled given the inlet's current and whatever she was tied to."

Mancuso found a golf shirt. "Look, let me get right to the point of why I want to talk to you." He used the shirt as a towel to wipe down his face and neck. "My partner of the past five years retired in July, and I'm pulling the pin in six months. So, to reward my thirty-plus years at the department, the chief of detectives is letting me sing my farewell song solo. Naturally, I'm flattered. But I'm thinking..." He leaned into Eli's personal space. "I can't stop you from looking for your niece." His tone was low, yet firm. "And I'm determined to end on a high note by finding who murdered Zoe. We can work separately or alone. I'm of the opinion two is better than one."

Eli raised a hand. "Hold on. Earlier today, Toussaint threatened to arrest me if I got involved. Now, you want to partner with me to find Tara and investigate a homicide?" A rush of adrenaline he hadn't felt since he'd left CID touched every nerve ending as Mancuso's request sunk in.

"Yep," Mancuso offered his hand as if to seal the agreement. "So, what do you say?"

THIRTEEN

Although the neighborhood was considered uptown, the corner of Harmony and Saint Thomas wasn't rich or vibrant or artsy or upper crust. Zoe Prevost's house was the same as the one in the photo of her and Tara in Eli's notepad—pale yellow, paint faded and peeling, the door and windows covered with rusting wrought-iron bars.

After knocking, Eli waited with Mancuso on the concrete stoop between two columns until the door cracked open with its security chain remaining latched. The pungent smell of pot wafted through the opening. A woman with cloudy eyes peeked out and hacked a wet cough. "Who is it?" Her voice rasped like her vocal cords had been grated.

Mancuso raised his badge. "Ms. Prevost, I'm Detective Mancuso, and this is Detective Colt. We have news of your daughter, Zoe."

The woman's eyes wandered, then focused on Mancuso. "You got my smokes?"

Eli's neck flushed warm. This woman, too concerned with

cigarettes and whatever else she planned on smoking, didn't ask if Zoe was okay. Eli flashed the two packs he'd picked up at a corner grocer. "May we come inside?"

Zoe Prevost's mother looked back into the house. "The place is a wreck."

Mancuso's face fell like it was he who lost a daughter. "Please, we need to talk to you about Zoe."

She blinked several times. Then the crack closed to the sound of sliding metal, and the door opened. The woman faded into the dim light inside. Eli and Manny entered the abyss.

The house reeked of stale beer and cannabis. The clanking of a window A/C unit drowned out Judge Judy on the TV. Clothes, shoes, and empty candy wrappers were scattered on the floor. Dirty plates littered the coffee table among spent beer bottles, empty cigarette packs, and leafy reefer scattered near a pipe and a plastic bag.

Zoe's mother, her hair matted, her complexion pale alabaster, tied a tattered terry cloth robe against her thin frame and plopped into a ragged upholstered chair. "Let's have it. Where did Zoe turn up this time? That horrible place in the Quarter?"

Eli remained standing halfway from the door to the chair. Mancuso sat on the adjacent couch, foam rubber escaping its worn edges. "What's your first name, Ms. Prevost?"

The woman tore open a pack of fresh smokes. "Emma."

Mancuso found a plastic lighter on the coffee table and pressed his thumb down to produce a flame. "I'm afraid it's bad news, Emma. Yesterday, we found Zoe's body in the Rigolets."

The news didn't reach Emma's emotional switch right off. She sat in silence for a moment. Blue cigarette smoke streamed from her nostrils. She clawed her fingernails into her forearm and expelled an audible breath. "Body?" She looked up at Eli, then back at Mancuso. "She's dead?" Her head shook slowly at first, then faster and faster.

With one hand, Mancuso pulled a handkerchief from inside his jacket. He used his other hand to wrap Emma's bony shoulder in a comforting touch. "My condolences."

"I told her this would happen." Emma's voice was filled with desperation, but her eyes produced no tears. "I told her to stay away from that...that...that gentlemen's club."

The hair on Eli's neck raised with a jolt. "Gentlemen's club?" he whispered. "What gentlemen's club?"

Emma pointed a crooked finger to a rickety bureau in the corner.

Eli moved to the cheap chest-of-drawers and found a blue and gold leaflet on top of a scattering of papers and opened envelopes.

Eli read the header out loud. "Gabriella's Gentlemen's Club—more than a lap dance."

"You sure it's Zoe?" Emma asked. "I mean, how'd you know?"

Eli produced the photo of Zoe and Tara. "This was taken right outside your house. From the photo, we were able to identify your daughter." He stepped closer and pointed at Tara's image. "Do you know this girl?"

Emma ignored the photo and Eli's question. "Why did my Zoe have to die?" She eyeballed Eli like he had the answer. "Why?"

Bile rose from Eli's belly to his throat. He wanted to spit on the floor and scream at the woman for not reporting the disappearance of her fifteen-year-old daughter.

Mancuso appeared more forgiving. "I am so sorry for your loss, Emma." His eyes roamed the living room and squinted at a dark hallway. "Is there anyone else here?"

"She didn't listen..." The lines at the corner of Emma's

eyes etched deeper. "She never listened to me." She buried her face in her open hands and convulsed in long drawn-out sobs.

A low whimper drifted in from the rear of the house. Eli stretched his neck and perked his ears to the sound, but the noise stopped.

Mancuso fixed his eyes on the direction of the noise. "Is there somebody we can call? A friend. The girl's father?"

Emma jerked her head up. Her pale skin darkened to an angry red. "He's never seen the girl," she said. "He disappeared when I was pregnant."

Mancuso offered a deep sigh and a thoughtful expression. "Maybe a friend or a neighbor? Someone who can be with you today?"

Emma's eyes filled like a ditch in a monsoon. Mucus bubbled from her nose.

The unmistakable whine of a baby fussing returned. Eli moved to the sound, but he couldn't see anything beyond the living room because of the poor lighting.

Emma brought a shaky hand to her forehead. "I can't deal with him now."

Mancuso shot a go-check-it-out thrust of his chin at Eli.

Eli ventured down the hall to the sound and entered a room scattered with dirty laundry. A twin bed sat on one side, a crib on the other with a rickety dresser between them.

Eli switched on the light and found the *him* Emma referred to—a gaunt baby lying feet up in the crib, hands clutching, nostrils flared, his face and bare chest pink with fury. The pitch of his cries grew louder and louder, then shifted to short staccato sobs. The sight of the bawling boy transported Eli back six years to Afghanistan.

The image of a naked, open-mouthed infant lying flat on its back on a dusty, war-torn road flickered in his brain like an old newsreel. Next to the child, a woman lay face down. From her shoulders, broad stripes of dark fluid had coursed down her flanks to pool beside her. The sound of small-arms fire receded in the distance, Eli's unit repulsing the Taliban. A medic rushed beside the child, then stooped to feel the mother's carotid. He took off his helmet and glanced at Eli. "She's dead."

Now, Eli's chest contracted. He backed from the crib. His knees weakened, his hands curled, his breathing labored—again. "Oh, God help me. Please help me." The knee-jerk appeal came without conscious effort.

"Eli. You okay, son?" Mancuso's warm voice eased Eli. His heart rate slowed. His breathing more natural.

Tears streamed across the boy's scarlet temples. Mancuso lifted the baby and held him. The seasoned detective cocked his head away in disgust. "Ugh...this boy needs a change." He grabbed a blue backpack with Baby X emblazoned across its front from under the crib. He opened it, then tossed it to the floor. "No diapers, no lotion, no baby powder. Plus, the kid looks malnourished."

Mancuso sat on the bed and ripped off the diaper. "Go check the bathroom and see if you can find clean towels. Look for skin lotion, too. This butt rash is so bad it's bleeding."

Eli found a clean towel, a clean face cloth, and a jar of Vaseline. He doused the face rag with warm water and returned to the bedroom. "This is all I could find."

Mancuso inspected the wares. "See if there's any baking soda in the kitchen. That breaks down the acid from the urine and stool."

Eli thought of Cedro while searching the kitchen. He found an unopened box of baking soda in the pantry and a bottle of hydrocodone on the counter. He brought the baking soda to Manny. "You moonlight as a nanny or something?"

"I've raised five children, and seven grandkids keep me in practice." Manny proceeded to powder the boy's bottom. "Go sit with Emma. Find out what else she knows. I'll need to make some calls. We can't leave this little fellow here."

Eli happily left the stench of the dirty diaper and the memory of war. He joined Emma in the front room, too angry to find words to question her.

Tear tracks lined her pale face. "I lost my little girl."

"What about the boy's dad?" Eli searched the room for photos, papers, or anything to help him find Tara. "Does he live here?"

"No. I don't know him that well. You gonna take Damian, ain't you?"

Of course, we'll take Damian, you stupid woman, Eli wanted to shout. "We're going to make sure both of you get the care you need," he said instead.

"Don't take my Damian." Emma bolted upright from the chair. "Please don't take him. He's all I got left."

What chance did Damian have growing up in this dump if he didn't die from neglect? Did poor Cedro, the boy Eli rescued in Solace, live like this when he was brought into this world? Would Damian end up cowering in some small-town storeroom after stealing food to survive? Eli pulled the photo of Zoe and Tara from his notepad and thrust it in front of Emma again. "Do you know the girl in this photo with Zoe? It's on your front porch."

Emma sat back down in her chair and ignored the photo once again.

The sound of Damian bawling burst from the backroom. Mancuso cooed like a pigeon in Jackson Square.

Emma screamed, "Damian. Shut up."

Eli wanted to grab this useless mother by her shoulders and shake her like a loose shutter in a summer squall. Look at the picture, damn you.

"What's he doing to my baby?" Emma asked.

"He's changing his diaper." Eli's voice was high-pitched and impatient. "He's taking care of your son."

Mancuso appeared with Damian wrapped in a towel and blanket, still wailing. "There, there. You want your mommy, huh?" Mancuso rubbed Damian's chin with this forefinger.

She reached for her son, and Mancuso surrendered him. "He's all cleaned up, but I think he needs a bottle."

"No bottles." Emma fiddled with the top of her robe.

Eli's heart slowed. His head throbbed.

Mancuso turned his back, and Eli did the same to allow Emma to breastfeed Damian.

The room settled into silence except for Damian's suckling. Eli proceeded to a dilapidated bureau littered with unpaid bills, junk mail, and business cards. He shuffled through the stacks and found a card that interested him.

The card read Dr. Lindsey Crenshaw, PsyD, Safe Harbor Home for Girls.

Emma continued to nurse Damian, whose head bobbed with zeal under the blanket.

Eli's skin crawled in disgust. The pot and the beer and the hydrocodone polluted the milk Damien drank without question. He lifted the picture of Tara and Zoe to Emma. "The other girl. Do you know her?"

Emma squinted bloodshot eyes to study the photo. "No." Her chin quivered. "Who is she?"

"I'm sorry, Emma." Mancuso's tone had a kindness Eli couldn't understand. "But we need to ask you a few questions. Is that okay?"

Emma lifted the blanket as if to check on Damien. "Yes."

"When did you last see Zoe?"

She rocked back and forth. "Three weeks, maybe. A month. Some man picked her up after dark. I was so mad."

Mancuso returned to his seat on the sofa. "Emma. Can

you tell us about this man who picked her up? We need to talk to him."

"Why?" Emma's mouth formed a spit bubble. "Did he kill my Zoe?"

"We don't know. But we'd like to talk to him and learn what he knows."

"I didn't get a good look. I told Zoe to stop riding in fancy vehicles with men I don't know."

Mancuso scooted closer to her. "Fancy vehicles?"

"Yeah, a fancy sports car."

"What kind of car?" Mancuso asked. "Can you give us the model?"

Her hand raked through her unkempt hair. "Foreign. Begins with a P."

Eli's adrenal gland shifted into high gear. "A Porsche?"

"Yes." Her voice expressed no emotion. "A Porsche."

Mancuso's eyes grew wider than cup saucers. "What color?"

"Uhm...red. Like a firetruck?"

Mancuso pulled out his notepad. "You're sure you didn't see the driver?"

"Not really. The car had really dark windows. You know, tinted. And Damian was fussing."

"What about a license plate?" Eli asked with little hope.

She shook her head.

"But it was a red Porsche," said Mancuso. "You're sure?"

"Pretty sure. As I said, Damian was fussing."

Intense fury clawed at Eli's insides. He couldn't look at Emma Prevost for another second. Her neglect for Zoe. For Damian. His breaths started to leave him.

Another episode.

He hurried out the door, pressed his hands against the porch column, and focused on his breathing.

How could this woman allow her teenage daughter to

leave with a stranger after dark? How could she let her infant son lay for hours in his feces, bleeding?

He glanced at his watch. It was time to meet Gina for dinner.

———

Outside the Prevost home, Eli waited at the curb. The sun broke through cumulus clouds and brought with it an oppressive humidity. His shirt clung to his shoulders and back. He needed a shower.

Finally, Mancuso came outside, his forehead wrinkled, his eyes sad. "I'll wait for social services to pick up the boy."

Eli handed Mancuso the business card he'd taken from the bureau inside. "What do you make of this?"

Manny put on his half-glasses. "Dr. Lindsey Crenshaw." Mancuso returned his readers to his jacket. "Well, what do you know?" He breathed in a deep breath as if he enjoyed this new development. "I know this place. It's a home for sexually abused girls."

Eli's heartbeat found its way to his ears. "Sexually abused?"

"I'll check on Emma." Mancuso handed the card back to Eli. "I hope social services hurries. I'm getting hungry, and you need to go."

"Won't you need this?" Eli offered the business card back.

"Nah. We'll regroup early in the morning."

"What then?"

"We'll visit my old friend, Dr. Crenshaw. If anyone can help us learn more about Zoe, it's Lindsey."

Eli peeked at his watch. He'd need to leave now if he were to make dinner on time. "My fiancée made reservations for dinner at Commander's Palace."

"Go ahead then. We'll pick it back up early tomorrow."

But Eli didn't want to go. The case had momentum. Sure, Gina expected him for dinner, and he'd always succumbed to her wishes in their carefree lives in Solace. But tonight, Tara's life was at risk.

He felt caught between two opposing forces—Gina's demands and Tara's endangerment. And there was something else—he felt empowered with information to move the case forward.

FOURTEEN

The afternoon sun tucked behind the two-story bed and breakfast in the Bywater. Badeau stood in the small courtyard behind the main building with the B&B manager, a raging migraine, and two C-notes in his hand. "Same deal as before, Marvin. I need complete privacy. A group of teenage kids is coming tonight, and I want this party to be off the grid."

Marvin, a slight man with clean-cut hair and a preppy wardrobe, kept his eyes on the money.

Badeau tapped Marvin's chest with the hand that held the cash. "No adults poking around, especially the police."

The manager's eyes bulged at the C-notes like a bulldog before meat scraps hit the floor. "Got it. No one older than eighteen back here."

Shoving the money in Marvin's eager hands, Badeau slapped the manager on the back. "Make sure of that."

A half-hour later, Freddy and his buddy Myles arrived, five girls with them, four Badeau recognized from the Jamboree. Two were tall and thin—one white, one Latina. Another was petite, and Shirley Temple cute. And one was an absolute knockout, with dark hair, dark eyes, and an innocence that rivaled Audrey Hepburn. The new girl kept her arms tight to her body, shooting glances at Badeau but never making eye contact.

To create an energetic vibe, Badeau bounced from one girl to the other and burst out in throaty laughter, "Come on in, ladies—*Mi casa, su casa.* We have chips and dips on the table, a keg in the kitchen, and tequila on the countertop. Plenty of ice in the freezer."

Freddy pumped the keg, filling red Solo cups with foamy draught beer.

Myles grabbed the tequila bottle, twisted off the cap, and lifted it to his mouth. Badeau snatched it from him, spilling a stream of the cheap liquor on the kid's dress shirt. "Ladies first."

All the girls accepted the tequila except the new one. Instead, she stood tall and erect, jaw tight, sipping her Solo cup like a nun at bingo.

Freddy and Myles had come through like Tom Brady in the fourth quarter. But this uptight chick wasn't helping Badeau's headache. She could cause trouble if she didn't get into party mode. Badeau chose a selection from his iTunes playlist and Bluetoothed it to an amplifier. "Let's get lit, ladies. I want this party to be dope."

He grabbed a bag of crystal meth from his pocket and signaled Freddy to a bedroom. "Use this to get the party started. When do the boys arrive?"

"Bout an hour or so," Freddy said.

"You did good, my man—real good." Badeau wrapped an arm around Freddy's shoulders. "Look. I need you full-time for a couple of weeks. I need you to go to Vegas."

Freddy thumped his chest. "Boo-yah. Vegas? You got it. How much does it pay?"

"Plenty if you stay sober and do your job right. But

tonight's different. I want you to get these girls high and into these bedrooms. I want you or your buddy between the sheets with one of these ladies when I get back, you dig?"

Freddy inspected the bag of meth. "No problem, Unc."

Badeau rubbed his temples. "You got any Oxy?"

"Nah, man. I'm bone dry except this meth you just passed me."

"I need to get me some Tylenol or Excedrin or something. My head's about to explode. You need anything?"

"I'm tight."

"When I get back, I wanna see some action going down. You feel me?"

"You got it." Freddy bounced back to the kitchen as if he wanted to celebrate.

Badeau made his way to the door. The new girl stood in the corner—quiet, observant. Not good.

He would flash his charms to get her right when he returned and had this headache under control.

———

At 7:28 p.m., Eli sat in his Jeep and crept with a long parade of vehicles on Magazine Street, heading to the Warehouse District and French Quarter's restaurants, bars, and clubs. His damp shirt and muddy boots had him feeling prickly. And he and Gina were sure to be late for their reservations at Commander's Palace.

Gina hadn't called or texted all day. He tried her cell and the hotel room, but she answered neither. A frightful feeling formed in his gut. Where was Gina, and why hadn't she called? Was she displeased in her demure, seemly manner? That made Eli feel more guilty than if she'd pestered him with calls every hour.

That is if she hadn't up and left and returned to Solace because he ignored her all day.

The slow pace gave him time to stew. He'd found Tara's friend, Zoe, murdered and washed ashore in the Rigolets. And he learned of three solid leads to pursue—a Bourbon Street gentlemen's club, a man of interest driving a red Porsche, and a mysterious psychologist on the Northshore. Eli wanted to follow this new evidence immediately. But because he'd convinced Gina to come to New Orleans, he couldn't allow her to dine alone.

Comparable to his days as an Army investigator, this current case was hard to put aside. Seeing Zoe Prevost's body raised the urgency to find Tara to DEFCON five. Was the man Emma Prevost last saw with Zoe responsible for her death? For Tara's disappearance? Was he the older boy Tara's friends reported to Julia?

The last clue nagged like a foot blister during a ten-mile run. And who was this psychologist to Mancuso, and how did she fit into this case?

Eli resisted calling his sister-in-law, Julia. He had learned plenty about Zoe but was no closer to finding Tara since they last talked. And if Julia learned about Zoe's murder, it may push Julia past her emotional limit. Besides, he had to get his head right, his mood more festive, so his and Gina's dinner at Commander's Palace would help her forget about Nashville.

The Jeep crawled at twenty. He cut over to Tchoupitoulas, but the traffic almost came to a stop. He pulled out his phone and speed-dialed Gina. Voicemail. The clock on his dashboard read 7:49. Gina had booked their reservations for 8:30. He'd be lucky to get to the hotel by eight.

Eli blew through a yellow light on Julia Street and turned right on Lafayette to Convention Center Boulevard. He sped the two blocks to the hotel and turned into the courtyard. He braked with a tire screech and tossed his keys to the valet.

He expected Gina to be waiting at the front door, in the lobby, or at the bar if he was lucky. She wasn't in any of those places. She wasn't in their room. But dark wool slacks, a silk shirt, and an Italian-cut sports jacket were laid out on the bed with a note on hotel stationery.

> I took an Uber to dinner. I'm meeting a couple who called out of the blue at the restaurant early. See you soon. Love—
> G.

What couple? Who did Gina know in New Orleans? Maybe a sorority sister from Ole Miss? That meant mindless chit-chat with a condescending husband while Tara dominated Eli's thoughts.

The warm shower rinsed away the sticky sweat and revived his energy. His new outfit fit like a James Bond tuxedo, which didn't surprise Eli due to Gina's shopping prowess.

Eli called down for his Jeep. His phone buzzed outside the elevator. He answered. The sounds of city traffic flooded the line. "You make it to dinner yet," Mancuso said.

"On my way to the restaurant. What's up?"

"I want to discuss our next steps if you have the time?"

Eli crammed into a packed elevator, hoping not to lose the connection. "Would that include checking out Gabriella's?"

The cell phone signal ebbed with static, but Eli could hear Mancuso. "You must have read my to-do list."

"Yes sir."

"Drop the sir and call me Manny. Look, I didn't know the chief of detectives put you bird-dogging Reggie."

Eli's adrenaline meter hit red. Would that be an obstacle to him and Manny working together? "Is there a problem?"

"Don't worry about Reggie. I cleared it with Captain Guidry. You'll be with me from now on."

Eli stepped into the courtyard and tipped the valet. "Okay,

let me do my husband-to-be duties tonight, and I'll see you bright and early."

"How long are you in town?"

"Supposed to be back in Solace on Tuesday."

"Well, unlike Reggie, I don't like grass growing between my toes. But this ole Creole will need a favor."

"What's that?"

"I'll need you to drive me around."

Eli took the phone from his ear, stared at it, and then returned it. "Drive you?"

"Yeah. I hate driving. Plus, my police cruiser has over 200,000 miles."

"So, you want me as your driver?"

"You mind?"

Eli shrugged to himself. He was on a murder case. Why make waves? "Not a problem."

"Call me in the morning," Mancuso said.

Twenty minutes later, the maître' d escorted Eli through a crowded Commander's Palace to its Garden Room. Gina sat adorned in a pastel green, bare-shouldered evening dress worthy of the Academy Awards. Across from her at their table was an older couple whose back was to him. Gina's eyes met his, and she flashed him a sly, closed-mouth smile, causing the couple to turn.

It was the first time he'd seen his parents in seven years.

———

Badeau returned to the Bywater B&B, his migraine under control, and happy to find his plan progressing. Two of his targets, high as satellites, danced to Lil Wayne and motioned with their fingers for him to join.

The tall Latina gyrated her hips like a dancer at Gabriella's. "Come dance with us."

Badeau flashed a well-practiced smile and lifted a finger. "One sec."

He peeked into the first bedroom. Its celeste white walls bordered with pale-blue wallpaper backdropped Shirley Temple nuzzling with Freddy. The second room had the tall white girl sitting bare breasted on the queen bed and Myles slipping out of his trousers.

Badeau checked his pant pocket for the digital camera and snapped a few shots before returning to the dancing girls. They pranced toward him, noticeably high on drugs or alcohol or a combination. The rapping at the front door couldn't have come at a better time.

With the Latina tucked under his arm and Audrey Hepburn rubbing his chest, Badeau stood in the doorway, and four guys stood outside. Three were average-sized, all white, all in jeans and tee shirts. The fourth, wearing baggy sweatpants and a wife beater, made his friends look small.

Badeau caressed both girls' shoulders. "You boys here for the party?" Every pair of eyes grew wider than twenty-two-inch rims.

"Yeah," said the big guy.

Badeau held out a hand. "Cost you twenty each to get in. I take Venmo and PayPal."

The big guy thrust out his chest. "Freddy didn't say nothin 'bout no cover charge, bruh."

"Follow me if y'all wanna smash." Badeau led them to the door of the first bedroom. He opened it just enough for the guys to get a good look inside. "These girls out here are ready for some action, too. Anybody wanna dance?"

The cell phones came out, and Badeau showed them the beer and the booze and gave them his account information. Then something vexed him. The uptight chick had disappeared. He went to the tall Latina who now struggled at dancing. "Where's your friend with the attitude?"

She squinted pink eyes, trying to balance herself against her dance partner's shoulder. "Oh, Kaitlyn? She left. She said this wasn't her scene."

Badeau's body temperature elevated. His ears burned from the inside. Why didn't he do something about this Kaitlyn situation before he left? "When did she leave?"

The Latina slumped, and the guy held her so she wouldn't hit the floor. "When Freddy and Makenzie went into the bedroom." Her words ran into one another.

Badeau winked at her dance partner and nodded to the bedrooms. The kid took the girl by the hand. Somebody pounded at the door. Badeau twitched at the sound, and the mental image of the police outside flashed in his brain. He peeked out the window, ready to run out the back door.

Thankfully, five teenage guys were waiting, with another two entering the courtyard. Badeau gave them the tour and had them transfer their money, then locked the front door and ran to the street. He passed a half-dozen boys on the walkway. "I'll be right back to let you guys in."

Two blocks away, Kaitlyn sat at the bus stop. Her head tilted down. A paperback spread open in her hands. And as if she had some premonition, she lifted her head, and her eyes met his.

Badeau spread his arms, palms up.

She stared back for three beats, then returned to her book. A city bus pulled in front of her like a solar eclipse. The bus pulled away, and Kaitlyn was gone.

Badeau's pulse pounded like a jackhammer on concrete. He blasted an F-bomb. He could run to his Escalade and follow the bus, but the party was full-on, and the key to his plan required his presence. He knew where Kaitlyn was going, and it would take time by bus.

Back at the room, another dozen of Freddy's buddies

arrived to get high and take a turn in the bedrooms. Freddy emerged from the bathroom shirtless, his pants undone.

Taking him by the shoulder, Badeau led him out into the courtyard. "We got a problem."

Freddy's eyes were glossy, his breath strong with cannabis, tequila, and beer. "Problem?"

"Kaitlyn took off."

Freddy zipped his trousers. "Kaitlyn?"

"The uptight girl you and your friend shouldn't have brought over."

"Don't blame me, Unc. You told me you needed five chicks from that home, and I brought five chicks from that home. How could I stop her from leaving if I'm in the bedroom doing what you said?"

Freddy was right. Badeau shouldn't have left because he had a headache. "Okay. Not your fault."

Kaitlyn leaving had Badeau's mind and body scrambling. He pulled his video camera from his pocket and handed it to Freddy. "Get some videos of the girls in action and make sure you get their faces, dig?"

"Yep."

"And have some of your buddies take videos on their phones. I want these girls trending by tomorrow. Got it?"

"Got it, Unc."

Badeau counted out four hundred dollars and gave the bills to Freddy. "When the party dies down, get rid of these dudes, but make sure none of the chicks leave. You hear me?"

"Yeah. Don't worry. They'll be here when you get back."

For the next twenty minutes, Badeau broke every traffic law to arrive at the group home in time to witness Kaitlyn stroll down the walkway and up the steps. Security lights lit up the two-story, white-bricked building. A forty-something man walked out the front door to greet her. The two spoke briefly.

Badeau's heart froze.

The man scanned the neighborhood like a sentry guarding a fortress.

Badeau's mouth got as dry as sand in a desert. Would Kaitlyn tell others about the party when her friends didn't return? Kaitlyn had seen his face at the B&B and the bus stop.

He shifted his Escalade into gear and headed to the French Quarter. He needed to speak to Javier and, if necessary, cut this potential catastrophe off.

————

Chardonnay dribbled into Eli's glass at the lavishly set table. He lifted the drink to thank the waiter, then swallowed every drop in one pull. What were his parents doing here, and why were they sitting with Gina?

"The funniest thing happened…" Gina refilled Eli's glass to the brim as if knowing there wasn't enough wine in Louisiana for him to get through this dinner. "I had just returned to our room from shopping when the hotel phone rang, and I thought it was you. I mean, who else knows we're here, right? To my surprise, it was your mother, Margaret, calling." Gina chattered like she and Eli's parents were old friends. "Margaret said she talked to you and wanted to invite us to their place for dinner."

Eli cursed himself for sharing the name of their hotel with his mother, then shot her a venomous glare. "Did she now?" So much for the romantic dinner.

Gina seemed to ignore the unmistakable tension that besieged their table. "So, there I was, talking to my future mother-in-law, whom I've never met, and I said to myself, why not invite your parents to have dinner with us?" Gina's tone was upbeat, as if she were the keynote speaker at one of her charity events.

Eli's temples ached. Why not indeed? It was Gina who argued his parents sent him to an emotional edge.

Gina steepled her hands as if praying and then spread them wide. "And here we are. One big happy family."

Eli signaled to a nearby waiter. "McClellan neat." The wine wasn't doing the trick.

And as if not to be outdone by his son, Eli's father raised his half-empty tumbler to the waiter.

"Isn't this nice?" Eli's mother said. "As I was telling Gina, your father and I have never eaten here before. Isn't that right, Tom?"

His father drained his tumbler and set it down with a thud. "Gina tells us you're looking for Tara," he said to Eli.

Eli unfolded his napkin and placed it on his lap. "More like I'm making sure the police do their job."

The waiter appeared with the drinks for Eli and his father.

His father angled his body at Eli. "What did Julia have to say?"

Eli tinkered with his silverware, trying to ignore his dad. "Not much."

His mother reached for his dad's elbow. "Tom. We're here to have a nice dinner, not to interrogate the boy."

His dad leaned back in his chair and crossed his arms. "I'm just trying to find out what happened to my grandchild. That woman won't speak to me."

Eli blurted a half-suppressed laugh. "Do you blame her?"

"What is that supposed to mean?" his dad said.

Gina picked up her menu. "I was thinking of ordering appetizers for the table."

"Yes ma'am?" said the waiter, who appeared as if on Gina's cue.

"How about...the potato dumplings and the stuffed blue crabs." She beamed at Eli's mom and dad. "What do y'all think?"

His dad looked uninterested.

His mom stared at her menu like it was written in Japanese.

Eli took another pull of scotch.

"Okay, and we'll have more chardonnay," Gina said. "Now, let's have a nice dinner, shall we?"

Gina didn't realize Eli and his parents had never done anything nice together. Never.

But that didn't stop his mother. "I agree. We are here to get to know Gina and see our only..." the words stuck in his mother's throat. "Living son."

"Son?" his dad spat the word like he'd cursed. "He hasn't darkened our door in years."

What was Eli doing here? Definitely not having a lovely dinner with his fiancée. Instead, he sat with people he wanted to avoid like a pandemic. And Gina invited them. She invited them.

"I want my granddaughter to be found," said Dad. "It's all I have left of your little brother. Don't you care about your only niece?" His lips curled, and he looked away.

That same line Eli had heard earlier from his mother.

Eli planted his feet under the table and leaned in. "Do I care about my only niece? I'm here, aren't I?"

He'd typically held his tongue in such situations, but the alcohol had numbed Eli's inhibitions. "The question is, do you care about me? You were never there for me. Not when I played baseball in High School. Not at my Ranger graduation. Not for at my bronze star ceremony. Not at the airport when I came home from Afghanistan. Let's face it, Dad. You've never been there for me my entire life."

People at other tables started to stare.

His dad fidgeted back in his chair and looked away, and like a bell at the end of a round, their waiter appeared with their red wine.

Eli asked for another McClellan.

Gina held her hand over her mouth, then moved it to her chest. "If we must get this horrible business out of the way to enjoy our dinner, tell us, Eli. What did you learn today?"

Instead of saying he'd learned his fiancée had betrayed him by inviting his parents to this dinner, Eli let his professional persona reign. "The missing persons detective on Tara's case is a joke. And they found a girl's body in the Rigolets."

Mom covered her mouth with trembling fingers.

Dad pressed a fist to his mouth and blinked.

A flutter of guilt forced Eli's hands up in surrender. "Not Tara. That's why I'm late. I wanted to make sure."

Dad growled deep in his throat like a bulldog. "I don't get the police in this town. I pay my taxes. Your brother paid his. And you...well, you're a decorated warrior, aren't you? Tara should get top priority."

The disconnect hadn't improved between Eli and his dad. "Why should that matter?"

"What should matter is she is Jacob's daughter. Maybe this wouldn't have happened if you had been here instead of out in the sticks."

Mom squeezed his father's arm. "Tom, be civil, or he'll just leave again."

"You know what, Dad?" Eli was primed for a fight. "I don't blame Julia for not letting you see Tara. Why would she? Heck, I wish I didn't have to see you right now. And spare me your attempt to pull my heartstrings. It won't work. When I find Tara, I hope Julia keeps her away from you."

"So, you'll find Tara?" his mother asked, her brow high on her forehead. "You promise?"

A chill crawled down Eli's neck. "What?"

"You said when you find Tara."

So that's why his mother called Gina and wormed into this

dinner. It wasn't to meet Gina or see Eli. It was about him finding Tara.

A soreness scratched Eli's throat. His appetite left the building. "To answer your question, Mother, I plan to find Tara, and I'll get back to it right now." He downed his scotch, kissed Gina, and stood. "I'm sorry, Gina, but you should've checked with me before inviting them."

Gina didn't appear too put off. Instead, like a little girl caught with a forbidden cookie, a satisfied smile tugged at the corner of her mouth.

Eli stepped back from the table. "I'm gone."

And he left—for Gabriella's.

FIFTEEN

Eli stood outside a daiquiri bar across from Gabriella's, the Bourbon Street gentlemen's club Emma Prevost linked to Zoe. A combined cacophony of jazz, rock-and-roll, and voices of French Quarter revelers coursed up and down Bourbon Street like summer rain hammering in drainage ditches.

A slew of men paraded through the club's entrance in the few minutes since Eli'd arrived but seeing Reggie Toussaint stumble out of the club quickened Eli's breath. He hurried into the shadow of an alcove until Toussaint turned the corner at St. Peter Street.

Toussaint said he'd be fishing this weekend. So, why was he at Gabriella's, a place of interest in Zoe Prevost's death?

"Been here long?" The voice came from behind Eli.

The question triggered Eli's defenses, but the McClellan from dinner fogged his brain. He wheeled with his hand sliding to his hidden weapon.

Manny Mancuso raised his hands, palms out, three paces behind Eli. "Whoa, son."

"Sorry." Eli straightened his new jacket and let his hand fall to his side. "I'm not usually this jumpy."

"I thought I'd come sniff around and see what this place is about." Mancuso indicated Gabriella's with a bob of his head. "What are you doing here? Dinner reservations got canceled?"

"I left after drinks."

"Everything okay with you and your lady?"

Eli didn't want to talk about dinner. "People I don't particularly care for showed up."

"Pity." Mancuso's inquisitive eyes swept over Eli. "You're dressed for the red carpet."

Eli decided not to tell Mancuso Toussaint had just exited Gabriella's. Eli wanted to trust Mancuso, but it was too early to trust anybody. "I wasn't sure you'd come tonight."

"Me either. My wife wasn't particularly thrilled, I can tell you." Mancuso winked at Eli. "Saturday night. Bourbon Street. Strip club."

Eli scratched his chin. "You told her you were coming here? Why not just say you had to work?"

Mancuso shouldered past Eli. "Because I tell my wife everything. Fewer problems that way."

A lump of remorse formed in Eli's throat. Should he have been that honest with Gina?

"We going to stand out here all night or go inside?" Mancuso treaded into the street.

Inside the door, the club boomed techno music that assaulted Eli's inner ears. He and Mancuso forked up twenty bucks each and followed a curvy woman in a short backless one-piece jumpsuit with a separate tuxedo collar that cut into her neck like a garrote. She seated Eli and Manny at a table the size of a dinner plate ten feet from the main stage.

"Monique will be out to dance next." The hostess said as if she brought earth-shattering news. "Ruby will take your drink order. Enjoy the show."

The performers on stage were young and beautiful, whirling bare-skinned bodies to music that continued to assail Eli's ears.

Ruby, their waitress, wore a pink negligee, high heels, and dark nylons.

Manny ordered tonic water with lime.

Eli, still reeling from the scotch at Commander's Palace, asked for a Diet Coke.

Waiting for his soft drink, Eli checked out the scene. Full-length mirrors hung on the left and front walls. A bar ran along the right side of the room, with bartenders pouring drinks for servers dressed like Ruby. A runway projected from the stage to the club's center. Pink neon flashed Champagne Room on the back wall.

Men fixated their eyes on nude women dancing. They howled. They gawked. They lifted cash between their fingers to stuff into colorful garters fitted on assorted legs.

A scantily clad dancer led an unsteady man, shirt untucked, unbuttoned to his breastbone, through a glistening curtain below the Champagne Room sign.

The MC announced Monique. The music changed from techno to Springsteen's "Born in the USA" as a tall redhead twirled onto the stage, draped in Old Glory, writhing her light-skinned body to the E-Street Band.

During his stint in the Army, Eli kept clear of the strip clubs that littered the towns around every state-side military base. Why did women do this? Didn't beauty help women avoid life's hardships? This woman, this girl who peeled away the Stars and Stripes, was stunning, yet here she was.

Maybe that's what drew men to a place like this. Not to bay at bare flesh. Not to fantasize about sex. Not to act a fool in the presence of naked women. But for the thrill of watching a woman yield to men's lusts and submit to her brokenness.

Maybe that's why these men bellowed like wolves at a full moon.

Ruby appeared and put down two tonics and two diet cokes. "That'll be thirty bucks, honey. Remember, two drink minimum." Another reason to avoid strip clubs.

Eli pulled his phone from his jacket pocket.

Ruby bent at an angle, exposing her cleavage, and scanned the mobile payment app on Eli's phone. "Let me know if y'all need anything else."

Manny showed his badge. "I'd like to see the manager."

Ruby disappeared.

Five minutes later, a stout man in crisp khakis and a maroon blazer appeared at their table. "Gentlemen. Please follow me."

Maroon Blazer escorted them through a doorway behind the main stage. They passed an open door where girls changed outfits and applied makeup. Their escort knocked on a panel door near the back entrance three times, then entered without waiting for a response.

"Gentlemen." A short man in his mid-twenties, his face shaped by high cheekbones and a fashionable beard, stood behind a massive wood-carved desk. A crushed cigarette smoldered in an ashtray. A fresh one hung unlit between his fingers. "Enjoying the show?"

A bank of security monitors covered the wall on the far right with sixteen live feeds to various sections of the club.

Mancuso sat in a plush leather chair across from the man before being offered the seat.

Eli positioned himself near the monitors for a better look.

"Not here to enjoy ourselves," Mancuso said. "We're on the clock. I'm Detective Mancuso. This here is Detective Colt."

The man lit his cigarette and offered his hand from across

the desk. "Marshall Aberdeen. Acting manager." Aberdeen appeared cocky, like a kid given power before his time.

Mancuso accepted his hand. "Acting manager?"

"The owner's on vacation."

"So, Javier Navarro's not here?" Mancuso said.

Aberdeen's mouth tugged into a contemptuous smile. "How can I help you gentlemen?"

"You can start by answering our questions," Mancuso spoke in an even, borderline-friendly tone. "So, is Mr. Navarro here?"

"He's unavailable, detective."

"Fair enough." Mancuso set his hands in his lap—relaxed, non-threatening. "We have questions about a girl you may know."

Eli handed Mancuso the photo of Tara and Zoe Prevost and stepped back to study the monitors.

Mancuso slid the image across the desk.

Aberdeen studied the picture. His eyes flashed recognition but immediately shrunk back into dark pools. He pushed the photo back to Eli. "Don't know 'em."

"You sure about that, Mr. Acting Manager?" A hint of disdain rose in Mancuso's tone.

Eli focused his attention on the monitors. A red Porsche sat in plain view on one of the visual displays from the outside. "Is this your back alley?"

"The service alley, yes," Aberdeen said.

Eli circled the Porsche with his finger for Mancuso's sake. "Parking in the Quarter must be difficult."

Aberdeen shifted in his chair. "Parking can be a mother."

"Do you have to park in the Quarter?" Eli said. "Or do you live nearby?"

Aberdeen pulled back his shoulders. "I live in the Garden District."

Eli almost asked if Aberdeen lived with his parents. The

plush Garden District was too expensive for a man Aberdeen's age. "So you drive."

"Yes. I drive." Aberdeen gloated like an uptown yuppie.

"I was admiring the Porsche parked in the service alley. What a magnificent car. Beautiful."

"It should be." Aberdeen pulled in a deep breath. "It cost enough."

"It's yours?" Eli turned, feigning surprise.

Aberdeen leaned back in his chair and folded his arms. "It is."

Eli stepped back in admiration. "What do you call that color? Fire engine red?"

"No, it's cherry metallic."

"What a fine piece of machinery," Eli said.

Aberdeen rocked in his chair. "That, detective, is an understatement."

Confident he'd found the fancy vehicle Emma Prevost last saw Zoe enter. Eli edged closer to Aberdeen and pressed his palms on the desktop. "Mr. Aberdeen." His tone was more assertive. "Why did you lie to us about not knowing one of those girls?"

"What are you talking about?" Aberdeen sat up and directed a nervous gaze at Mancuso. "I don't know them. Besides, they're too young to work here?"

"Yeah? How old are you?" Mancuso said.

"That's none of your business," Aberdeen said.

Mancuso laughed. "Like I can't find out your age in about twenty seconds. You being the acting manager and all. You're on the liquor license, I presume?"

"Uh...liquor license?"

Mancuso stood and inspected the walls. "Yeah. You know. That piece of paper you're supposed to have displayed so I can make sure you're legal."

Aberdeen took a deep breath and swallowed. "Uh...look, man...I've got—"

"Don't worry about the liquor license. I'll just show this photo around to your staff and your customers. In fact..." Mancuso pulled out his phone and wagged it. "I'll get a dozen uniformed officers here to pass out some prints."

"You can't do that." Veins bulged on Aberdeen's neck and temples. "Having a dozen cops in here will kill our business."

"Too bad," Mancuso said. "I've been humping all evening investigating the murder of a girl whose body we found in the Rigolets. And check this out..." Mancuso pushed the photo back to Aberdeen. "The last time her mother saw her, she was getting into your cherry metallic Porsche."

Aberdeen's eyes bulged, then flitted to the live feed of his car.

Eli leaned in, his nose two feet from Aberdeen's face. "Congratulations, you've just become our prime suspect."

"I didn't kill anybody." Aberdeen rolled back in his chair, creating distance from Eli. "And you can't prove that I did."

"Not yet," Manny said. "But once we close this place down and search every crack and cranny. Who knows what we'll find?"

"I can't let you do that." Aberdeen pulled at his beard.

"How are you going to stop us?" Eli said.

"I have rights."

"Really. Do acting managers have rights? Where's Javier Navarro?"

Aberdeen stiffened. "Don't you hear good? He's not available, I said."

Mancuso pulled out handcuffs from his jacket. "If I were you, I'd see if I could make him available, seeing as we're about to haul you to the station."

Aberdeen peeked at his watch. "It's late. Too late."

"We need information about this girl. If we can't talk to

someone who can answer our questions, I will call for those uniforms—now."

Aberdeen waved both hands like he was trying to stop traffic. His chest hitched, and his voice quaked. "Look. You guys should leave right now."

Mancuso sat and examined his fingernails. "We leave. We leave with you under arrest for the murder of Zoe Prevost."

Eli took the seat next to Mancuso. Mancuso couldn't hold Aberdeen for murder for more than a few hours. The evidence of his involvement was too thin. Emma Prevost, a drug addict and alcoholic who just had her only surviving child taken from her for neglect, was their only witness. And she could only tie Zoe to a car that could be Aberdeen's. He'd be out by sunrise, if not sooner.

Aberdeen paced the floor, wiping his hands on his pressed shirt. "I need a smoke." He grabbed his cigarettes and lighter and left the room.

On the monitors, Aberdeen hurried out of the office and down the hall. Then he moved out of that frame into the live feed of the alley.

Eli rose to pursue the young punk, but Mancuso held up his arm. "He ain't going nowhere." Mancuso leaned his head back and closed his eyes. "I almost wish he would."

And as if to prove Mancuso right, Aberdeen lit a cigarette outside and paced, stopping to consider his car in irregular intervals.

"Kid's dimmer than a night light, I tell ya," Mancuso said like he could see the screen with his eyes still closed. "Don't he know we can see him?"

Eli focused on the monitor. "How's talking to this Navarro gonna help us find Tara or Zoe's killer?"

"Probably won't. But you have to turn over rocks to see what's underneath. Besides, Navarro is the most powerful pimp in New Orleans. Has cops, politicians, and probably judges in his pocket like they're loose change."

Eli reflected on Reggie Toussaint at the club earlier but still said nothing.

"I've got a feeling about this place," Mancuso said. "My gut tells me the answer to poor Zoe's murder is here."

"And Tara?"

Mancuso finally opened his eyes. "Tara too."

"So what now?" Eli asked.

Mancuso stood and strolled to the monitors. "Haven't a clue."

A dark Escalade appeared on the alley's livestream and parked behind Marsh Aberdeen's cherry metallic Porsche.

Sixteen

Badeau watched as Marsh ground a cigarette butt into the blacktop beneath the sole of his Cole Haan in Gabriella's service alley. He gave Badeau a small nod, but there was panic in Marsh's expression. His lips curled into a weak smile that didn't quite reach his eyes.

Eight years earlier, he'd recruited the fourteen year old Marsh on the French Quarter streets where he and his older brother danced for loose change. Although their dancing did little to produce revenue, his older brother fed his heroin addiction by selling young Marsh to pedophiles found in the crowd.

Badeau attempted to purchase Marsh to work at Gabriella's, but his brother rejected the offer. Five days later, Marsh approached Badeau at the club with the news his older brother had overdosed.

When Javier first laid eyes on Marsh, the pimp said the boy looked like an angel, often having Marsh come to Javier's room. The lad procured good revenue in Gabriella's underground business, which sold young boys to a particular clientele.

After Marsh aged out of his usefulness as a child prostitute, he transitioned to a recruiter. Although he could charm like a male gigolo in a women's prison, his work ethic was poor. But Javier didn't seem to mind. He'd fallen in love with Marsh, and Marsh took advantage.

Badeau exited his Escalade. "Something wrong?"

"No...nothing." Marsh's hand trembled as he lit another cigarette. "Uh...what brings you out tonight?" Marsh's words stumbled over each other in a nervous stammer.

"Somethings bothering you. What is it?"

Marsh glanced back to the club, then closed his eyes. "There's a couple of detectives in Javier's office."

Badeau's shifted his focus to the security camera mounted on the club's exterior. "Do they have a warrant?"

Marsh leered as if he lived above such scrutiny. "No."

Badeau grabbed Marsh by the elbow and led him inside.

Marsh tried to free himself. "Get your hands off me."

"Shut up you idiot." Badeau shoved Marsh past the office door, down the hallway, through the dressing room, and up the stairwell to the second floor.

Out of the watchful eyes of security cameras, Badeau pinned Aberdeen to the wall with a forearm across the throat. "You allowed the police in here without a warrant?"

"Yeah, so what?"

An unleashed fury raged inside Badeau. The long day caught up to him. "What do they want?"

"They're asking about missing girls. Nothing to do with us."

"If they're here, it has everything to do with us. Wait..." No way the police could be searching for Badeau because of Kaitlyn. She knew nothing about Gabriella's. "You said they were asking about missing girls? How many?"

"A dead one and a live one. The dead one is Zoe, but Javier

sold her to Commodore a few weeks back. I've never seen the live one before."

"Who's Commodore?" Badeau asked, surprised Javier used someone he wasn't familiar with.

Marsh flashed a satisfied grin. "I thought you knew everything. Didn't Javier tell you about the Commodore?"

Badeau shoved Marsh harder against the wall. "No, he didn't. Why don't you?"

Marsh's eyes gleamed like he had exclusive knowledge. "He's some crazy clown who dresses like a rear admiral and buys underage kids to work on his yacht."

"What did you tell the detectives?" Badeau said.

"Nothing. I told them nothing. They said they will show their pictures to our customers whether we let them or not."

"They're bluffing." Badeau loosened Marsh from his hold. "Get rid of them."

Marsh tucked in his shirt. "Who do you think you are ordering me around? I'm in charge when Javier's off."

"First rule of survival..." Badeau advanced on Marsh, forcing him to step back. "Never talk with the police without a lawyer sitting next to you. Rule number two—never let them inside without a warrant. Now, get rid of them."

Instead, Marsh rushed into Javier's apartment and tried to shut the door.

Badeau pressed through the door to Javier's apartment, using his larger and stronger frame.

"What's going on?" A husky feminine voice from the den. "Whose there?"

"It's me, Charisse," Marsh said. "Everything's fine. Just checking on Javier."

Javier's gravelly voice erupted. "Who's making that racket?"

"It's Marsh," Charisse said. "Go back to sleep."

Charisse had been Javier's friend and confidant for over

forty years, starting when she had been Gabriella's main attraction in the club's early years. Now retired, Charisse became more of a fixture in Javier's apartment as his health declined.

"Sleep?" Javier let out a series of coughs. "How can I sleep with a scuffle in the hallway and voices in here? Who's with you Marsh?"

"It's Andre. I'm sorry to disturb you. Listen to Charisse and go back to sleep."

"Andre. Oh, Andre. Come here my boy. Let me see you."

Badeau entered the dark room, grabbed a chair from a small desk, and sat beside Javier's reclined body on the chaise lounge. "How are you feeling?"

Javier looked older than his seventy-eight years. His cotton-white hair. His milky, moist eyes. His timeworn skin creased like crumpled parchment. "Great. Just taking some time off from the business."

An uncomfortable wedge formed in Badeau's throat. "Can I get you anything?"

"You being here is enough. How long has it been? A month? Two months?" Javier's eyes drew together into a pained expression.

Badeau had hoped he could've avoided this subject. Regrettably, it had been closer to four months since he'd seen Javier. "I need your advice." Badeau glanced over his shoulder at Charisse and Marsh. "Can we speak in private?"

Charisse grabbed her purse and moved toward the door. "I've got to get home and feed my cats. Good to see you Andre. Don't be such a stranger." She blew Javier a kiss. "I'll see you tomorrow."

Marsh hadn't moved. Instead, he fluffed a pillow and placed it beneath Javier's head.

Javier touched Marsh's wrist gently. "You need to be downstairs running things. Andre can see to my needs." Javier smiled at Marsh. "Leave us."

Badeau lifted his hand. "Hold on. Two city detectives are in your office on police business."

Javier's eyes flashed rage. "What?" He struggled to sit up but withered with the effort. "Do they have a warrant?"

Marsh lowered his head like a cowering puppy and said nothing.

Javier's face flushed. His ears reddened. He hawked discordant coughs. "Get rid of them, Marsh. Get rid of them now."

Marsh stormed out and slammed the door like a grounded teenager.

It took a minute for Javier to recover. "The boy dotes on me but has too much to learn."

"Perhaps," Badeau said. "But some things can't be taught."

Javier ignored the comment. "What brings you to see me?"

"Different reasons. Business."

Javier's eyes searched the ceiling like a question nagged at him. "Why are those detectives here?"

"It's about two girls. They found one dead."

"What does that have to do with me?"

"Marsh told me you sold the dead one to some wannabe navy commander." Badeau fluffed another pillow and placed it on top of Marsh's. "I'm guessing they tied the other girl to the dead one. You need to take this seriously."

"Zoe." Javier stroked his white hair and grimaced. "Commodore. He pays well but is a brutal cuss. Look, I need a favor."

"Anything."

"I want you to hide a camera in my office..." Javier spoke in a hushed tone. "Don't tell Marsh, but I want to watch what goes on down there. I may be slowing down, but I still need to know what's happening in my club. In my office."

Javier sat straighter. "In the meantime, I'll call some friends to see if I can get this Zoe business slow-walked or squashed." The dimmed light in Javier's eyes brightened. "I still have my contacts in the police department. City Hall too. But enough about me. How's your business doing? Prospering, I hope."

"Business is good," Badeau said. "But you know the score. It's a grind."

"And you have something you want to discuss?"

"Yes," Badeau leaned closer. "Leon from Vegas reached out. He needs more girls, and he wants me to supply them."

"How many?"

"Five for starters," Badeau said.

"You got 'em?"

"Working on it as we speak."

Javier leaned back on the pillows and closed his eyes. "Why's he need them? Leon ain't got enough of his own?"

"He lost half his inventory in a police raid," Badeau said. "And there's a big MMA fight next weekend."

"Well, expansion takes planning and a lot of guts." Javier pulled Marsh's pillow from beneath his shoulders but kept Badeau's in place. "You're a good businessman. You've learned much. But be wary of Leon. I did business with his daddy. He'd kiss a baby to get close enough to steal his lollipop."

That much Badeau knew. He didn't trust anybody except Javier. Not even Freddy—and he was family.

"It's likely a good move." Javier placed a blue-veined hand on Badeau's forearm. "It's about time you spread your wings outside New Orleans. But don't get too busy. When I'm gone, this place is yours."

Badeau's thoughts spiraled like a tornado. He'd thought he'd get something from Javier after he died. But the club?

Javier's head leaned to one side. "You looked surprised."

"I thought you'd give it to Marsh. I mean, he stayed, and I left."

"Marsh will be taken care of, and you'll have a hand in

that. But he's not ready to run an operation this big." Javier's jaw loosened. He emitted an audible sigh. "I doubt he ever will."

Badeau's exhaustion transformed into robust enthusiasm. The rigors of his day—the planning, Freddy, Kaitlyn escaping, all seemed so small.

"Don't tell Marsh," Javier said. "Better he finds out after I'm gone."

Ideas flooded Badeau's brain. Ideas about how to expand and maintain the club's integrity. "That's gonna create a big rift between Marsh and me."

"A small price to pay for Gabriella's, I think." Javier frowned. "I don't have the heart or the balls to tell him."

"Is the succession in writing?" Badeau asked.

"Yes. I finalized my new will this week." Javier offered his hand. "You get the whole enchilada. But there's something else. Something you'll need after I'm gone."

Javier grabbed a pen and a tablet from an end table, scribbled on the paper, then tore it off and handed it to Badeau.

"What's this?" Badeau said.

"The combination to the safe in my office. Inside are some personal items I set aside for you. And the full weight of the power I use to keep this business running—video recordings of the city's most powerful men and women in...let's say... compromising positions."

Badeau didn't have to ask what that meant. Videos taken in rooms just down the hallway. He stifled an exuberant smile with the realization of the power he'd soon possess. "So that's how you kept the police from breaking these doors down."

"You and I are the only ones with access to those videos. They're the keys to my kingdom. Guard them with your life." Javier wrapped his cold fingers around Badeau's hand. "Now, why'd you come to see me?"

Badeau hated to pump the breaks on his exuberance. "I lost a girl I was recruiting."

"Happens."

"She left, but four of her friends stayed."

"You know where she is?"

"Group home for foster girls."

Javier showed no emotion. "Leave her. If she causes a stir, we can use our connections. Might be a good lesson for when you take over."

Our connections. Not Javier's. Badeau's long-term expansion plan became more real. But first, he had to get five girls to Leon in Las Vegas by Thursday. He had four at the B&B ready to close. That left him one short and not enough time.

Tara? His sweet personal plaything all nestled at home in his condo. He'd hate to loser her, but the news he'd learned tonight softened the blow. Besides, Leon might pay extra for that particular piece of merchandise.

SEVENTEEN

Eli slipped on his Costa del Rays against the morning sun's brutal reflection off Lake Pontchartrain. The trip with Mancuso across the twenty-four-mile Causeway Bridge to the lake's north shore had been quiet. Neither he nor Mancuso had spoken for an hour except exchanging good mornings when Eli had picked up Mancuso at his Mid-City home.

The night before, after leaving Gabriella's and recording the Porsche and Escalade tag numbers, they'd argued over coffee and donuts at Café du Monde about not bringing Marshall Aberdeen in for questioning.

Eli still struggled with Mancuso's reasoning for not wanting to interrogate a prime suspect in Zoe Prevost's murder.

But Mancuso argued he wanted to avoid "stirring the gumbo," meaning not alerting Javier Navarro's network of corruption until Mancuso had built a stronger case. "Emma Prevost is our only link between Zoe and Aberdeen," he'd said. "A first-year law student could destroy her as a witness, not to mention the well-paid attorney Navarro will send. Aberdeen will be out before we can get him fingerprinted."

And Eli contended Navarro had already been alerted by Aberdeen. But Eli's frustration with Mancuso didn't rest solely on the case and Mancuso. Gina's manipulation at dinner, which had pitted Eli against his parents, had his insides still quivering.

Thankfully, he hadn't talked to Gina since leaving the restaurant. Her snoring was in full force when he arrived at the hotel last night and left this morning. A sign of too much chardonnay and that nothing short of the apocalypse would wake her.

"Tell me about this psychologist, Dr. Crenshaw," he said to Mancuso, his voice cracked from not using it all morning.

Mancuso's head flinched as if he broke free from deep thought. "I'm sorry. My head is somewhere else. What'd you say?"

"Dr. Crenshaw," Eli said. "The psychologist. What's your connection to her?"

"Oh..." Mancuso sat straighter. The corners of his mouth crept up in a smile. "I've known her for twenty years."

Eli pictured a matronly woman with grey hair in a bun wearing winged glasses and orthopedic shoes. "You've worked with her before?"

"Never," Mancuso said without changing expressions.

"Never? So, why—" Eli cut off his own words and bit the inside of his cheek. If he asked why Mancuso had Eli take a ninety-minute round trip to see an old friend instead of hound-dogging Marsh Aberdeen, last night's friction would resurface. "Never mind."

Mancuso settled back in his seat, seeming to return to his mysterious reverie.

———

Sitting at her desk on a Saturday morning, thirty-one-year-old Dr. Lindsey Crenshaw frowned at the notes from her latest counseling session. Her patient had made little progress since arriving at Safe Harbor Home for Girls almost two months ago. But that wasn't unusual. Physical and emotional traumatization requires long-term therapeutic treatment to achieve optimal results. And all of Lindsey's sixteen patients required extensive therapy.

Sexually abused survivors had not been under the care of psychologists until the latter part of the twentieth century. But to Lindsey, these girls had been the focus of her entire career. Moreover, she had one advantage that helped her professionally—her own history. She'd been a victim of child trafficking and came to Safe Harbor as a patient at age thirteen.

Looking up from the file, outside her window, she saw Manny Mancuso getting out of a Jeep parked next to her faded blue Civic. She felt her pressed lips surrender to an upward turn at the pleasant respite from her morning doldrums. What was Manny doing here on a Saturday?

A striking man about her age appeared from the driver's side. Manny approached him, pointing to the distant dormitories and talking. The attractive man stood with his hands in his pockets, his shoulders low and loose.

Her heart squeezed and her stomach fluttered like her old Civic at fifty miles per hour—the familiar signs for her to pay attention. Then she heard God's gentle voice in her ear. "This is the man I've chosen for you."

She'd heard God in the same inner voice in that rundown warehouse so long ago. But then she'd been desperate for help. And then, Manny had appeared. This was different.

What is this about, Lord? You know my fear of intimacy, and You know why.

Yet God's words came again as if He stood behind her and leaned down to her ear. "This is the man I've chosen for you."

The men disappeared behind the building on their way to the entrance. Knocking echoed through her office's open door. She strode to the mirror beside her bookcase to fuss with her hair. "I'm coming," she shouted. Why did she decide not to wear makeup today? She scowled at the constellation of faint freckles across her nose and under her green eyes. She rushed to the entrance. Her legs shook. She unlocked the door and stutter-stumbled back.

Manny entered. "Hello kitten. How's my girl?" Her old friend embraced her like a father. "We were going to your apartment. Then I saw your car parked here."

She peeked at Manny's companion. He had dark blue eyes that seemed to study everything in the foyer but her. "You know me. I spend more time at work than home."

Manny puffed out a gust of frustration. He'd always encouraged her to be more social ever since she'd been in high school. Finally, he turned to his companion. "This is Eli Colt, a detective from Mississippi. He's helping me with a case, and that's why we're here."

Eli Colt nodded blankly. Then, his gaze shifted to the Safe Harbor logo on the wall.

Did he just ignore her? How rude.

Lindsey turned and led the detectives into her office. "Why didn't you call ahead?" She motioned to the couch in the consulting area.

Eli Colt remained standing by the door.

Lindsey took a seat in her usual leather chair.

Manny sat across from her. "Some things you shouldn't share over the phone. I'm afraid I bring bad news." He produced a photo.

In the picture, Zoe stood with a younger girl, tall, lithe, blonde, and budding. And with the same dark blue eyes as Eli Colt. An ache throbbed in Lindsey's throat. "The girl in the front is Zoe Prevost. She's one of my patients." She looked away from the photo as if that could prevent the inevitable bad news Manny had mentioned. "Where did you get this picture?"

"The girl beside her is Detective Colt's niece. She disappeared late Wednesday."

"And Zoe?"

"I'm sorry kitten." Manny hesitated as if trying to regain control of his voice. "We found her body yesterday."

The ache in Lindsey's throat swelled into a painful knot. Although Zoe's death shook her, it was not wholly unexpected. She handed the photo back to Manny and glanced at Eli Colt.

He showed no emotion and avoided her eyes with cruel indifference.

"How'd she die?" Lindsey kept her tone neutral.

Manny breathed in a quick audible breath. "I'm afraid it's a homicide. Somebody killed her then tossed her into the Rigolets."

"Poor Zoe. If only she'd stayed here where it was safe." It wasn't the first time the police sat across from Lindsey and told her one of her girls was dead. The risk of trafficked girls overdosing or meeting their end with violence was high, as was not finishing high school, teen pregnancy, and homelessness. But at Safe Harbor, they had more chance for a future without violence.

"We're hoping you could share information about Zoe that could help us track down her killer," Manny said.

Eli Colt finally moved from his position at the door and sat on the couch next to Manny. "And to help us find Tara." Eli Colt's voice made Lindsey's muscles twitch. Eli. Short for Elijah? She liked the name. Courageous. Biblical.

What's wrong with you, Lindsey?

She'd just learned somebody murdered Zoe, and she was swooning over this Eli Colt like she was in high school. This feeling inside her was so strange, so unfamiliar. And it threatened to absorb her heartache for Zoe. She stood to get Zoe's file from a drawer at her desk, but not because she needed it. She had to hide her curious fascination for this Mississippi detective and start acting professionally.

"Have you ever heard of a Marshall Aberdeen?" Eli Colt asked.

At her desk in the next room, Lindsey thumbed through her patient's folders. "No. I don't think so." She glanced up to see if he was watching. Nope.

He looked up at the ceiling while talking with her.

"Zoe came to us over a year ago." Lindsey pulled the file and Zoe's journal and returned to the consultation area. She made a show of studying a document from the file until her heart rate slowed and the trembling in her stomach settled.

"Who brought her here?" Manny asked. "Her mother?"

Lindsey shook her head. "Zoe's grandmother Sylvia. She recognized Zoe's mom struggling to raise her because of—"

"Drugs and alcohol." There was disgust in Eli Colt's tone.

"So, you've met Emma," she said.

"Yep," Manny said. "And I had to call Social Services to pick up Zoe's little brother."

Zoe having a little brother was news to Lindsey but not a surprise. Zoe shared in her therapy sessions that men came and went, drinking, doing drugs, and having sex with her mother. Some came into Zoe's room after her mother passed out.

"So, Zoe came here because she was sexually abused?" Manny's face looked like it was ready to crumble—the same expression Lindsey had seen when Manny had rescued her in the warehouse over twenty years ago.

She confirmed with a nod. "Zoe's grandmother saw what was happening and took Zoe home."

Eli Colt leaned back on the sofa and scratched his jaw. "And grandma brought her here?"

"Not at first. Sylvia tried to raise Zoe and make sure she attended school, but Zoe proved too difficult. She rebelled, from her grandmother, and at sixty-seven and suffering from fibromyalgia, Sylvia found she couldn't handle a teenager with severe psychological wounds. So, Sylvia followed her church's advice, and she and her pastor brought her here."

"When did she leave?" Eli Colt asked.

"Which time? She left three times. Found her way back twice." Lindsey grabbed a tissue from the coffee table. "It was the fourth of July when she last ran."

"Did she say anything about a red Porsche or a gentlemen's club called Gabriella's?" Eli asked.

"No, but I suspected Zoe had options other than Safe Harbor. Most girls her age do."

"She didn't like it here?" Manny asked.

Lindsey's heart started shrinking. Why couldn't she help Zoe? "We have rules for girls to follow and try to enforce them with love. Some girls find us a safe space. Others can't get away fast enough."

"Like Zoe?" Eli Colt said.

"Yes." Lindsey handed the journal to Manny. "It's her diary. She'd had it when she first arrived, and she'd never left it behind before."

Manny accepted the book and thumbed through it. "What's in it?"

"I haven't read it. I must maintain trust with these girls, and reading Zoe's most intimate thoughts would've not gone over well."

Eli Colt flexed his hands open and shut. "Did she leave anything else?"

"No." Lindsey felt the thrum of her pulse. Why was Eli Colt so angry?

Manny stood first, then Eli, and finally, Lindsey hauled herself up. Eli walked to the door.

Manny stepped close to Lindsey. "I'm sorry for your loss kitten. Let me know if I can do anything?"

"Any leads on his niece, Tara?" Lindsey asked.

Manny whispered. "She ran too. According to Eli, the father died a while ago, and her mom's shacking up with a loser."

Lindsey peered over Manny's shoulder to find Eli Colt roaming outside in the hallway. "What's his story?"

Manny's head pulled back. "Now kitten...don't tell me—"

"Forget it." Her face warmed. She walked with Manny and caught up to Eli by the entrance.

Lindsey caught a whiff of Eli's masculine scent and she felt a bit queasy. But she raised her chin and her courage to fix her eyes on his. "If there's anything I can do to help, detective. Please don't hesitate to call." She inched closer and offered her hand.

Eli Colt didn't react for three heartbeats. And then his hand took hers. His touch sent a warmth through her arm that lingered. Then he blinked and shifted his focus to Manny. "You ready?"

Manny's arm wound around her waist, and she offered her cheek. He kissed it, moved past her, and the two men left the building.

The unexpected visit had her numb all over. Zoe murdered. It was an all too familiar drawback of her job. But the gentle voice she heard earlier was rare—its message extraordinary. And Zoe's death had brought him to her.

Why had God chosen a man who hadn't seemed interested in her? She watched Manny and Eli Colt get into the Jeep, then glanced at her computer.

Who was this Eli Colt?

———

Eli's heart thumped like a heavy metal bass guitar the second he laid his eyes on Dr. Lindsey Crenshaw. She wasn't the librarian type he pictured on the drive over. She looked nice, smelled nice, and did selfless work for kids who needed it. He looked out his windshield to the girls' dormitories, trying to shake the pleasant ache he felt inside. Because he was engaged to Gina—the most beautiful, the most sophisticated, the most alluring girl he'd ever met.

They would be married this spring. They would raise beautiful children in the country. They would live as the perfect family, with few worries in their carefully constructed world. Eli didn't need this distraction.

Manny buckled his seat belt. "What do you think about my girl Lindsey? Isn't she what my grandkids call—dope?"

Eli started the Jeep. "She seems nice."

"Always good to see her. I like to get out here every chance I can."

Driving off the property, Eli headed south. "You two seem close."

Manny relaxed in the passenger seat, closed his eyes, and tilted his head back on the headrest. "We are. What she's accomplished, the girls she's helped. My Lord. She turned chicken salad out of...well, you get my point."

"I'm not sure I do?"

"Let's just say Lindsey was trapped in a rough childhood. And Safe Harbor is where she got saved. And now she works there."

"So, you've known her twenty years? Since she was a kid?"

Mancuso set his shoulders back and pushed his chest out. "I've been a part of her life since she was thirteen. And she makes me feel prouder than my wife's Cockapoo after a trip to the doggy salon."

"Cockapoo?"

Manny laughed. "A cocker spaniel mixed with a miniature poodle."

"Sounds like a mutt to me."

Mancuso's eyes narrowed. "Try buying one."

"Is Dr. Crenshaw your godchild or something?" Eli found himself curious about this woman and hated that he did.

"Godchild?" Manny cupped a hand over his chin. "Let me put it like this. She's someone special who God has chosen to put in my life."

"I don't understand."

Mancuso stopped smiling. "She's proved to me what God's grace can do for a life that's been destroyed. Twenty years ago, I found her in an abandoned warehouse."

"Warehouse? Was she trapped or something?"

Mancuso dipped his chin to his chest. "No." He paused for several seconds, then raised his head. "Sorry, not my story to tell."

———

Lindsey sat at her desk and typed Eli Colt into the search engine. A tingling settled at the base of her neck as articles popped up concerning the man God promised her. She clicked the first article.

Local Warrior Awarded Silver Star with Valor for Risking Life to Save Others

NOLA.com. Published July 12, 2011

Sergeant Elijah Colt fought through blinding pain and refused to leave his fellow soldiers. The citation reads: "Despite being wounded during heavy enemy contact, Sergeant Eli Colt of the 1st US Ranger Battalion acted by single handedly encircling enemy insurgents and destroyed them. In addition, he eliminated two assault vehicles firing on his team. In the process he saved the lives of five of his fellow soldiers and helped to prevent serious injury."

After his team came under a rocket propelled grenade ambush in Helmand Province, Afghanistan, Sergeant Colt suffered severe shrapnel injuries to his thigh. He spent six weeks recuperating at Brooke Army Medical Center at Joint Base San Antonio, Texas.

Colt has since returned to his unit and redeployed to Afghanistan.

"Oh God," Lindsey whispered. "He's a bona fide hero."

She scrolled down to the next line to find a bridal registry website. The caption read:

Virginia Barrow and Elijah Colt to Wed

Their photo took up almost the entire webpage. Eli Colt and an attractive dark-haired woman with an olive complexion were in an intimate embrace and smiled into each other's eyes, their noses touching, her left hand holding the back of his head, fingers opened, displaying a diamond of at least three karats.

Lindsey set her jaw into her open palms and whispered, "The Lord gives, and then He takes away."

She continued reading.

The Wedding
 Saturday, May 8
 3:00 p.m.
 Attire: Formal
 Ceremony: St. Stephen's Church, Solace, MS.
 Reception: Barksdale Plantation Country Club, Solace, MS.

Lindsey didn't know if she was disappointed or relieved. She'd met a man who God revealed He'd chosen for her, only to find this man was engaged to someone else.

She closed the website and returned to her patient files. And then, for the third time in less than an hour, God spoke to her again.

"Don't be afraid. This is the man I've chosen for you."

EIGHTEEN

Exhausted, Andre Badeau leaned against his kitchen counter, breaking eggs for Tara's omelet. She'd been pouting since Badeau got home at 4:30 this morning. He tired of playing nice and placating the girl with all his other responsibilities pressing at him. "What would you like to do for lunch?"

Tara slumped at the breakfast bar with rounded shoulders, frowning at the plate. "Eat," she said as if her sarcasm could injure him.

Badeau would have to suffer this childish behavior for now. He had so much to do before Wednesday that he didn't have time for juvenile antics. "I need to step out for an hour or two—"

"Andre, nooo," she moaned like a wounded puppy. "You were gone for like all night. I was sooo bored."

Badeau felt his headache returning. "I'm sorry. But it's been a crazy weekend. I promise to make it up to you. Be ready to leave when I get back, and I'll take you to lunch, then we'll shop for new clothes." He needed to entertain an adolescent like he needed another Kaitlyn on his plate.

She pursed her lips and shifted her shoulders. "Oh, alright. Being a commodities broker must be hard. I've barely seen you since I got here."

"I know, honey. But we'll have a great time today." He slid the perfect omelet onto her plate. "Promise."

The weekend had been crazy. But Badeau's plan for getting five girls to Vegas was going well except for Kaitlyn's unexpected exit from the B&B last night. It had been stupid to leave because of a headache. Stupid. Stupid. Stupid.

He couldn't worry about that now. He only had five days to get five girls to Leon. And because Kaitlyn bailed while he left for Tylenol, Tara had to be one of those girls. He'd work on the four from the foster home this morning, then Tara after lunch.

———

The smell of stale cannabis, tobacco, and alcohol hit Badeau as he entered the B&B cottage.

Myles snored on the couch, surrounded by a sea of crushed Solo cups.

Restful breathing hummed from each bedroom. Freddy lay tangled with the tall white chick under the sheets in one bedroom while Audrey Hepburn slept peacefully beside them. Shirley Temple and the Latina huddled together in the other bedroom, abandoned by whoever last took advantage of their inebriations.

Time to close the deal.

The tall white chick stirred. Badeau entered the room, and she scrambled to get dressed, stumbling, mumbling, and cursing after her long night of drinking, drugs, and intercourse.

He offered her a loaded meth pipe and a lighter. "Try this. It'll make you feel better."

She took it. "Can you give us a ride home?" She flicked the Bic to light the pipe. "We came with Freddy and Myles."

She wasn't bad looking. Put her in a tight dress and make up her face, and she could look fairly hot. But in six months, she'd be an addict, probably living on the streets. There's nothing worse than a hooker who's always high. They're unreliable and become ugly and desperate. That'd be something Leon would need to deal with, not Badeau. "What's your name?"

"Madison."

Audrey Hepburn's eyes fluttered, then split open.

Freddy turned, pulling the sheet with him.

Audrey Hepburn lay nude and exposed.

Madison gave up putting on her pants, now high from the rock. "We need to go home, Hailey." She nudged her friend. "Let's go."

"What's your hurry?" Badeau produced a roll of cash. "You can stay here with me."

"What's he talking about?" Hailey tugged at the sheet to cover herself. "What time is it?"

"I tell you what I'm talking about," Badeau said. "I'm talking about a new life for you girls."

Madison's eyes were vacant—zoned out.

Hailey rose from the bed and grabbed clothes from different mounds of pants, shirts, and shoes scattered across the floor.

Badeau snatched the pipe from Madison and handed it to Hailey. "Look here, girls. I know where you live. I got friends that used to live there. Some are working for me now. And if you know what's good for you, you'll stay away from that place."

Madison sat on the bed next to Hailey, whose eyelids hung low. He hunched down to their eye level and snapped his fingers. "You think you can go back there now?"

Hailey toked on the pipe and coughed.

Shirley Temple staggered in with wobbly legs.

Badeau continued. "Don't you know what happens to hookers?"

Madison looked at him with a glazed stupor. "We ain't hookers."

"No? What'd y'all do last night? Do you remember? You go back to school, and you'll find out. There were about fifty dudes up in here, and y'all serviced most of them. Man, cell phones flashed, taking pics and videos. Look here." Badeau pulled out his phone and played a video from social media. Hailey's eyes bulged and teared up.

Madison covered her mouth, muffling a series of high-pitched whines.

"Who shot that video?" Shirley Temple's voice trembled like a widow at her husband's funeral.

"Does it matter? What matters is the guys here paid for you. You made 500 bucks." Badeau waved a roll of twenties. "You know what that means, right? Sure, you do. The police ain't gonna help you. Their job is to arrest hookers. And your rich little friends at school? Who do you think you were hooking up with last night? Their boyfriends, that's who. Them girls home right now watching videos of you screwing their wannabe-prom dates."

Badeau paused to allow his words to hit their mark.

Shirley Temple walked into the hall. "Natalia, wake up. You got to hear this."

"And don't even think about going back to that group home," Badeau said. "They can't be housing hookers."

Despite the meth, a light went on behind Hailey's eyes.

"But here's the thing, ladies. You can stay with me, and I'll give you fine clothes and put money in your pocket, starting with this." He threw the roll in Hailey's lap. "And y'all can stay together, like peas in a snug condo, making your own cash."

Madison buried her head in her hands, and a low, unearthly squeal followed.

Hailey inspected the money, probably the most cash she'd ever seen.

"Why don't y'all just relax? Sit back and talk about it. I can give y'all a good opportunity." Badeau felt the sweat building on his scalp. He needed this to work. Needed it bad. "I'll take y'all out for breakfast. On me. After that, we can talk about Vegas."

"Las Vegas?" Natalia, the tall Latina, entered the room. "What about Las Vegas?"

Bingo.

"Freddy's going to Vegas on Wednesday, you know, to see the shows, hit the tables, play the slots."

"But what about all our stuff? Our clothes?" Hailey asked.

"I'll hook you up. Fine clothes. Not like those rags laying all over this place." Badeau grabbed Freddy. "Yo, bruh. I need you to take these girls shopping. On me. You know where."

"How long will we be in Vegas?" Natalia said.

"Couple of weeks unless you want to stay longer. Lots of money to be made in Vegas. Who knows, y'all could end up as models or movie stars."

Madison whispered in Hailey's ear.

Hailey's eyes fluttered, and she nodded.

"Go on now, talk it over," Badeau said. "I'll be back in a half-hour to take y'all to breakfast. I know a place around the corner that serves omelets, waffles, and café au lait."

"I don't know," Hailey said.

"That's why I said think about it. And while you're thinking, I'll buy you breakfast."

"Where's Kaitlyn?" Hailey asked.

"She bailed early, "Badeau said. "But that's cool. We all make our choices."

"Stuck up toad," Natalia stared at the pipe in Hailey's hand.

"Yeah. But what's she saying back at the home?" Hailey hit the pipe again.

Badeau agreed. What was Kaitlyn saying, indeed?

NINETEEN

At the north end of the Causeway Bridge, Eli paid the toll booth attendant and shot a side-eye glance at Mancuso. Eli struggled to shake his encounter with Dr. Crenshaw, her winsome beauty, her comely form, the fervor that remained inside him since he'd touched her hand.

Mancuso sat erect, absorbed in Zoe Prevost's diary since they left Safe Harbor. "Zoe was not your typical teenager," he finally said.

Eli eased his foot on the accelerator to merge into the bridge traffic. "What do you mean?"

"Kids her age don't write in journals anymore. They put their life on Facebook, Twitter, or that one from China?"

"TiK ToK," Eli said.

"Yeah, that's the one."

"Maybe she didn't have access to a cell phone or a computer." Then, a careless oversight dawned on Eli. He hadn't thought to search Tara's social media accounts. His neck flushed hot at his stupidity. "Son of a—"

"What's wrong?" Manny looked up from the journal. "You just thought about searching Tara's online footprint."

Eli hit the steering wheel with his palm. "Yep."

"Don't worry." Mancuso licked a finger to turn a page. "I checked her social media when you were at dinner. Tara's accounts are private, which is typical of kids her age. Don't want their mommy or daddy reading what they post."

"You could've told me earlier."

Mancuso removed his readers and rubbed his eyes. "You didn't seem to be in the mood for much talking this morning."

Eli cursed his lack of judgment about Mancuso's actions the night before. He'd done what Eli'd failed to do. He'd gotten rusty, not working major crimes during his time in Solace. Mancuso was right—two is better than one.

"I texted our IT geek, and he's secretly working on hacking Tara's accounts as we speak. It's not legal unless we get permission from your sister-in-law."

"I'll get Julia to email her consent." Eli glanced at the journal. "Anything of interest in there?"

"Lots. Zoe wrote more than John Grisham. Almost every detail of her life is in here but with little organization—no times or dates." Mancuso replaced his glasses. "Plenty of complaints about her mother."

"I'll bet." The adrenaline surge of a case moving forward hit Eli like a flood, washing away his infatuation with Dr. Crenshaw.

Mancuso turned the journal back a couple of pages. "There's mention of Tara too."

Hearing Tara's name sent a nervous shudder through Eli. "Anything that would help us find her?"

"Not yet. But I don't think I'm near the time of her murder. Like I said. No dates. Just random thoughts." Mancuso slumped in his seat. "Zoe tried to commit suicide right before her grandmother rescued her."

Eli couldn't respond.

Murdered at sixteen. Tried to off herself a couple of years earlier. What chance did Zoe Prevost have for a normal happy life? And what chance did Tara have for surviving whatever or whoever she was into?

"How does..." Mancuso seemed to stumble for words. "How does Lindsey deal with kids like Zoe every day?"

Eli's brain shifted from awe of the psychologist to sympathy for her demanding job. "I suppose it takes a special person to do what she does."

They rode in silence for fifteen miles. Then, still reading the journal, Mancuso said, "Well I'll be."

"What?"

"Looks like Zoe thought of Marsh Aberdeen as her boyfriend." Mancuso's voice rose a decibel or two. "And hold on to your socks. There's more."

"Go on."

Mancuso pointed at the page. "'Today, Tara went with me and Marsh to the French Market to shop for jewelry. We met this hot older guy near the linens and lace place."

Eli interrupted. "Julia told me Tara's friends had seen her with an older guy."

Mancuso's phone buzzed, but he ignored it and continued. "'He offered to buy us lunch at Central Grocery, but Marsh wanted a chili-cheese omelet at Camellia Grill. So we piled in Andre's Escalade and drove to Carrollton.'"

Mancuso stopped reading and scrolled on his phone.

"Andre's Escalade," Eli said. "A buck for a beignet, that's the Escalade we saw at Gabriella's."

"And look what my geek got off Tara's Instagram." Mancuso raised his phone so Eli could see the screen. On it was a picture of Tara, the rear end of a black Escalade behind her with the license plate visible. Below the image: I go everywhere in style.

TWENTY

Eli followed Mancuso into the Broad Street police station early Saturday afternoon but late enough to find the squad room empty and dark, except for a glow emitting from the same corner where Eli had met Reggie Toussaint the day before.

Mancuso had learned that according to the DMV, the Escalade they'd seen at Gabriella's and on Tara's Instagram belonged to an LLC formed in the Cayman Islands. "This Fleur de Lis' is a shell company."

He and Eli marched to the break room for coffee.

"We should've run those plates last night," Mancuso said. "I knew that guy in the Escalade was dirty."

In the break room they found Captain Guidry, hands on hips, leaning over a single-serve coffee maker. "Thing hasn't been here six months, and it's already on the blink."

"Should've never got rid of the Bunn," Mancuso said. "Thing would have outlasted me."

Guidry turned, his arms flexed at his side to widen his outline and set off an imposing posture. "Sorry, Manny. I thought you were Reggie." The captain relaxed his stance and glanced at Eli. "Good evening, Detective Colt."

Although Mancuso had told him Captain Guidry had cleared Eli and Mancuso to work together, a tense chill struck Eli like he'd been caught trespassing.

Mancuso raked his thin hair with open fingers. "Looks like if we want a caffeine fix, we'll have to hit PJs around the corner. You want us to grab you a cup, cap?"

"Naw, I'm leaving soon. You two burning late hours?"

"Caught a plate number on the Prevost case," Mancuso said. "Belongs to a company in the Caymans."

Toussaint stormed into the room with a look of level-ten irritation. Eli's presence seemed to catch him unawares. He squinted at Mancuso and turned to Guidry. "Just came for some coffee."

"Coffeemaker gave up the ghost," Guidry said. "Maybe you play nice with Mancuso and our friend from Mississippi, and they'll pick you up an espresso from PJs."

Toussaint said nothing. He stepped out of the room and returned to his desk.

Guidry focused on Eli. "I heard about your dust-up with Detective Toussaint. I'm sorry about that." He leaned his head to Mancuso. "Hope you don't mind working with this old salt. He's been here longer than the furniture."

"Not at all," Eli said. "Working with a veteran like Detective Mancuso is an honor."

Guidry's lips formed a smile. "Well, ain't you two like a Hallmark Bromance." Then his eyebrows drew together. "You may want to stay clear of Reggie. He's not happy he has to work this weekend to get his clearance rate in line."

Mancuso exhaled, causing his lips to flutter. "Any way we can roust somebody from forensic accounting to go over this shell company?"

"I can try but make no promises," Guidry said. "But first, I need to ask a favor from you both."

Eli and Mancuso followed Guidry to his glassed-in office, where he shut the door and closed the blinds. Guidry waved at the two seats by his desk and sat in his chair.

A slight shiver sifted through Eli.

Mancuso sat in his seat stiffly. "What's up, cap?"

Guidry leaned back and rubbed his chin. "Look, I don't like talking inside baseball with outsiders, but I think I can help all involved with your case."

"I'm all for that," Mancuso said.

Guidry continued. "You both have a stake in solving these investigations." The captain sat straight and rested his forearms on his desk. "Look, I know this is unprecedented and maybe not the smartest thing I've ever done. But I need to do something for Reggie, or he'll be demoted to auditing arrest reports by the end of the month."

Guidry opened the side drawer of his desk. "You know how many cases run across Reggie's desk? Him being the most senior detective in missing persons?"

Eli could only compare the number of cases he'd handled with CID in a year. That number averaged about seventy.

"I have no clue, cap," Mancuso said.

"Well, let me tell you." Guidry lifted a stack of folders from the open drawer and plopped him on his desk. "He handles about six cases per month, and he's closed about a third. And I don't have to tell you, most of those closed themselves. Kids coming home after a week or two on their own or the odd husband not missing, only shacking up over the weekend with his paramour."

Mancuso shrugged. "What does that have to do with me..." Mancuso glanced at Eli. "Us."

"It's more about me and my numbers. To be frank, Reggie's dragging my clearance rate down. To date, I'm one case short of fifty percent clearance. I need your help, Mancuso. Your's too, Detective Colt."

"You want us to handle Reggie's cases?" Mancuso said.

"I've reviewed his open cases." Guidry tapped the top of the files on his desk. "Here are four teenage girls who've gone missing from a foster home. The case is red hot, reported early this morning. They should be easy enough to clear. And to help with the numbers, I opened a file on each girl."

Manny lifted his hands as if somebody trained a gun on him. "I'd love to help you, cap, but I'm a Homicide detective in the middle of a case. Why not ask someone in auto theft or robbery?"

"Because they're not my best. Look, I've got a sloppy detective who's in drop and can't pull his weight. So I cut him loose before he makes his twenty in a few months, or I help out a fellow cop. And there's another reason."

"What's that?" Mancuso said.

"I checked out your temporary partner here." Guidry jerked a thumb at Eli. "Seems like he's one fine detective. According to the Army, Detective Colt's clearing rate is still revered. And they hated losing him to his former captain, now his current chief of police."

Mancuso chuckled. "I told you he had skills, cap."

"This skills I'll need to help me out of my current dilemma." Guidry's eyes studied Eli. "Why he's wasting his talent in a small town in Mississippi is a mystery, but I would sure like to put them to work for me."

"I like Solace," Eli said. "I'm getting married this spring and plan to make it home. I'm just here to find my niece, sir. Not here to help your numbers. Sorry."

Guidry's expression melted into a mixture of friendly and firm. "Let's call it quid-pro-quo then. I pulled you a solid by opening my department and partnering you with one of my best detectives. If you think you can find your niece faster without my help, go ahead and try." He drummed his fingers on his desk. "But you'll need a hand along the way. A hand you might find less forthcoming if you don't return the favor. Like I said, quid-pro-quo."

And there it was. Help Guidry with his numbers or find the NOPD more enemy than ally.

How could Eli tell Gina he'd agreed to more investigating and less time with her? Or should he keep his mouth shut? He looked at Mancuso, who offered no help. "Say I agree to work the cases. If I find Tara before finding these other girls, I'll be heading back to Solace."

Guidry stood and offered Eli his hand. "Fair enough. Welcome to the NOPD."

TWENTY-ONE

Military training had taught Eli that sleep was a weapon. Never stand when you can sit, never sit when you can lie down. And most important, never stay awake when you can sleep.

So when Mancuso found an NOPD forensic accountant willing to review Fleur de Lis Limited, but not until the following day, Eli returned to his hotel to crash for five or six hours to refresh his brain and recharge his determination.

The elevator in the Four Seasons was empty up to Eli's floor. He was tired. A yawning-every-ten-seconds tired. A falling-asleep-standing-up tired. A not-thinking-or-walking-or-speaking-straight tired. So tired, he could make out the dark circles under his eyes in his obscured reflection on the brass elevator door.

He entered the suite and almost tripped over stacked luggage. The night was slipping into the early morning, but Gina wasn't in bed. Instead, she sipped white wine on a plush white couch, waiting.

Her eyes fluttered, displaying her perfectly mascaraed

lashes. "You ready?" Her tone was somewhere between expectant and demanding.

Dropping down next to her, Eli sunk into the couch. "Ready for what?"

Gina waved him off. "I'm fed up with spending every moment in this city alone. I'm going to call for a bellman, have him pack your Jeep, and you and I—my husband-to-be—are going home."

Eli leaned his head back and closed his eyes. "I need sleep."

"Of course you do," Gina said in an unsympathetic tone. "You stay out all hours of the night. You don't call."

Eli expelled all breath. He had no energy to argue.

"You can sleep in the car while I drive," she said.

Going home and sleeping until Tuesday didn't sound bad. But Eli had never left a mission before completion, and he wouldn't start now.

Besides, he hadn't felt this much juice during an investigation since he'd left the Army. But he needed to sleep bad.

His mind scrambled, trying to think how to diffuse Gina's assault demanding he abandon Tara. "Gina, I'm close. And we found out Tara could be in the hands of some evil people. I have to stay."

"No," Gina said with authority. "I know I gave you the weekend and tomorrow is Sunday, but I'm done, you hear me? Done." She rose to her feet. "Now don't give me a fuss. I want to be home before breakfast."

Eli's heart rate elevated. He'd had commanding officers give him direct orders with more tact. He sat straighter and gave Gina a what-did-you-say gaze. "I'm not going home. Not now. I have work to do here."

"I don't want to be unpleasant. I don't." Gina fiddled with her engagement ring as if it were hot on her finger. "But I've talked to Daddy. You remember my daddy. The mayor and your boss' boss. "She walked with long steps to the fully stocked bar.

Eli thought about having a drink. A good stiff one. But he'd be out before his second pull.

Gina topped off her wine, strolled to the room's phone, picked up the receiver, but didn't dial. "It was noble for you to come down here this weekend and look for your niece. But New Orleans is an open sewer, and it leaves everything it touches with a foul smell. Our weekend is over, and it's time to go home. I didn't pack your toothbrush or razor. In case you want to shave or brush your teeth." She sipped her wine, her eyes giving Eli a penetrating, imperious gaze.

Eli's shoulders collapsed under the weight of his exhaustion and Gina's demands. "I'm not leaving, Gina. Not until I find Tara. "He could hear the fatigue in his voice.

"Please, I don't want to sound mean or like a spoiled little daddy's girl." Gina pointed the phone's receiver at Eli like it was a weapon. "But you will leave with me this morning. Now. No argument. I've had enough."

Eli's anger flared, vented like flammable gas leaking through a fractured pipe. He set his jaw tight. "What is it about me finding Tara that has you so upset?"

She hung up the phone. "Because I fear this city is putting a spell on you and drawing you into its wickedness. I'm afraid if I let you stay here another day, you may never leave." Gina's face registered pain and displeasure.

"Believe me. I don't want to spend a second more than I have to here. Once I find Tara, I'll be back in Solace. I told as much to the NOPD captain last night."

"I'm sorry?" Gina's brow shot up in mild indignation. "What does a New Orleans police captain have to do with you leaving or staying?"

"He doesn't. I'm just working with him and a detective to find Tara, and—"

"And what?"

"Nothing." He paused, knowing that with the next phrase he was about to stick his size twelve boot down his throat. He really needed to get some sleep. "There's another case linked to Tara's disappearance."

"Another girl missing?" Gina asked as if she'd stumbled into some deep secret Eli held.

"Ah...not exactly."

"What case then?"

"A homicide." Eli could taste leather.

"Homicide." Her tone was ripe with rancor. "And why am I only hearing about this now?"

"Because it's the first time we've been alone since we got to New Orleans." He shifted his voice into high gear.

She leaned over him, her eyes cold and cunning. "And who's fault is that?"

His irritation exploded like an active volcano. "I wasn't the one who invited my parents to dinner last night, was I?"

She turned from Eli and sauntered back to the bar. "I'd never met them."

"I know you haven't, and there's a reason. And now that you've spent time with Mom and Dad, I expect you know why."

Gina raised her arms and pleaded like a politician for a vote. "That's why I need to get you out of New Orleans. This place, these people. It's not good for you."

"I'm not a child. And I know this place and these people a lot better than you."

"Maybe." She took a generous pull of her wine. "But it's sucking you into its filth. I can see it even if you can't. If we're going to be soul mates and lifetime partners, then you need to understand that I'm wiser than you in most things. So, you need to trust me and come home with me tonight."

Eli squared himself to face her, his anger rising above his hurt. "Are you giving me an ultimatum?"

"Call it what you like. But if I go home alone tonight, don't bother coming back to Solace. There will be nothing for you there. No job, no place to park your crappy Airstream, and no me."

Was he hearing his fiancée correctly? Was she willing to scorch Eli's life because he was trying to do the right thing? If that's the hand she wanted to play, fine. He dragged his bags to the bedroom to call her bluff, then fell into bed without removing his clothes.

Gina called for the bellman.

He fell asleep within thirty seconds, too exhausted to care.

———

Eli's phone buzzed repeatedly, but the sound seemed distant. The pillow-top mattress had swallowed him, the warm comforter so cozy he never wanted to leave. The phone kept chirping over and over like artillery right before a battle.

Five more minutes, please.

The phone's insistence forced his eyes open and a streak of sunlight sliced through a crack in the curtains. Where was he? The Four Seasons. Gina. The argument they had last night. He snatched his phone off the nightstand but dropped it.

"Gina," he shouted while it vibrated on the floor. "Hello," he said, getting the phone to his ear.

"Good morning buttercup." Mancuso's voice was as cheery as a camp counselor. "Up and at 'em. Early bird gets the snake in the weeds."

"What time is it?" Eli's voice was rough and raspy.

"Eight hundred hours for you military types."

Eight in the morning. "Give me half an hour."

"You got it. My forensic accountant is working on Fleur de Lis."

Eli hung up. He stalked around the suite but couldn't find a trace of Gina. He stood under the hot shower, then shocked his system by turning the faucet cold. He used this trick while in the Army, during a challenging case or after a night of too much to drink.

He dressed, packed, and rushed to the lobby, stopping by the front desk.

The clerk handed him a note. "Our system said your wife checked out at three this morning, Mr. Barrow. I hope you both enjoyed your stay."

"Thank you. Can you have my car brought down." Eli opened the small envelope.

Eli—I hired a car to take me back to Solace. Hope you find what you're looking for—G.

He threw his bag in the Jeep and tried to call Gina, only to get her voicemail.

He left a message. "Please call me and let me know you got home safe."

Why had she left in the middle of the night. Couldn't she see he was in no condition to have the conversation she forced with her power move?

Ten minutes later, Eli parked and walked to the Broad Street Station. His phone chimed a text alert.

Arrived home safe and sound—G.

Blood drained from his head at the elevator. How could things go so wrong so fast? But his mission hadn't changed. He needed to find Tara soon and get home to repair his relationship with Gina.

In the squad room, a few people milled about—detectives on the phone at their cubicles or talking amongst themselves.

Mancuso called out from the break room. "You get enough sleep?" He held a steaming Styrofoam cup. "Cap felt sorry for us and picked up a Mr. Coffee. Ain't a Bunn but it gets the job done. Here, you look like you could use this."

"Thanks." Eli took a gulp of the coffee. Just like he liked it, strong enough to dissolve a spoon. "Where's your accountant?"

"At home. He's working remotely."

They found an email from the accountant at Mancuso's workstation and printed the attached document.

Mancuso scanned the report. "Says here Fleur De Lis Limited has some large assets. The Escalade we know about. And..." He whistled." A fifty-foot Marquis Sports Coupe."

"What's that, a boat?" Eli asked.

"No, son. That there is a yacht that costs about eight times my annual salary." Mancuso shuffled to another page. "Okay, what else we got? A storage warehouse on Tchoupitoulas, and..." Mancuso gazed at the document for another moment, then slapped it with the back of his hand. "A riverfront condo."

Eli extended his hand for the paper. "There's a good chance Tara's there."

"And an equally good chance she could be on that yacht or at the warehouse," Mancuso said. "I'll broadcast a BOLO for the boat and get warrants for all three. I should have everything by noon."

"I thought your go-to judge was at the beach?"

"No sweat. He'll do it by email."

Eli was in no mood to wait. "I'll go to the condo and see if I can worm my way inside."

Mancuso picked up his desk phone and dialed. "I'll get there as soon as I can with the warrant."

———

Monday morning Badeau drank coffee in the kitchen of his French Quarter property with Jewel, a stunning black woman, with dark skin, dark eyes, and a dark demeanor when needed. She once worked as a hooker, but now managed Badeau's whores.

He came to arrange a place for the four new girls to stay until Freddy brought them to Vegas. The house was quiet, with his hookers still sleeping after working late. There were three conventions in town.

The home housed his whores but he didn't think of it as a traditional brothel. Ten girls currently lived in the three-story structure on Dauphine Street, with its high ceilings, brick walls, oak floors, and private courtyard. By adding another four girls the home would be cramped, but not for long.

Badeau saw to it that his hookers didn't have to hustle the streets. Jewel would schedule their tricks in homes or hotels or vacation condos, safer than some dark corner in the Quarter or Mid-City. And with Loto, a Samoan who once played defensive tackle in college, they had live-in security and a driver to take them to and from their appointments. Loto also served as muscle for johns trying to get more than they paid for.

For the most part, selling their bodies to conventioneers and tourists was relatively safe for his girls, although disease and the occasional beating were still hazards of their trade.

Badeau poured himself more coffee. "Separate the new girls. Bunk each one with an older girl."

"They ain't gonna like it," Jewel warned.

"You kidding me. They'll love it. I saw the house they came from. This place is a palace compared to that dump."

"I ain't talking about the new ones. I'm talking about the ones who have to share their room."

Badeau's rage meter ticked up. "Well, they don't have to like it, do they?"

"You ain't got to hear them get all mean and nasty neither." Jewel lifted her arms in protest. "And break up the fights that will be happening sure enough. These hos get real territorial about their space up in here."

"You're right, I don't have to listen to these whores." His tone was as sharp as a stiletto. "That's why you don't turn tricks anymore and live high on a really fat hog. Besides." Badeau didn't know where his anger had gone so quickly. Probably because he needed Jewel more than he cared to admit. "It's not gonna be for long. We're moving the new girls to Vegas on Wednesday."

"For real?" Jewel said, adding a bark of laughter. "You pimping for that no count Negro Leon now? That brother dirtier than a martini on Bourbon Street."

"I need to expand."

"So, you expand to Vegas?" Jewel dipped into dissension. "Why not expand right here?"

Badeau thought about his conversation with Javier. "That's in the works too."

Jewel cocked her head back. "What's going on Andre? What you up to."

"I'm expanding the business, which means more opportunity for you."

Jewel cupped her ear like she couldn't hear. "What you say?"

"I'm getting Gabriella's when Javier dies."

Jewel's eyes lit up like sparklers. "I thought Marsh was Javier's prince of perverts next in line for that throne."

"So did I." Badeau sipped his coffee. "Javier figured Marsh couldn't run anything bigger than a snowball stand. So, he's giving it to me. Paperwork is all signed, stamped, and recorded in probate."

"Whoeee, sugar." Jewel drummed the counter with both hands. "That's hitting the lottery. Bam!"

Smiling at Jewel's elation, Badeau took a moment to enjoy the excitement. "Javier's practical. He wants to leave a legacy that will last longer than ten minutes after he's gone."

"And that's you?" Jewel said. "The legacy I mean."

Badeau shrugged at the thought but liked it. "What do you think?"

"I suppose." Jewel poured herself a cup of coffee. "As long as you got ole Jewel to manage your hos for you."

Jewel did speak the truth. She had proved to be loyal and efficient and capable of managing this house despite the constant complaining of ten hookers living in tight quarters. And for those qualities, she had been well compensated.

Not only did Badeau pay her well, but he'd given her the down payment for her house in Carrollton and bought her an electric Prius to hum around town.

"I need you to get these new girls ready for the road by Wednesday," Badeau said. "Freddy will drive them and a crown jewel I've just acquired straight through."

"Crown jewel?"

"I just landed a high-end piece of merchandise."

"She polished?"

Badeau shook his head. "She's a fifteen-year-old pure as Everclear."

"Why you want to sell young girls to old men." Jewel's mouth rolled like she bit into a lemon. "Leave that to Javier and Marsh."

"This one's special. She's like a brand-new Mercedes in a lot full of used Fords."

Jewel grimaced with an air of disgust. "I know you can make plenty of money with those young'uns. But dealing with those sleazy perverts who like little boys and girls is a gamble." She touched Badeau's arm. "You get caught, you going to

Angola for decades. And these other hos may get righteous. They be up in your grill for exposing little girls to this kind of life."

"Who says they gotta like it?" Badeau said with venom. "Besides, these kids will be in Vegas within a week."

"Well, what about the PO-lice. You know they leave us alone with the girls we got working. Bring in underage hos— they might be breaking down the door."

"I hear ya." Badeau rested a cheek on his palm. "But I'm committed. I can't let Leon down now."

"With Leon them new girls lucky if they survive two years."

"Again. Not my problem. I'm getting my cash up front." Badeau poured himself more coffee and topped off Jewel's cup. "I'll come back from Vegas flush with capital. Then we can start preparing to take over Gabriella's and we'll entertain our high-end johns here." His thoughts turned to his old mentor and a flutter of guilt tickled his insides. "I saw Javier last night. I don't think he'll make spring."

"When you bringing that crown jewel in?" Jewel asked.

"I'm not. She'll be staying with me till Wednesday."

Jewel chuckled as if Badeau was outside his lane. "You gonna hold out with a teenage girl that long?"

"We've all got to make our sacrifices."

Badeau's cell phone rang. Javier.

TWENTY-TWO

"Answer the damn phone," Badeau screamed into his cell after the fifth ring on his third attempt to contact Freddy. Badeau paced around the fountain in the courtyard of his French Quarter property, his phone jammed against his ear. Javier had warned Badeau of a warrant issued to search his condo.

A warrant. A freaking warrant. This was Aberdeen's fault. Letting cops into the club was as stupid as stupid could get. Badeau stopped pacing and considered racing back to the condo to get Tara, but he doubted he could beat the police there. Instead, he called the B&B to ring the cottage.

"Hello." The voice was low as a mosquito buzz and female.

Badeau couldn't determine which of the four girls answered. "Put Freddy on the damn phone."

Silence.

"Hello?" Badeau shouted the word, a coldness crawled through him despite the damp New Orleans heat. He recalled the cottage as he left it on Saturday. Freddy sprawled on the couch. The girls napping the night off. The pungent odor of weed, alcohol, and sex still strong. He should have moved the girls then, but the whore business was booming with the conventions in town.

Now, this oversight was causing him to look at twenty years in prison.

"Hello," Badeau shouted again.

Finally, a wet cough, followed by Freddy's gruff voice. "Yeah?"

"Tell me you're not sleeping," Badeau said.

"Wha—what time is it?"

"Time for you to get up. I've got a job for you."

"Huh?"

"Wake up, Freddy." Badeau tapped his right shoe on the brick floor. "I need you to run to my condo. Like now."

How did the police put together Tara and his condo? Badeau had multiple layers separating him from his home. "Freddy, you still there?"

More disgusting sounds of Freddy coughing and spitting. "Yeah."

"Get up. I need you on the road now."

"Why?"

Other voices started talking to Freddy.

"Don't worry about why.," Badeau said. "Get going."

"We're leaving for Vegas already?"

Badeau slammed his foot into a wrought iron chair knocking it on its back. "No. We ain't leaving for Vegas. Get in that hotrod and go."

"What about these chicks? Ain't I supposed to bring 'em to Dauphine Street?"

An adrenaline rush overwhelmed Badeau. This was taking too long. "I'll get Loto to take care of that. Just get over to the condo as soon as you can. I need you to grab a girl that's staying there, then call me."

"Another girl?"

"Yeah, but she's special. And Freddy, in and out. Don't hang there. Just get the girl and her stuff and leave immediately."

Badeau heard Freddy moving and pictured him stepping over Solo cups and discarded clothes. Then, the familiar sound of urine hitting water.

Badeau used his shirt sleeve to wipe the sweat from his forehead. "Let's move Freddy."

"I'm moving. Where do you want me to bring her?"

"I don't know yet. Just go."

"Okay, okay. But can't this wait an hour or—" Violent retching.

Badeau lowered the phone to his thigh. He envisioned the police going up his private elevator with a warrant. After finding the girl, they'd put out an all-points on Badeau. He'd have to leave town. Maybe the country.

He raised the phone back to his ear. "You okay?"

"Yeah. I'm good now. Must have been something I ate."

More like pounding beer, booze, and weed on top of molly. "You get this done," Badeau said. "And there's a bonus for you. A big one." He heard fumbling, then a toilet flushing.

Badeau's internal clock set off resounding alarms. "Get that girl out in less than forty-five minutes, and I'll give you a big chunk of cash."

"How much?"

"Double what you got last night."

A brief hesitation, then Freddy spoke. "Let me brush my teeth, and I'm out of here."

"Freddy." Badeau spoke slow, emphasizing every syllable. "Forget your teeth. If you don't get moving right now, I swear—"

"I'm going, I'm going. I'm walking out the door. How do I get in your place?"

"I'll text you the code. And Freddy..."

"Yeah."

"Don't touch her. Don't put a finger on her."

"Don't worry bout that, Unc. I've been getting down with these freaks here for the past two nights."

The roar of Freddy's Mustang's five-liter engine thundered. "Let me know when you have her out of the condo, you hear? And I'll see you soon."

"Uh, okay. I'll call in about twenty minutes."

Badeau hung up. He hoped he had twenty minutes.

————

When Tara first arrived at Andre's condo, she thought an elevator opening into the living room weird. "What happens if someone pushes the wrong button?" she'd asked Andre.

"They can't. Didn't you see me enter a passcode on the keypad?"

She didn't. She'd been digging through her overnight bag searching for her iPhone she'd lost while escaping home.

But now, standing in Andre's great room, she looked at her reflection in the brass doors inside Andre's condo, tempted to go downstairs to find something to eat. There were no potato chips or other snacks in the pantry. Just organic this and organic that and packaged foods in the refrigerator with names she couldn't pronounce.

Andre should've been back hours ago and now her stomach howled. The low-tech flip phone Andre gave her rang.

She answered. "Hello."

"It's Andre." The voice was Andre's but something was off.

"Where are you? I'm starving." She didn't mean to scold Andre. But she'd waited around all morning for him to return.

"Something's come up, baby. I can't get away." His voice was different. Hurried. He sounded scared.

"What do I do for lunch?" Tara resisted raising her voice. Andre acted strange.

"I've got my nephew coming to pick you up. He'll bring you anywhere you want."

"You were supposed to be here hours ago." Her tone softened from angry to pleading.

Silence.

"Andre?" Something is bad. Really bad.

"Tara." He sounded like his mind was on something else. "I need you to pack your things. Pack everything. Toothbrush, makeup, everything."

A tingling of fear made Tara's legs restless. "You're kicking me out?"

"No. Not at all, baby. Look—"

"What then? What's going on?" Tara body trembled. She stepped a leg back to brace herself from falling. "Why do you want me to leave?"

"I'm taking you on a trip, honey. I'm taking you shopping...yes, shopping. You need clothes, right? I mean, you left most of your stuff behind." They'd talked about him buying her a new wardrobe. But why did he sound so troubled?

The tension in Tara's chest relaxed and she let out a giggle. "Shopping? Where?"

"I need to be in New York tomorrow and I want to take you. We can hit Fifth Avenue and I'll buy you whatever you want."

Tara bounced on her feet. "New York." She shrilled at max volume.

"Just go with my nephew. His name's Freddy. He'll be there soon. Be ready to leave. He'll take you to the airport."

Tara rushed to her room to toss what little she had into her bag. "You'll be at the airport?"

"I'm on my way there now. I'll see you in an hour. Hurry up. Freddy should be there by now."

———

Eli arrived at One River View—high-end condos for the one-percenters, including a few professional athletes. No one sat behind the security desk.

"Hello." Eli's voice echoed through the lobby of marble, brass, and steel.

No response.

He looked for a directory, but there was none. Rich people don't advertise where they live. But tucked near a phone on the security desk was a printed list of names. Eli panned his eyes from one end of the lobby to the other.

Nobody.

He pulled the list and ran his finger down a column of condo numbers and corresponding names. Alongside 1201—Badeau, Andre.

Eli found the elevators and pressed the call button over and over, as if that would hurry the car.

The elevator arrived. He entered but the panel only had buttons for floors one through ten. He needed 1201, likely the penthouse suite. He exited and to his right a young, disheveled male stood outside an alcove down the hall, his hoodie pulled over his head.

Ding.

The kid disappeared inside the alcove.

Eli strode to the area and found two elevators—1101 over one, and 1201 above the other—no call buttons, only keypads. That's the elevator he needed but who was that kid? He tried the stairwell, but the door was locked.

He returned to the security desk, and an attendant in a maroon blazer sat at the desk.

"Excuse me." Eli bent to read the silver name tag on his lapel. "Sam." Eli flipped opened his jacket and revealed the police badge on his belt. "I need to get up to the twelfth floor now," he said with authority.

Sam stared at Eli's badge, then lifted his gaze. "That's a penthouse suite. It has a private elevator."

"Yeah, I figured. You got the code?"

"No, but my supervisor does."

"Where's your supervisor?" Eli said with a sense of urgency. That grungy kid didn't belong in an upscale place like this.

"Making his rounds?"

Eli tapped his knuckles on the counter. "This is a police emergency. I need access immediately."

Sam lifted an old-school rover from under the counter. "Mike. I got a cop here looking to get up to twelve?"

"What for?" Mike's response crackled.

"Says it's a police emergency."

"They got a warrant?"

"Be here in a minute," Eli said. "My partners right behind me."

Sam relayed the message to Mike.

"When his partner gets here, I'll come down. I got two more areas to check."

Mike set down the radio. "He said—"

"I heard." Eli adopted a challenging tone. He pressed both palms on the counter and leaned in. "Tell him there may be a young girl in danger."

"Hey, Mike, he said there may be a young girl in trouble up there."

"That warrant there yet?"

"Nope."

"I'll see him when it arrives."

———

Tara packed in ten minutes, brushed her teeth, dropped her head to the faucet to rinse her mouth—

Ding—the elevator.

"Hello," she called.

"Where are you?" The voice came from the elevator. Muddled and male. Andre's nephew.

"I'm back here. In the guest room."

She looked around the bathroom checking if she'd left anything.

A tallish, thin boy about eighteen or nineteen peeked into the bathroom. His clothes were wrinkly, and his hair tangled in a matted mess.

Tara honed in on his appearance. "Are you Freddy?" This scruffy person can't be related to Andre.

"Yeah—" A look of panic covered his pale face. He rushed to the toilet, pulled the seat up, then puked something orange that had a horrible smell. Freddy spat twice, gagged, and threw up again.

Tara turned away, memories of Mom retching after drinking vodka gimlets all day.

Freddy pushed Tara to get to the sink. He lapped water like a dog from a ditch.

"Are you okay?" Her stomach rolled from the disgusting smell.

"Yeah." He sucked in more water, then spewed it back into the sink. "Something I ate."

Tara crossed her arms. "You already ate? You're supposed to take me to lunch."

"You all packed?"

"Yes, I'm packed." How could Andre send this cretin to bring her to lunch? "I guess you can take me right to the airport. I'm too excited to eat anyway."

"Huh?"

"The airport. Are you coming with us? If you're going, you should take a shower. You don't smell good."

"What did you—"

"Andre said we should hurry. He'll be at the airport soon."

Freddy stared at her like she had three noses. Then his phone rang and he answered it. "Yeah?"

He grabbed her bag and headed out of the bathroom and to the elevator. "Got it."

Tara followed Freddy into the elevator, his phone still at his ear.

"Where?" he said, his face contorted. "What about the other chicks?"

Other chicks? He must be talking to one of his friends. She pulled out the phone Andre gave her but decided against calling him.

"Okay," Freddy said. "See you in twenty."

She swallowed a giggle, hiding her enthusiasm. She wanted to appear like a sophisticated grown-up on her way to New York. Like those girls at school who lived in St. Charles Street mansions. Or better yet, like Taylor Swift or Cardi B or Selina Gomez.

———

Eli'd waited ten minutes for Mancuso to arrive at Badeau's building with the warrant. Another five minutes for Mike, wearing a maroon blazer that matched Sam's, to enter the lobby.

Mike strolled to the desk with unfettered confidence and no urgency. "You the detectives?"

"Yep," Mancuso said. "Let's go."

Mike peered over his glasses that rode low on his nose. "You got the warrant?"

Mancuso handed the warrant to Mike, who studied it. His lips moving silently, his eyes moving side to side. He reached for the phone behind the counter.

"What are you doing?" Eli asked.

Mike picked up the receiver and turned his body as if to hide.

Mancuso grabbed Mike's collar and pulled his ear to Mancuso's lips. "You make that call, and I'll arrest you for obstruction."

"What?"

"Get us into 1201. Now," Mancuso said.

"All right, all right."

At the private elevator Mike entered a code, the doors opened, and the three of them stepped inside.

"You see a young girl come in or out of here in the last two days?" asked Mancuso.

Mike pushed out his bottom lip and shook his head.

They rode the elevator to the twelfth floor. The doors opened into a massive room.

———

Tara wanted to ask Freddy a zillion questions, but he didn't seem too interested in talking. Since she'd met him, he'd thrown up, hurried her out of Andre's condo, and pulled her out of the elevator, not in the lobby but on the third floor.

"Why are we getting off here?"

"Shortcut." His voice was not polite or kind or gentle like Andre's. What a jerk.

They rushed down two flights of stairs like the building was on fire, then into the garage. A bright yellow Mustang sat where Andre had parked his Escalade Thursday night.

Tara pulled her seatbelt over her shoulder. "Do you work for Andre?"

Freddy glared at her with bloodshot eyes.

She really didn't like Freddy, who seemed a younger version of Mom's butthole boyfriend, Rick. But she was too wound up to stop talking. She would meet Andre at the airport and fly off to New York. How freaking awesome. "You didn't tell me. Are you going to New York?"

Freddy ignored her and pressed the ignition. The Mustang's engine roared.

Tara covered her ears. "I've never been to New York." She had to shout over the noise. "But I always wanted to go. Andre's taking me shopping for cool clothes for when we eat in fabulous restaurants. Have you ever been to a Broadway play?"

Freddy pressed his lips together so hard that all the color left.

"Well, have you?"

The Mustang sped out of the garage, but on the street, they cruised slowly past a four-door sedan at the curb near the front double-glass doors. Freddy ran a shaky hand across his sweaty forehead. "Cops."

"Cops?" Tara looked back. "How do you know?"

"The car." Freddy flinched his chin at the sedan. "It's a police cruiser. I can spot them a mile away."

Freddy's eyebrows drew together like he was trying to look inside his brain. Then his face contorted like Rick's when Tara talked back to him. "Freakin' Andre."

Twenty-Three

The Mustang swerved in a wild turn onto Canal Street, pressing Tara against the passenger door. She clutched the necklace Andre had given her to cool the craziness of the past twenty minutes. "Are you mad at Andre or something?"

Freddy kept his eyes ahead, his scowl intense. "Don't worry about it."

"Tell me, or I'll tell Andre you puked in his condo."

"Go ahead." His voice was loud. His tone was angry. He turned off Canal Street and entered the French Quarter.

"Where are you going?" Tara's heart banged against her ribcage, her confusion turning to fear. "Andre's waiting for me at the airport."

Freddy's face pinched, his eyes fierce like a wild animal ready to pounce. "Shut up. He's not meeting you at the damn airport, you stupid girl. He wanted you out of his condo before the cops broke down the door."

Panic caught Tara's breath in her throat. But Freddy was lying. She was Andre's girlfriend. They were going to New York.

And what did Freddy mean about the cops? Could Mom have called the police? Reported her as a missing person? Nah, Mom was too busy with Rick. But how'd the cops even know where to look? No way. Freddy was drunk or stoned.

She hated Freddy. Hated. Hated. Hated. Wait till she told Andre he'd called her stupid. Then Freddy would find out who's stupid.

Andre would probably fire him or suspend him or dock his pay. Maybe Andre would punch Freddy in the face like boyfriends are supposed to when standing up for their girl. And she was Andre's girl.

Pastel-colored buildings passed by. She rolled down her window and tried to slow her breathing. The smells of stale beer and urine hit her nose worse than day-old crawfish.

She'd been to the French Quarter on school trips to the Cabildo and the St. Louis Cathedral, and to the Aquarium with her mom and dad. But that was years ago.

Dad. No one had made her feel as special as Dad did, not until she met Andre. She rubbed the necklace again. It was real. Andre had given it to her. Andre was her boyfriend and she was his girlfriend.

Freddy slowed for a corner, slid into a space under a no parking sign and cut the engine. "C'mon. Andre's waiting."

Tara shivered against a sudden coldness. She couldn't get out of the car. "Andre's not here." Alarm sounded in her tone. She worked at putting calm in her voice. No use getting Freddy madder. "He's at the airport, I told you. Take me to the airport."

Freddy opened the passenger door and stuck his head even with hers. "If Andre hadn't told me not to touch you, you'd be bleeding by now. Move before I forget how much money he's paying me to bring you here." He spoke the words low, but they were wet with spit and fury.

The back of Tara's neck bristled. A blackness as if she'd

entered some sci-fi wormhole enveloped her. "What are you t-talking about?"

"Move." His hand bit into her bicep. He undid her seat-belt and yanked her out of the car.

Hot blood warmed her cheeks and neck. She clung to the door handle, squirmed, and coiled like a twisted knot. She tried to break free. "Let me go. Let me go." She lashed her nails at anything Freddy. But she couldn't match his strength.

Freddy pulled and pushed her. "Now walk you little tramp."

The few people around in their dirty jeans and do-rags couldn't care less how Freddy treated her. She should just run.

Then Andre walked out on a balcony, two floors up, a half-block away. A tall black woman behind him.

Tara's stomach fell and left a bitter hole. Why was he with this woman? Why wasn't he at the airport?

———

The elevator to Badeau's condo slid open. Eli clutched the handle of his Sig Sauer but kept it holstered. He stepped onto the highly polished wood floor for a better vantage of the space.

"New Orleans police," Mancuso called from the elevator. His words filled with authority. "We have a warrant to search the premises."

Nobody answered.

Mancuso turned to Mike from building security. "Go to the lobby and wait. We'll need a statement if this is a crime scene."

"My shift is over." Mike's voice had a hard edge. "I'm going home."

Mancuso leaned in and Mike shifted to the back of the elevator. "If I find you held us up downstairs so the psychopath that lives here could escape with an underaged girl, you'll be spending the night in a cell with a con who'll send you Valentines for decades." Mancuso drilled his index finger into Mike's chest. "Now go downstairs. Wait by your desk. Until I say, you can go home."

Mike lifted his hands as if to fend off Mancuso's obvious agitation. "Hey, now. There's no need for—"

"Thanks for your cooperation." Mancuso joined Eli outside the elevator. He ambled right, to a ten-foot table with matching chairs set against the full view of the Mississippi West Bank.

Eli unholstered his Sig and maneuvered around a huge plush white sectional sofa, then through a maze of chairs and weird sculptures on his way to search the bedrooms.

The hallway was wide and furnished with framed art of Louisiana landscapes hanging on pale-beige walls. Eli followed his gun into the first bedroom and caught a whiff of vomit. He eased past a queen-sized bed, its covers tucked tight, its pillows aligned straight and balanced, so precise, so like the bed in Tara's room. But this was a guest room not the master, but it did have an adjoining bath.

Eli switched on the bathroom light. The stench of vomit so strong he covered his nose. Water was spread over the marble counter. Hadn't had time to dry. Recent.

A pink toothbrush lay on the floor. Pink. Not the toothbrush of a pimp. Eli holstered his gun, pulled a plastic bag from his back pocket, and placed the toothbrush inside. The towel by the shower was damp. He'd just missed them. There were no women's or girl's clothes in the walk-in closet.

He continued down the hall to a larger bedroom, its king-sized bed made up, but not with military precision like in the guest room. Men's essentials littered the ornate bathroom— razor, hand wash, and hair products scattered.

The guest bedroom had Tara's tidiness. A single man less

inclined to neatness occupied this room. Eli's stomach clenched to the lingering vomit stench and his own disappointment. He'd been close. So close.

Eli found Mancuso at the breakfast bar.

Mancuso stared out the large window with a view of the Mississippi. "Who'd you say this place belongs to?"

"According to the directory I found at the security desk, an Andre Badeau."

"Nice place." Mancuso relaxed his shoulders and tugged on his chin. "How much do you think a high-end condo like this costs?"

Eli turned, took in the obvious extravagance. Being with Gina, Eli knew high-end, and this was high-end. "I'd say it's about three-thousand square feet with a high-rise river view. Five mil would be my guess."

Mancuso grimaced. "My entire net worth ain't a tenth of that. Who says crime doesn't pay?"

"You still have your health. I doubt Badeau will boast the same when I find him." Eli lifted the evidence bag with the toothbrush. "This was in the guest bath."

Mancuso put on his glasses. "I'm not an expert on toothbrushes, but I'd say that could belong to a teenage girl."

"I'll text a pic to Tara's mom, see if it looks like Tara's."

Mancuso returned his gaze to the winding Mississippi. "Tell her to collect a hairbrush or clothing for fingerprints and DNA. We'll need a sample from the mom too. We may need it for court at some point."

Experience told Eli, he and Mancuso were nipping at the heels of Badeau and Tara. "You can smell puke in the guest bath, a towel's still wet, there's water on the counter. Tara was here and somebody took her out in a hurry. And it was minutes, not hours. They bolted before we came up that elevator."

"Building has security cameras." Mancuso started for the

exit. "Let's go check out the stairs, then give Mike another chance to cooperate."

———

Tara walked ahead of Freddy, disoriented and her body numb.

Not the same numbness she'd experienced when Mom grounded her for cutting classes. Or when Mom announced she and Tara would move. This numbness accompanied body shivers and helplessness, like when Dad died.

But she straightened, and strode through a courtyard, past an algae-stained fountain with water flowing into its round pool.

Freddy opened a scuffed-up door and shoved Tara into a narrow stairway that spiraled up to the second floor. The tall black woman met them at the top and led them into an apartment. Andre paced the outside balcony with the New Orleans skyline behind him, his phone to his ear. He rubbed his pained face nonstop. His voice was loud, panicky, out of control. This was not the same man who took her to dinner and cooked her breakfast and promised to bring her to New York.

The black lady fumbled with the knot tied at the bottom of her white shirt. "What's up, Freddy. Heard you guys been raging in the Bywater the last couple of days."

"Sort of." Freddy shot dark eyes at Andre. "I need to talk to him."

"You'll need to wait." She gave Tara a what-do-we-have-here going over. "He wants to talk to little girly here first."

Andre appeared and he looked like he'd sounded when he called Tara at the condo earlier. Nervous. Afraid. Panicked.

The black lady stood six feet tall and she leaned down to Tara's eye level. She had green eyes with yellow flecks, skin the color of coffee and cream, and a face prettier than Rihanna. "So, you's what all this fuss is about, huh?" The lady clutched Tara's chin and stared eye-to-eye. "Lookie here, girly. My name is Jewel. I'm the goddess around here. You feel me." Her tone was even, direct, and mean. "You behave, we cool. You don't, you feel the back of my hand. The quicker you learn that the better for both of us. But mostly for you." Jewel glanced at Andre. "Now, go talk to Andre. He got some questions for you."

Tara had seen enough TV to know what was happening. She knew what a hooker was. Jewel was a hooker. Which made Andre her pimp. Freddy was right—Tara was a stupid girl. Totally stupid. And getting played by Andre's kindness and promises was super-stupid, kindergarten-stupid, naive-twit stupid.

She'd been conned. Andre wasn't a loving and attentive boyfriend. He'd sucked her in to be a hooker, a ho, a slag.

She thought the past six weeks had been awesome. But today, she got a reality slap. Time to kick her Harlequin fantasies and figure out how she to get out of this sick mess.

With shaky knees, she wobbled onto the balcony, but kept her mouth shut, her shoulders hunched, her chin down. She had to get over her middle-school pity party. Nobody here cared.

Andre towered over her like Thanos in the movie *Endgame*. "Answer me honestly, or you'll get hurt. Do you have an uncle who's a cop?" His tone was harsh like nothing she'd ever heard before.

She'd been so dumb.

Yes, she had an uncle, but why would Andre care?

"Tell me." His tone was keyed-up with fear. Creepy.

"I. Don't. Know." She slung the words at him in a loud whisper.

He grabbed her shoulders, tight and rough. "You don't know if you have an uncle?"

A squirming cat clawed inside her throat. And now her eyes filled with idiot-girl tears. "I don't know if he's a cop."

"What's his name?"

"Eli." The name slipped out like a two-year-old's whimper. But somehow saying his name calmed her. She raised her chin. "Eli Colt."

"Are you two close?"

"I haven't seen him since I was eight." Her tone surprised her. Some of her fear had left.

"Is he a cop?"

"Maybe. I think he was in the Army. A detective. He got a medal for bravery. It's on the Internet." She didn't know why she added that. Maybe it'd scare Andre, and he'd let her go.

"Great. Just great." Andre stalked back to the balcony railing and gripped it with both hands. He swayed.

Tara counted ten seconds.

Without turning, Andre waved at Jewel. "Take her."

Tara's heart fluttered. Take her where?

"We two beds short." Jewel grasped Tara's arm.

Tara cringed.

"Figure it out," Andre said, his focus still out in the street. "I've got stuff going down. Just don't let her out of your sight."

"I do have a home, you know," Jewel said. "I don't live here anymore."

"I do know." Now Andre turned and glared at Jewel with demon eyes. Eyes Tara had never seen. "I gave you the down payment, remember. You can take her with you when you leave here."

Tara's mind grasped at this info. Going to Jewel's house? Was that a good thing? Could be easier breaking free from Jewel without Freddy and Andre around.

"We still a bed short," Jewel said.

"Take the Brit with you. She's intelligent. She can help you with this one."

Jewel flung her hand up. "I got a business to run. I need to earn."

"Don't I take care of you?" Andre said the words short and snappy, as if to get rid of them. "The cops may know I have her I can't have her close."

"Sage got a high roller at the Ritz," Jewel said.

"Work it out with Loto," Andre said. "He can drop Sage at your place after she's done at the Ritz."

Loto? Who's Loto? The name sounded male and mean.

"This girl." Jewel tightened her grip on Tara's arm. "She got a name?"

"Tara," Andre said. No emotion in saying her name. Not kindness or caring, and definitely not love.

"We'll change that. Never knew a ho named Tara." Jewel dug her fake fingernails into Tara's skin.

Tara flinched. Her heart slammed into overdrive and sent terror to her belly. A bitter taste rose in her mouth. Change her name? To something whorish? She needed to cut loose from these people.

But how?

Twenty-Four

L indsey pulled into the empty church parking lot. Unlike most New Orleans churches, the building didn't have the splendor of the large, ornate cathedrals built in the eighteenth or nineteenth centuries—no high-reaching steeple, no old arches, no muted frescos, no mosaic walls. Instead, Mid-City Community Fellowship featured a double-gabled brick building, a raised concrete porch, and an eccentric pastor, Reverend Justin Vincent who was Lindsey's best friend.

And like the church building, Justin didn't appear as expected. He wore his reddish-brown hair back but slightly unkempt, blending with a matching beard that formed a point below his chin. His eyes were green and serious. His clothes said musician more than preacher—blue jeans, tee-shirt, Birkenstocks.

He and Lindsey had a long history that went back to that riverfront warehouse. So, Justin understood Lindsey more than anyone else. They talked at least twice weekly, but she wanted to speak with him face-to-face today. Life had thrown her a curve, and God was on the pitcher's mound.

She parked in the rear of the building near Justin's office. He stood outside the side entrance as if waiting for her. She opened the car door, and he approached, all five foot six and one hundred forty pounds of him.

"Good to see you, Lin." He hugged her tight. "What brings you here?"

"Do I need a reason?"

"Not at all, but I'm sure you have one." He kissed her on the cheek. "Come on in. After you called, I asked Mrs. Necaise to make us some lunch. She should be ready for us in the fellowship hall."

Mrs. Necaise was Justin's secretary. A seventy-two-year-old, stout firebrand, who doted on the pastor of her church. She would show protective fury if anyone said or did anything against Justin. And, as if she was his mother, that same anger could be levied at Justin if she thought he stepped out of line.

In the fellowship hall, Mrs. Necaise spooned mounds of chicken pot pie on plastic plates.

"Good afternoon, Mrs. Necaise," Lindsey said, always a bit intimidated by the older woman.

Mrs. Necaise poured iced tea into plastic cups. "'That the Lord keep you from all harm—that he watches over your life.'" Her half-lidded eyes found Lindsey as she quoted the Psalm. "'That he watch over your coming and going both now and forevermore.'"

The peace of the Holy Spirit washed over Lindsey. God's intimate connection graced her as if He spoke to her through the old woman.

Justin's eyes followed Mrs. Necaise as she hurried off to the sanctuary. "Preparing our lunch bled into her prayer time," he said. "Every day like clockwork she starts at high noon. He straightened his shoulders, bowed his head, and blessed the food.

Justin unfolded his napkin and placed it on his lap. "So, what do I owe the pleasure of your company?"

Lindsey pulled in, then let out a deep breath. "Well, life's been good. In fact, up until yesterday, I couldn't have been happier. I have my work which is fulfilling. And I was quite content."

Justin arched an eyebrow. He blew on a steaming fork full of food before placing it into his mouth.

"Then, out of nowhere," Lindsey continued. "Manny brought this handsome young detective to Safe Harbor, and my whole world is turned upside down."

Justin dropped his fork. "Handsome young detective?" He raised his fist to his mouth and let out a gleeful laugh. "Could it be? Could it really be? You're finally attracted to a man?"

The heat of embarrassment flushed Lindsey's face. "Excuse me? What are you talking about?"

"Come on now. I've known you since we were knee-high to dachshunds. How many times have you been interested in a man?"

"Ninth grade," she said with a defiant smile. "I had a crush on Mr. Inglewood, my English teacher. He introduced me to *To Kill a Mockingbird*."

Justin shook his head as if trying to shake something off. "Forget your childhood crushes. Tell me about this detective who seems to have lit that dormant fire inside you."

"Just so you know, I had nothing to do with it. It's Manny's fault." Lindsey sipped her iced tea.

Justin pointed his fork at Lindsey. "Don't blame it on Manny. I've introduced you to dozens of eligible men who would make perfect husbands. Only you wouldn't give them a smoker's chance in a marathon."

"I was nice to them."

"Pfft."

"I was."

"Go on." Justin waved his fork. "Tell me about Prince Charming."

Lindsey paused, considering how to best explain her encounter with Eli. "Look, you know me. I'm not on a mission to find a man."

"That's an understatement."

"Like I was saying, Manny came by with this detective— Eli Colt. They actually brought bad news about a girl of ours whose body washed ashore in the Rigolets."

"Oh no." Justin grew still. "Did I know her?" His voice was two octaves lower.

"I don't think so. Her name was Zoe. She was only with us for a couple of weeks."

Justin touched Lindsey's hand. "Oh, Lin, I'm sorry for your loss."

"Thank you." Lindsey turned her head and rubbed her wet lashes. "Every time something like this happens, I thank God we were saved when we were."

"Thank God for Manny."

They shared five beats of silence, then Justin gave her a keep-talking hand gesture. "So, tell me about this detective."

"Well, I didn't think much about him at first. I mean, he's cute. Kind of rugged but handsome. But that wasn't what got my attention. I felt something. From inside." Lindsey clutched her chest with both arms, like hugging herself.

Justin perked up. "You felt something?"

"Um-hm."

Justin slid his chair closer to the table and leaned in. "And?"

Lindsey picked up her fork and poked at her food. "Like a spiritual awakening. Like God telling me this man is the one."

Justin leaned back, cupped his elbow with one hand and tapped his lips with the other. "That's what you felt?"

"Yep. And I gotta tell you. It threw my whole world into a tailspin."

"How's that?"

"The guys engaged to be married. In the spring."

"That may be a concern." Justin's eyes squinted and flashed a twinkle of mischief. "But he ain't married yet."

"Neither am I." Her hand covered her mouth. Why did she say that?

Justin jerked his head back. "So, what's this guy think about you?"

Lindsey's hands flew up. "Doesn't seem the least bit interested."

A relaxed smile crossed Justin's face. "Do I detect some disappointment?"

"You would think if God picked a man for me, I would attract some attention once or twice. It's not like I've been praying about finding someone. I was happy with my life. At least I was when I woke up yesterday."

"And now you're smitten." Justin's voice was soft and gentle.

"Yes." Lindsey glanced toward the hall to ensure Mrs. Necaise was not nearby. "To someone getting married in May," she whispered.

"And what do you want from me?" Justin went back to his lunch, like he'd lost interest.

"To give me some advice. To do what pastors do. That's why I'm here."

"I'm not your pastor. You go to church on the Northshore." Justin ate the last bite of his lunch.

Lindsey wadded her napkin and threw it at him. "You're my best friend, Justin. Tell me what to do."

Justin laughed. "Sure. That's easy."

"Go on."

"This may sound ridiculous, but it's quite simple. In fact, it's the easiest advice I've given in a consulting session in months."

"If it's so easy, why can't I figure it out?"

"Because you don't have years of seminary training and a deep, intimate relationship with the Holy Spirit."

Lindsey crossed her arms and dropped her chin. "Okay Billy Graham, what do I do?"

"Nothing. You don't do a thing."

"What?"

"Like you said." Justin stacked his empty plate and plastic utensils. "Until yesterday you minded your own business. Then God throws a wrench into your boring content life. The way I see it, it's not your problem to solve. It's totally God's idea, so let Him deal with it. We accept offerings on our website, thank you very much."

Lindsey sighed heavily. "Do nothing?"

"You might want to mention this issue while you're praying." Justin rose calm and casual to toss his plate in the trash. "But, other than that—yeah. Hang tight."

With her Eli Colt dilemma less constraining, Lindsey's body relaxed. "Okay. I can do nothing. Nothing is easy."

Justin filled his glass, then Lindsey's with more iced tea. "Uh...any chance of you seeing this fellow again?"

"I'm going to the morgue to make a formal identification of Zoe's body. Manny tells me Detective Colt will be there."

"Oh, Lin, shouldn't one of her family members do that?"

"I talked to her mother earlier. On top of losing her daughter, Social Service just took her son." Lindsey swallowed her revulsion of the morgue, a fate she'd surely dodged as a child. "She's not up to it."

"I'm sorry you have to do that." Justin's eyebrows drew together in a pained expression. He'd been saved from that warehouse too.

"Well, it's not like I haven't done it before. And who knows, maybe my Prince Charming will act like I'm in the same room."

Twenty-Five

Tara went with Jewel through Andre's French Quarter building into a room of exposed brick walls, dimmed lighting, two couches with plump pillows facing each other, and a glass table stacked with different video games and consoles between them.

On one couch, two women, not much older than Tara, both blondes but one with dark roots, scanned their phones with crossed legs, wearing tee shirts that barely covered their sheer panties. On the couch sat a burly man in a 'sleeveless wife-beater exposing warrior-like tattoos. His long dark hair bobbed over the light brown skin of his shoulders as he jerked a controller, killing zombies on a monster TV on the wall.

"That's Loto. He's Samoan." Jewel threw out the words to the whole room. "He drives the girls around and protects us."

Jewel and Tara pressed on to the kitchen where an ebony-skinned girl with high cheekbones and closely cropped hair scrambled eggs in a skillet. Two other girls sat on stools in provocative dresses and stiletto heels, eating crisp bacon with their fingers at a breakfast counter.

A heaviness crowded Tara's chest, and she struggled to

breathe. Is this place a preview of her future—lounging around with your business hanging out, and eating breakfast late in the afternoon?

How would her Uncle Eli find her? Could she escape on her own?

Jewel snapped her fingers and raised her voice. "You hos need to hurry up with your breakfast. We got tricks lined up, and there's money to make."

The girls were not the least bit insulted, as if each one accepted being called a whore.

Jewel addressed the girl cooking. "Brandi. Downtown Hilton in ninety minutes. I don't want you late for the van again."

Brandi stifled a yawn with an open hand.

Up the stairs to the third floor, Jewel guided Tara through a long hallway, beyond the sound of a shower, to a door at the end. Jewel opened the door and entered. "Sage."

The running water stopped. Then, a super-gorgeous lady draped in a thick robe stepped out of a hall doorway in a cloud of steam, rubbing her hair with a towel.

Jewel stood erect like a strict teacher. "Get dressed and get your things together. When you finish at the Ritz, you'll stay with me."

Sage's violet eyes blinked, and her gaze wandered between Tara and Jewel. "Staying with you? At your home? Why?" Her accent sounded like a character on *Game of Thrones*.

Jewel crossed her arms. "Get hopping now. You're due at the Ritz."

Sage entered the room and focused on Tara. "Who's the child?"

"New talent," Jewel said. "She's staying with me too."

"How old are you, love?" Sage smiled a kind smile that calmed the thumping in Tara's chest.

Jewel's face lit up like a gas stove. "Never you mind that. Get ready, I say."

Sage's pale cheeks flushed a deep pink. She opened her mouth to say something, then hesitated as if she'd thought better. She stood and edged to the closet. "She's too young for this, is all I'm saying."

Jewel's head tossed side to side. "You ain't here to give your opinions. You here to turn tricks. Now get moving."

————

Tara rode shotgun in a cramped Prius. She turned in her seat a full ninety degrees, ear flattened against the headrest so as not to look at Jewel. Tara's mind was still numbed from Jewel calling her a whore. Then, the familiar screeching of metal braking against metal and the clanging of a streetcar bell awoke her numbed brain.

She searched the median and found the green-colored streetcar. Red streetcars rolled up and down Canal Street. Green ones ran uptown. Tara was close to home.

Home.

Tara wanted to go home. She missed home and her mom. Rick might get drunk and scream, but he was weak and harmless. Jewel was dangerous and mean.

Tension built in Tara's shoulders, tight like a bowstring ready for release. Thoughts raced through her mind of what could happen to her in the next few days. She had to escape. Today.

Jewel turned right onto Oak Street and then, three blocks later, took a left. If Tara jumped out and hopped on a streetcar heading downtown, within a half-hour, she could walk home. But streetcars cost money, and Tara had none. Plus, Jewel could chase her down. Probably run her down.

Five minutes later, Jewel pulled into a driveway. Her house

was not fancy—a shotgun—narrow across and went straight back. The yard was overgrown and the iron fence rusted.

Jewel unlocked the storm door with a key attached to her Prius key fob. "Sorry for the mess. If I'd known I'd be having company. I might have tidied up."

Mess didn't describe the interior. Unfolded laundry strewn on the couch and empty beer bottles littered every table.

Jewel stepped past the mess and into the next room. "I'm going to have a cold one."

The next room was the kitchen, where the mess continued —dirty dishes piled high in the sink, food splattered inside the microwave, and the stove covered with oily film. A skillet lined with solid white grease sat on a burner. The frying pan reminded Tara of Rick's drunken stupidity of setting off an ear-piercing alarm a few months back.

Tara looked from the stove to the ceiling and found the smoke detector. She held her breath to control her runaway pulse. "I need to pee."

"Nobody stopping you, sugar. Go to the hallway, first door on the left."

Tara found the bathroom dirtier than the kitchen. Sitting on the toilet, Tara scrutinized the white-tiled room with a white tub with a curved top and a curtain draped around it. The one-sink vanity had a mirror above it and shelves on each side. Makeup, shampoo, and body wash lay scattered on the shelves. Soiled, wrinkled towels were on the floor. Two clean towels were on the shelves.

After flushing, Tara pried, hoping for anything that could help with her plan. First through the mirrored medicine cabinet, she inspected the shelves, closed the door, and rifled the cabinets, but there was nothing she could use.

She almost turned to leave, but something jutted from under the bottom towel—a five-dollar bill.

The money sat there like a gift from heaven—enough to jump on a streetcar and get Tara home. She barely got the cash in her pocket when the bathroom door flung open.

Jewel filled the doorway, her arms crossed. "Dang girl, how long you gonna take?"

The money in Tara's back pocket burned her butt. "I'm done."

Jewel looked around the room and curled her upper lip. "You know how to clean?"

"Yes ma'am," Tara said with the manners her mother never could drill into her.

"Good, I might put you to work if you stay awhile. You finished in here?"

"Yes ma'am."

"Yes ma'am." Jewel chuckled as if the words were a punchline to a joke. "C'mon, I'll show you where you'll stay."

The bedroom had two twin beds. Both had magazines, clothes, and shoeboxes piled on them.

"Just toss that mess in the closet," Jewel said. "I'm hungry. You like pizza."

Pizza woke an empty gnawing in Tara's belly. "Yes, please."

"Pepperoni with extra cheese?"

Tara smiled like she loved being in this pigpen. "That's how I like it."

"Great, sugar. Me and you gonna get along fine."

"Yes ma'am."

"No need you callin' me ma'am. I'm still young and fine. You call me Jewel like everyone else, you hear?"

"Yes ma'am...I mean, yes Jewel."

"I'm gonna order that pizza. You get yourself settled."

And that's what Tara did for fifteen minutes—cleared off the beds, pulled straight the bedding, and worked out a plan to escape and get home.

———

Everyone from New Orleans knew streetcars were scheduled to pass every ten minutes. Night or day, weekday or weekend, streetcars were among the few things that did what they promised. Now that she had money Tara could get home.

But to do that, she had to cover three-and-a-half blocks between Jewel's house and Carrollton Avenue. And that could only happen if something kept Jewel busy long enough before that big hunk Loto arrived back with Sage.

Tara needed to gain Jewel's trust. She'd cleaned the bedroom—folded clothes, put shoes in shoe boxes, threw empty containers in a bin in the closet. The room didn't sparkle, but it looked a ton better. Next, she'd do the same in the living room.

Jewel reclined on the couch watching TV and drinking beer, with the front door open but the storm door closed. Did Jewel lock the storm door after they'd come inside? Did it lock from the inside? Tara couldn't remember.

Tara found trash bags in the same place her mom kept them—under the sink in the kitchen. She cleared the counter-tops and the kitchen table of trash and went to the living room to pick up bottles.

"You alright girl?" Jewel said.

"I like cleaning," Tara lied. "I did it for my mom at home."

"For true." Jewel sat up, appearing to be interested in having a conversation. "My mom was so strung out when I was a kid. She didn't know if the house was dirty or clean. Guess that's why I got used to living like this."

Tara dragged the garbage bag to the door and pushed on the storm door handle. Locked.

"What you doing? You can't go outside."

Tara lifted the bag. "It's full. Thought I'd take it out."

"Put it in the kitchen. We'll take it out when we done eating."

"Yes ma'am. I mean, yes Jewel."

"Don't sweat it. You clean my house. You call me what you want."

"May I have something to drink, please?"

Jewel looked away from the television. "Don't get many *mays, I'd,* or *pleases* hanging around hookers. Help yourself. There're cold drinks in the fridge. Grab me a beer while you in there…" Jewel suppressed a laugh. "*Please.*"

The fridge was empty except for two Barqs and two six-packs of Dixie. In anticipation of pizza, Tara unearthed a couple of plates and a stack of napkins. The doorbell rang.

"Pizza's here," Jewel shouted.

Tara set the plates, napkins, and drinks on an end table between the couch and an armchair. Jewel paid for the pizza, grabbed the cardboard box, and, with the luck Tara needed, left the keys in the storm door lock. Her heart stuttered. So far, everything went Gucci.

"Look at you, girl." Jewel set the box on the coffee table and eyeballed Tara. "You set us up with plates and all. I might talk to Andre about you living here full-time. Be like my roommate."

"Andre said he was taking me to New York." Tara frowned like a too-dumb little girl. "But I don't know if that will happen now."

"Yeah, we all been lied to in this business." Jewel sipped her beer. "Andre ain't no better or worse than most pimps. But he knows how to lie good. That's for sure."

Jewel grabbed a plate and a slice. "Sit down, grab some pizza, and tell me about yourself."

Tara sat and slowed her breathing to slow her heart. The key was in the door, the first piece of her plan, but for how long? Jewel was sure to notice soon or when Loto and Sage arrived.

If Tara was to escape, she had to act now.

Tara finished her pizza and offered to clean up. Jewel laid back on the couch, sipping another beer. Tara lit the gas burner on the stove under the grease-coated skillet and waited.

Soon smoke rose from the pan. A needle-like, high-pitched alarm sounded, overpowering the tiny house.

"What the— "Jewel jumped from the couch and dashed to the kitchen.

Tara flew to the storm door, turned the key, and then, using the same key, locked the door behind her. She jumped off the porch, staggered across the pavement, got her feet tangled, and fell onto the neighbor's lawn.

Jewel's curses penetrated the screen door, but Tara refused to look back. She picked herself up and bolted to Oak Street.

Three blocks to go.

People packed the sidewalk, going in and out of clubs and restaurants. Parked cars lined the street. Traffic crawled in both directions.

Tara weaved in and out of the crowd. She dared to peek over her shoulder.

No Jewel.

Two blocks to go.

Feeling confident, Tara slowed, blending in with college students and teens her age. But a half block later, the crowd thinned past the cluster of bars and clubs.

A green trolley snuck across the intersection less than a block away. She cursed. Did she have another ten minutes to catch the next car?

She glanced over her shoulder toward Jewel's street. Still no Jewel.

Her belly fluttered like hummingbird wings, but she broke out in a full sprint.

Ding, ding, ding. Another streetcar approached. It's early. That means the next one could be late. She had to get on that trolley.

Tara took another hurried look over her shoulder.

Oh God. Jewel. A block and a half away. Her frantic head swung side-to-side, scanning. Her angry eyes probed like searchlights. They found Tara.

Tara's body pulsed with full tremors. Her legs weakened like limp spaghetti. But she wouldn't get dragged back to that horrible house. She jumped into the first lane, ignoring oncoming traffic.

A silver Camaro braked hard. The car fishtailed. Horns honked. Rubber screeched, and gridlock happened.

Tara darted into the second lane. A motorcycle roared past her, the driver swaying to remain upright. Tara felt its wake as she flung herself on the median grass.

She made it. Only yards now.

Ding, ding, ding, taunted the streetcar, its doors closing.

"Nooo." Tara hobbled to her feet, ran, caught up, and beat on the trolley's side panel. "Wait, wait, please wait."

The car dallied for a few yards, then stopped. The doors folded open. She raced up the narrow steps to the driver and slipped her money in the slot.

"I can't give you change, Miss," the driver said.

"That's okay," beamed Tara. "Thank you for stopping. Thank you so much."

She moved to the rear. Jewel stood on the other side of Carrollton. Her dark face glowered. Her fists pressed against her hips.

Had Tara made it? Could Jewel find her? Tara glanced down at the key still in her hand. The key she'd used to lock Jewel inside her house. The key on a ring with Jewel's Prius' fob.

Tara inhaled a deep nervous breath and plopped into a

bench seat. Her plan had worked. She felt older. Wiser. Next stop home. She couldn't wait to see Mom.

Twenty minutes later, she stepped off the trolly on the corner of St. Charles and Washington and thanked her good fortune—the grease skillet, the stove, the smoke alarm, the money in the bathroom, the key left in the storm door.

She hurried down Washington, all her nerve endings jingling. She would be home in minutes. Sure, she'd be in trouble for leaving. But that'd be okay. She would be home— safe from Andre and Freddy and Jewel.

What would she do if there was nobody home? Andre knew where she lived. She could squeeze through the gate and wait in the backyard. They'd never get her there.

Her house came into view. Less than a block now. Mom's red RAV4 was parked out front and her bedroom light was on.

Tara trotted, then sprinted, barely feeling her bag jostling against her back. She passed the last corner, only two houses away. She'd made it. She'd made it. She'd really—

Thick warrior-tattooed arms wrapped around her. Her feet left the ground. A massive hand covered her mouth before she could scream. Her entire body reeled and throbbed in unearthly terror.

Loto shoved Tara into the backseat of a white van where Jewel waited.

The beautiful Sage, her kind eyes watering sat there too.

Loto got behind the wheel.

Jewel clung to Tara so hard she struggled to breathe.

The van jerked forward.

The lights in her mother's bedroom window flicked off.

PART THREE

TWENTY-SIX

Eli and Mancuso searched the stairway of Badeau's building. Every nerve in Eli's body surged from the near miss of finding Tara and the influence of the man who had her. His breathing accelerated to function like pure oxygen and fuel the fire of his PTSD.

Mancuso reached across Eli's shoulders. "You okay, son," he said in a fatherly tone.

Restlessness overwhelmed Eli. "Tara was here when I got here. I know it."

Mancuso directed Eli down the stairs to the next floor. "It's not your fault. Badeau knew we were coming."

Frustration swelled in Eli's throat and his heart rate hit the red zone. Of course, Badeau knew. "Who told him?"

Manny rubbed his jaw. "Only two sources I can think of. The judge or someone at the Broad Street police station."

Eli had figured NOPD was not free of corruption. But corruption typically stemmed from lucrative crimes like drugs, not missing persons. Unless— "You think we've uncovered something more than a simple kidnapping."

Mancuso lifted his brow. "Say again?"

Eli's gut instincts kicked in, his mind quickened, and his pulse slowed into its regular rhythm. "You said it upstairs. Crime does pay. But only certain crimes pay well enough to afford a five-million-dollar condo."

Mancuso tilted his head. "The only crimes that pay that well are drugs and—"

"Human trafficking."

On the third-floor landing, they found a small book, lying there as if dropped.

Mancuso snapped a photo on his phone, then scooped up the new evidence with his gloved hand. He shuffled through the pages. "Think this confirms it." He handed the book to Eli.

Eli opened it and inside were pictures like the ones on Tara's dresser—Tara with her father, Tara with her mother, Tara with Eli when she was four.

Eli's legs lost all strength. He sat down on the stairs. "No need for a DNA test on that toothbrush."

"She didn't go through the lobby. So, somebody drove her out of here. Let's search the garage."

In the dank, humid parking garage, two empty spaces for unit 1201. And the entire garage was covered with security cameras.

"Let's go talk with our friend Mike." Mancuso strode to the garage entrance leading to the building's lobby. "I bet he can't wait to help."

Mike sat at the security desk where Mancuso had sent him.

"We'll need to see your security footage on the twelfth floor, the stairwell, and the garage for the past twenty-four hours," Mancuso said.

"Your warrant doesn't specify those areas." Mike had revived his non-compliant attitude. "Sorry about that." Mike's tone suggested he was in no way sorry.

Mancuso raised his thick dark eyebrows. "Sorry is what you'll be if you don't show us those tapes right now."

"Company policy requires a warrant to review anything that may infringe on an occupant's privacy." Mike knocked his wrists together as if to be handcuffed. "My hands are tied."

"If you don't cooperate. . ." Manny reached inside his jacket. "You'll find those hands of yours zip tied."

"You can't do that?" Mike said.

Mancuso crossed his arms. "Maybe you're right. But you want to know how me and my partner got a warrant to search Mr. Badeau's condo?"

Mike waggled his shoulders in a who-cares shrug.

"The work of a forensic accountant sent us here. And I'm thinking. . ." Mancuso tapped his index finger to his temple. "If I can get a judge to issue a warrant to search a condo, I can get a subpoena to look into your feeble finances."

The mention of Mike's finances knocked his indifference back a step. "My finances?"

"Do you pay taxes on those Christmas gifts from Mr. Badeau?" Mancuso said.

"They're in cash." Mike fidgeted at his shirt collar.

"There you go," Mancuso glanced at Eli while pulling out handcuffs. "Our friend Mike here just admitted to accepting a bribe."

Mike drew his head back. "I did not."

"It's a felony to accept cash payments to obstruct a police investigation." Mancuso pulled out a zip tie and reached for Mike's arm. "I can sell that to a DA."

Mike's gaze ping-ponged between Eli and Mancuso. "C'mon, guys," he pleaded.

A roiling heat rose from Eli's belly. He lowered his chin and raised his voice. "The video feeds from the garage and the twelfth floor. Now."

Mike slumped his shoulders. "Okay, okay."

Eli sat in Captain Guidry's office at the Broad Street station, listening to Mancuso report to Guidry about their search of Badeau's condo and what they'd learned from the building security tapes.

"Sounds like this Badeau character knew you were coming." Guidry tone showed interest, but his half-lidded eyes betrayed a certain lack of concern. And he had little reaction to the soft knock at his door. "Come in."

Reggie Toussaint entered. A surprised flush crept across his cheeks when he glimpsed Mancuso and Eli. "You wanted to see me?"

"Grab a chair, Reggie. This concerns you too."

Toussaint shuffled into the office and slid down in a chair.

A tsunami of distrust rolled in with Reggie Toussaint. What was Toussaint doing here? Didn't Guidry just agree someone tipped off Badeau? And wasn't Toussaint a likely possibility?

Guidry reviewed with Mancuso what they'd discussed as if Toussaint had been there all along. "So, you have evidence Tara Colt had been in the condo moments before you gained entrance. Also, you've seen video evidence of her leaving with..." Guidry referred to the notes he'd taken. "Freddy Badeau in a yellow Mustang."

Guidry scanned the information, then shifted his attention to Toussaint. "As you know, Manny and our guest, Detective Colt have agreed to help with a few cases you're working." Guidry emphasized the word *guest* as if any concessions Eli currently enjoyed could be stripped straight away. "And as you've just heard, they've made progress with your Tara Colt case, and they've agreed to help with the four girls missing from the Orleans Parish Center for Girls."

Toussaint's docile demeanor differed considerably from

the insufferable arrogance he'd displayed when Eli first met him. And he kept his mouth shut.

"I'm sending Manny and Colt to the shelter to interview a witness." Guidry handed the paper from Manny to Toussaint. "You'll stay here to review RTTC (Real Time Crime Center) images and see if we can figure out where this Mustang went after leaving One River View."

"Reviewing traffic photos at intersections?" Toussaint groaned in resignation but accepted the paper. "I'd rather interview the shelter witness."

Guidry ignored Toussaint and turned to Mancuso. "The witness was with her friends, the four girls, the night they went missing. According to the shelter director, the witness can fill you in on when and where these girls were last seen."

Eli cleared his throat to get Guidry's attention. "I don't mind reviewing the photos." The work was mundane, but it would keep him focused on finding Tara. "Reggie can go with Detective Mancuso—"

Mancuso stood. "As you suggested, cap. Eli and I will interview the shelter witness." Mancuso walked to the door. "Reggie, let us know what you learn about that Mustang."

All energy drained from Eli's body—a powerlessness he hadn't experienced since working with Afghan intelligence. Toussaint was a lazy detective and Eli had been pulled from Tara's case just to improve Toussaint's clearance rate. He rose from his chair and left with Mancuso, his nails digging into his palms.

He and Mancuso walked out of the station. "Toussaint won't look for that Mustang." Eli couldn't keep the anger out of his tone. "He'll stuff his face with donut holes and search online for lonely middle-aged women."

"Listen to me." Mancuso's expression exhibited under-standing. "I had to bail you out in there. You get crossways with Guidry, and I can't help you. He's like an armadillo, digs in, and nothing you do will pull him away. It's best we stay on his good side."

Mancuso was right but Eli had to vent his temper. "So we go chase four girls who may be on a bender while Tara is in the hands of some well-funded pimp?"

"No, we stay in Guidry's good graces and work Zoe and Tara's cases the best we can." Mancuso flicked his head toward the parking area and Eli's Jeep. "So, let's interview this witness and hope Reggie finds that Mustang."

————

Jewel eased her grip and Tara rolled onto her side to look out the window.

Loto drove down Tchoupitoulas carefully, likely not wanting to attract any police attention. Passing colorful murals on the flood wall didn't brighten Tara's deep sense of dark danger.

Loto was big, muscular, and could flatten her with one hand. Escape from the van seemed impossible.

"Can't go back to my house now," Jewel said. "Li'l hoe like to burn it down."

Tara wasn't stupid. Not now.

Forget being a whore. Andre likely wanted to kill her. And Tara didn't doubt Jewel or Loto or even the beautiful Sage sitting in the front seat would do it. They had nothing to lose. And they had Andre's favor to gain.

But Tara wasn't going to give up. She twisted and kicked and lashed with her arms. Jewel grabbed Tara's hair and forced her nose to the seat.

"Let me go." Tara's words were smothered in stinky vinyl. "Let me go home."

"Shut up." Jewel smashed a fist into Tara's ribcage and

then spun her over like she was a stuffed toy. Jewel slammed her knee in Tara's gut.

Air shot from her lungs.

"Little girlie, you've been nothing but trouble since I laid eyes on you," Jewel said. "Shut up, I tell you, or I'll throw you off the Mississippi bridge."

The Mississippi River didn't scare Tara as much as being in this van.

She kicked wildly, aiming for Jewel.

But Jewel was quick. She shifted and easily rammed her fist into Tara's belly so hard, Tara stopped breathing. Another blow to her gut. Tara coughed, moaned and bit her bottom lip until it bled.

"Leave her alone." Sage stretched and tried to wrench Tara from Jewel. "If you want to kill her. You'll have to kill me too. But remember, I'm Andre's best earner."

"You ain't all that hoe." Jewel's tone held authority, like some kind of whore-queen. "Don't get all uppity with that pretty face, fine body, and so-phis-ti-cated way of talking. You just a hooker like all the others. Here today, gone tomorrow. And I can make that *gone* happen real soon."

"Be that as it may," Sage said in her posh accent. "Andre won't fancy you killing us both, will he? Especially if he didn't give the okay. I do know Andre's the boss."

Jewel pulled out her phone. "You let me worry about Andre and keep your limey mouth shut."

Jewel said two words into the phone. "She's trouble." She listened, then terminated the call. "Loto. You holding?"

"Never touch the stuff," Loto said.

"We gonna need to drop off Sage and pick up Freddy. Little girly here is gonna take a little nap."

TWENTY-SEVEN

Eli scanned the reception area of the Orleans Parish Center for Girls. Windows overlooked a playground filled with playhouses, slides, and swing sets. Two hallways funneled toward the back of the facility. Guarding the halls was a reception desk manned by a teenage girl in a New Orleans Saints tee shirt.

Mancuso pulled out his badge. "We're here to speak to the director."

The young girl tapped a button on her desk phone and spoke directly at it. "Ms. Jackson. The police are here."

One minute later, the echo of hard heels clacking on the tile floors announced the director's entrance from the hallway on the right. A plump black woman wearing a smart navy pantsuit and a serious expression spoke in a commanding tone. "Right this way, gentlemen."

Introductions were made in the hall, and Ms. Jackson ushered Eli and Mancuso to her office. Inside, photos of girls from diapers to cap-and-gowns hung on the walls. "Can I offer you coffee?" Her tone had demurred almost to a southern hostess.

"No thank you," Mancuso said.

Eli said, "None for me, thanks."

Ms. Jackson sat behind her desk. "I expected you earlier." Her brow arched in steely indignation. "We called two days ago."

Eli relaxed in a chair and stifled a smile. This woman was no uncaring bureaucrat. On the contrary, she looked after these girls like a stern but loving aunt.

Mancuso sat in the chair next to Eli. "I apologize for the department. There's no excuse. But my partner and I were just assigned the case yesterday, and we've been busy with another girl who's missing."

The director shot a glare at Eli, then Mancuso. "Another girl missing? Too many vulnerable children are out there alone. It's a crisis in this city, and it's getting worse."

Mancuso gave her a concerned and somber expression. "I was told you have a witness."

"Yes," Ms. Jackson said. "Kaitlyn. She was with Hailey, Madison, Isabelle, and Bridget the night they were taken."

A quick hit of shock stung Eli. "Taken?"

"Yes, detective," she said with unwavering eye contact. "Taken."

Mancuso rubbed his forehead. "And Kaitlyn somehow escaped?"

"She said she left before things got weird. Those are her words." Ms. Jackson pushed a button on her phone. "Sheryl. Do you know where Kaitlyn is?"

"Where else? The library," Sheryl answered.

"Okay, gentlemen, please follow me." Ms. Jackson led the way out of her office.

———

Badeau glowered inside the office at his Dauphine Street property. It didn't have the amenities consistent with a corporate executive, high-powered politician, or chairman of the board—no antique desk, no state-of-the-art technology, no private area to make private calls.

Instead, Badeau had hookers coming in and out, looking for lingerie or prophylactics, and a back door to a rat-invested alley that smelled of piss.

He deserved better.

He'd worked hard and should enjoy the same perks his privileged clients took for granted. Those starched shirts had power, prestige, and pretty secretaries. Badeau had whores, late nights, and Jewel.

They were entitled.

He was blood and sweat.

But if the cops caught him in his crimes, his power broker clients would offer no sympathy, no mercy, no help. They'd run from him faster than a SpaceX rocket climbing into the cosmos, then pound their chests and demand justice.

Justice. What a joke.

Tara. The stupid little girl wasn't so stupid after all, making a fool of Jewel. If not for Loto and blind luck, the police would've banged down Badeau's doors by now. And if Badeau was lucky, the ones with the battering ram could easily be the same cops who took his bribes and enjoyed the pleasures of his girls for free.

Andre's phone buzzed.

Marshall Aberdeen. "Heard you had some trouble with the cop's niece. She almost got away."

This condescending jackleg loved to poke. "Keep it up, Marsh, and you'll get a visit that'll make you wish you never left the streets."

"Javier's not happy with the situation," Marsh said. "You may want to call him and smooth it over—if you can."

Badeau's cheeks flared hot. "Why are you calling me Marsh?"

"Just trying to give you a heads up. You know, I worry about you."

Badeau pictured the smirk on the little twerp's face. "Worry about your own mistakes. Like the other night when you let those cops into Javier's office. Your stupidity put those hound dogs on my trail." Badeau's insides tightened. "Because of you, I got detectives from Louisiana and Mississippi sniffing."

"Naw, naw, naw." Marsh laughed out the words. "Should have checked your girl's history. Heard her uncle's a detective and a war hero." His tone was goading. "So now, this Eli Colt has NOPD stirred up like a sloe gin fizz. And Javier is mad. He wants to know what you're going to do."

"I'll call him. I have a plan."

"What should I tell him?"

"Tell him I'll call." Andre disconnected and tossed his phone on the desk. He'd rather share his plan with Tara's uncle than tell Marsh.

A clatter in the hallway. He froze. Was somebody out there listening to snitch to the police? A few days ago, he moved around New Orleans with complete impunity. Now the threat of cops loomed like a rain cloud over a street festival.

He edged to the back door, breathed in the stench of urine, and jerked it open. The gold eyes of a calico cat stared back at him. He shook his head, closed the door, and returned to his desk. He had to solve this Tara problem, or he'd be looking at thirty years.

But he had little ready cash. He needed money to get out of New Orleans, relocate, and plan.

Badeau considered calling Commodore. He'd never done business with the man, but Javier had. He'd warned Badeau although Commodore paid well, he was a psychopath. But desperate times and because Badeau couldn't send Tara to Leon—she was too hot to whore out, and he wasn't about to show Javier he couldn't handle the business—he had no choice.

Getting rid of Tara was the only option. No Tara. No body. No charges. Badeau would disappear for a few weeks until things cooled down, then return to take what was rightfully his and build an empire.

He'd manage his kingdom from a high-rise office at the Place de St. Charles or buy a plush building in the Warehouse District or Uptown. His business would operate incognito, bribing and extorting powerful officials as Javier did now. Badeau had learned from the best.

Badeau had become untouchable and very, very rich. Yes, this transaction with Commodore would work out well. He grabbed one of his burner phones, punched the number, and waited.

"Hello," a macabre voice answered.

"It's Andre Badeau. Javier Navarro shared your number."

"Andre," the Commodore's voice changed to Sunday-church polite—the sounds of wind, gulls, and splashing waves in the background. The man was on his yacht. "How pleasant of you to call."

Badeau got straight to it. "I've got my hands on some merchandise. It's quite beautiful."

"How old?" Commodore's quick question relayed he was interested. Very interested.

"Not very," Badeau worked to keep relief out of his voice. "No wear and tear."

"And you want to sell it to me? How delicious." He hissed the *s* at the end of the word.

Badeau had heard Commodore was a genius. But Badeau's mind conjured a demon with wings and talons and sulfurous vapors dashing from its nose. "You were my first call."

"Was I?" Commodore's tone reeked of mocking. "I'm always looking for young people to complete my crew. We've recently had a young girl leave us. A young boy too."

Marsh's screwup that sent Eli Colt to Gabriella's. Badeau wasn't stupid enough to spill the Marsh mistake to Commodore.

"When can I take delivery?" A clinking noise followed Commodore's question.

Badeau imagined Commodore putting down a glass of fifty-year-old scotch or a pewter mug of snake blood. "That depends on how much you're willing to pay?"

"I see..." Commodore's words trailed off as if something else had caught his attention. Then the line went silent. Badeau's heartbeat counted the seconds.

"I have to say," Commodore finally spoke. "I'm interested in the proposal. How much do you want?"

Badeau didn't want to leak desperation. So, he kept his answer short and vague. "Plenty."

"No worry." Commodore half-laughed, half-bragged. "Plenty is what I've got."

————

The library bore little resemblance to the libraries Eli had known as a kid in school. Libraries where he'd spent countless hours devouring hard-boiled detective novels by writers like Hammett, Spillane, and Elmore Leonard. This open space environment replaced the quiet book depository feel. There were computers instead of encyclopedias and no Dewey Decimal System.

A young girl sat alone at a table, her jaw resting on her fists. She swept her eyes across an open book between her elbows. A pen lay on the right side, her dominant side, of the book.

Ms. Jackson approached first. "Kaitlyn, these are Detectives Mancuso and Colt from the police. They're here to ask you some questions about Friday night."

Kaitlyn didn't even look up from her book.

Mancuso reacted fast. "Excuse us." He steered Eli to the other side of the library. "What's your sense on this girl? You want me to take the interview, or you?"

Eli quenched all his misgivings about being here and calmly said, "You know how I feel about this case. You can't really want me to take the lead?"

"I do." Mancuso set his jaw firm. "You military types are well-trained in this field of interrogation, and I'd like to expose myself to your technique."

Eli lifted a skeptical brow. "Don't give me that crap. You're retiring in a few weeks. You don't need to learn a technique. What's the real reason?"

"Alright." Mancuso pointed in Kaitlyn's direction. "I want you involved in this case. Heavily involved so you don't mope because we're not pounding the streets for Andre and Freddy Badeau. We're stuck on this case and the quicker we solve it, the sooner we get back to Tara full-time."

Mancuso made sense. What good would it do for Eli to sulk, even if he knew Toussaint would be scouring the internet for lonely women and ignoring Tara's case?

"I'll do it." Eli pulled out his phone and opened the recording app. "It's obvious Kaitlyn doesn't trust police." He punched on the recorder and walked to Kaitlyn and Ms. Jackson.

Kaitlyn sat erect and closed her book. Her face revealed no hint of her thoughts or feelings.

Ms. Jackson sat to Kaitlyn's left.

Mancuso sat across from Ms. Jackson.

Eli put his phone on the table and sat face-to-face with

Kaitlyn. "I'll be recording our conversation, Kaitlyn, because it might help us later to review what you have to say."

Kaitlyn remained silent. Her expression unreadable.

Eli pulled out his notepad for effect. "How long have you been here at the Center?"

Kaitlyn clicked her tongue, showing disinterest. "Five years." She shifted her posture but displayed no irregular blinking or nervous ticks.

Eli jotted down a few words. "And how old are you, and where are you from?"

"Sixteen. I grew up in Gentilly." Kaitlyn's eyes focused on Eli and didn't look down to her dominant right side. Eli had his baseline.

"Did you have anything to do with Hailey, Madison, Isabelle, or Bridget's disappearance?"

Kaitlyn's eyes caught fire. "Hell no. What the—"

"Hold on, Detective." Ms. Jackson's voice shook with suppressed anger, her hands swept the air in big circles. "Let's go outside."

Eli expected nothing less from this Mama Bear director. He probably should've explained.

But outside the library, Ms. Jackson closed in on Eli's personal space. "What are you doing accusing this girl of a crime?"

Eli held up his palms. "I know Kaitlyn had nothing to do with your girls' disappearance," Eli said. "These questions I'm asking set an interrogation pattern."

Mancuso had followed and confirmed Eli's words. "He's right. If we wanted a confession from Kaitlyn, we would've read her her rights. She's not a suspect, but she's clearly not a cooperative witness."

Ms. Jackson tugged the lapels of her jacket and shot Eli a glassy stare. But she didn't stop the interview and the three retuned to the table.

Eli eased back in his chair and relaxed to pose an empathetic posture. "Okay, Kaitlyn. What can you tell us about Friday night?"

"Not much. It was...like...boring." She stretched out the last word.

No tics. No blinking. No touching her face. No lies.

"How so?" Eli asked.

"We went to this rundown B&B in the Bywater. In a cottage in the back, you know?" Kaitlyn talked fast, as if she thought it would end the interview faster. "They pumped a keg, cracked a bottle of tequila, and I leave. Not my scene. End of story."

"What do you mean by *not your scene*?" Eli put down his pen and made full eye contact. "You don't like parties. You don't drink?"

Kaitlyn rolled her eyes as if the question was dumb. "I ain't into those quicky romances, you know, like some of the sluts in this place."

"Language," Ms. Jackson said.

"Look. Isabelle, one of my roommates asks me to go to this party, you know?" Kaitlyn leaned back. "Supposed to be a place to meet guys, she says. But I'm not interested in meeting some dude at a lame party. I'm more than that." Kaitlyn lifted her book. "I'd rather read than skank at some party."

"So why'd you go?" Eli said.

"A favor."

"Eli glanced at Mancuso, then Ms. Jackson, then back to Kaitlyn. "You went to a party for a favor?"

"Yeah. Isabelle—agreed that if I went, she'd like do my chores around here for two weeks." Kaitlyn's lips formed a fierce frown. "I went. She's gone. And I'm stuck cleaning toilets."

Eli checked his phone, still recording. "Tell me everything from how you got there, until you got back here."

"I've said all I can remember." Kaitlyn turned to Ms. Jackson. "Can I go to my room?"

Ms. Jackson visibly bit her bottom lip.

"No. You can't. Not yet, Kaitlyn," Eli said. "In fact, I'm thinking about bringing you to juvie and having them hold you overnight. We can pick up this interview first thing in the morning, maybe when your memory's a little—"

"Stop harassing me," Kaitlyn said. "I didn't do anything."

Eli leaned over the table. "And you're not telling me anything either. Tell us the whole story, and then you can go back to your room."

"Okay, okay." Kaitlyn raised her hands in surrender. "I'll tell you."

Eli settled back. His leaning in and out was a subliminal technique he'd learned from what seemed like thousands of hours of interviewing subjects. First, lean in to invade the space that's all theirs. Then, lean back when you get what you want. He may've been harsh on a sixteen-year-old girl with tactics he'd used on hardened soldiers, but Kaitlyn didn't whimper or burst into tears.

Kaitlyn began to spill. "Myles, this guy Isabelle used to date, calls her on Thursday about a party on Friday. He asked her to bring four other girls from the Center."

Ms. Jackson clutched a fist to her chest. "Why the Center?"

Eli gave Ms. Jackson a cool-it look. No more questions until after the story is out.

"I don't know why, but I said no. My nickname is... "Kaitlyn places her hand on the book. "Bibliophile. And that's a big word around here. They all know I like books best."

Kaitlyn continued. "So, Isabelle makes a deal to take my turn cleaning bathrooms if I go with them to this party. Myles picks us up with his friend, and we go in two cars. When we get there, this older guy is being like the life of the party. He's jumping around and acting all MC-like, real fake if you ask me."

Eli wanted to ask about the older guy but didn't interrupt.

"After a while, the older dude leaves, and Myles takes... uh." Kaitlyn looked at Ms. Jackson and hesitated, then clammed up.

Mancuso sensed what Eli knew. Kaitlyn wasn't going to say more in front of Ms. Jackson. He stood, "Ms. Jackson, I'll take that cup of coffee now."

"W-what?" Ms. Jackson glanced at Kaitlyn, Mancuso, then Eli. "Okay. Yes." She rose from her chair and left with Mancuso.

When the door shut, Kaitlyn went on. "I really couldn't say this stuff in front of Ms. Jackson."

Eli nodded. "I understand, go on."

"Isabelle goes with Myles into a bedroom, and I figure my job is done. So, while everyone was dancing or diving under the sheets, I left." Kaitlyn flashed a smug smile as if she'd finished.

Eli sensed there was more. "And?"

"That's it." Kaitlyn's eyes darted down and to the right. Telltale sign of a lie.

Eli leaned in again. "Don't lie to me, Kaitlyn. I'll know. What else did you see?"

Kaitlyn blew out a long sullen breath. "Fine. I went to the bus stop, across the street from the B&B. While I'm there, I noticed a bunch of guys on our school football team arrive. Must've been ten or more coming in different groups, you know? Then I see the older guy come back in his big SUV. An Escalade."

Eli's heart pushed up to his throat. "Tell me about the Escalade."

"It was dark," Kaitlyn said. "Black, maybe blue."

"And what about the older guy? Did you get a name?"

"You mean Freddy's uncle?"

"Freddy?" An adrenaline-laced edge tinged Eli's voice.

"Yeah, Freddy is Myles's friend. Didn't I say the old guy's name?"

Eli leaned in. "No, you didn't."

"Freddy mostly called him Unc," Kaitlyn said. "But sometimes called him Andre."

TWENTY-EIGHT

Lindsey arrived early at the Orleans Parish Coroner's Office to identify Zoe Prevost. She hated this place. Hated its bland décor. Hated its sterile furnishings. Hated its chemical smell to mask the scent of death.

She'd been here before to identify three other patients she'd treated at Safe Harbor—Latricia Adams found in a dumpster in the Calliope Projects. Consuelo Carrillo, who overdosed above a seedy bar in the seventh ward. Chung Cha Park, who was hit by a minivan after escaping a sex trafficker by the bus station. Girls, who like Zoe, Lindsey had shown love and compassion. But, also like Zoe, left before Lindsey could fully connect and treat the traumatic impact of their abuse.

Manny had told her Eli Colt, the man God chose for her, would be there for Zoe's autopsy. The same man who, the first time they met, ignored her like she'd had the latest Covid variant. The thought only heightened her apprehension.

And to make her visit to the morgue more repulsive, she'd see Zoe right out of cold storage—matted hair and bloated body, her expression unchanged from when she departed this life.

Lindsey agreed to identify Zoe because her mother, who'd recently lost her son to social services, refused. And because Lindsey came from the same sexual abuse as Zoe and Latricia and Consuelo and Chung Cha. Only by God's grace, had she been spared a similar fate.

Down the hall, she spotted Manny and Eli Colt talking to a medical examiner easily identified by the man's full-length white apron.

Manny spoke with his hands and his mouth and his changing expressions.

The ME listened with a friendly grin.

But Lindsey focused more on Eli who rocked back and forth, arms hugged tight against his chest.

As a detective, Eli must've witnessed an autopsy or two. Police academy students had to attend at least one to graduate. But his detached expression was a clear tell he was not looking forward to seeing Zoe's body sliced open.

His gaze wandered from Manny and the medical examiner's conversation, then stopped on her. His stare lingered, his face flushed slightly, then he flashed a smile that made her arms erupt with goose pimples.

Eli ambled to her. Her throat narrowed to the size of a pinhole. She thoughtlessly reached in her purse for a breath mint.

He extended his hand. "Dr. Crenshaw. What a surprise." His tone was friendly enough, even comforting, inflaming the warm coals in her body to white hot. Why the change in his attitude? What had happened since they'd last met?

"Please, call me Lindsey." Her voice came out all breathy and nervous. "Nice to see you too."

"What brings you—" He scanned their surroundings. "Here?"

"You mean, what's a girl like me doing in a place like this?" A wave of embarrassment toasted her cheeks at her corny cliche.

He tipped his head as if to stretch the tension from his neck. "Um...yeah. I guess so."

He didn't want to be at the morgue any more than she did.

"Manny didn't tell you?" Lindsey said. "I'm here to identify Zoe."

"Oh," Eli scratched his cheek. "Shouldn't her mother do that?" He asked like he knew the answer.

Lindsey responded with an awkward shrug.

An uncomfortable silence followed for several seconds, then Manny appeared with a boisterous, "Hey there."

"Hey there yourself," she said. "Another friend of yours?" She motioned toward the young ME.

Manny glanced over his shoulder. "Oh, Lenny? Me and his dad go way back. Was an ME back when I was a rookie, retired about five years ago." His expression softened into empathy. "You ready for this?"

Latricia and Consuelo and Chung Cha's corpses swarmed her mind like moths on a flood light. Could she ever be ready to identify the body of one of her patients?

"Sorry about it falling on you," Manny said. "Last check, her momma is three sheets to self-medication since losing her boy to social services."

"And Zoe to—" Lindsey stopped herself from saying murder. "If Zoe would've just stayed at Safe Harbor. It's crazy how these pimps take a hold on these girls."

Manny shifted his gaze to Eli, reminding her about his niece.

"I'm sorry, Detective. That was insensitive of me."

"No reason to apologize," Eli said. "And please, it's Eli."

A young technician in a clean white lab coat approached Lindsey. "Dr. Crenshaw, we're ready for you."

Manny touched her shoulder. "You want me to come with you?"

She didn't want to go in that room. And certainly not alone. "Please."

Manny covered her shoulders in the crook of his arm. "Lead the way," he said to the technician.

Her emotions swung from delight to despair—Eli Colt had been kind to her. And now, she would see Zoe dead.

Manny opened the door to the dimly lit room, its window blocked by a drawn curtain. "You ready?"

She lowered her head and thrust her shoulders forward, as if preparing to walk into a strong wind. "I am."

———

Eli put on the paper apron, cap, and footies he'd pulled from a cardboard box outside the autopsy room. Lindsey had left ten minutes earlier, sobbing, Mancuso's protective arm around her shoulders.

Mancuso returned and pushed through the double doors to the autopsy room. He and Eli entered, the smell of death and disinfectant mingled, and death had the upper hand.

Too bright, too brash LED light fixtures illuminated the room. Tiled floors and tiled walls were dull and dingy from years of spilled blood. Rows of cabinets lined the walls, behind their glass doors, electric saws and bone splitters. Disposable face shields like welding helmets hung in a straight line over polished sinks. Along another, six steel tables, each with gutters running alongside its edges and drain holes in the corners waited like fresh dug graves in a cemetery.

On table seven, beneath the medical examiner's probing eyes, lay the naked pale body of Zoe Prevost.

Unlike the corpse of a battle-hardened soldier or aged prostitute or combatant from a foreign land, Zoe's nudity mortified Eli. She was an underaged girl from his hometown who got mixed up with an evil that killed her. And her death stare too similar to the dancing boy in Shurandam whose horror had followed Eli for over eight years.

Sweat dampened Eli's back and armpits.

The medical examiner reached for his camera and photographed Zoe's body from head to foot. Then he rolled a cart of stacked cutting tools next to the table. He switched on a voice activated recorder, picked up a scalpel and surgical shears.

Eli stepped back, leaned against the wall to avoid a potential blood splatter. Next to him, on a counter, was a plastic bag containing the blue cord found around Zoe's ankles at the crime scene. He picked up the bag.

"Let's get started." The medical examiner's voice was monotone and uncaring. "The body is that of a well-developed Caucasian female, measuring sixty-five inches in length and weighing one-hundred and nine pounds. Except for the skin damage from prolonged water submersion, her appearance is consistent with the noted age of sixteen years."

Eli thought he'd developed an emotional numbness from witnessing dozens of autopsies with his work at CID, but his hands shook, his stomach swirled.

He distracted himself, opened the evidence bag and pulled out the blue cord. What secrets did this evidence, the only evidence found at the crime scene, have for Eli to find?

The medical examiner cut a standard Y-shaped incision across Zoe's chest, moving to the sternum from the lower tip of the Y, then down to the pubic region.

The sight of cut flesh pulled back the curtain on Eli's recurring nightmare—the dancing boy lying in the dusty alley with his throat slit.

Vomit filled Eli's mouth. He gagged and caught a dribble with his palm. What's wrong with him? Puking at an autopsy? He wasn't a rookie.

Mancuso edged close. "You okay?" His tone was low and sympathetic.

Eli swallowed the bitter bile before responding. "Fine." The word came out like a gurgle.

"The spleen weighs one hundred sixty grams," the medical examiner said into his microphone. "The capsule is intact. The parenchyma is trabecular and pale purple."

Most of what a medical examiner said during a post-mortem exceeded most detectives' vocabulary. Usually, Eli would be impatient for the bottom line, the all-important information—cause of death. But now, his getting out of this room verged on panic.

Eli took in a deep breath and fixed his eyes on a spot on the ceiling. "It will pass in a minute. It will pass in a minute," he repeated his mantra.

"The gallbladder wall is of normal width," the medical examiner continued, stealing Eli's attention. "It contains minimal greenish bile with no stones."

The blue cord. Eli fixated on the cord. It seemed vital. Not to Zoe's autopsy but to finding Tara. He rubbed sweat from his forehead.

"The bladder mucosa is intact," the medical examiner said. "There's only an ounce of pale urine. And there are petechiae internally on the epicardium and visceral pleura." He held his hand over the microphone and glanced up at Manny and Eli. "That's red spots on the heart and lungs for you dumb detectives." The medical examiner chuckled, his first display of any emotion. "Whoever called asphyxiation at the crime scene gets a gold star."

Eli didn't want a gold star. He wanted to get out. It was as if his nightmare had found him. Here, standing over this present reality of another child being abused and murdered.

The whirring sound of the circular saw ripping into Zoe's skull closed the walls of the room in on Eli. His pulse pounded. His breathing exercises failed.

He peeled off his paper apron, wobbled to the double doors and split them open. He staggered in a zig-zagging pattern down the hall. His lungs shrunk. His breathing reduced to short shallow gasps.

"Eli? Are you okay?" Lindsey's gentle tone behind him.

He tried to laugh off his terror from the room and his guilt from Afghanistan. The fear of not finding Tara. And the horror of the possibility of seeing her on one of those steel tables.

"Uh...I'm fine. Just been a while." He waved at the doors he'd just stumbled through.

"I'm sure it's a terrible thing to witness." Her soothing voice and scent failed to soften Eli's horror.

"You're right." He filled his lung with air, tried to slow his breathing. Uncontrollable gasping pants shook his chest.

. Panic. Tears. Sobs. Tara.

He must find Tara.

TWENTY-NINE

Lindsey waited at the coroner's office to learn more about the man God had chosen for her. About his relationship with his niece, Tara. And about his impending wedding in May.

But when he'd blasted past her. He wore panic and fear on his face. She hurried to catch him in the open-air parking lot.

Lindsey had experienced many harrowing sessions with abused girls with PTSD—their intrusive memories, their flashbacks, their emotional distresses. Most of her girls avoided talking about what brought on their attacks, but after persistent treatment, those who'd share the event that triggered their anxiety would eventually find relief.

Eli wasn't her patient, but she'd easily diagnosed a PTSD episode outside the autopsy room. Now, in the parking lot, she coaxed him into her Civic to assess him further.

His pulse throbbed against the skin near his carotid artery. His eyes were half-wild, half-scared. His breathing was erratic and his hands trembled.

Seeing Zoe spliced open must have triggered a flashback. Perhaps the source of his disorder.

"I must find her, you hear me." He spoke in a breathless, desperate tone. "I must find Tara today. They don't care about her. None of them. Do you hear me? Can you help me find her?" There was hyper vigilance in Eli's voice. Not PTSD anger Lindsey had often seen with her girls.

Lindsey knew if Eli exhibited hostile behavior, there'd be little she could do to protect herself. But something inside her quelled this fear—as if God placed her there to hear what Eli needed. And to share with her what triggered his attack.

Lindsey lifted his upper eyelids. "Eli. You remember I'm a psychologist. Right?" His pupils were dilated as she suspected.

He looked at her with extraordinary blue eyes, anxious eyes, cords flexing in his neck.

Lindsey clutched his wrist and estimated 150 beats per minute. "The best thing you can do right now is get your breathing and your heart rate under control." She placed her palm on his warm cheek and spoke softly. "Then we can talk about what you're going through. I won't interrupt, won't judge, and I won't tell you what you need to do. Okay?"

Eli lifted his hands to his face. "Not here," he said between his fingers. "I can't do it here. It's too much. Do you hear me? It's too much."

Lindsey had an idea where to go. She texted Manny where he could find them.

———

At the Aquarium of the Americas on Canal Street, Eli grounded himself in the present by soaking in the splendor of his surroundings. And walking with Lindsey's help through the thirty-foot tunnel of rounded acrylic walls, its soothing backdrop of rainbow-colored fish, schooled in near perfect formation, allowed him to slow his breathing.

He and Lindsey continued to the Amazon Rain Forest, past a shark tank, then stopped at the Seahorse Gallery where he realized his heart rate had returned to normal.

They ended the tour at the food court where Lindsey suggested ice cream. She chose vanilla. Eli got rocky road.

Lindsey chose a somewhat secluded table. "Are you feeling better?"

Eli winced an embarrassed grin. "I'm sorry you had to witness that." And he was sorry. What would've happened if Gina had seen him in such a state?

A sweet smile blossomed across Lindsey's face. "It's best to talk about what's bothering you. I make a living at listening to what upsets people."

His Army therapist had also stressed the importance of sharing his condition with a friend. Was Lindsey a friend? Was her help more personal than professional?

Outside of Zeke in Solace, Eli had few companions. He couldn't count on Gina, who it was clear to him now, was too self-absorbed. But what about Lindsey Crenshaw. He barely knew her, but she was a psychologist. Professional help—couldn't hurt too much.

And without her showing him kindness, he might now be in his Jeep, balled up like a newborn sucking his thumb, instead of inside this calming environment of marine life. "Are you on the clock?"

"You paid for the ice cream." A flash of excitement played in her eyes and a swift rush of color to her cheeks. "That should cover my cost."

Eli felt lighter, more in control. He dug his plastic spoon into his rocky road. The past couple of hours had been rough, but oddly he found comfort in Lindsey's company, and the cool sweetness of ice cream.

She poked her spoon into her vanilla. "You know, my job

at Safe Harbor is treating girls who've suffered physical and emotional trauma. So don't be embarrassed about what happened today. I've seen it before. And I've struggled with it myself."

Eli arched his eyebrows, surprised she was sharing something so personal. "I remember Manny starting to tell me something about how he and you met."

She stiffened as if a confidence had been betrayed. "What did he tell you?"

Eli lifted a spoonful. "Not much. Said it wasn't his story to tell."

Lindsey blinked back tears.

Could Eli have pried into some dark despair she wanted to keep buried? A trace of guilt spread through him. "Manny bragged about you that's all. He didn't tell me anything about your past. He did share how much he respects and admires you."

Lindsey brushed her index finger across her damp lashes. "Let's just say I didn't have a traditional upbringing. I never knew my father, and my mother was...uh, different."

"I see," Eli said. But he didn't. Lindsey Crenshaw was an enigma. A young, beautiful woman who nestled herself away like Mother Theresa in Calcutta, giving herself selflessly to kids who needed help. So, why was she now in New Orleans with him?

His posture perked and he slid his chair closer to the table. "I'll tell you my secret if you tell me yours."

She laughed a soft, lilting melody. "I'm afraid that's not how the doctor-patient process works, detective. You're to tell me what's bothering you. I assess and determine how to proceed with your treatment."

The sound of her laugh, the sound of her voice engulfed him like a tidal wave.

"What I share about myself does not fall under doctor, patient confidentiality." She lifted her cup. "And, since I accepted ice cream as my fee, what you say does."

"Okay then, here goes."

Eli's words flooded from some deep, dark place like raging waters after a spring thaw. He shared the horrors of Afghanistan—the ambush, the wounds he'd suffered in combat, the dancing boy dead in the alley, and the guilt he felt for doing nothing to save the boy. He'd talked for twenty minutes and spared nothing. And as she'd promised, Lindsey didn't interrupt or judge or tell him what he must do.

And the weight of his failure to act fluttered away like dandelions in a stiff breeze.

Her phone buzzed and she checked her screen. "Manny just texted me. He learned something new about Zoe's murder at the autopsy. He wants to meet up."

———

Eli and Lindsey met Mancuso among the azaleas and artists in Jackson Square, the iconic New Orleans landmark named for the bronze statue of Andrew Jackson located in its center. Mancuso sat on a metal-slat park bench tossing popcorn to pigeons clamoring at his feet.

"What did you find?" Eli asked.

Manny pulled from his jacket a section of the blue cord Eli had examined during the autopsy. "This cord we found on Zoe's body, forensics has no idea what kind it is or where it came from."

"How does that help?" Lindsey asked.

Eli took the cord from Mancuso and rubbed its smooth coated surface. "Because if forensics can't identify it, it's rare. And if we learn what this cord is, it may be easier to trace it."

Mancuso stood and tossed the popcorn bag in a nearby trashcan. "You used to work with the Feds, right Eli?"

Eli lifted the cord to eye level. "Back when I was an Army detective. I can reach out to my former contact and ask Quantico to take a look. The worst he can say is no."

THIRTY

Eli paced the slick marble floor inside the lobby of the FBI building on Leon C. Simon Boulevard. He stalked back and forth between the mahogany reception desk to the smoked glass windows blocking any sunlight from outside. His FBI contact in Washington had arranged for a local agent-in-training to put the blue-coated cord—Eli's only viable evidence—in a pouch bound for Quantico today. And then, by tomorrow, Eli would have an analysis that would hopefully get him closer to finding Tara. A long shot—but his only shot.

Almost forty minutes later, the elevator doors opened, and a too-young male with a faded tan, sun-bleached hair, and an ill-fitted suit strode into the lobby.

This had to be Eli's agent-in-training. "Agent Sutcliffe?"

Sutcliffe, hands in pockets and wearing a not-a-care-in-the-world expression, meandered to Eli. "You Colt?"

Eli offered his hand. "I am."

Sutcliffe's grip was firm. "I'm supposed to get some kind of evidence from you?"

"Yes, more than a half-hour ago. Aren't we pressed for

time to get my evidence into that pouch?" Eli held his disgruntled tone in check.

"Not anymore." Sutcliffe's carefree expression changed to one of frustration. "The pouch already left. We're too late."

"Not *we*." Eli emphasized the last word, his aggravation building. "I'm not late. I've been here. Where were you?"

Sutcliffe stood tall and ignored Eli's obvious reprimand. "Not my fault. My supervisor had me in another boring seminar. The class was as inspiring as a general anesthetic." His face flashed with rebellious indignation. "I tried to get down here on time, but my supervisor hit me with a big fat veto."

"Does your supervisor know a young girl's life hangs in the balance? And this evidence is our only lead?" Eli turned, shifted his attention to the grandmother-like receptionist, a distraction to avoid another panic attack. The receptionist returned Eli's glance with a smile as sweet as a French macaroon.

Eli reigned in his unease. "Okay, I get it. Not your fault. You have a first name?"

"Dakota."

"So, Dakota. Can we somehow catch the pouch?"

"Even if we could, it's a sealed pouch," Sutcliffe said. "Nothing can go in or come out."

"Is there another pouch heading to Quantico?"

"Not for forty-eight hours."

Eli inhaled slowly and exhaled even slower. "So, Dakota. What are our options?"

"Like I said, I'm new. So new, you're one of the few people in this building who knows my first name." Sutcliffe held out his hand. "Why don't you give me the evidence, and I'll check with one of the special agents. They may know a way."

Eli dangled the evidence bag at eye level. "It's only a sample."

Sutcliffe's eyes flashed with recognition. "Holy crap, dude. Where'd you get this?"

"Off a murder victim."

Sutcliffe snatched the bag and opened it. "No. Where'd you get this? Near a river or a lake?"

"The Rigolets."

"I'm from Florida, man. Speak English."

"It's a channel between Lake Pontchartrain and the Gulf."

Sutcliffe studied the cord. "They do much skiing in the Rig-ah-whatever?"

"Maybe. Why?"

"This is a high-velocity tow line for water skiing."

"How do you know?"

"Like I said. Grew up in Florida—Winter Haven. Been skiing since I was six, and this line costs about three-hundred bucks for a hundred-foot line. Typically sold with a wakeboard handle." Sutcliffe rubbed the cord with his thumb. "It's specially coated, so it doesn't explode, which will happen with a cheaper cord pulling a skier."

New information. Not just a cord but expensive water ski line. Eli wanted to hug Sutcliffe. "You're sure?"

"I may not have much of a voice in the FBI choir here, but when it comes to water-skiing—I'm Bruno Mars." Sutcliffe tugged at his lapels. "I'm also in the Coast Guard reserves."

"Coast Guard reserves?" Eli said, a little confused. "Why are you in the FBI?"

"Daddy issues. He's convinced my career will go farther on dry land."

Eli's father came to mind. "I can empathize. What kind of boat would you find this line on?"

"I'd say a killer ski boat like a MasterCraft ProStar or a Malibu Response."

Eli patted the kid's shoulder. "Get this to Quantico to

confirm what you just told me. And I'm gonna search for a killer ski boat somewhere in the Rigolets."

———

Eli met Lindsey and Mancuso at the Morning Call Coffee Stand across from the iconic St. Patrick Cemeteries on City Park Avenue. He passed the distinctive nineteenth-century mirrors, arched-shape counter, and swivel stools to take a chair beside Lindsey near the rear wall. Mancuso sat across the table, munching on a powdered beignet.

The coffee and fried dough aromas were tempting but not nearly as gazing at Lindsey. Eli kept his eyes on her for too long.

Manny cleared his throat. "What'd you find out?"

Embarrassment warmed Eli's face. "Uh...unofficially, the line you pulled off Zoe's body isn't your average baling twine. It's a," he pulled out his notepad, "high-velocity ski line typically sold with a wakeboard handle. The special blue coating keeps the rope from exploding under tension."

Manny sipped the last of his coffee. "Ski rope? In the Rigolets?"

A server stopped by. Eli ordered beignets and a cafe au lait.

Lindsey declined a refill.

Mancuso lifted his cup. "I've fished them inlets for years. Not from those pricey camps, mind you, or off their custom-built piers. I caught many a red snapper casting a line right from the bank."

"Ever seen anyone skiing?" Eli said, trying to keep his eyes off Lindsey.

"Never," Mancuso said. "And if somebody had the cojones to ski those waters, I'd hate to see what'd happen if those good ole boys caught them. The guys in those camps live to fish and think they own the inlets. Put a ski boat speeding through their waters, and it will be like the Gaza Strip."

"So you're saying a ski boat in the Rigolets would get noticed?" Eli teemed with excitement. "Sounds like we should canvass the Rigolets for a ski boat."

"Can't," Mancuso said. "Have a meeting with an assistant DA on another case."

Eli fished his wallet out of his back pocket, and flashed Lindsey a warm smile. "Care to take a ride?"

THIRTY-ONE

Tara woke on a soft mattress, her stomach turning, her mouth dry and tacky, her head pounding like she'd slammed into a brick wall. She opened her eyes slowly. Everything around her was fuzzy shapes and blurred colors. Where was she and why did she feel so weird?

She tried to sit up, but the room spun like the Tilt-a-Whirl ride at last year's school fair. Was she in the hospital? There were no voices over an intercom and no strong disinfectant smells.

She'd never felt this strange—not when she smoked a joint with Zoe, not when she drank too much from the bottle of vodka she stole from Mom's liquor cabinet. And not when the doctor gave her that red cough syrup for bronchitis two years ago.

Her nostrils twitched to the smell of pan-fried fish, which usually made her mouth water, but now sent sour puke up to her mouth. She fought through her nausea and rolled onto her back.

After the room stopped spinning, she sat up. Things in the room started to come into focus. She could make out the furniture—dresser, chest of drawers, nightstand next to the bed. But they all were still hazy.

She eased her legs off the mattress and tried to stand on the spongy carpet. She burped and almost vomited like that jerk Freddy in Andre's apartment.

Freddy.

The airport.

New York.

He came to get her to meet Andre. Did she fall asleep on the plane? This room didn't look like what she saw on the Plaza Hotel's website.

Spreading her feet wide, she stood, her muscles not fully obeying her brain. Curtains came into focus on the far wall. She swayed, stumbled to the window and opened the blinds.

Outside, a strange boat like a rocket ship hung under a pitched roof. Tied to the pier alongside it, was a boat more than twice as long and twice as wide, and looked like someone could live on it.

The room and its outdoorsy decor came more into focus and, unlike Jewel's messy place, was tidy and clean.

Jewel.

The French Quarter.

The streetcar.

Home.

Heat surged through Tara's veins. Andre was not her boyfriend. Jewel called her a whore. Tara ripped down the curtains, then violently puked on the carpet.

She rushed to the door nearly losing her balance. She tried the knob, but it wouldn't budge.

Muffled male voices outside the room. The creep Freddy, and someone else—not Andre.

Tara pressed her ear against the wood panel.

"Andre sure screwed me on this deal." Definitely Freddy.

"Like to get me arrested getting that underage slag out of his condo."

That jerk called her a slag.

"Then we find from our plant with the police, the whore has a Pit Bull uncle sniffing around trying to find her," Freddy said. "I almost ran into him at the penthouse."

Hearing her Uncle Eli had come to New Orleans to look for her lit her like New Year's fireworks.

The throwback image of her on her uncle's lap gave her a better vibe. Her headache faded and she saw everything clearer.

It was as if Dad was still alive.

THIRTY-TWO

Eli accelerated his Jeep over the Chef Menteur Pass. The afternoon sun spawned orange clouds near the eastern horizon. To the north emerged empty lots with concrete foundations left bare since Hurricane Katrina. Next, a splattering of businesses—churches, strip malls, dollar stores, and a beat-down motel, passed by.

Beside him, Lindsey tapped her thumbs across her phone screen.

Eli concentrated on the dull throb from his old thigh wound to ignore his persistent curiosity about Lindsey, the woman who calmed him outside the coroner's office.

He'd bared his soul at the Aquarium but knew so little about her. Perhaps on this drive, he could connect, learn more about her, maybe understand her like he never could understand Gina. "You writing a novel over there?"

Lindsey clicked the screen a few more times, then stopped and looked up. "I'm letting my assistant know I'll be taking more personal time and giving her instructions on adjusting my calendar."

Eli steered through a stretch of road dominated by live

oaks Cheniers, tall grass, and hundreds of birds on power lines. "I really opened up to you at the Aquarium. It's almost embarrassing." What was it about this woman that stirred him to bare his soul? "You know so much about me, and I know so little about you."

She exhaled to almost a murmur and removed her sunglasses. "I'm not that complicated, really. I love my work at Safe Harbor. My childhood was less than ideal, but I meet kids who've had it worse almost every week."

Worse than what? he wanted to ask and pry further. "I understand sharing horrible things is difficult. You're the only person I've shared what happened to me with that Afghan boy. And that includes the Army head shrinkers." Eli felt Lindsey's eyes on him, and he winced at his headshrinker remark. He slowed and made eye contact. "Look, all I'm saying is I'd like to know more about you."

Lindsey folded her arms.

Eli shifted his focus back to the road.

"I was put into the foster care system near Dallas when I was five," Lindsey said. "I don't recall ever seeing my father. And what I remember of my mother left little doubt she struggled with alcohol."

Lindsey fidgeted with an elastic band on her wrist, then bound her hair in a ponytail. "I bounced around foster homes from kindergarten through middle school. I never felt like I fit in where they put me. So, when I turned thirteen, I ran."

Eli pulled over to the shoulder and parked. He leaned back against his door. "You were on your own at thirteen? Where'd you run to."

"I didn't have much of a plan or money. I got as far as Shreveport." She shifted her weight showing her discomfort. "There I met this guy Rex at the bus station. He was cute, and I was desperate. It took me five seconds to fall in love." A faint smile tugged at her mouth, but her eyes filled with sadness.

Eli's attention heightened, as did his curiosity about Lindsey. "How old was this guy, Rex?"

"He told me he was twenty. Manny learned later he was thirty-five." Lindsey tightened her arms across her chest. "Manny also found out Rex had a long record of pimping girls in Dallas and Fort Worth. Then he left Texas to solicit girls my age in Louisiana."

"I'm so sorry." And he meant it. He could sense the horrible place this story was headed.

"Compared to what many of my patients have suffered, it's not so horrible." Her voice wavered, lacking conviction. "Treating others who've suffered the same type of trauma is good therapy for me."

"I can imagine your time with Rex is painful to think about. I didn't mean to make you relive that trauma."

"Like I said. I revisit it with my girls pretty regularly. And like I told you outside the coroner's office, talking helps most people."

But Lindsey was visibly uncomfortable.

"Since I started sharing my sad story," she said with a half-laugh, likely meant to put Eli at ease. "I might as well finish." Her gaze focused on the floorboards. "Rex brought me to New Orleans for the Super Bowl. He said he had reservations for a penthouse suite at a high-end hotel. We would sleep in a bed as big as a swimming pool, eat crab cakes, drink Hurricanes, and have a blast." She kept her eyes down, avoiding eye contact.

"Let me guess. No penthouse." Eli said.

"Nope." She nervously twirled the edge of her ponytail. "We stayed in an abandoned warehouse. My bed was a flattened cardboard box on concrete."

Lindsey's breathing turned short and shallow. She pulled a Kleenex from her purse and patted her moist eyes. "He brought men to have sex with me. Most smelled like whiskey and sweat. Then there was a time he took me to the park near the river and left me on a bench holding a balloon."

She crossed her arms into a defensive posture, like forming a shield around her heart. "A man came and took me to that fancy hotel Rex promised. But he beat me, tore off my clothes, and then..." She didn't finish what was likely too horrible for words.

But he knew what happened. A heavy force, like a mortar round, slammed into his chest. He regretted his prodding and pressing and prying into her horrid childhood. "I'm so sorry."

Lindsey released a tense sigh. "Then he snuck me back to the park after midnight. I was bleeding so bad Rex wanted to kill him. Instead, Rex just took me back to the warehouse and gave me a roll of paper towels."

Eli clenched his fists. "These men who abuse kids for sexual gratification. Monsters."

"Yes, they are. But unlike poor Zoe and many others, I survived."

Eli cranked the ignition and shifted the transmission in gear. "But I have a niece who's likely out there with another monster like Rex, and his name is Andre Badeau."

Lindsey set her jaw in determination. "That's why I came with you. Helping girls like Tara is what I do. And you just heard why."

———

Rigolets Bait and Seafood sat across the bridge just east of the channel. According to its yellow signage on pale-blue weatherboards, it offered live shrimp, beer, tackle, and fuel. Eli turned into its gravel parking lot. "Manny told me about this place. Says the owner knows everything that happens in the Rigolets."

Eli held the door open. Lindsey entered the building, and

the smell of live bait wafted out. Inside were aisles labeled fishing lures, rods and reels, safety equipment, and boating line.

Boating line. "I'm going to check for ski cord," Eli said, heading to the aisle.

Lindsey walked to the front of the store.

The rope selection was extensive—marine double-braided nylon, high-quality dock rope, and trawling line, among others. But the one rope they didn't have was a blue, high-velocity ski rope sold with a mainline wakeboard handle.

He joined Lindsey at the counter where a man wore a yellow mesh cap, looked older than the cypress floorboards, and appeared quite taken with Lindsey.

"Mr. O'Sullivan, this is my friend, Eli," Lindsey said with a bright smile, obviously recovered from their conversation on the drive. "Eli, this is Dermot O'Sullivan, the proprietor of this business."

"Pleased to meet you, Mr. O'Sullivan," Eli offered his hand.

Dermot O'Sullivan's handshake was rough from hard calluses, and his eyes remained on Lindsey.

"We're looking for a boat you probably don't see often in the Rigolets. A ski-boat. Can you help us?"

"Naw. Ain't seen hide nor hair of no ski boat in these waters," O'Sullivan said in a husky drawl. "But I got something fur 'em if they come tearing through the channel, mucking up the water, and scaring the fish." He nodded at an ancient spear gun mounted on the wall. It resembled a rifle he'd once seen in a Sylvester Stallone movie, but from its muzzle protruded a metal spearhead that looked like it could kill a whale.

O'Sullivan rubbed his jaw. "Although...seems somebody told me of some fancy-schmancy boat barreling across the channel causing all types of consternation. But I thought they was pulling my leg."

Eli's heart rate rippled. "Really? Do you remember who told you?"

O'Sullivan shook his head. "Can't remember what I had for breakfast. And I eat here most days." He slapped the counter and guffawed at his joke.

"This is very important, Mr. O'Sullivan," Lindsey said. "We're looking for a girl who's been kidnapped by sex traffickers."

O'Sullivan slid his cap off, then put it back on his head, his expression turning thoughtful, almost concerned. "You know I talk to dozens of people every day. Some I know, some I don't. But now I recollect someone said they saw a ski boat south of here, 'bout two or three miles."

"Sir, I appreciate your help," Eli said. "And I'd like to ask for some advice if you don't mind?"

"You can ask," O'Sullivan said.

"If you were looking for a ski boat in this area, how would you go about it?" Maybe the old codger knew more and would offer more help.

O'Sullivan leaned back and tugged on his hat brim. "Well, I'll tell ya. I'd get in a boat and cruise the coastline south of here." His speech was slow and measured. "It's still hot, so nobody's got their boats in for the winter yet."

"What if you don't have a boat and are in a hurry? Is there an accessible road we could take?"

"Naw, son. The Rigolets is more water than land. You'll need a boat." O'Sullivan pointed to a sign behind the counter displaying the various leasing costs. "So I'd rent one."

———

Eli grabbed his rucksack from his Jeep, then met O'Sullivan behind the bait shop. O'Sullivan led Eli and Lindsey down a dock, past Bass Boats, Crestliners, and Boston Whalers. He stopped at a tiny skiff that looked like it belonged in a boat boneyard. Its maybe fourteen-foot aluminum hull had more dents than a tin roof after a hailstorm, and the engine hatch lay bent and unfastened, likely from countless repairs.

"This thing seaworthy?" Eli asked.

O'Sullivan tucked his thumbs in his pant pockets. "Sure is. Never stranded me once."

"What about the customers who leased it?"

O'Sullivan stepped into the skiff but said nothing.

"Is this the only boat available?" Lindsey's tone spilled over with concern.

"Yep." O'Sullivan spat in the channel and gave the Evinrude engine a quick inspection. "Other two are out for repair." He flipped closed the engine cover. "Now, don't you worry yourself about *Little Lizzie*. She'll get you where you need to go."

O'Sullivan squeezed a rubber bulb in the fuel line, twisted the throttle, then turned the key. He pushed down the choke and cranked the engine in one motion. After releasing the choke, the engine sputtered, caught, and coughed foul-smelling black smoke.

"There ya go," O'Sullivan said. "Try to have her back before sundown. It gets pretty dark at night around here."

Lindsey hesitated, then eased herself into the skiff.

With a rocking thud, Eli sat in the skiff's rear, gripped the engine's throttle, and turned. Too much throttle, it sounded like a possessed lawnmower. Too little, and it threatened to shut down. After a few minutes, he found the RPMs that seemed to suit the engine. But what would happen if it stalled? The two oars in the hull did little to boost Eli's confidence in this mission.

But he quelled his fears. He needed to find a ski boat with a blue ski cord—his only solid lead.

THIRTY-THREE

A spark of irritation flickered inside Eli. Darkness was fast approaching. He and Lindsey had traveled at least five kilometers in *Little Lizzie*, talking with fishermen along the way. But no one had seen or heard anything about a ski boat in the Rigolets.

With daylight quickly fading, nervous energy coursed through Eli's veins. He drummed his fingers on the throttle. "We should call it a night and return to the bait shop. We can come back at first light."

"Let's give it another half hour," Lindsey said with a tinge of urgency. "I hate the thought of Tara out here with a monster."

Laughter and camaraderie disrupted the natural noise of the channel. Eli accelerated around a slight curve in the shoreline. Ahead, a family of four fished in a clearing from the tailgate of a pickup backed to the water's edge.

Eli pulled the boat closer.

Lindsey balanced herself and stood. "Excuse me. Have you seen a strange boat in this area?"

"You mean besides yours?" asked a teenage boy that brought laughter from the entire clan.

"No. A ski boat," Lindsey said.

"Oh, oh." A girl about nine raised her hand and waved as if she had the answer at school. "We seen that last week, huh, Mama? Right out there." The girl pointed farther south.

"Yeah, that's right," her mom said. "Come screaming like a low-flying airplane. Had a girl up front baring her business in a skimpy bikini. A boy was driving, and another one was skiing behind it."

Lindsey's body swayed slightly, causing the boat to rock. "And you saw it last week?"

"Yep," said the girl.

"Do you know where the boat came from?" Lindsey asked.

The man nodded. "Sure do. My cousin does odd jobs now and again at a big house up about a mile yonder. Same as we seen. Say they had a fancy boat, purple and black. Got Malibu something or other written on its side."

"Wakesetter," said his wife. "Malibu Wakesetter."

The man pointed south. "Go up a piece and turn into the next inlet. The only house in there. Can't miss it."

"Thank you." Eli followed the directions and turned into the inlet. The purple ski boat with Malibu Wakesetter on the side was suspended on a lift inside an open boathouse.

A Sea Ray was docked alongside on a pier—over fifty-feet, blue and white, luxurious. Eli pulled out his phone to call Mancuso but had no signal.

————

The sun disappeared below the horizon. A partial moon pitched a dim glow with minimal visibility on the property and its manicured lawn. If the boathouse and boats were impressive, the house was spectacular. Mind-blowing.

From his rucksack, Eli pulled his military-grade night vision binoculars.

Lindsey leaned forward in the skiff. "Good place to get away and embrace the simplicity of nature, wouldn't you say?"

"I could rough here for a few days." Eli scanned the immense grounds and structure. Huge square columns elevated the building only yards from the shoreline. An expansive waterfront porch encased in glass dominated the property.

"We're exposed out here in the open," Eli said, searching for better cover.

"How about there." Lindsey pointed to a cluster of leafy bamboo a few yards from the boat house.

Eli throttled *Little Lizzie* behind the natural cover.

"I need to check that ski boat in the boat house and the Sea Ray docked at the pier," Eli said. "I won't be but a few minutes." He sloshed through the bamboo to dry land, rushed to the pier, then pushed through a creaking door inside the boat house to the smell of aged wood, brackish water, and marine fuel. The inside was spacious, with walls adorned with brass portholes, an ancient sextant, and weather maps for decoration. And alone on the floor in the corner, a roll of blue high-velocity ski line, a wakeboard handle attached.

Eli rubbed his thumb against the ski rope—same thickness, same smooth coating, same line found around Zoe's ankles. And to make the evidence more convincing, the line was cut clean on one end. His chest thumped in rhythmic triumph. He pulled out his phone and took a photo.

He slipped to the Sea Ray and placed his foot gently on the gangway. A glow from the house flickered in his peripheral.

A window.

A girl's form through partially drawn curtains.

He abandoned the Sea Ray and hurried back to Lindsey. "I found the same ski line in the boathouse. And I saw a girl's shadow in that window."

The light had gone dark. Eli peeked through his binoculars, but the girl was gone.

Lindsey tucked a small strand of hair behind her ear. "We need to get word to Manny, but there's no cell service."

Eli grabbed a flashlight, a dark skull cap, and a dark pullover for concealment. He checked his weapon, then holstered it. "Hang tight while I check this place out."

Lindsey touched Eli's arm, sending a surge of energy to his belly. "Be careful. This place is nice but still kind of creepy."

"Zoe's body washed up only a few clicks from here. I can't leave without finding out what or who's inside."

"You think Zoe could have been killed here?"

"Possibly. Keep trying your phone. If you contact Manny, tell him where we are and what we found."

The army taught Eli two reconnaissance techniques. One was to avoid detection from enemy threats, and the other called for an overt observation with force. Of course, this situation demanded the former, but the latter, was more appealing.

He waded through bamboo into warm ankle-deep water. With his shoulders hunched low, he hustled to the east end of the property, careful to stay clear of lighting.

He stuck close to the building and found an outer elevator door. He listened. No sound. And no movement in his night vision.

Next, he skulked around to the roadside. A bright-yellow Mustang parked on a circular drive. And the neighborhood wasn't a neighborhood because there were no neighbors. According to the distance finder built into his night vision, the closest crossroad was a half-mile. This house sat at the end of a dead-end road on a dead-end inlet.

The roadside of the building was like the waterside, with an antebellum-style stairwell leading up to another expansive porch. He was tempted to climb to the second floor, but he would encounter blind spots that would make him vulnerable. He was here to observe and assess, not get caught.

He slithered back through sparse foliage toward *Little Lizzy* and decided the elevator would be where he'd enter.

————

Badeau's eyes shot open to near-pitch darkness in the stateroom of his fifty-five-foot Sea Ray docked at Javier's fishing camp. The put-put-put of a small craft engine in these fishing waters shouldn't be alarming. But lately, every sudden clap, clang, or clamor had him as jumpy as a swamp rabbit near a gator pond.

The boat shifted. Someone on the gangplank? Minutes later there were voices.

He lifted himself from the king-sized bed and peeked out the porthole. In the dim moonlight, he made out two shadows in a small skiff in a patch of bamboo.

One shadow sat still, slender neck tapering into the subtle slope of the shoulders. Curved lines and a ponytail. A woman.

The other silhouette had broad shoulders and a strong jawline. Something mechanical jutted from his eyes. Binoculars.

Heat flushed through Badeau's chest, neck, and face. He fingered his Glock 17 on the nightstand. Best to learn more about the intruders and their intentions.

Badeau didn't want to kill anyone and feed their carcasses to the Rigolets like the Commodore had done with Marsh's little trollop Zoe. That's what brought Tara's uncle into Badeau's current dilemma. Could that be who's in the skiff? The commando uncle from Mississippi.

No. That'd be a big stretch.

Was it a mistake to have Freddy and his wimpy friend Myles guard Tara upstairs in the house? Javier had taught Badeau never to take risks that could land you in prison. So, if Freddy and Myles got caught...those were the breaks. And if Badeau lost Tara to the police before cashing in with the Commodore, at least Badeau would survive for another day.

The masculine outline left the skiff like a cat on the prowl. This guy was military. Tara's uncle was military. No stretch now. Within seconds he vanished into the darkness.

Should Andre remain on the Sea Ray and see what happens? There was Freddy to consider. If only Badeau could make a call in these forsaken wetlands. No phone service or internet on the boat or in the building.

Damn you, Javier.

Hang on. The war hero was back.

THIRTY-FOUR

The minutes waiting onboard the small skiff had stretched into a lifetime for Lindsey. Eli'd been gone for twenty minutes. Was that too long?

Thumping footfalls startled her. She tensed.

Barely visible in his black pullover, Eli emerged in a swift, fluid motion. His feet splashed in the shallow water, and he heaved himself into the boat. The skiff swayed, and she clutched against the hull's edges.

"Thank God you're back." A surge of warmth broke through her, and her heart rate steadied. "You find anything?"

"I found a way inside. There's a freight elevator. But it's probably louder than an F-35. And there's a car in the driveway. Did you reach Manny?"

She showed him her phone's screen. "Still no signal."

Eli grabbed his bag. "I'm going in."

Beads of sweat spread across Lindsey's upper lip and forehead. Was Tara in the house? There was no way to tell. An emotional conflict erupted within her. Should she stay with Eli or leave him to find help? "I could take the skiff. Find cell service. Get hold of Manny."

It took five pulls for Eli to restart the engine. "Go call the cavalry. I'll meet you at the bait shop when I'm done here."

A gnawing unease gripped Lindsey. "How will you meet me at the bait shop?"

"I've got options. Like I said, there's a car out front, and I'm a fair hand at hot-wiring. Something I learned in the shadier side of my military career." He lifted his chin to the fifty-footer on the pier. "Or I can use that floating condo."

"Okay then. But if you find a phone, call me. You have my number," she said through a smile.

A glimmer illuminated Eli's eyes. "I do."

"I'll be praying for you." The words blurted out of her lips. "I know that may seem trivial to you. But it's the most powerful thing I know to do."

Their eyes met. A fervent sense of intimacy unfolded inside her.

Impulsively, she encircled him with her arms, then pulled him in, conveying she cherished the hours they'd spent together—a time she didn't want to end. With her lips near his ear, she whispered, "Come back to me."

Eli pulled her tighter and held her for a long moment. Then, he broke free, leaped off the skiff, splashed through the water, and climbed back onshore.

———

The elevator lumbered up to the second floor like a heavy freight train on a steep incline. Eli disabled the elevator's overhead light and stooped low into a firing position. He aligned the front and rear sights of his Sig Sauer at the stainless-steel door and waited.

The lift stopped with a loud clank. His neck pulsed. He breathed in, exhaled partially, then held his breath to minimize body movement. Ready to fire.

The door slid open.

No one.

He stepped into a dimly lit kitchen with shiny chrome appliances and the smell of cooked fish.

Dirty dishes cluttered the counter. He checked the stove. Partially solidified oil clung in a soupy layer to the inside of a cast iron skillet. Greasy white residue was splattered on the stovetop. He rubbed the semi-solid grease between his thumb and index finger. The remnants of oil and fat felt warm.

Somebody had cooked within the last hour.

From the kitchen, Eli entered a sizable room, Sig Sauer first. His flashlight illuminated leather armchairs, plush sofas, and a well-stocked bar. He swung the beam across the walls where several stuffed fish were mounted, from Spanish mackerel to yellowfin tuna to amberjack. Then he honed the light on the magnificence of a glassy-eyed mako shark. Its imposing presence loomed like a guardian above an archway leading into a darker hall.

He resisted the urge to rush in, banging down every door to find Tara. He kept to his Ranger training, slow walked, his eyes scanning, his finger stroking the Sig Sauer's trigger guard.

Shadows danced on the walls playing tricks on his perception. His senses exploded. His breathing echoed in his ears. Every creak in the wooden floor beneath him seemed amplified. A shadow seemed to move on the wall ahead.

He directed his light to three evenly spaced doors. He maneuvered swiftly with anticipation and caution, following his gut.

Arriving at the last door, his hand quivered. Clutching the cold metal door handle sent a shiver through his arm. With a firm grip, he turned and pushed open the door.

The flashlight's beam illuminated Tara, her arms and legs bound to a chair and her mouth gagged.

Eli struggled to ignore his heart palpitations, his shortness of breath, the pressure in his chest. He kept his gun extended, eased himself inside the room, ran his hand across the wood-paneled wall near the door, found a light switch, then flicked it on.

Glistening tears tracked down Tara's cheeks, her eyes wide with desperation.

A young male, his own expression a mixture of confusion and terror, stood, hands in the air, as if caught in a situation beyond his control.

Eli's gaze darted from corner to corner, his senses on high alert. "Face down on the floor."

The kid's legs wobbled beneath him, but he lowered himself, knees sinking, hands extending, until he lay flat on the wood floor.

Tara's gaze focused on the wall that butted flush with a bookcase. Her eyes bulged. Fear? Didn't she know Eli was her uncle and was here to take her home?

He glared at the kid who showed no resistance. "Hands behind your head, then thread your fingers."

The kid obeyed like a trained circus animal. His body shook. He whimpered.

Eli holstered his gun in the small of his back, pulled flex cuffs from his rucksack, pinned his knee against the kid's spine, and zip-tied his wrists.

Then a swoosh of a door opening on well-oiled hinges.

Tara stomped her feet.

Wham. A solid thwack into his right shoulder.

Pain shot through his torso. He crumpled face down on the floor but rolled on his back to face his attacker.

His assailant stood over him, wild eyes inflamed. An aluminum bat circled his head like a violent tornado.

A deranged psychopath—hell-bent to kill.

THIRTY-FIVE

A symphony of sounds serenaded Lindsey—frogs croaking, crickets chirping, water gently lapping against the skiff's aluminum frame. A cooling breeze swept across her bare arms and raised goosebumps. Her bottom lip quivered with misgivings for letting Eli go back to the house. She looked up to the stars and prayed.

"Lord Jesus. Empower Eli against the evil that seeks to destroy Tara. I pray he'll see Your help clearly and recognize who You are. Release the spirit of protection and bring me back the man You promised me, alive and unharmed."

She revved the skiff's engine. Something flashed on the yacht docked by the boathouse.

Then a splash.

Just a fish?

Or an alligator?

Or something thrown overboard off the yacht.

But Eli'd been on the dock—in the boathouse. He would've known if anyone was onboard. Wouldn't he?

She needed to get to cell service, so she backed the skiff out of the bamboo and into the channel. She twisted the throttle, but the engine sputtered, then died. "No, no, no, no."

Like Eli and O'Sullivan, she tried restarting the engine pulling, once, twice, maybe ten times. The motor refused to turn over. Desperation seeped through every tendon, every sinew, every nerve ending.

She looked back to the sky. To God. "Precious Lord, please help me."

————

The bat swung down. Eli rolled. Again.

Whack.

The wood floor beside his skull splintered.

Tara gushed muffled moans into her gag.

Eli dug his heels against the floor and with his feet and one hand, backpedaled until he hit a wall.

The red-eyed attacker laughed and banged the bat twice on the floor.

Eli reached for his weapon pressed between the floor and his back, but his right arm couldn't clear it.

The psychopath stiffened his legs.

Curled his shoulders.

And swung like a major league slugger.

Anticipating the blow, Eli lean-lunged left onto his good shoulder. The strike landed inches from his head.

Time slowed.

His attacker coiled like a cobra.

Raised his weapon again.

His knuckles white with a savage grip.

His arm pulled the metallic bat high.

The aluminum reflected faint light.

Eli's primal fear for survival kicked in. He slung his Sig

Sauer from its holster, now free as he lay on his good side, raised it as high as his wounded shoulder allowed, then fired.

Pop. Pop. Pop.

Three poorly aimed rounds. But one hit the bat wielder's knee.

He fell. Landed in a sprawl next to the restrained kid on the floor. Blood streamed from the batter's knee like thick chocolate syrup.

The bat rolled. Pain coursed through the right side of Eli's battered body, but he grabbed the bat with his left hand and kept his gun level with his right. The bookcase was open. A hidden door on the wall. That's how his attacker ambushed him.

Eli ignored the batter, got to his feet, pulled out his utility knife, cut Tara's restraints and gag.

She clutched his waist, buried her head in his chest. "I knew you'd find me Uncle Eli. I just knew it."

"Tara," he spoke her name, but didn't know what else to say.

The reality of finding Tara sparked relief, joy, and a profound sense of purpose. He squeezed his eyes shut, trying to block away any past regrets. At last, he said the only thing he could bring to mind. "Sorry it took me so long to find you. You ready to go home?"

She beamed like the four-year-old he remembered. "Yes, yes, yes."

Eli tapped the restrained kid on the floor with the end of the bat. "Anyone else in the house?"

"No sir," the kid said like a boot in the Army.

"What's your name?"

"Myles."

"And his?" Eli pressed the bat into the wounded man's chest.

"Keep your mouth shut, Myles," the batter said with defiance.

"It's Freddy." Tara's tone spewed venom. "Freddy Badeau."

"Badeau, huh." Eli stood over Freddy like a conquering gladiator. "You kin to Andre?"

Freddy sat up but said nothing.

Eli waved the bat near his wounded knee. "Tell me."

Tara stood with a narrow-eyed glare. "He's his uncle."

"Where's your uncle, Freddy?"

"Not here." Freddy rubbed his thigh above his bleeding knee. "I need a doctor."

"That you do, boy. But talk first."

"Get me to an emergency room, or I'll bleed to death."

"Maybe. But your uncle, Uncle Andre. Where is he?"

"I don't know." Freddy's tone carried a challenging edge, a refusal to be intimidated. "He brought us some lunch and left. That was hours ago."

Eli turned to Tara. "Is Freddy telling the truth?"

Confusion clouded Tara's face. "I don't know. I haven't seen him here. And I don't really know where here is."

"How long have you been here?" Eli asked.

She blinked with, what Eli noticed for the first time, dazed and bloodshot eyes. "I don't know. I can't remember things."

Eli tensed, sending pain to his shoulder. He glared at Freddy. "You drug her?"

A flicker of audacity danced in Freddy's eyes. "Not me." But a smirk tugged at his mouth.

"You think you're a tough kid, don't you, Freddy? Drugging girls and swinging bats."

"Surprised you, though." Freddy jutted his chin at Eli's shoulder. "Messed you up real good."

"I'd be more worried about that leg of yours. Might have

to be amputated if we can't stop that bleeding. Now, when's your uncle coming back?"

"He was supposed to bring dinner," Myles said. "But he didn't show,"

"Shut up, Myles," Freddy shifted, tried to stand. He gasped in pain and slumped back on the floor.

Eli cut Myles' restraints. "Take your belt and wrap it tight above his knee. And Freddy, call your uncle. I need to have a word."

"Can't. There's no cell or internet out here." Freddy's eyes radiated a confident bravado. "But you'll see him real soon."

THIRTY-SIX

Eli's shoulder wrenched with the weight of his Sig Sauer, heavy as a howitzer in his hand. Shockwaves of razor-like pain reverberated through his torso with each step down the grand stairway from the front porch to the driveway. In front of him, Freddy used Myles for support. Tara, beside Eli, clung to his good elbow.

Tara stopped, and Eli searched her face. Her color drained, her pale complexion like a porcelain doll on the verge of shattering. She shuddered, her eyes wide and fixed. "Andre," she whispered in a shallow, ragged gasp.

Eli followed her gaze to the corner of the house. Lindsey.

And a man with a gun pointed at her head. Badeau.

The world around Eli faded into a blur. His mind raced. Every thought fixated on saving Lindsey.

Badeau shielded himself behind Lindsey. "Good evening, detective. Let's not do anything rash."

Detective? Badeau knew?

Eli summoned his will and stood taller. The agony in his shoulder seared, but he aimed his Sig Sauer on Freddy.

He slid himself in front of Tara. "I got my niece. She's all I wanted. Take your crew and leave. There's an army of cops on their way."

The corners of Badeau's lips curved into a mocking smile. Your girlfriend never got to make that call." Badeau's voice was steady, clear, confident.

Eli's every nerve ending hummed with dread. First, the bookcase. And now the floating condo where Andre had to have been hiding out. Why didn't he clear it?

Freddy limped toward Badeau. "He shot me."

"Stop right there," Eli said. "Or I'll shoot you again."

Badeau clutched Lindsey's hair in a tight fist and snapped her head back.

Lindsey's eyes flashed desperation. Her mouth fell open in a silent scream.

Eli's arms and shoulders tensed. He needed a plan, and quick.

"You shoot my nephew. I'll shoot your girlfriend." Badeau pressed his pistol's muzzle against Lindsey's temple.

Lindsey's lips trembled, her chest rose and fell erratically.

A knot twisted with a sickening potency in the pit of Eli's stomach. Nausea returned, clawed its way up his throat, threatening to betray his confident stance. The taste of regret lingered on his tongue, a bitter reminder of his stupidity.

Badeau's eyes sharpened like the tip of a dagger. "Drop the gun, now, or she's dead."

Trapped, caught in the web of his own mistakes. Mistakes that could prove irreversible. A heavy stone sat in his chest. He grappled with the harsh reality that if he chose to fight over surrender, two women he cared for, one family, one more than a friend, could die.

A cold sweat trickled down his temples in rivulets of panic. His heart and lungs fought each other for space inside his chest. But Eli knew. Knew what he had to do.

He flipped on the Sig's safety and tossed it to the ground.

—————

For Lindsey, this moment was as terrifying as when she was raped as a young girl. Her neck strained against Badeau's vice grip hold on her hair.

But as soon as Eli surrendered his gun, the chilling death touch on her temple disappeared.

Still, her heart shattered at the sight of Eli in obvious pain and the emotional strain of surrendering his weapon.

Tara clung to Eli. A petrified expression plastered on her face.

A whirlwind of stress overwhelmed Lindsey. She fought against her fear, her mind raced to God's promise and prayed to hold Him to His Word.

Freddy hobbled, picked up Eli's gun. "Tara, get over here."

Tara trudged to Freddy like she wore weighted shoes, passed him, and walked to Badeau.

Freddy aimed Eli's gun at Eli's head. "You should've never shot me, you son of a—"

"Freddy, no." Badeau's voice cracked in Lindsey's ears like a thunderclap. He let go of her.

A coldness froze every limb. A surge of helplessness washed over her. She reached out to Eli.

Bang.

The shot rang through the thick air like cannon fire.

A mist of blood puffed above Eli's head.

He rocked backward, fell hard on his back.

Lindsey's breath caught. A strangled gasp escaped. Sharp shards of terror pierced her heart. The ground beneath her collapsed, leaving her suspended in a hellish void.

She dropped to her knees and covered her face. "No, Lord. Please, no."

"You idiot," Badeau bellowed the words. "You killed a cop."

"He shot me." Freddy argued.

"Yeah, and they got lethal injection up in Angola. Get the girl on the boat."

"What about my car?" Freddy asked.

"We're leaving it."

"What about this one? We can't leave her." Freddy said.

Lindsey dropped her hands. Freddy had Eli's gun aimed at her chest.

She didn't care if Freddy shot her. Eli was shot. Dead?

Still on her knees, Badeau walked close. Though his eyes held a glimmer of empathy, they also betrayed that a job must be done. He raised his gun six inches from her face.

Lindsey closed her eyes and braced for the pain of a bullet. Would there be pain? Or would she die immediately? Would God allow this? Would she meet Eli in heaven instead of spending a lifetime with him on Earth?

A peace that surpasses all understanding fell over her. She was ready.

Whack. But not a gunshot.

Pain fired into her skull.

Darkness swallowed all her senses.

PART FOUR

THIRTY-SEVEN

The boat docked behind the house loomed over her. Tara couldn't remember if she'd walked or been carried to the pier. Her mind, trapped, suspended, stuck on one thing—Freddy shooting Uncle Eli in the head. Was he dead? He had to be—the shot, the blood, how he fell, how he didn't move after collapsing on the driveway.

Freddy was evil. Like Joaquin Phoenix in *The Joker*. Or Hannibal Lecter in *Silence of the Lambs*. But this was not a movie. Freddy was not an actor. He'd killed her uncle easily and for no reason. Even Andre had freaked.

But Andre was no better. He'd held who he called Uncle Eli's girlfriend at gunpoint. Was she dead too? Tara hadn't heard another gunshot.

"Upsy daisy. Get onboard." Freddy interrupted her one nightmare for another. "Take hold of that rail and hoist yourself up." Freddy grabbed her butt, squeezed, and pushed her forward onto the yacht.

He and Myles dragged her into a room at the front of the boat with a large leather-covered steering wheel surrounded by blinking lights and gauges. The lights seemed like warning signals, counting down to her death. But why bring her here to die when they could've just killed her on the driveway like Uncle Eli? Like his girlfriend?

Freddy flung her on a couch and flopped down beside her to inspect his bleeding knee.

His presence suffocated Tara. She wanted to run, scream, flee from his closeness. She shifted uneasily, inching away to increase the space between them.

Yet, Freddy seemed oblivious to her. His eyes fluttered and then closed.

Andre entered, his face was a mask of detachment, the skin around his eyes tight. "Freddy, have you been hopping on dope all day, or are you naturally that stupid?" His voice was fast and rough. "As if things weren't hot enough with the police already—you have to go kill a cop?"

Andre, confirming Uncle Eli's murder, shattered Tara's world into a billion pieces. Tears blurred the room, the blinking lights, Andre, Freddy, and Myles.

"But he shot me, Unc." Freddy sniffled like a five-year-old. Tara wished he'd been shot in the heart, not the knee.

"He should've killed you. Now I'll have the FBI crawling all over my tail."

Andre studied the lights and gauges beside the steering wheel, flicked a few switches, turned two keys. The boat motor kicked in.

"Myles. Go free the lines," Andre ordered.

For a half hour, the boat lunged forward. Andre sat at the wheel.

Freddy fidgeted. His blood-soaked leg extended.

Myles wheezed like he struggled to breathe.

And the boat sailed farther and farther away from New Orleans, away from home.

Every few minutes, Tara lifted herself a few inches to peer out the window. Her heart spiraled into a maddening frenzy at the sight of endless grey water—the shoreline a faint smudge on the horizon. The compass pointed southeast. They were still in the Rigolets but headed to the Gulf. Tara's mind raced through millions of unanswered questions.

She'd witnessed at least one murder, probably two. She could ID Freddy and Andre and be a witness at their trials. Where were these killers taking her?

Were they going to shoot her and dump her body overboard? Or were they going somewhere far away where they'd force her to be like Jewel—a prostitute?

And Uncle Eli was dead. There was nobody else—nobody to save her.

"How much farther?" Myles's voice pierced the stillness.

Andre shifted his gaze to Freddy, who'd passed out on the couch. "Not long." His tone was now concerned. "We'll offload Tara, and she'll be Commodore's problem, not mine. I'll need you to come aboard with me to help." Andre pointed straight ahead. "There's his yacht, *Leviathan*."

———

Lit up like a Walmart parking lot, the boat called *Leviathan* floated on calm water under a sliver of moon. Tara's gut twisted. The old ship appeared eerily like Dragonstone Castle on *Game of Thrones*.

Three figures stood near a railing—a plump man dressed in white, a red-headed man wearing all black with a gun strapped to his chest, and a tall, gangly girl who looked about Tara's age dressed a lot like the fat man.

Herded to a kind of bridge that connected the two boats, Tara trudged across to *Leviathan's* deck. The smells of fresh paint and pine invaded her nostrils.

Eerie shadows moved like demons across the wood decks.

With watery eyes, she surveyed the ship. Her muscles tensed. She kept sinking deeper into this never-ending nightmare.

Andre shook hands with the fat man.

Myles stood next to Tara like a timid puppy.

Freddy had remained on the smaller boat, sleeping.

Andre grabbed her elbow and pushed her to the fat man. "Here you go, Commodore. Just like I promised."

"Yes, she'll do nicely. Nicely indeed," Commodore said, his voice low, husky, hair-raising.

A scream threatened to escape her lips, but she stifled it, afraid of unleashing more viciousness.

Commodore turned to the redhead in black. "Riley, take the boy below."

"What, boy?" Myles's voice cracked on a tremor.

Riley whistled, and two men, also in black, both bearing guns, appeared.

The men seized Myles and hauled him to an open door.

Myles clutched its frame.

The men pulled Myles through the door. His high-pitched scream grew faint and then disappeared.

Riley handed Andre a briefcase.

Andrea beamed a satisfied grin, shook Commodore's hand, and strode away.

Gone. Andre was gone.

And Tara. Abandoned.

Commodore's eyes, beneath pudgy pink eyelids, traced Tara's form. "We all have our roles on this ship. In time, we will find yours."

He tilted back his black-brimmed hat and glanced at the doorway where Myles had disappeared. "It appears your friend may need more persuasion. But then, he didn't antici-pate his coming with us." Commodore took a handkerchief from inside his jacket and dabbed his sweaty forehead and cheeks. "Molly will show you where you will sleep, and I'll see you bright and early tomorrow. You have much to learn."

"Learn?" The words came out almost as a whistle.

"Yes. You'll learn what we're all about. And how we plan to change the world. In the meantime, you'll serve me, this ship, and before long, all of humanity." He turned his chubby frame and walked into the darkness.

———

Tara followed Molly to the lower deck. Their shadows danced on the worn and weathered staircase into a dimly lit corridor. A loud, annoying sound like an air conditioner rumbled.

Molly's long arms swung like loose spaghetti. "What you hear is the engine room. Don't worry. You'll get used to the noise."

The air in the lower deck was stagnant. Light bulbs flickered. In an open room, they passed tattered sofas and armchairs. Then, into another hall, Molly stopped at a door. "Shhh." She pulled a key from her pant pocket, unlocked the door, and entered a room filled with soft snores.

The scent of lavender and dust mingled around three bunk beds. Two were filled with four sleeping girls, faces buried in pillows. The third bunk bed was empty.

"Come on in, silly," Molly whispered. "What do you think?"

Tara followed Molly to the bunk and said nothing. Questions, concerns, alarm could show weakness. Weakness is what got Tara here—allowing Andre to con her and Freddy to drug her. And then to be exchanged for whatever was inside that briefcase. She would not be weak or stupid or naïve anymore.

"Hey." Molly's voice was friendly.

"Hey." Tara tried to sound unafraid. But she couldn't shake the thought of the briefcase. Did Andre sell her to

Commodore? Did he plan to use her for sex? Like these other girls? Like Molly?

Molly pointed to the empty bunk bed. "I'll give you a boost. You're on top." She leaned over and threaded her fingers together.

Tara planted her foot into Molly's hands and lifted herself into the upper bunk. For now, this room seemed safe enough.

"There's a pillow and sheets and PJs up there," Molly said.

Molly undressed and slipped on pajamas.

Tara collapsed onto the bed and lay exhausted, her mind whirling with burden and blame. Uncle Eli and his girlfriend would still be alive if not for her and her dumb need to run away.

"I'm so glad you're here," Molly said softly. "I love making new friends."

Molly's warm tone didn't warm Tara.

"What did you think of Commodore? Isn't he wonderful? He's the smartest man I've ever known." There was a sparkle in Molly's voice.

Molly seemed to shift and roll in her bed, then said, "I'm so stupid. We've just met, and you've just arrived. Believe me. You'll understand what I'm talking about soon enough." Her words bubbled with excitement. "So, after your class in the morning, Commodore will assign you a mentor."

"What do I need a mentor for?" Tara sure hoped it wasn't to teach her how to pleasure fat Commodore.

"Another girl to teach you our way." Molly's voice rose and fell with every syllable. "I hope the Commodore pairs us together. I recently lost a student."

How did Molly lose a student? Did Commodore kill her? Was there an accident? No. No more questions. Not tonight. Tara had been through too much.

"Oh, I so hope you and I will become good friends." Molly's tone brimmed with delight.

The more Molly talked, the more the unknown weighed on Tara like a heavy blanket. It was too much for one night.

Watching her uncle murdered.

Andre dropping her off on this floating Jonestown.

But despite the fear, a spark of defiance burned. She must be brave. Must survive.

Must escape.

———

Eli slipped into a blur of colors and shapes. His body limp, battered. Pain. Deep pain. Pain in every cell. Every breath a struggle. Tight chest. Labored gasps.

The thump of helicopter blades.

Chaos and motion all around him. Chatter. Medics.

Afghanistan?

No.

The skiff.

Tara. He'd found Tara.

The blow to his shoulder.

The shot.

Faces.

Lindsey.

Tara.

Alive?

Dead?

He'd failed.

Failure had consequences.

Dark seeped in from the edges.

Defeated.

Broken.

Ashamed.

Blackness.

Thirty-Eight

Aboard *Leviathan*, Tara awoke to a bright light from a fixture above her bunk.

"O-five-thirty. Time to get up, ladies," Riley blared like a bullhorn from the open doorway.

The room appeared smaller than it did last night. The ceiling was low, the walls were dingy, and ZP, among other initials, were etched into the wall beside Tara's bed.

ZP—Zoe Prevost? Tara's best friend from school?

Her bunkmates launched from their beds in their pajamas, then lined up to grab folded white uniforms from a dresser drawer.

"Don't lay there all morning, girly," Riley barked at Tara. "Get these on." He tossed her a folded white blouse and pair of pants, just like Molly wore the night before. Then a white hat with CMRE embroidered on the front. "Your class with Commodore starts in half an hour. Molly will take you."

Tara lifted the hat with the CMRE logo to Riley. "What does this stand for?

"Commodore. What else?"

She followed Molly and the other girls in silence down the

dim hall into a compact bathroom with faded grey walls and black-and-white checkerboard floors. Tara waited in line to rinse her face in a white porcelain sink with pale yellow stains. She changed, then hurried up the stairway to the main deck with Molly.

The sky was covered with gold traces of early light. A soft breeze cooled Tara's skin and played with her hair. The distant shoreline moved by faster than when Tara came aboard. At least a mile swim to land. Impossible.

Each of the other girls darted across wood planks to some designated destination.

Boys in stained white tee shirts and shorts dashed to the edges of the main deck—some with ropes, others with buckets, scrub brushes, or painting equipment.

A man dressed like Riley lurked in a doorway.

Molly led Tara up a polished wooden stairwell, through an open-air lounge, and into a room that reminded her of an uptown mansion—paneled walls, expensive rugs, and artwork that belonged in a museum.

"Wait here for Commodore." Molly giggled like she knew something Tara didn't. "I'll see you after."

Commodore, in pressed white uniform like the night before, stepped through a double doorway holding a cup and saucer.

An edginess settled in Tara's stomach.

"Good morning," Commodore said without emotion. "Let's start our lesson with the proper protocol. When you come into the presence of a superior, you salute him. Understood?"

Tara took a deep breath. "Okay."

Commodore's pasty white face reddened. He stuck out his sagging jaw. "Never respond with *okay* to me or any other officer, young lady. It's *yes sir* or *aye-aye*. Understood?"

His words cut through the air like a sharp slap across Tara's face. "Uh...yes sir. Commodore. Uh...aye-aye."

His face faded back to pasty. "Now, let's try the salute."

She lifted her hand to her forehead.

"No, no, no. Palm down towards your shoulder. Forearm and hand should form a straight line." He shuffled to her with a stern expression and corrected the angle of her arm. His moist, cold hand on her arm made her skin tighten and sent a bitter tang to her mouth. "Try again."

After three more attempts, he appeared somewhat satisfied. "Practice with the girls in your quarters until it becomes second nature. Failure to salute properly will garner demerits."

"Demerits?"

"Yes, demerits. We meticulously track your behavior on *Leviathan*. You earn enough demerits and punishment will be administered." Commodore pointed at a chair with thick cushions under a library of shelved books. "Now sit."

Tara sat at the wood-grained table with the odd feeling she was playing the victim in a psychological thriller.

Commodore paced the width of the room. "Your presence here will be what you make of it. I'll give you an overview, and Molly will drill down what we expect from our crew. Pay close attention to her and follow her instructions in detail. You'll be her assistant so she can ensure you obey the rules." Commodore jingled a small silver bell with a curved slender handle he lifted from an end table.

A guy about Tara's age, wearing clean white shorts and tee shirt, appeared through the double doorway and saluted. He handed a manilla folder to Tara, and a legal pad and pencil.

Commodore sipped from his cup. "You'll find the nautical terms we use on this ship in that material. Please learn them by tomorrow. And I do mean all of them. There will be a test."

She opened the folder but couldn't focus on the words. "Aye-aye Commodore."

"Excellent," Commodore said with approval. "More coffee, Marco. And get the girl some water, will you?"

Marco snapped a salute. "Aye-aye, Commodore."

Commodore's eyes followed Marco to the door. "Our main emphasis on *Leviathan* is for you to have more joy in your life. In time you will learn to appreciate our intentions are pure."

If Commodore's intentions were so pure, why did he have to buy Tara? And why did he have to take Myles by force?

Marco returned with a tray. He filled Commodore's cup from a silver pot, served water to Tara, saluted Commodore, and left.

"Now you must understand, Tara." His tone was kinder, almost like a dad. "I'm the one who can get you to a place where your life has meaning. You see, I have been tested as a genius. The highest score ever recorded in human history."

Tara resisted rolling her eyes at Commodore's arrogance. She couldn't tell who thought higher of the man, Molly or himself.

Commodore stepped to a colorful painting of an ocean landscape with a serene coastline and gave the canvas an approving glance. "I was talking in full sentences at age one, excelled in sports as a young boy, winning the Midwestern martial arts championship at ten. I earned degrees in microbiology, mathematics, and physics, all before my twentieth birthday and all within three years."

He moved away from the painting and tasted his coffee. "I joined the Navy after college because of a deep love of the sea. At thirty-five, I was the youngest to earn my second star as a rear admiral."

If this guy was some kind of Einstein, why doesn't he cure cancer or start a colony on Saturn? And let Tara off the ship so she could go home.

"But I plan to give more to humanity than a military

career," Commodore said. "I'm destined to be a supreme force on this earth. Supernatural forces have sent me here to change the world, and girls like you will help me."

———

Once Tara's meeting with Commodore had finished, Marco led her to the polished wood staircase.

Molly waited with wide cheery eyes. "Commodore assigned me to be your mentor. Isn't that fabulous?"

"I heard." Her voice was flat and uninspired.

"First thing we'll do is get you familiar with *Leviathan*." Molly clutched the brass handrail and bounced up the red carpeted steps.

Tara followed, then stepped with Molly into a glow of sunlight and the gentle breeze of open air. Long cushioned seating and several pillows lined the side rails. A Jacuzzi tub sat in the wooden deck's center with five closed umbrellas over five tables positioned around it. The area had the look and feel of a resort.

"This is the sundeck, my favorite spot on the entire ship." Molly tilted her head back. Sunlight illuminated her face. "I hope you learn to love it up here like I do. After all, this ship will be your new home."

"You mean, you live on this boat all the time?"

"Of course, silly. Commodore avoids the inferior laws of governments. Here, we live as we want."

"Sounds like I'll be living as Commodore wants." Tara said with a mocking tone.

"Shush…" Molly scanned the deck, searching as if somebody might be listening. "You don't want to be put on report your first day, do you?"

"Put on report?"

"Yes." Molly cupped her hand, place it to Tara's ear, and

whispered into it. "Anyone on this ship can report you to ship security if you say or do something that goes against the code."

"Ship security must be Riley and his goons." Tara said with a warm smile.

"Shhh…" Molly put a finger to her lips. "You don't want to get on their bad side."

A rebellious fire smoldered inside Tara. A deep sigh, heavy with pent up frustration escaped her lips.

Molly's eyes narrowed to a steely glare. "It's my job to teach you. You're my priority. That and being the chief stewardess." Her expression softened and her upbeat tone returned. "And you'll be my assistant—second stewardess. Isn't that lovely?"

"Why me?"

"Because I need help and all the other girls have their own responsibilities."

"And what does a second stewardess do?"

Molly's face lit up. "Stewarts are responsible for making Commodore comfortable. You will assist me in ensuring his meals are delivered, and his cabin is clean. Make certain the ship and its services serve him to full capacity."

"So we're his servants?"

"Yes, silly. And we're lucky to serve him. He's our leader. He'll bring stability to the human race. And you've been chosen to help him. It's your privilege. Your destiny."

Molly must have drunk too much of Commodore's Kool-Aid.

"Where is this boat headed?" Tara said. "Do you know?"

"Commodore wants to go to the African coast and help some country that's fighting a civil war."

Tara's shock mixed with a sense of helplessness. She gazed at the distant shoreline, resisting the temptation to jump overboard and swim. "Africa?"

"Yes, and I'll be sharing with you everything about the incredible life you'll enjoy. And we can start now."

Tara joined Molly on the lounge cushions but couldn't shake the thought of sailing to a third-world continent. What about her friends and her mother?

"The first thing you should know," Molly said, "Commodore will enlighten your spirit. Things may seem a little different at first, but you'll eventually realize that you're a product of a corrupt environment."

Tara's shoulders stiffened. "How could you know about my environment?" She averted her eyes to the sea.

"Don't take it personal, silly. Everyone in this world is the same until we're pure. What you'll learn on *Leviathan* is a precise path that leads to the complete understanding of your spiritual nature. The relationship between yourself and the supreme being."

"I don't understand." Tara said with loads of uncertainty. "Who's the supreme being?"

"Why, Commodore, of course."

No. Freaking. Way.

"Don't worry. You'll learn," Molly said. "There's so much to learn."

Way too much. "I don't think I'm cut out for this," Tara said, defeated.

"Let me be honest, Tara. You don't have a choice." Her words stung like sand in the eye.

A concerned smile formed on Molly's lips. "You are an immortal spiritual being. Your experience will extend well beyond one lifetime. Don't you get it? Your capabilities are unlimited, even if you don't understand them now."

Molly talked like her brain had gone through a car wash. But that could be to Tara's advantage. Maybe Tara could lead Molly to slip and reveal when, where, and how to escape this floating nightmare.

"It's like this." Molly's tone became more expressive as if she were teaching a child a vital lesson. "You are basically good. Your spiritual salvation is totally dependent on yourself and those around you."

Tara relaxed. She leaned slightly to Molly to make her feel heard and valued.

"Molly's eyes sparkled with radiant energy. "We're not some legalistic, demanding religion. We don't ask you to accept anything on faith alone. You'll discover for yourself that our code is sound by using its principles and experiencing the outcome."

Molly went on like she could talk for hours about this stupid code. But Tara widened her eyes to show interest. "So, what is the outcome? What's in it for me?"

Molly's posture straightened. "Great question. Our roots lie in the deepest beliefs of all great religions and encompass a heritage as old and as varied as the human race. Commodore has absorbed the wisdom of centuries. He has isolated the fundamental laws of life and developed a workable process we can apply to achieve a happier and more spiritual existence." Molly recited this tripe with conviction like it'd been drilled into her head since kindergarten. "His code was developed by the advances in the physical sciences over history. Commodore has bridged Eastern with Western philosophies to produce a real application of spiritual awakening."

Tara squinted to fake confusion. "I'm sorry, can you explain that?"

Molly placed her hands on Tara's shoulders. "It's really simple. We're all about what we do, not what we believe."

Tara knew what she wanted to do. Get off this ship.

THIRTY-NINE

Refreshed by a hot shower at the University Medical Center hospital room, yet still overwhelmed by the emotional overload of the past twenty-four hours, Lindsey applied concealer to hide the bruise on her cheek and the welt under her eye. Her skin wasn't broken where Badeau slammed his pistol, and according to the ER doctor, Lindsey suffered only a mild concussion.

Last night, she'd regained consciousness outside the remote mansion. The sulphur smell of a gunshot still lingered. The distant echo of boat engines faded away.

Eli lay still on the driveway where Freddy had shot him. Tara was gone.

Lindsey rushed to Eli. Her ears thumping in the erratic beat of her pulse. Recounting God's promise, she knelt beside him. "You can't be dead," she whispered.

Eli's hair was matted with blood. His eyes were partially open, fixed on the sky yet without focus. But his carotid artery registered a pulse. Thank God.

She needed to get him to a hospital. Quick.

Lindsey clasped Eli's hands with both of hers. "Hold on, Eli. I'm going to get help."

She'd jumped into the skiff and repeated what Clancy had shown her and Eli at the launch, and by some miracle, the engine started with one pull. Minutes later she'd found the family who gave them directions, cooking their catch over an open fire. The father drove her to an area where she called Manny and 911.

It'd taken a half-hour for the police to arrive and airlift Eli to the hospital.

Earlier that morning, Manny had informed Lindsey of what he'd learned from the ER—Eli had a fractured clavicle and a grade four concussion he'd suffered from Freddy shooting him. Thankfully, the bullet only creased Eli's skull and wasn't fatal.

Ready to check herself out of the hospital, she took slow, methodical steps to the ICU and found Manny in the waiting room. "How's Eli doing?"

Manny's eyes were underlined by dark circles. "He's in and out of consciousness, but the doctor says he should be coming around soon."

"I need to see him, Manny."

"Afraid that's not possible." Manny's tone sounded constricted, concerned. "From what I've just heard, they'll be moving him to another hospital."

"Why? What's wrong with this one?"

"Let's sit down." Manny's voice was soft—protective. "You look exhausted."

"I don't want to sit down. Why are they moving him to another hospital if he's not fully conscious? Who made that call?"

"Seems the mayor of Eli's hometown has some pull in our fine city. He feels Eli will get better care back in Solace. He's going back to Mississippi."

"Mississippi?" Lindsey forgot to breathe for a moment. "So, they're going to drive him, what? Five hours in an ambulance?"

"He's being airlifted. Right from the roof of this hospital."

"When?"

"Now."

Lindsey leaned her head back to fight the nausea from her concussion, then bore her eyes into Manny's. "What about Tara?"

Manny's mouth opened and closed as if he struggled to find words. "We've notified the Coast Guard of course and given them your description of Badeau's boat. Let's pray they find it soon."

"That boat could be halfway to the Yucatan Peninsula by now."

The doors to intensive care split open. An orderly pushed a gurney carrying a comatose Eli with a uniformed officer alongside. Following them, a stylish woman in a chic dress tapped away at her phone. The woman on the wedding website with Eli—Gina Barrow.

Lindsey ignored her crippling headache and Manny's hand on her shoulder. Her heart lurched and her legs weakened as she hurried to catch up with Eli.

Only yesterday she was comforted in Eli's embrace. Gina was harmless. But today she was a threat. Jealousy gnawed at Lindsey's insides, fueled by the fear of Eli slipping away forever.

Yet, determination ignited inside. She would do whatever it took to keep Eli here.

The gurney slid into an open elevator.

Lindsey closed the fifty feet between her and Gina to introduce herself. "Excuse me, Ms. Barrow. My name's Dr. Lindsey Crenshaw. I was with Eli last night when he was shot."

Gina Barrow crowded in next to the policeman and reached down to press the floor buttons. "I heard something about a woman with my fiancé out in that dreadful swamp. Thank you for getting him to this hospital. If you contact Bethaven Plantation in Solace, Mississippi, I'll make sure you're well compensated."

The policeman stepped forward extending his hand like a roadblock. "Excuse us ma'am, we have a helicopter waiting."

A smile crept up on Gina's lips as the stainless-steel doors slid closed.

Gina taking Eli threatened to crush Lindsey's spirit. The demon of doubt whispered cruel questions about her place in Eli's life. She hit the elevator button to race up and stop this nonsense, but the nausea that hit her in the waiting room threatened to spill on the hospital floor.

She stepped to the ladies' room, wet a cold napkin, and wiped her face and neck.

She pulled her phone from her back pocket to call Justin. But what could he do? What could anyone do to keep Eli in New Orleans. To find Tara?

Lord Jesus, I'm in an impossible situation. I need your help.

FORTY

Eli had no sense of time between his short stints of consciousness. But now, he woke to a tortuous piercing like a drill grinding through his shoulder. His face contorted. His eyes stung with tears.

Determined, he forced his eyes open to a blurred vision that took a few seconds to come into focus.

Gina.

She gazed at him through her long lashes, lowered her full lips to his ear, and whispered, "Welcome back."

He tried to speak. Impossible.

"Water. Now," Gina's commanded someone in the room. Within moments, she lowered a glass with a bent straw in front of his face.

He sipped, and the cool water drenched his parched throat. He managed to ask, "Where am I?"

"You're home, darling."

Home? Solace? How?

He scanned the room, but the eye movement made him nauseous. "Hospital?" He squeaked out the word.

"No. You're at Bethaven, so I can take care of you," she

said triumphantly. "We have a full-time nurse, and the doctor is only a phone call away. She should be here soon."

"How did I get here?" He struggled to get the words out of his thoughts.

Gina stroked her manicured nails over him. "The local paper picked up your being shot on the wire. Daddy got a call from the editor. I called your parents, and we got you out of that dreadful public hospital in New Orleans. Daddy chartered a helicopter and had you airlifted here."

Eli reached to rub his head, but it was heavily bandaged. His shoulder exploded with pain. "How long have I been here?"

Gina paused for a moment and bit her lip. "Took us two days to make the arrangements, and you arrived home yesterday."

Three days? And that word again, *home*. Not his home. His head throbbed without mercy.

Tara.

Lindsey.

"Tara?" he asked. "Where is she?"

Gina averted her eyes. "I'm afraid she's still missing. You were injured in the middle of some awful swamp. It was reported that a female psychologist found you."

"Lindsey Crenshaw." The name came out as a slow groan. "Is she okay?"

Gina's posture stiffened. "Apparently. Do you know her?" Gina's lips pursed into a dubious frown.

His heart raced for a moment before stopping—his joy for Lindsey's survival tempered by his failure to save Tara. "Lindsey treated Zoe. The girl found dead in the Rigolets."

Gina jutted her lip and adjusted his covers. "You no longer need to worry about that evil in New Orleans. Look what happened. It almost killed you." Her frown changed to a bright smile as if she recalled a fond memory. "Now, you will stay here, and I will nurse you back to health. The doctor says your recovery will take a few months, bringing us into spring." She adjusted her hair and smiled a bit shyly. "Just in time for our wedding."

Wedding? Gina had called the wedding off, called their relationship off. And there was Lindsey.

If only he'd checked that fifty-foot yacht. Badeau wouldn't have surprised him. Tara would be safe. And he'd be in New Orleans with Lindsey and not stuck in Gina's family home.

How could he get out of this antebellum clinic? Zeke. Zeke would help. Zeke could help him get back to New Orleans. But Gina would never allow it. And Gina was in control.

Doc Leena, the physician who treated Cedro, entered the room.

"There you are," Gina said. "I called twenty minutes ago."

"Simmer down, Gina. I've other patients, you know." Doc Leena walked to the bed and flashed a pin light into each of Eli's eyes. "Follow my finger." She moved a finger in front of his face. "Haven't seen you since you brought Cedro to see me. How's he doing?"

Eli followed her finger. "Haven't seen him since. I've been out of town."

"So I've heard." Doc Leena flicked off the light and clipped it inside her front pocket.

A smile tugged at Gina's mouth, and she stood over Doc Leena's shoulder. "Now that he's awake, we can get some home cooking inside him. I'll go to the kitchen and get the cook started." Gina slipped out of the room and closed the door behind her.

Doc Leena pressed her stethoscope against Eli's chest and listened. "Sounds good and strong. Your eyes are clear and focused. How's your head feel?"

"Like I've been hit with a mallet."

Doc Leena's eyes flared a mix of fascination and concern. "Doesn't surprise me. That's quite the part you got on your scalp from the bullet."

Eli lifted his hand, but Doc Leena caught hold. "Leave it be. Your head is bandaged and healing nicely."

"How bad am I hurt?" Eli said, his voice hoarse and weak. He tried to sit up, but a sharp pain shot through his right shoulder, causing him to groan.

Doc Leena gently pushed him back onto his pillow. "You've got a serious concussion and a broken collarbone. My best guess as to why the bullet didn't do more damage is you must've turned at the last second. The slug glanced off your frontal bone without penetrating your skull." Doc Leena flashed a confident grin. "But you did suffer a traumatic brain injury, which is medical speak for your noodle got scrambled at impact."

"What's wrong with my shoulder?" Eli said. "Every time I move, the pain's so bad I can hardly breathe."

"You have a fractured clavicle. You'll recover fully but will be in discomfort for several weeks."

"I need to get back to New Orleans now." His voice choked with desperation.

"Not possible." Her voice was low but firm.

Eli must stay calm and make her understand his sense of urgency. If she didn't help him, he'd never make it to New Orleans. "Do you know why I was there?"

"I read the paper."

"Then you know a young girl's life is at stake. And that young girl is my fifteen-year-old niece."

"I'm afraid that shoulder severely compromises your mobility. And another blow to that head right after a concussion could cause irreparable brain damage. And given your current physical limitations, you can do little to help her."

Miracle. A miracle saved her husband.

"Like you with your husband?" Eli said.

She gave Eli a side-eye glance and reached into her medical bag. "See, your noggin is healing just fine." She held out two pills. "For the pain. And like I told you. I had nothing to do with my husband making a full recovery."

"You prayed for a miracle. I didn't believe you when you told me, but I'm desperate now."

She tilted her head, her face a mask of curiosity. "Sounds like God has you where he had me when my husband had a heart attack."

Eli washed the pills down with water. "Where's that?"

"Depending only on Him."

"I have nowhere else to turn. Even if I get to New Orleans, like you said, my mobility is shot."

"Yes, but your faith isn't." Doc Leena's face was aglow. "The Bible says that 'the earnest prayer of a righteous person has great power and produces wonderful results.' Are you seeking God's help with your current dilemma?"

"Yes, because my niece needs my help. And there's this wonderful woman..." Eli searched the room for his phone. "I need to call her. I need my phone."

"I'm afraid your fiancée has confiscated it."

Gina was taking advantage of his disaster for her best interests.

"Could you call Zeke and tell him I need his help," Eli said.

"I can. But you'll need more than Zeke. I'd get to praying if I were you."

Feeling lost with no control around his situation, he said, "I'm not sure I even know how to pray."

"Let me get you started." Doc Leena touched Eli's good shoulder. "Lord Jesus, please show my friend Eli how awesome You are and protect his niece and the good woman who needs

Your help. And while you're at it, could You show him why You made him and how he should live his life? Amen."

Eli breathed out, long and deep, almost a sigh. "Uh...that's it?"

"What do you want, a sermon?"

"No, but it seems inadequate for such a big ask."

"It's not the size of the prayer, Eli. It's the size of the One you're praying to." Doc Leena packed her stethoscope in her bag. "And for Jesus, it's...what do you detectives like to say... elementary?"

"That's Sherlock Holmes."

"Oh...so then...a piece of cake."

"Is that how you pray?"

"Every day. Like I'm talking to my best friend." She stepped to the door. "But remember, Jesus is a friend that sticks closer than a brother. Nothing's impossible for those who believe."

Eli sunk into his pillow and closed his eyes. "Nothing's impossible," he whispered. "That's the kind of friend I need."

———

Eli tried to pray like Doc Leena suggested. But he felt he lacked sincerity. As a kid, he only prayed for certain Christmas gifts or getting out of trouble. And later, God didn't answer Eli's prayer for his brother, Jacob, who died too young because of Eli.

Maybe it was the pain or the drugs, but Eli slid back eight years to the memory when a surge of patriotism took hold of Jacob following Eli's war wounds. With a wife and his four-year-old daughter, Tara, Jacob chucked his promising law career and, like Eli, enlisted in the Army.

From his hospital bed at Fort Campbell, Eli tried to reason

with him. Eli pleaded with Jacob not to make such a radical life choice.

But once Jacob Colt decided, no one could deter him.

Only a few weeks in, during Ranger parachute training, Jacob was slammed against a cinderblock building when the wind shifted. He died two days later. Jacob's death left Julia a widow, Tara without a dad, and Eli's relationship with his family fractured.

No miracle for Jacob.

And Eli lost faith in God.

Now Zoe Prevost's killer had Tara, and Eli was stuck in bed. But Doc Leena believed in God, in miracles, in prayer. And from what he could determine from their last conversation, so did Lindsey.

Eli was alone, lost. He needed help. He needed faith. He needed God.

So he prayed.

God, if You're real, get me out of this room and back to New Orleans to find Tara and bring her home to her mom.

A tense argument seeped from the hall.

"How'd you get in here." Eli recognized his nurse. "Ms. Barrow said no visitors."

The door swung open.

Zeke, showing no bedside concern, said, "You ready to get out of here?"

Relief and hope jammed Eli's tongue to the roof of his mouth, but he managed a faint, "Yep."

Without another word, Zeke sprung to Eli's side and offered his arm. "Let's do this."

Eli gritted his teeth, determined to push through the pain. He took a deep breath and swung his legs to the floor. Then, a delicate dance with Zeke and Eli stood on his two feet once again.

"What's going on here?" Gina's fists were pressed against

her hips. "Put him back in that bed. He's under strict doctor's orders not to get up or to leave this room."

"That's funny," Zeke said. "Doc Leena called me to come get him."

Gina stepped into the room, her eyes full of disbelief and betrayal. "That's not possible. Look at him. He can barely stand. He needs several weeks to heal. Did the good doctor tell you that?"

"Didn't come up."

Eli summoned strength and let go of Zeke. "I'm okay. Doc Leena said I'll make a full recovery. I'm fine."

Deep lines etched between Gina's eyebrows. "Don't you tell me you're okay. Do you know what Daddy and I did to get you out of that cesspool and back here to Bethaven?"

"I know and appreciate all you and your family have done. But I need to find Tara." Eli searched the room for his clothes. "That hasn't changed."

"Of course, things have changed." Her cheeks flushed red. "You were shot in the head and have a broken shoulder that needs more time to heal. You go back to New Orleans, and you'll probably be killed."

"I'm a soldier, Gina. I analyze, and I take calculated risks. It's part of the job."

"You used to be a soldier. Now you're a small-town cop who will soon be part of this wonderful community. The future master of Bethaven can't be prancing to Louisiana to rescue some irrelevant relative from a family who discarded you years ago." You have a responsibility. A responsibility to the Barrow family and a responsibility to me."

Like a jigsaw puzzle after finding a missing piece, Gina's outburst made her motives wholly visible. Even the fog of his concussion couldn't hide her intentions. She didn't love Eli. She loved only herself and her family's legacy. Eli was to be just like the groundskeeper, the cook, the housekeeper, who were there for Gina and her father's pleasure to ensure the plantation remained and ran smoothly.

"Sorry, Gina. I must find Tara. And I'm a detective. She needs my help."

"Eli Colt, you leave, and you and I are finished. You'll lose your position with the Solace Police. You'll lose the land where you park that horrid trailer. You'll lose all the riches you could have had with this." She waved her hands wide as if to point out everything in Bethaven, including herself.

Eli took the full weight of Gina's words. "I figured as much back at the Four Seasons. Don't you understand, we won't work?"

Gina rushed from the room, arms flailing, high heels clicking on wood floors.

Eli glanced at Zeke with fierce determination but unsure what his future held. "I feel like a barrier has been broken. Now get me back to New Orleans so I can find Tara."

FORTY-ONE

With his arm in a sling and a wave of dizziness threatening to pull him back into unconsciousness, Eli slid into the passenger side of Zeke's pristine '55 Chevy pickup. He closed his eyes, gripped the edges of the seat, and took deep breaths to steady himself.

Zeke turned the ignition and the engine thundered like it was NASCAR-ready.

"Sounds like you've done some work to her." Eli strained to make his voice less pain filled.

"You know me. Always tinkering." Zeke radiated contagious feel-good energy. "But I've had some help."

Zeke never let anyone touch his prized truck, not even a professional mechanic, so Eli had to ask. "Who?"

"The kid Clancy roughed up. Cedro." Zeke backed out of the driveway. "He's living at the Anderson farm. And he loves to work on engines. He's like that guy on *Vice Grip Garage*."

"What's that?"

"A YouTube channel where this dude finds abandoned cars, gets them running, then drives them hundreds of miles home."

The comparison between discarded cars and Cedro was not lost on Eli. "How's Cedro doing?"

"Great, thanks to you and the Andersons. They good people."

"You should know."

Zeke's eyes softened. "Yep. Who'd have figured a down-and-out orphan would grow up to run his own business? I owe Bob and Carol a lot for stepping up and raising a no-count gangbanger from New Orleans."

Eli laughed, then winced at the pain only slightly dulled by Doc Leena's meds.

Zeke turned right at the end of Bethaven's driveway. "Speaking of Cedro, you gonna see him today. I got to run by the farm to drop off some clothes. He starts school next week."

Eli looked down at the blood-stained shirt he wore the night he was shot. "Can we stop by my Airstream? I need to pick up some things."

Zeke's shoulders shook with suppressed laughter. "We better hurry before Gina has it towed to the dump."

The road to Eli's camper sloped up and down hills alongside a narrow creek that meandered to the property where Eli had lived for the past five years.

He slow-walked to the Airstream's exterior storage panel and, one-handed, unlocked the compartment where he kept his small arsenal packed with assorted ordnance.

He selected an AR-15 rifle equipped with a Vortex Strike Eagle scope and a Beretta nine-millimeter pistol to replace the Sig Sauer Freddy Badeau used to shoot him. He winced at the thought of his blunder by not clearing Badeau's Sea Ray and losing Tara. He couldn't afford to make another mistake if he found Tara again.

He had Zeke stuff a gear bag with extra magazines, binoculars, handcuffs, flex-ties, and tactical communications set. He resisted adding a ballistic vest and Ops-Core helmet, their weight too much for his wounded head and shoulder.

Zeke secured the bag in the truck bed beneath a canvas covering.

Eli showered and changed.

Then they headed east, past quaint farmhouses and countryside for ten miles until Zeke broke their silence. "He asks about you, you know."

Eli glanced at Zeke. "Who does?"

"Cedro. He appreciates what you did for him at Clancy's."

Eli chuckled. "Did you tell him nobody likes Clancy around here?"

"Don't matter to him why you did it. Just that you did. Not too many people have shown that boy kindness. He's been roughed up plenty in his young life."

"You ask him about his past?"

"I did. But he's pretty tight-lipped. He did let slip that he passed through New Orleans. Something happened there that freaked him bad."

"He say what?"

"Nope. And I don't think he's gonna."

Eli took out his phone. Could Lindsey help?

Zeke honked the horn as he pulled into the Anderson's gravel driveway.

Eli opened his phone screen. "You ever talked to a psychologist when you were a kid?"

"Nope. Randy and Carol don't trust 'em. Say they're all quacks."

Eli pocketed his phone.

A white gabled house with a wraparound porch snuggled amid sprawling live oaks. A boy and a girl about nine or ten ran from behind a cluster of azalea bushes, laughing. Cedro lagged a bit behind them.

Like Santa at Christmas, Zeke pulled a bag from behind

his seat and distributed candy and dime store toys to the younger kids. Then he pulled out an overstuffed bag from Old Navy for Cedro.

But Cedro's attention was not drawn to the bag. Instead, he fixed his gaze on Eli's shoulder sling and bandaged head. "Y-you okay?"

"I'll be okay. How about you?"

"I'm good, but what happened to you?"

Zeke patted Cedro's back. "Where's the Andersons?"

"They went to the feed store."

"Let's hop on the porch," Zeke said. "And catch up."

———

Lying half-prone on a cushioned lounge chair, Eli sipped iced tea flavored with lemon, mint, and honey. The cool drink slid down his dry throat like a soothing balm. The pain in his shoulder didn't bother him much if he remained still.

Zeke rocked in a wooden rocker.

Cedro swung on a porch swing, his face grimaced as if he could feel Eli's discomfort. "Can I get you some Tylenol?"

"Or something with a greater kick?" Zeke said with an amused smile.

A greater kick meant medicinal moonshine, a popular analgesic in rural Mississippi. Eli had a prescription from Doc Leena but chose a clear head over blocking the pain with alcohol. "The iced tea is doing just fine." He took another long sip.

"Country life agrees with you, Cedro," Eli said.

A telling blush crossed Cedro's face as if he couldn't contain his good fortune. "Yes sir. I love it here."

Zeke leaned forward in the rocking chair. "The Andersons tell me after high school you thinking about Mississippi State."

Cedro's face beamed with self-assurance. "I've always liked

animals. Mr. Bob says it's one of the best colleges in the country for animal husbandry. And with my knack with engines, he said someday I could run a farm."

Eli was encouraged by how this once timid teen had found his self-confidence and was looking at a bright future. Eli reached to put down his glass, a spasm of pain assaulted his shoulder like a blast of cold air.

Cedro's brow pressed down. "What happened to you?"

Eli cast a sidelong glance at Zeke. Zeke shrugged as if to say, "Why not?"

"You know I'm a police officer, right?" Eli said. "Sometimes my job puts me in dangerous situations."

"Dangerous?" Cedro surveyed the countryside. "Around here?"

"No. In New Orleans. It's my hometown," Eli said. "Zeke tells me you passed through there before coming here."

"Something like that," Cedro's relaxed expression faltered as if he wanted to avoid talking about his past. "So, you got hurt in New Orleans?"

"I did."

"But you're a cop here."

"This was for a personal matter. My niece was taken." Eli closed his eyes to mask his failure and fought through his physical and emotional pain.

"Did you find her?" Cedro asked.

Eli opened his eyes. "I did. But then this happened." Eli raised his sling. "Now, my niece is in the hands of a dangerous person."

Cedro hunched and lowered his eyes. "How old is your niece?"

"About your age. Fifteen."

"I knew a girl in the hands of bad people." Cedro's eyes glistened with what seemed like lingering emotional pain. "Just outside New Orleans."

Eli leaned forward, ignoring the rippling discomfort from his head and shoulder. "Can you be more specific?"

"Not really." Cedro shrugged. "I was on a ship."

"On the Gulf?"

Cedro shook his head.

"In Lake Pontchartrain?"

"No."

"The Mississippi River?"

"Nuh-uh."

Eli pulled out his phone. "Cedro, I'm going to show you a picture." He scrolled through his phone until the photo of Tara and Zoe Prevost appeared. He turned the screen toward Cedro.

Cedro stood, walked over, bent low for a closer look. His face turned pale. Then he turned, ran across the porch, threw open the screen door, and flew inside the house.

FORTY-TWO

Lindsey sat behind her desk at Safe Harbor Home for Girls, her fingers on her keyboard, her computer screen touring Gina's Bethaven Plantation, her heart as heavy as a locked chest with no key. She'd been pleading with God for guidance for three days, and for three days, God's answer was the same.

Wait.

That's what the Holy Spirit instructed. Her pastor friend Justin confirmed the same when he talked her through her crisis of faith. But the weight of her worry hadn't diminished an ounce. She remained frustrated, lost, and fearful for the future.

Lindsey hadn't asked God for a husband, yet He promised her Eli, lifting her hopes to the clouds only to have them free fall when the hospital elevator doors closed, cutting her off from Eli and his fiancée, Gina Barrow.

God saved her when she was thirteen. He reached down, snatched her from the squalor and abuse at that horrible river-front warehouse and placed her here at Safe Harbor. Now, she served God by serving young girls who had suffered like she did.

So why would God promise her something that would never, could never, happen?

Justin had reminded her that Abraham had waited twenty-five years for Isaac. And David struggled under the threat of death for fifteen years before he'd been crowned king. Would she have to wait years before God's promise would be fulfilled? It had been only, what—ten days.

She swiveled in her seat to look outside her office window to the place she'd first seen Eli. What were he and Gina doing now?

What would Lindsey do?

Call Bethaven and check on Eli? What if that demon with the condescending smile answered the phone? The nerve of that Gina Barrow offering Lindsey a reward.

Or she could drive to Solace, Mississippi, and confront Queen Gina in her fiefdom. Or Lindsey could do what the Spirit had told her and what Justin confirmed.

Wait.

Her phone danced across the desk. Eli Colt's name illuminated the screen. Her heart leaped the height of Mount Sinai.

"Hello." Her voice sounded tentative.

"Lindsey." Eli's voice sounded strained.

A sudden cheeriness in her soul had her almost giddy. "Eli. Thank goodness you called. I've been so worried."

"I'm sorry it took so long." Eli's words were punctuated with gasps for air. "I just got my phone back a few hours ago. Are you hurt?"

"No. I'm fine." She rubbed her wet eyes on her sleeve. "Just a bump and a bruise. And you? How are you?"

"I took a little damage from our encounter with Andre and Freddy." Eli paused. "But the doctor here says I'll be fine."

Lindsey struggled not to burst into sobs. "I just missed you before you left the hospital for Solace."

"I know." Eli's breathing sounded more raspy. Turbulent. "But right now, I could use your help."

A wave of relief washed over Lindsey. Her stomach somersaulted. "Of course. Anything."

"There's a boy here, Cedro, who could help us find Tara," Eli said with a hint of trepidation. "I think he was with Zoe when she died."

"Where are you? At Gina's?" Her tone sounded a bit prickly.

"No," Eli said. "I'm with Zeke, a friend of mine."

Lindsey's muscles relaxed. Her body uncoiled. "What do you need me to do?"

"Could you come to Solace and talk to the boy?"

"Text me the address." A newfound trust in God's promise emerged. Lindsey grabbed her purse. "I'm on my way."

———

Lindsey's headlights glimmered over the dark Mississippi road. Its faded white lines barely showed where the asphalt ended, and the ditch began.

"Three miles to your destination," her GPS said, alerting her to how far to the Anderson's farm.

The five-hour drive had her raging, then repentant. What could've happened between Eli and Gina that he was no longer with her?

"Two miles to your destination."

And what about Cedro? Did he know Zoe? Could he lead them to Tara? Anticipation and anxiety swirled like a tempestuous storm.

"One mile to your destination."

Lindsey slowed her Civic and studied the mailbox

numbers reflected by her high beams. The GPS announced, "Your destination is on your right."

She turned and followed a driveway for fifty yards to a quaint two-story farmhouse.

A black man came off the front porch.

She parked and opened the door.

He waved. "You Dr. Lindsey?"

"Yes, and just Lindsey is fine."

"I'm Zeke." He dipped his chin. "This way."

Lindsey followed Zeke onto the porch and through an open screen door.

———

Cedro sat in his bedroom on the edge of his soft bed. Through his open window, he heard whip-poor-will calls.

Why did he have to see that picture of Zoe? He'd been trying to forget about the *Leviathan*. What would happen if he refused to answer the detective's questions? Cops got pretty angry when you didn't cooperate. Vindictive too.

Cedro stood and paced the floor. Eli Colt seemed interested in what happened to Cedro from the start. When he'd stood up for him at the convenience store, when he took him to breakfast at Zeke's diner, and when he arrived earlier looking broke down like a car in a Miami chop shop. But if Cedro's experience had taught him anything, it taught him cops were all the same.

Tires crunched the gravel driveway. High beams flashed across his bedroom wall. Cedro peeked outside and saw Zeke talking with a pretty woman. No doubt, a social worker ready to send him back to Florida. Or take him to juvenile detention for stealing that food in town. He should have answered Eli's questions instead of moping in here all night.

He could climb out the window and run. But he wasn't in

north Miami, where he could disappear in an alley or blend into a crowd. There were few people out here in the country. And Mr. Randy said there were dangerous animals once you got deep in the woods, like rattlesnakes, bobcats, and bears. He'd seen a bear at Jungle Island in Miami and didn't care to meet one in the woods.

———

Lindsey sensed tension thick as morning fog inside the Anderson's home. A plain, no-nonsense couple in their sixties waited in the living room, the woman's demeanor uninviting. The man stood as if they'd been waiting for a battle.

Faces of a young boy and girl spied her from a doorway, each with welcoming smiles.

Eli sat slumped on a worn leather chair, his face etched in pain and exhaustion. "Hello, Lindsey. Welcome to Solace."

Lindsey gaped at his bandaged head and his arm strapped in a sling. She resisted rushing to him, especially in front of this stern couple. "Shouldn't you be in a hospital?"

Zeke snickered like a schoolboy. "I just broke him out of one of the finest private facilities in Mississippi where he had round-the-clock care."

"I'm fine." Eli's voice was low and gravelly. "Thanks for driving all this way."

Zeke introduced the couple. "This is Bob and Carol Anderson. They have a few questions."

Carol Anderson's icy blue eyes held a sharpness that could cut glass. "I'm sorry, I don't approve of all this. Cedro didn't talk for three days when we first got him. And he was happy this morning until Zeke brought Detective Colt to our home. Then the poor boy completely shuts down."

Lindsey's pulse pounded in her neck. "I'm sorry, Ms. Anderson—"

Carol's voice arched into a high pitch as she spat out the words, "I prefer missus, not *miz*." She stressed the last word.

Lindsey's cheeks flushed hot with embarrassment. "Forgive me, Mrs. Anderson. I came here to see if I could help."

"Help?" The woman's intense face demanded a reckoning. "The only way you can help is to get back in your car and head back to where you came from."

Lindsey felt her insides twist with frustration but kept her voice calm. "I understand your concern, Mrs. Anderson, but I'm a licensed therapist. I specialize in working with children who have experienced trauma. I assure you I could help Cedro if you allow me to."

Carol's expression didn't soften. "You government types are all alike. You say you come to help, only to leave a big mess behind. Then we've got to spend days, if not weeks, cleaning up."

"I'm not with the government," Lindsey said.

Mrs. Anderson's rolled her unbelieving eyes up to the ceiling.

Eli lowered his gaze. "I'm sorry, Miss Carol." His voice was soft and reluctant. "I'm to blame here. Lindsey works for a non-profit organization that helps kids like Cedro."

"Helps how?" Carol said.

"I'm a clinical psychologist," Lindsey said. "I work at a home for sexually abused girls."

The older woman smirked. "Here we go. Another bleeding heart from Social Services that thinks she knows more than we do."

"Hold on, Carol," Bob said. "The detective said she's from a non-profit, not Social Services."

Lindsey locked eyes with Carol with a softened expression. "Look, Mrs. Anderson. I understand your concern. I do. I've had my run-ins with Social Services more than once. And I assure you, my intentions with Cedro are no different from yours. I want to help."

"So you say. What makes you different than those other government do-gooders?" Carol crossed her arms and looked away.

"Because I'm fairly certain there's little difference between my childhood and his. I've been where he's been. Would you care to hear?"

————

Cedro stood by his closed bedroom door, listening. Miss Carol was hotter than Florida asphalt. He imagined her aiming her eyes like gun barrels, but he couldn't make out what she said.

Next, the pretty woman did most of the talking. Probably laying down the law of what Social Services could do and what the Andersons couldn't. Not the first time he experienced foster parents wilting to the will of the system.

The knock at the door made him flinch.

He didn't move or answer.

"Cedro. It's Miss Carol. Can we come in?" Her tone was surprisingly friendly.

He didn't answer.

"Cedro?"

He remained quiet.

Whispers, then the door opened. Miss Carol entered with the social worker.

"Cedro." Miss Carol's face was as soft as when he first met her. "This is Miss Lindsey. She's a doctor, and she wants to talk with you."

The hair on his arms and neck lifted. "Sh-should I pack my things?"

Miss Lindsey's eyes were warm, not threatening. "No Cedro. This is your home."

A light quiver flickered in his stomach. "S-so, why are you here?"

"To learn what happened to a girl I once treated. Her name was Zoe. I hear you might know something about her."

Cedro felt the blood rush from his head. He collapsed onto the end of his bed.

Miss Lindsey pointed at an armchair by his bed. "May I sit?"

Cedro remained quiet and still.

"I'll leave you two alone." Miss Carol closed the door behind her.

Miss Lindsey was prettier up close. Definitely not a social worker whose only concern was hauling him to a shelter.

"Like I said, Cedro. I just want to talk." Miss Lindsey's gaze remained gentle.

Cedro's breath hitched in his throat. Why was this woman and the cop so interested in Zoe?

"You know," Miss Lindsey said. "Zoe once lived where I live."

He couldn't contain his curiosity. "She lived with you?"

Miss Lindsey lifted her shoulders. "Well, sort of. I work at a girl's home."

A knot burned in his belly. "A shelter?"

She tilted her head. "No, not a shelter? A home for girls. Girls who need help because of what they've been through. You know what I'm talking about, right?"

He did. "Miss Carol said you're a doctor."

"A psychologist actually. Do you know what that is?"

"Yes. I talked to one at a shelter in Miami."

"By your expression, I bet it wasn't a pleasant experience."

"No, it wasn't pleasant."

Miss Lindsey's face turned serious. "I don't work for social services. I work for a Christian organization that helps girls who were abused."

"Like Zoe?"

Her eyes got sad. "Like Zoe."

"Do you know what happened to her?" Cedro asked.

"Do you?"

He held onto his answer but then whooshed out the words he'd been holding in tight. "She died."

Miss Lindsey kept her eyes focused on Cedro. "I know. I identified her body in New Orleans." She paused. "Can you tell me how she died?"

"Why should I?" His defiant tone surprised him.

She remained calm. Patient. "Because another girl is in danger. And Eli and I are trying to help her." Her tone stayed calm and patient.

Cedro's resistance softened. "The girl in the picture?"

"Yes."

"Why do you care so much?"

"Because I know what she's going through." Lindsey reached out and touched Cedro's shoulder. Her face slackened. "I know what it means to live in fear." Her words came out slow and heavy.

"How?"

Lindsey averted her gaze to far outside the window. "Because when I was thirteen, I ran from a foster home in Dallas after bouncing around in the system for six years."

Miss Lindsey's story triggered the haunting reminder of Zoe's death stare on the deck of the *Leviathan*.

"But I was saved, Cedro. Like you, I found people who love me. And now I need your help so the girl in the picture doesn't end up like Zoe. Can you help?"

Cedro's eyelashes warmed with his tears. "What's the other girl's name."

"Tara. She's Eli's niece."

Cedro clinched his fists. "You need to find a ship named *Leviathan*. It belongs to a man called Commodore."

FORTY-THREE

The old Civic shook like a rollercoaster on rough rails, sending shockwaves through Eli's wounded head and shoulder. He shifted, attempting to find the most comfortable position to minimize the pain.

The distant New Orleans horizon was a distorted canvas in his blurred vision. Buildings bled into one another, forming a bizarre cityscape. Eli wanted to stop, take potent painkillers, and sleep. But he had to find Tara.

"You okay," Lindsey said from behind the wheel, concern lines etched into her face.

He strained a smile to mask the pain that plagued him. "I'm fine. A little discomfort. But nothing I can't handle."

Lindsey's brow and forehead crunched into deeper wrinkles. "I can see it's more than a little discomfort."

"This bumpy bridge isn't helping." Eli tried to soften his lie. "I can feel every shimmy and thump in the road."

Lindsey stole glances at Eli's bandaged head and arm sling. "You won't be much good to Tara if you're in excruciating pain."

"Let's find this yacht first." His voice trembled slightly.

"Which yacht?" Frustration crept into Lindsey's tone. "Badeau's Sea Ray or the *Leviathan*?"

"I called Manny from the Anderson's," Eli said. "He has a call into the Coast Guard to get them looking for both."

Lindsey pulled off the interstate onto Canal Street.

His phone buzzed. He pulled it from inside his arm sling.

"It's a no-go with the Coast Guard," Manny said. "They've got their entire fleet on a major drug operation."

The weight of disappointment crushed down on Eli's bad shoulder and his mood. "Tara's out there somewhere, and we don't have much to go on. We can't waste any more time." His words came out sharp and impatient. He terminated the call, then turned to Lindsey for some semblance of strength.

She reached over and clutched his left hand and squeezed. "It's not Manny you're mad at. It's the situation. We'll keep searching, and I'll help you. I'm convinced God will lead us to Tara." Her voice held assurance, acting like an elixir to his wounded head and shoulder.

His heart formed a deep bond with the beautiful Lindsey Crenshaw and a ray of hope sparked within his broken body. Somehow, they would find Tara. Together.

His phone buzzed again, and again it was Manny. Eli put the call on speaker. "Manny, some good news I hope."

"I just got word from Reggie Toussaint." Manny's voice was urgent and slightly breathless. "A woman called our Crime Stoppers hotline about Tara's disappearance."

Eli's and Lindsey's eyes met in a shared moment of eager curiosity.

"When?" Eli said.

"Two days ago."

"Two days?" Eli couldn't stifle his irritated tone. "Why did he wait until now to come forward?"

"He didn't wait. The hotline just called him a few minutes

ago. They just found out. The crime stopper message was left on their recorded line."

"What'd the woman say?"

"The woman, who has an accent—"

Eli's phone alerted him of an incoming call. "Hold on, Manny." The number was slightly familiar, but he refused the call. "Sorry. Go on. A woman with an accent..."

"She claims she has information about Tara and will only talk with you."

"Me?"

"That's what she said. She'll only talk with the girl's uncle, Eli Colt."

Eli coiled like a spring. "What kind of an accent?"

Manny's snort resounded through the line. "Knowing those who work at the call center, it could be anything from Texan to Tunisian."

"Do you have the woman's phone number?" Eli said.

"I do."

"Did anybody call the number?"

"Nope. She asked for you, and I don't want to spook her."

"Who knows about this call?"

"Me, the captain, and..." Manny let out a long sigh. "Reggie, of course."

"Okay. Text me the number, and I'll call her." Eli terminated the call and glanced at Lindsey. "What do you think?"

"We have more now than we did two minutes ago."

"A break?"

"An answered prayer." Lindsey's tone exuded strength and conviction.

Eli called the number. No one answered. He left a message to call his cell.

———

Lindsey paid for their coffee order at the register of Mardi Gras Perks. A coffee café tucked away on Decatur Street, its air filled with smells of roasted coffee beans, baked pastries, and the sounds of soft jazz piped through an audio system. She glanced at Eli, sagging in a leather chair, his eyes squeezed shut, agony across his face.

She watched him. An alliance of awe and admiration glowing in her chest. Even in pain, his was jaw set firm in determination, the deep creases in his forehead showed a man who'd steeled himself against whatever life threw at him. A man who, when confronted with a mission, did what was necessary without pause, despite any setback.

She carried the cups to their table. The clock on the wall said 11:20, ten minutes until the woman informant with a British accent was due to arrive.

"She should be here soon." Lindsey set her and Eli's cups on a coffee table, then sat in another leather chair.

"Hope my appearance doesn't scare her away," Eli said, his eyes still closed.

Lindsey bit her lip to suppress her nervous energy. "Are you sure you're up for this?"

"No. But you're here." Eli opened his eyes to gaze at Lindsey a long moment. "I'm sure about you."

His reply sent warmth through her, trekking to her cheeks and ears.

Then, a curious presence in her periphery—a striking woman wearing dark glasses and a baseball cap pulled low on her forehead sat near the exit, observing them. She wore a white, loose-fitted blouse and casual jeans draped over a well-rounded figure, and despite the unassuming attire, her beauty was obvious.

The woman stood and walked over. "Are you Eli Colt?" she said with an unmistakable British accent.

Eli nodded with a pained smile. "Yes."

"Who's this?" The Brit raised her brow and stared at Lindsey. Her eyes wary with distrust. "We were to meet alone."

"She helps me get around," Eli said. "As you can see, I've had an accident."

"I heard." She took a seat at the table. "Freddy shot you. Your bandaged head is how I knew it was you."

"Heard from where?" Eli's voice cracked with an edge of caution.

The Brit glanced over her shoulder. "A friend of mine works at a club."

"Gabriella's?" Eli said, his voice tinged with surprise.

"That's the one. Freddy's uncle is close to the owner."

Eli's face displayed his amazement. "Javier Navarro."

"Seems like you know a lot," the Brit said.

"We don't know where Tara is." Lindsey's tone was terse. "She disappeared with Andre and Freddy Badeau the night Eli was shot."

Eli attempted to sit straighter, his expression clenched. "You know where they took her?"

The Brit gave a single, slow nod. "Yes."

Adrenaline and caffeine jolted through Lindsey's system. "How?"

"I overheard Andre negotiating to sell her."

"Sell?" Lindsey narrowed her eyes. "How can we be sure what you're telling us is true?" Lindsey's tone was sharp with doubt.

"Because I know who Uncle Eli is," the Brit said with no hesitation. "Tara told me about him."

"You've seen Tara? Spoken to her?" Lindsey said.

"Yes."

"When? Where?" Eli lips tightened.

"At Andre's brothel in the French Quarter," the Brit said. "The day before you two lost her."

"Why not tell the police what you're telling us?" Eli said.

"Because the police work for Badeau. At least some of them do."

The words sent a cold sensation throughout Lindsey.

Eli quirked a single brow. "Do you know a Reggie Toussaint?"

The Brit offered a subtle shrug. "No. Never heard of him."

"What else can you tell us?" Lindsey said, her curiosity surging.

"I know the man who bought Tara." The Brit lifted her chin high, asserting candor. "Andre called him Commodore."

FORTY-FOUR

Eli shuffled into an elevator at the NOPD station with Lindsey holding his elbow.

Manny waited on the second floor where Captain Guidry was expecting them. Manny had asked Eli to debrief Guidry on their progress in finding the four teenagers who went missing from Orleans Parish Center for Girls. Eli and Lindsey had learned from the Brit where they were being held —Badeau's French Quarter brothel. He hoped Guidry would feel more compelled to help Eli find Tara now that they could close four of Toussaint's missing persons files.

Guidry sat in a conference room with Toussaint and motioned for Eli, Lindsey, and Mancuso to sit. "Manny tells me you have information about those four missing girls."

Lindsey gave Guidry the address of Badeau's brothel.

Guidry passed it to Toussaint who snatched the paper like a squirrel does a nut. Then he scurried out of the room.

"I've put out feelers for the yachts you uncovered in the Rigolets. Badeau's Sea Ray and this..." Guidry referred to his legal pad. "*Leviathan*. But so far, nothing."

"What do we know about this Commodore character?" Eli asked.

Guidry shuffled through his notes. "It's not much but seems he's a former investment banker who fancies himself a rear admiral. Rumor has it, he tried to buy a World War Two destroyer out of mothballs, but the Navy turned him down."

"And he buys teenagers from pimps?" Eli asked, not masking his gut-wrenching urgency.

"If that's true, the guys a first-rate nut job." Guidry clinched his hands behind his head and leaned back. "I'm stumped on how to find these boats."

"What's your usual protocol?"

"Coast Guard," Guidry said. "But as Manny already told you, that's not happening anytime soon."

"The next call goes to the Feds," Manny said. "They have technology that morphs ours."

Guidry wagged his index finger. "But the FBI doesn't play well with others. They'd rather big foot your case and roll in like John Wayne."

Mancuso turned to Eli. "What about your connection in D.C.?"

Eli blasted a short breath. "I called him but no help."

"Hit you with budget restraints and how his hands are tied?" Guidry said.

Eli nodded. "He explained the only possible way they could find a boat in open water was with a satellite search. According to him, a CubeSat is the way to go. But there's only a few in orbit, and time on one is expensive. DOJ only uses the CubeSat for cases of national security."

"I can try Homeland Security," Guidry said. "But the last time I contacted them, it was three days before they called back."

Lindsey hunched her shoulders. "The *Leviathan* could be

halfway around the world by then." She wrapped her arms over her chest. "What can we do right now?"

"We've hit a dead end." Eli said weakly.

———

Eli languished in the lobby of the Holiday Inn on Loyola Avenue.

Lindsey sat across from him, her chin down to her chest.

Mancuso paced behind her, grating on Eli's last emotional nerve.

Eli hadn't expected human trafficking, a horrid level of wickedness responsible for Tara's disappearance. He figured he'd track her down through friends and teachers and deliver her to Julia within hours. And maybe, get on better terms with his parents.

His phone's vibration shook him from his gloom. For the third time, it displayed the same unknown number. And for the third time, his thumb hovered. Why not?

"Thank heaven you answered. I've been calling for days." It was agent-in-training Dakota Sutcliffe of the FBI.

"Sorry Dakota. I've been preoccupied."

"So I've read. Shot in the Rigolets. It's all-over social media. I hope I'm not responsible."

Eli's gaze followed Mancuso pacing the lobby. "Why would you be responsible?"

"Wasn't it my ski line info that sent you to the Rigolets?"

"It was and thank you," Eli admitted. If it wasn't for Stucliffe, the case would have died days ago. "It led us right to the house where Tara was being held."

The muffled "whoo-hoo" had Eli imagining Sutcliffe ready for a congratulatory fist bump. "You did good, Dakota. Real good."

"Thanks. But you should've taken me with you. I've had Coast Guard and Quantico training, remember."

"I doubt the Bureau would've let me have you for the evening."

"Are you kidding me? They barely know I'm here, except to pick up lunch or get coffee or fetch paper clips. I lead a bane existence here, Detective. I'm the Ned Stark of the FBI."

Eli cracked another smile. Although Dakota lifted his mood, Eli wanted to stop talking, stop thinking, be alone with a bottle of single-malt and get pie-eyed.

"So what's your plan?" Sutcliffe said.

Eli didn't have one. "We've hit a dead end." Eli's breathing got heavier. "Dakota, there's nothing else you can do. We're stuck."

"Try me." Sutcliffe crowed like Steph Curry before launching a three.

The hair on Eli's neck stiffened. "It's no use, trust me."

"You're acting like my supervisor." Sutcliffe's tone turned bitter. "Zero faith in my abilities."

The kid identifies one ski line, and he thinks he's Philip Marlowe.

"Tell me what you need," Sutcliffe said. "Give me a chance."

"Fine," Eli said with no small amount of irritation. "What we need is time on a CubeSat to find a yacht called the *Leviathan*." The words spit out of Eli's mouth like bullets from an assault weapon. "We've confirmed that Tara is on this ship with some madman called Commodore. Its last reported location was in the Rigolets about three weeks ago." Eli paused before piling on. "Oh, and we need that CubeSat now."

"You have a color?"

Eli's mind got stuck in neutral. "What?"

"The yacht. What color is it? Never mind, I can find it."

Keyboard clicks followed. "There it is. Hmm. Looks white. Registered in the Cayman Islands."

More clicking and a strange confidence emanated from the other end of the line.

"Where are you?" Sutcliffe asked like they were discussing when to meet to tee off.

"Holiday Inn on Loyola."

"I'll get what you need. Meet me in four hours at Willie Mae's restaurant in the Pythian Market. Order me the fried chicken with red beans and rice."

FORTY-FIVE

As if Tara's previous interactions with Commodore weren't weird enough, today she sat in his over-the-top stateroom with wood-paneled walls, the floor covered in plush carpet, and furniture fit for an English mansion.

Today was the fifth day of her training. Commodore sat in front of a big-screen television, then showed her a video of six black-hooded men with machetes beheading four women.

Tara stared at the screen, paralyzed by terror. Fear pulsed through her body. Her mind raced with confusion, struggling to wrap itself around the horror. Time froze for the seconds the women died. Tara's breaths quickened. Her chest tightened until her ribs felt like they'd break with each gasp. She turned her focus to Commodore, who watched her intently, hunger in his eyes. A wave of heat flushed over her skin.

Commodore asked rapid-fire questions. "What were the perspectives of each person in the film? What was the man giving the orders thinking? How about the kid who couldn't use the machete properly? The old woman who died? The young girl? What were they thinking? What do you feel?"

Tara knew better than to not answer. "I...I think the man giving the orders was...he was...I don't know, maybe he was angry or...or..." she stammered. There were no words for this nightmare she was forced to watch.

Commodore leaned forward. His gaze drilled into her with a heightened intensity. "Come now, Tara. You must have some idea. What was going through their minds? What were they feeling?"

Tara shook her head to refocus. Her eyes returned to the television screen. "I don't know. I can't even imagine. It's...it's just too much." Tara covered her mouth with her palm to muffle a gasp.

Commodore chuckled low, like a prankster reveling in his mischief. "Oh, but you must try, my dear. It's the only way to truly understand the human psyche. You must put yourself in their shoes, think what they thought, feel what they felt." He flashed a confident smile. "Take the rest of the day to meditate on what you've just seen."

————

An hour later, on the sundeck, Molly brushed off the video. "It's real life, Tara. Crap like that happens, and you can't be naive. This is a dangerous world. Commodore monitored how well you could handle it. Don't worry. You did great."

"Did great?" Tara blurted. How does someone do great when subjected to sadism? She couldn't, wouldn't conform to this insanity. But she didn't want to test this psychopath. Escape was the only rebellion that made sense.

She could play the faithful disciple and plan an escape when they docked for supplies.

How far could she swim if they got closer to shore?

No chance of escaping during daylight. They'd catch her with the dingy.

No, nighttime was the only time to go.

———

Eli called the menu selection at Willie Mae's Restaurant country cooking. Lindsey called it soul, and Manny called it Creole. But no matter how the cuisine was identified, it seemed odd that the Florida-born, once competitive water skier, FBI agent-in-training Dakota Sutcliffe would select Willie Mae's for dinner.

Eli couldn't get comfortable in the plastic chair. He and Lindsey ordered the red beans and fried chicken. Manny chose fried catfish with okra and butter beans.

Lindsey and Manny retrieved their dinners from the pickup counter. A half-minute later Sutcliffe strutted through the door.

The kid was right on time.

Sutcliffe picked up his order, sat across from Eli, and immediately crunched down on a drumstick, running a napkin across his chin. "I found her."

"What?" Eli's pulse raced like Jimmy Johnson at Daytona.

"*Leviathan*. I found her."

"How?" Eli said.

Sutcliffe peered over his drumstick and frowned. "You don't look so good, Detective. Shouldn't you be in bed."

"Don't worry about me. Go on."

Sutcliffe broke off a piece of cornbread. "I served in the Coast Guard Reserves during college, my roommate at Cape May was this techno geek. He scored off the charts at MIT and now sits at the controls of a CubeSat in New London, Connecticut."

Eli pushed his plate away. "How did you get permission to do a satellite search."

"Permission? I didn't have permission." Sutcliffe shoved the beans in his mouth.

Manny looked up from his catfish. "Oh, I like this boy." Manny set down his forkful of beans. "Where's the ship?"

"Close." Sutcliffe checked his watch. "As of five minutes ago, she was in the Chandelier Sound north of Bay St. Louis. She's moving east by southeast at ten knots headed out into the Gulf."

"Can the Coast Guard rescue Tara now that we know where she is?" Lindsey asked.

Sutcliffe shoveled a forkful of red beans and held it halfway to his mouth. "Not enough information to warrant that. And by the time I get through the red tape, the boat will be long gone."

"So, how to catch and board that ship is the challenge," Eli said.

Sutcliffe discarded a chicken bone. "Yes, and we need to hurry. I have a boat ready in Gentilly big enough for four."

———

Tara sat at the white table in *Leviathan's* galley in her ridiculous white uniform, poking at the tasteless white potatoes on her plate. The clatter of dishes and silverware competed with Molly's babbling about some sorority-type group Commodore wanted Tara to join.

Tara trusted no one. Especially Molly, who never tired of training her. All Tara's other bunkmates were true believers. All worshiped Commodore as if he were some god. And all told her not to cause trouble. Troublemakers were disciplined. Some disappeared.

Molly had explained Commodore's teaching was a university for the soul. "You'll learn to expand the inner light within you, and your spirit will be a beacon for all humanity."

It sounded like church, but it felt dark and devil-like. Especially after watching a mass murder on film.

And why were there no ugly girls on board? No fat ones, no thin ones, no girls with bad acne or stooped shoulders. Every girl was pretty. And so were the boys. Marco and Myles and every kid that slung a paintbrush or scrubbed a deck were attractive.

A gleam of delight danced in Molly's eyes. Her lips stretched into a wide grin. "It's so exciting. You'll be one of us."

"Uh, sorry," Tara said. "My mind was somewhere else."

"I said you'll be part of us."

Tara shifted her weight and slow panned the galley. "I thought I already was."

Molly patted Tara's arm. "No silly. I mean you'll be part of our select group. The inner circle. The women Commodore truly trusts."

Part of Tara wanted to punch Molly, the other part wanted to run to the deck and jump overboard. "What does that mean?"

Molly lowered her voice. "It means you've been chosen to take his mark."

Tara gazed at Molly with sudden focus. "His mark?"

Molly's lips formed a soft *O*. "It's a great honor that you've been chosen this soon."

"What kind of mark?" Tara held her arms tight against her body.

"Oh, don't worry," Molly said. "It's like a tattoo."

An inner alarm bell rang inside Tara. "A tattoo of what?" No way she was cool with this.

"I can't say."

"Do you have one?" Tara asked.

"I do."

"Can I see it?"

"Not until you have your own."

Bad vibes sent the hair on Tara's neck to stand on end. "Where would they put it?"

"Sorry. Not until you get it yourself."

An uncertain sigh escaped through Tara's pressed lips. If she wanted to escape, she must be trusted. Plus, what's a tattoo—right? Most girls at school had one. "When?"

Molly's eyes gleamed like stars on a clear night. "You'll do it?"

"If it makes Commodore happy." Tara strained to say the words. "Why not?"

FORTY-SIX

In the damp afternoon heat, Eli lay sprawled in the backseat of Sutcliffe's F-250 pickup, his muscles tense and rigid, his damp shirt clung to his back like a second skin.

Lindsey turned in the front passenger seat, her cheeks flushed pink, likely with worry. "Tell me again why I'm here and Manny's not."

"Manny needs to be at police headquarters where he can manage resources should we need them." Eli's concern for Lindsey's well-being was at odds with the calm her presence gave him.

Sutcliffe turned off Old Gentilly Road, then stopped at a chain-link gate guarded by a Coast Guard seaman garbed in blue shirt, blue trousers, and a nine-millimeter holstered on his side.

"Be right back," Sutcliffe said as he exited the truck to speak with the guard.

Sutcliffe continued to prove himself more valuable than he appeared. He'd showed an inquisitive mind and an insatiable desire to impress. He also demonstrated an aptitude to influence others in his Coast Guard world to keep Eli's mission of finding Tara moving forward—like the Coast Guard tech who'd found the *Leviathan* on the CubeSat and the seaman who was opening a gate to a military installation without searching his truck for weapons.

And then there was the injection.

Sutcliffe had stopped at Tulane University's athletic center, where he knew the athletic trainer. The trainer injected Toradol, a potent anti-inflammatory into Eli's shoulder, which eased Eli's discomfort and delivered near maximum mobility.

But Sutcliffe's top-tier contribution was the military-grade boat he'd commandeered—a Coast Guard small unit inflatable attack boat equipped with two ninety-horsepower Suzuki engines. The twenty-four-foot Ocean Craft was a whole lot better than the battered aluminum skiff Eli and Lindsey had braved in the Rigolets.

And in addition, Sutcliffe had acquired an updated schematic of the ninety-year-old *Leviathan*.

Time to find Tara and bring her home.

Sutcliffe sat in the pilot seat. Eli positioned himself to Sutcliffe's right. Lindsey took the seat behind Eli. The engines propelled them through the grey waters of the narrow inlet, then due east into the choppy Lake Borgne, toward *Leviathan's* last reported CubeSat position.

Eli's confidence in Sutcliffe's abilities seemed to invigorate the young man. A determined demeanor replaced the frustration Eli had witnessed during their first encounter at FBI headquarters. Within two hours of leaving Willie Mae's restaurant, they were gliding across Lake Borgne at forty knots to intercept *Leviathan* and, hopefully, Tara.

"Forty clicks to the ship's last known position," Sutcliffe said through the tactical headset Eli'd brought from his arsenal. "Half hour. Over."

"Copy," Eli said.

Lindsey focused on Sutcliffe, her hands gripped the seat.

A half hour later, Eli scrunched down in a small well at the boat's bow and searched the waters of Chandelier Sound.

"Two miles to destination," Sutcliffe said.

No sign of *Leviathan*.

"One mile." Sutcliffe's tone quivered with excitement.

Still, no *Leviathan*. Nor at a mile, a half-mile, or a quarter.

Eli blew out a frustrated sigh. "Leviathan's nowhere in sight."

"We'll catch her. The old ship can only top end at fourteen knots," Sutcliffe's said through the comm. "Time to see what this glorified floatie can do."

The Suzuki engines thundered. The boat's front end elevated as it gathered speed, then leveled. Eli's hair whipped against his forehead. He scanned the waters with his night vision goggles. His belly came alive with a quiver reserved for impending battles. He'd been longing for this fight. Longing for pay back. Longing to rescue Tara since he'd been bested in the Rigolets.

Their assault boat flew past Grand Island. Still no sign of *Leviathan*.

Sutcliffe pulled out his satellite phone, dialed. Whatever he asked, the answer had him turning due east with increased speed.

"Where is the damn ship?" Eli boomed, his impatience bordering on anger.

Sutcliffe focused ahead. "Fifteen minutes."

Fifteen minutes later the Sea Craft entered the Gulf of Mexico within sight of Waveland, Mississippi. The seas were calm, the horizon canvassed with orange clouds streaked with purple. But no ships were visible. Eli's heart sank to his gut. Did Sutcliffe get bogus information from his geek friend in Connecticut? Could the old yacht make it to international waters before they caught her?

A flicker of distant, indistinguishable light caught Eli's attention. He abandoned his goggles for binoculars and pressed them to his eyes. The hazy light transformed into a floating façade of a long white vessel. Painted in cursory script on the stern above the waterline was the ship's name—*Leviathan*.

"There she blows. A hump like a snow hill." Sutcliffe's words filled Eli's earbuds.

"Is that Melville, from Moby Dick?" Lindsey said with an exuberant chuckle.

Their engines decelerated to match speed with the white whale. Their boat bobbed over the Gulf's choppy waves, cresting and falling in sync with Eli's pulsing energy.

"See if you can get close enough to see what we're up against." Eli's voice buzzed with anticipation.

Sutcliffe flashed Eli a thumbs up and steered the boat within two hundred yards of the yacht's starboard, cloaking their presence in the shadow of the Mississippi coastline.

The *Leviathan's* hull gleamed against the dark sky, its towering multi-deck profile, its masts, staterooms, berths, and open-air spaces illuminated by yellow-hued lights.

A pilot and watchman in classic naval whites manned the bridge. A handful of men clad in black slacks and shirts scattered about the ship like spiders in a dark attic. Handguns strapped across their chests identifying them as ship security.

Over a dozen teenage boys in an open-air lounge on the main deck ate like a pack of wolves consuming a fresh kill. And there was a familiar face among them. Myles, the scared kid Eli encountered with Freddy at the Rigolets mansion.

Adrenaline jazzed through Eli's body. This time he would succeed. He would find and rescue Tara.

He joined Sutcliffe and Lindsey in the boats aft. "Okay, here's what we got..." Eli laid out his rescue plan on the Leviathan's diagram.

"We go now—right?" Sutcliffe said without hesitation.

Eli grabbed his AR-15. "Let's wait for those boys to finish dinner." He studied the sky awash with millions of stars. "Wish we had more cloud cover."

"Don't worry. We're practically invisible." Sutcliffe lifted his chin. "And I can dock this boat as subtle as a minnow on a cruise ship."

"Remember." Eli checked the magazine of his nine-millimeter before strapping it to his hip. "We capture the bridge. We control the ship. They'll have to come to us to retake it."

"Works for me." Sutcliffe pulled the slide on his Glock 40.

Eli checked the horizon. Only a faint hint of sunlight remained. "Lindsey, you good to drive?"

"Yes. I've been watching Dakota since we left the base." Her voice had a nervous quiver. Her eyes darted to the *Leviathan*.

"Good. Sutcliffe and I will board. We'll need you to come get us after we find Tara." Eli glanced at Sutcliffe. "We start in half an hour."

Eli reconnoitered *Leviathan* once more and discovered three members of ship security leading six teenage girls through a doorway that, according to the ship's schematic, was to the lowest deck.

And Tara was with them.

———

Tara marched with Molly and four other girls to the lower deck of *Leviathan*. Riley and his thugs trailed. A tingling sensation crept up and down Tara's neck, partly from anxiety but mostly from a curiosity about what would happen next.

She ignored the fear. Participation in this ridiculous tattoo ritual could be an opportunity for escape.

Riley unlocked a door, opened it, and switched on the light. He positioned two men outside as guards and led everyone else inside. The compact room had carpeted floors and varnished walls the color of old furniture. The sparse furnishings included a hospital gurney, a small podium, and a clay-colored urn.

Commodore, dressed in a thin white linen robe, open at the front revealing his paunch belly, white briefs, and a knife sheathed on his calf waited by the podium. His personal attendant, Marco, entered from the hallway carrying an iron rod and a small lumpy bag.

Tara leaned into Molly. "What's Marco's stick for?"

Molly's eyes widened, totally fixated on Commodore. "Shh. The ceremony will start soon."

Commodore stepped behind the podium.

Marco poured the contents of the bag, which looked a lot like barbecue coals, into the urn, squeezed a stream of noxious fluid from a can, then tossed a lit match into the urn. A whoomph of orange flame flashed.

"Dominus Obsequious Sororium," Commodore chanted.

"Dominus Obsequious Sororium," the girls replied.

Latin? What did it mean?

"I am lord over women," the Commodore said.

"You are lord over us," the girls replied.

Commodore sipped water from a plastic container. "Tonight, we welcome Tara into our elite circle. Although she's only been with us for a short time, she's made tremendous strides. So, to promote her journey of spiritual enlightenment and personal freedom, we accept her into our group of special believers." Commodore's lips parted slightly. His gaze moved up and down Tara's body. "Please, Tara, disrobe."

An icy jolt prickled Tara inside. Disrobe for a measly tattoo? "Why?"

Molly's hand took hold of Tara's shoulders. "It's part of the ceremony."

Outrage and violation coursed through Tara. "It's just a tattoo."

"It's more than that." Commodore undraped his robe and commanded. "Ladies."

Hands grabbed Tara, unbuttoned buttons, unzipped zippers, pulled off her blouse and skirt. She tried to break free but too many girls restrained her.

Tara struggled to focus on what was happening. Fear in the face of physical aggression had her uncertain, powerless to defend herself.

They forced her to the gurney stripped down to her bra and panties.

The scent of smoldering coals filled the room. Commodore stood naked, his skin pale and luminescent except for mottled pink skin on his left breast, an anchor overlaid with the letters CMRE.

———

The attack boat engines purred like a panther. Eli hunched low in the bow.

Lindsey piloted the boat to the *Leviathan's* starboard side.

Sutcliffe stood ready. A rubber-coated grappling hook hung from his right hand. He slung the hook toward the railing. The nylon line uncoiled at his feet, and a soft thud sounded.

Eli scanned his scope along the railing to search for enemy targets. None appeared.

Sutcliffe scampered to the attack boat's stern and threw another hook, securing the boat to the towering *Leviathan.*

Eli hung his rifle over his good shoulder and positioned his body perpendicular to *Leviathan's* hull. His tactical boots gained traction against the slick, painted wood slats. Then he pulled himself upward with barely an ache. God bless Toradol.

Sutcliffe scurried alongside him like a squirrel on a tree trunk. Reaching the wood railing first, he helped Eli over onto the main deck, then lowered the grappling hooks back to Lindsey on the boat. And as planned, she steered the boat off starboard, where she would match *Leviathan's* speed from 200 yards.

Eli set his feet in a stable shooting position on the smooth polished decking, aligned his sight forward, and scanned *Leviathan's* main deck, its towering masts, its sleek curves, its deck lights revealing a path to violence.

Sutcliffe, with his Glock 40 steady, stood in the glow of the ships lighting with a grin as wide as the Gulf Stream. "Having fun yet?"

"A blast—"

A blur crossed to Eli's left. He wheeled and aimed. A man —ship security—stood under a beam, his pistol extended, aimed at Eli. Orange light flashed. Two shots—tchew, tchew.

Eli's hip caught fire.

He lined for a head shot, and double tapped his trigger.

Whop, whop.

Two rounds placed high on the scalp and above the right eye, propelled the tango back to the railing where he slumped to the deck, motionless. Dead.

Sutcliffe rushed to the midship stairwell and Eli followed. Blood dribbled down the side of his calf. The plan was to secure the double doorway to below deck to eliminate any threat from that area. Eli reached for the zip ties to lock the doorways, but each was bolted shut with two-by-sixes slid into metal brackets.

"Why would they do that?" Sutcliffe said.

Eli navigated to the wheelhouse, climbing the stairs to the second level, his wounded hip numbed by adrenaline.

Reaching the top of the staircase, he slowed his breathing, paused three seconds, then charged the wheelhouse with Sutcliffe at his six.

Another shot flashed from the sundeck, the yachts highest level. The deck splintered between Eli and Sutcliffe.

Sutcliffe's Glock 40 erupted. One shot. One distinctive thump of a bullet hitting flesh. And one heavy splash in the Gulf waters.

Using his Ranger training, Eli positioned himself near the wheelhouse entrance for a clear line of sight. He extended his AR-15 to engage any threat inside. Sutcliffe pressed in behind Eli, tapping his shoulder to confirm he was ready.

Certain he'd lost the element of surprise, Eli swiftly breached the wheelhouse door, and slipped into the room, lit mainly by the lights on instrument panels.

The watchman, eyes bulging, chin trembling, stood six feet away, a .45 pistol pointed at Eli's head.

———

"Dominus Obsequious Sororium," rang through Tara's ears.

Marco fanned the flame inside the urn. He shoved the black stick with a rubber handle and wedged it inside the urn.

The other girls continued to force her to the massage table and tightened a strap across her belly. Fear clenched her with confusion and disbelief, struggling to grasp the horrifying mystery of what would happen next. Restraints wrapped around her wrists and ankles, pulling her legs slightly open, like stretching her across an altar, as if she were a pagan sacrifice in some low-budget horror flick.

"It's alright," Molly said. "It's natural to refuse once you've committed. That's how you know this is good for you. It's how you know Commodore's teachings are working for your personal growth."

Good for Tara? Like a tattoo? She wanted to kill Molly. Kill her, kill her, kill her.

"Dominus Obsequious Sororium," Commodore chanted, his face a mask of undisguised lust. He signaled to Marco to hand him the smoldering rod. Commodore blew on the white-hot plate at its end. A metallic aroma hit Tara's nostrils. Tiny flecks of shimmering sparks fell from the metal plate.

"Dominus Obsequious Sororium," the girls repeated in harmony.

Pain invaded Tara's chest and lungs. Her throat bubbled with salvia and bile, stinging her tongue with an acidic tang. Finally, a primal scream escaped from inside her.

"No, no, no. Don't do it. I'm not ready. I'm not."

FORTY-SEVEN

Time slowed inside *Leviathan's* wheelhouse, and Eli's Ranger training took over.

The .45 shook in the watchman's hand like a flag in a summer gust. The man closed his eyes.

Eli dropped to one knee.

Kaboom.

Eli's ears rang from the .45's explosion in close quarters.

The shot missed high and left, clanging against the metal wall.

Eli double tapped the AR-15 trigger, hitting the watchman's starched shirt with a tight grouping on his left breast. Crimson orbs blossomed into one another on the white fabric. The man crumpled to the wood deck, convulsed, then went dead still.

The pilot threw up his arms. "Don't shoot. I'm not armed."

Sutcliffe rushed past Eli, secured the man's hands and feet with zip ties, then gagged his mouth with duct tape.

Eli checked his wounded hip—no damage to bone or major tissues. The bleeding had slowed to a trickle. "I'll clear what I can from here to the main deck. You get this boat turned around."

"You got it." Sutcliffe tilted his pistol to the pilot. "I have all the help I need."

Eli moved aft into battle position, swinging his rifle in horizontal 180-degree arcs. He first cleared a massive stateroom furnished with walnut paneling, expensive furnishings, and a big-screen television. Then he searched the main deck—its staterooms, cabins, and berths. He found the teenage boys with Myles among them, crouching in the narrow galley. "Take a lifeboat and get off this ship," Eli said. "Head north off the starboard."

The boys rushed out of the galley as if they'd found salvation.

Eli grabbed a handful of Myles' grease-stained shirt and jerked him close. "Where's Tara?" His rigid tone conveyed no forgiveness.

Myles' face was pale, weak, shaken. "Down below with Commodore and the other girls. They're doing some kind of weird ceremony." Myles' full body tremors made him believable.

"How many of the crew are armed?" Eli pressed his face closer. "The ones in black."

"Six, including Riley. He's the worst of them all."

"Is he the redhead?"

"Yes, and he's down below."

Eli shot a glance to the stern. Three combatants, including Riley, had gone below with the girls. Three were left upstairs. Eli and Sutcliffe put two down, which left one on the upper decks. Eli released his grip. "Get off the ship with the others."

Eli stalked in a crouch to the rear of the dining area to establish a fatal funnel—a kill zone for any combatant coming up the lone stairwell from the lower deck. He glanced back to the galley. No cover.

He trained his rifle aft despite the armed combatant to his rear. With the tension in his neck rising, he gritted his teeth and steeled himself for the impending fight.

The wind shifted with *Leviathan's* slow arcing turn. Eli pressed his ear pod. "Dakota. I've got the stairwell covered, but there's a threat somewhere on my six. Everything secure up there?"

"Yeah. I'll do a concentrated sweep on my way down. And I have intel. The pilot tells me there's an arsenal midship. AK-47s."

———

Below deck, Tara struggled like a trapped animal to loosen herself from the girls' clutching hands. "Please, God. Help me."

Commodore's tongue glistened his upper lip. "Dominus Obsequious Sororium."

"Dominus Obsequious Sororium," the girls responded over the deafening drone of the nearby engines.

Marco pulled the black iron from the urn. Its flat head blazed white hot with flecks of red.

"Nooo." Tara screamed her throat raw.

Marco handed the iron to Commodore.

He focused his eyes on the glowing red metal, then found hers. His brow dropped, and wrinkles formed on his forehead.

Commodore inched the iron closer to Tara's naked skin.

The area between her hip and bellybutton grew warm, hot, and hotter.

Then, Tara's weight shifted. The heat on her flesh disappeared.

Commodore stepped back and braced his hand against the wall.

The *Leviathan* was turning.

Commodore handed the iron to Marco and glared at Riley. "Why are we changing course?"

Riley glanced at the doorway. "I don't know."

"Go find out, you idiot."

———

Eli controlled his breathing to sight his scope on the dark opening leading below deck.

A man clad in black emerged from the stairwell with his pistol low at his side.

Eli lined his sight to the man's forehead for a quick kill. "Don't move a muscle," he said with calm authority. "On your face, now."

The gunman raised his pistol at Eli.

Eli fired.

The round appeared like a red decimal point on the man's forehead. He fell.

Behind him a patch of red hair ducked down in the stairwell. Riley.

Eli's body shook with an adrenaline rush. He took a deep breath and peered over to the galley opening.

Nothing.

———

At the crack of a gun firing, Tara sensed the hands that clutched her arms and legs let go.

Commodore gaped in the gunfire's direction. "What the hell?"

Riley came through the doorway, his eyes crazed and shaken. "There's trouble up top." He pointed to the stairwell as if to emphasize the problem. "I have a man down."

"Who's out there?" Commodore said.

"Not sure." Riley's nostrils flared in panic. "But we're pinned down here. There's no way out except up those stairs."

Commodore raged. "Why aren't your men fighting up top?"

"I have to assume they're down," Riley said. "Whoever's out there has control of the wheelhouse."

A sliver of hope coursed through Tara only to be met with the image of Freddy killing Uncle Eli.

Commodore pushed Molly to Riley. "Use her to rush whoever's out there."

Molly went without protest or struggle, like a trained dog following its master's command.

––––––––

Eli kept his aim at the stairway opening. Two forms bobbed up from the lower deck, slow and methodical, one in front of the other.

Leading was a young female, long and lean, her chin tucked to her neck, her brow up, her eyes probing like a soldier taking point in a recon patrol. Patches of red hair lurched from behind her as the two moved. Riley's .45 glinted at the end of his arm, oscillating over the girl's right shoulder.

Eli locked his scope on Riley and the girl, hoping to eliminate Riley. But the girl, as if by choice, prevented him a clear shot. Eli lowered his aim to the girl's legs—no shot at Riley beyond them.

Riley's muzzle found Eli.

Eli took cover behind an iron bulkhead to his right and glanced to the galley behind him.

Rhythmic footfalls grew closer as the girl and Riley approached within thirty feet. Five seconds and Eli would be exposed.

There was movement at the galley opening—the missing combatant with an AK-47.

Orange flashes.

Duka-duka-duka-duka.

Chunks of metal flitted from the bulkhead.

The deck exploded into splinters.

Eli dove, then crawled alongside the gunwale, leaving his rifle behind.

From the aft, Riley shed the girl as cover, and with both hands, aimed his .45 at Eli.

Eli took comfort he'd leave this world doing the right thing. But his thoughts became overpowered with an image of Lindsey.

He wasn't ready to die.

FORTY-EIGHT

From the Coast Guard boat, 200 yards south of *Leviathan*, Lindsey watched two armed men attack Eli. Helplessness and desperation overtook her. She closed her eyes and clutched the binoculars so hard her fingers throbbed, but she prayed.

Lord Jesus. You are my strength and my shield. In You, I put my trust.

She'd learned the psalm as a young girl at Safe Harbor. Word's that carried her through many long nights of worry for girls under her care.

Now she prayed for a lifeline from heaven.

Save Eli from the hands of his enemies and deliver him from harm.

The thud of shots fired.

Her spirit spilled out like a river cresting. Her prayers intensified.

Father, I declare that the Spirit of the Lord is with us and that no weapon forged against us will prevail.

Tears formed, but she blinked them away. She stood and shouted. *I command the enemy to bow to Your name and be subdued. You are the Alpha and the Omega, the Beginning, and the End, the First and the Last. You are the One who is, was, and is to come. You alone have the keys to hell, death, and the grave.*

———

Eli stared aft, into the squinting eyes of the girl behind Riley, then into the dark hole of his .45. Eli glanced at the galley and the AK-47 trained on him. He clutched his Glock in its holster. Too late.

A tremendous explosion of light and thunder erupted from the galley. Sutcliffe.

The man with the rifle made an "uunnh" sound, and his weapon fell from his grasp. His head twisted to the side. A long thin breath rattled from his lips, and he collapsed like an accordion.

Sutcliffe burst from the galley like an avenger in a Marvel movie.

The red-headed Riley's face contorted into a mixture of fear and uncertainty. His gaze shifted between Eli and Sutcliffe.

Would he surrender now that he was outgunned?

"Come here Molly." Riley jerked the girl to the front of him, blocking any clear shot.

Molly's eyes flared contempt at Eli, her lips curled into a sneer. "Shoot him," she screamed to Riley.

Riley raised his pistol at Eli, arcing it up with a stiff arm.

Eli's nine-millimeter blast sliced the humid air. The scent of freshly exploded gunpowder filled his nostrils. A thick swirl of blue smoke rose from his Glock's muzzle into the Gulf breeze.

Molly stood stoic.

Riley lay behind her on bloody wood planks.

"What a shot." Sutcliffe's voice seemed distant through

the ringing in Eli's ears. "I don't know how you missed that idiot girl."

Eli pushed himself up from the deck and slow walked to Riley, his Glock ready. Riley's dark sweater grew darker in an ever-increasing patch.

Eli kicked away Riley's .45, checked his carotid artery, and felt it stop. "He's dead." He glanced at Molly.

She displayed no fear—no mouth open, no hands shaking, no eyes widened in terror. Instead, she remained the discordant calm she displayed while acting as Riley's shield.

Suddenly, six girls poured out from the lower deck, with one boy dressed in starched whites. The last armed man in black was with them, his .45 pointed at Sutcliffe.

Sutcliffe aimed his Glock.

Eli did the same.

Their pistols fired in a deafening salvo.

The two slugs slammed into the gunman's chest like a wrecking ball, knocking him back. His face slackened and he fell into the stairwell and disappeared.

Eli leaned low and scurried through the six frantic girls to the stairwell. The man lay sprawled halfway down the stairs.

Sutcliffe organized Molly, the other girls, and the boy in the covered dining area. "How many more are down there?"

One girl blurted, "Just Commodore and Tara."

Molly's eyes blazed. "Shut up, Marcie."

Sutcliffe glared at Marcie. "Keep talking."

Marcie kept talking about the room where Commodore had Tara and what awaited Eli and Sutcliffe below.

Eli didn't hesitate. He descended into the lower deck, his rifle prone, his finger outside the trigger guard.

On the bottom step, he found the room Marcie identified, the room that flickered with a shifting glow caused by the ripple of burning coals—coals to heat a branding iron, Marcie had said.

Eli sensed the same ominous darkness he'd felt in the house two kilometers outside of Shurandam. It was evil below deck on *Leviathan*.

The worst kind of evil.

———

Lindsey pressed her eyes against the binoculars. Eli and Sutcliffe had survived. Then Eli disappeared into Leviathan's lower deck. She prayed out loud.

"Jesus, you said to suffer the children, that their angels see Your Father's face. You said to uphold the fatherless because they're Your heritage."

She swayed. "You protect the widow and the orphan in Your holy habitation. You bring the wicked to ruin."

She pointed her finger skyward. "It would be a shame on Your name if You didn't protect Tara and the other kids on that boat. In the name of Jesus Christ, I beg you take command of this battle and bring Your chosen safely home."

———

Eli's hip burned. Five feet from the door to the room, he stopped, held his breath, and listened to Tara's sobs. He heard footfalls behind him.

Sutcliffe took a knee beside Eli, his pistol up to his shoulder.

From inside, a nervous laugh. "Who's out there? The police? The Coast Guard?" More laughter. "Welcome to my worship."

"Commodore. This is Detective Eli Colt. Send the girl out."

"Uncle Eli," Tara cried.

Tara's voice made all of Eli's suffering seem small—the

struggle with Gina, his injuries at the camp in the Rigolets, the near-death experience upstairs.

The ominous feeling was replaced by an ample supply of hope. Something was different. A powerful, but tender presence Eli had never experienced was nearby.

"I don't think so, Uncle Eli," Commodore said. "You come in, and I'll kill your niece. I've got a very sharp knife at her throat."

"Commodore, listen. Just let Tara come out, and I'll come in. We'll trade. Me for her."

"No, thank you, detective. I like how things are now. If I die, Tara comes with me."

Eli tested the door handle. Unlocked. "We need to talk, and there's not much time. A SWAT team is on its way," Eli lied. "Send the girl out and save yourself."

"Save me from what? I'm eternal." Commodore's tone became more assertive. "When I leave this world, so will Tara."

Eli calculated the odds of Tara's survival. "There's no way out for you, Commodore. You don't have to die, and neither does Tara."

"I'm not scared of dying, detective. That's why I sent everyone up and stayed down here. When I leave this world for the next one, I'll take this special girl to tend to my needs."

Keep Commodore talking. Keep him engaged. "Tell me about this next world. Is it heaven or hell?"

"Oh, that's easy to answer," Commodore said. "Me and your niece will be born again into the flesh of another body. We'll shed these bodies we now possess and live out eternity with immense power over the physical world. Today, I will complete the cycle of birth and death and become pure. Your niece will assist me, as will others who've gone before me and have become incorporeal souls themselves."

Sutcliffe circled a finger around his ear—the universal sign for crazy. Then he pointed a flat hand to inside the room.

Eli declined rushing the room with a shake of his head. "Commodore, I want to hear more. I'm coming in." He touched his Glock at the small of his back, held his AR-15 to his side, non-threatening, and entered the room leaving Sutcliffe in the hall.

The dim amber light of the burning coals revealed Commodore behind Tara, a knife held to Tara's throat. They were propped against the wall near an urn, a rod poked out.

Eli was familiar with the fast pulse of battle—the dry mouth, the heightened senses, the adrenaline rush. But he'd never experienced the pure evil he saw in Commodore. His eyes were black and hollow. His teeth flared behind lips pressed wide to pull up loose jowls. This man was a demon and wanted to die and take Tara with him.

Eli placed his rifle on the floor, then slid it just out of reach of Commodore.

————

Tara didn't dare move. The knife blade Commodore held to her throat, seared into her skin. The room blurred. Her heart fluttered like a captive bird.

Then Uncle Eli tossed his rifle to the ground. She wanted to scream *noooo*, but a sudden surge of courage swept into the room, fueling her spirit with strength.

Commodore bent, reached for the gun. The blade's pressure on Tara's neck eased. She slumped back and let her legs buckle and slid down Commodore's body.

Commodore reset his grip on Tara's shoulders and pulled the knife away.

Tara closed her hand around the branding iron's handle and pressed the hot metal through the robe at his hip.

Commodore wailed.

Tara tore herself away.

———

Eli drew his Glock from behind his back and shot the Commodore, hitting him center mass and slamming him into the wall.

Commodore's eyes went wide, then lost the light that separates life from death. His chin dropped, his head tilted forward, he fell, and his lifeless body toppled the urn.

The burning coals ignited the plush carpet, and the flames flashed like wildfire in a dry forest, setting the paneled walls ablaze.

———

Intense heat hit Tara. The acrid scent of burning carpet mingled with choking black smoke. She rushed away from the crackling inferno into Uncle Eli's arms.

He pushed her into the hallway, into the hands of another man. "Get her out of here, Sutcliffe. This boat's like dry kindling."

Sutcliffe grabbed Tara's wrist and hurried her to the stairs. "The ship's engine holds about 12,000 liters of diesel," he shouted over the hissing of burning wood. "When those tanks get hot enough, this ship will blow."

Eli followed Tara and Sutcliffe up the stairs. "The crew took the lifeboats. We'll need to jump overboard, and hope Lindsey will come get us."

They sprinted to the midship starboard railing and shed their shoes for the swim.

"Where's Commodore?" A hysterical voice screamed from the shadows. Molly held a stainless-steel pistol like the one Riley had carried.

Everybody froze.

Finally Sutcliffe shouted. "Down in the belly of this whale, you stupid girl. And if you don't come with us, you'll be broiled like a shrimp dinner."

"He's dead?" Molly bawled with maddening anger.

"He's reborn." Tara feigned a shaky voice. "He's shed his body and is now pure."

Molly lifted the gun and aimed at Tara. "I should have stayed. I'd be with him now and for all eternity."

Tara forced an affectionate smile. "You can still join, him." She touched Molly's gun with her left hand and directed it down.

Molly dipped her head and sobbed. "How?"

Tara swung her angry fist, hitting Molly flush on the cheekbone, sending her to the wood planks.

Sutcliffe grabbed Tara, preventing her from swinging again.

FORTY-NINE

Lindsey stared through her binoculars at the second lifeboat, but no sign of Eli, Sutcliffe, or Tara on board. Alarm gripped Lindsey. She struggled to breathe. "Where are they? Where's Eli?" Panic rose from her belly.

Should she catch up with those kids in the lifeboat and ask what they knew? Should she maneuver closer to *Leviathan*? Should she wait here? Her mind darted between options, each carrying its own risk of her not being ready when Eli and Sutcliffe needed her.

Movement on *Leviathan*. A figure in white stirred in the shadows—a tall, lean girl.

Lindsey edged the throttle forward.

More movement. Sutcliffe and another girl in white running across the main deck. Tara? Eli limped behind them.

Black smoke rose to the heavens from the ship. Then orange flames billowed, mirrored in the calm water.

Lindsey shoved the throttle full forward. The boat sped to *Leviathan*. Painful thoughts ran through her head. Eli was injured—again. The smoke. The fire. Would he get off the ship alive?

One hundred yards from *Leviathan*. Eli now at the rail. But he didn't jump. They didn't jump.

Please, Lord, get them off that boat.

———

Tara helped Uncle Eli into one of the lifejackets, then put on her own. Together, they leaped and hit the inky water.

Uncle Eli threw back his head and let out an insane wail.

Tara's heart lurched. "Let me help you. You're hurt." Water spilled over her bottom lip.

Sutcliffe and Molly splashed beside them seconds later.

Uncle Eli scissor-kicked and paddled with one arm. "I'm fine. Swim to the boat that's heading this way."

The man Uncle Eli called Sutcliffe swam behind them with Molly in tow.

Tara wouldn't leave Uncle Eli to swim alone. She grabbed his shirt, kicked her legs, and stroked her free arm alongside him. Grasping for air, she waved at the boat speeding toward them and screamed, "Hurry."

The boat coasted nearer. The pretty woman, Uncle Eli's girlfriend was behind the wheel.

Tara forced her legs to kick harder, harder, until finally, she felt the rubber hull.

Sutcliffe climbed in first, pulled in Molly, then Tara, and then Uncle Eli.

Uncle Eli clutched his shoulder and winced. "Get this boat out of here."

———

Eli collapsed into Lindsey's arms, the effects of the Toradol injection had worn off. His shoulder seared, his hip burned, his entire body heavy with exhaustion. His discomfort pulsated with every winded breath.

But with Tara sitting beside him, his joy burned brighter than his pain as they sped away from the fiery *Leviathan*.

Tara appeared to recognize Lindsey and Eli's affection. She gifted him with an approving smile.

Lindsey's eyes lit up like a constellation. "You made it. You saved Tara and made it back to me alive." Her voice rang like a melody.

Eli looked back at *Leviathan*, flames licking the night sky.

A massive boom. The shockwave rumbled through him.

Lindsey pulled him closer. He felt her breath on his neck. With a tender turn of his face, she leaned in and pressed her lips against his.

An electric surge ignited a fire that warmed Eli from his lips to his very core. It was a kiss that awakened his heart and confirmed what he'd tried to deny when he'd met her. His and Lindsey's future would be lived together.

FIFTY

Amid tall pines reaching skyward and the distant hint of briny saltwater from nearby Lake Pontchartrain, Eli stood at the back of the rented lot beside an old single-wide trailer. Hands up, he directed Sutcliffe, who maneuvered the Airstream attached to his F-250 pickup.

"Turn your wheel a touch to the left to catch the ramp," Eli said over the rumble of the truck's engine. "Now, straighten her out nice and easy."

In the side mirror, Sutcliffe's reflection, brow wrinkled in concentration, nodded. The camper mounted onto the blocks and straightened into a perfectly parked position.

Eli clenched his left fist. "Whoa."

The camper stopped. Sutcliffe shut off the engine and jumped from his truck. "Nice place," he said with abundant sarcasm. "Real private-like."

Cedro came out of the camper's front door carrying a bubble level. "Trailer's level."

Zeke gathered the unused blocks and ramps and set them in the back of his pickup. "This place ain't so bad. At least Gina can't kick you out."

"I'd call that a bonus." Eli pulled out an ice chest from his fully packed Jeep, then pointed at the picnic table set in a patch of grass to the side of his camper. He hadn't seen Zeke or Cedro in over a month. Not since he'd escaped Gina's plantation. "I have a realtor looking for a couple of acres for me to buy in Madisonville, not far from Safe Harbor and Lindsey."

Sutcliffe sat across from Eli. "That's pretty ambitious, you being unemployed."

Eli grabbed a Diet Coke from the ice chest. "I'll land on my feet. Maybe Madisonville PD could use an ex-Army detective."

Sutcliffe snapped open a can of Pepsi. "Ask if they want an FBI-trained agent who made a big splash on the evening news."

"Who would've thought a 150-foot yacht catching fire and sinking less than a mile from shore would get so much media attention?" Eli said with his own brand of sarcasm.

"Or that the FBI is more concerned about their image than actually solving crimes." Sutcliffe air quoted "*solving crimes.*"

Cedro scrunched his forehead. "So, what the FBI said on the news wasn't true?"

Sutcliffe sipped his Pepsi. "Let's just say their involvement may have been a bit exaggerated since I was the only one there from the FBI."

"Then why weren't you on TV?" Cedro asked. "Y'all saved all thirteen kids on board. Some of them were my friends."

"My guess would be politics." Zeke rummaged through the ice in the chest. "Dang. No Yoo-hoo?"

Sutcliffe frowned. "Let's just say what the bureau's public relations said in front of the news cameras ain't what they told me behind closed doors,"

Zeke's eyes narrowed into thin slits. "They fired you?"

"Not fired," Sutcliffe said. "Promised I'd never see a

promotion in my lifetime, which had Dad almost disowning me."

The full force of Sutcliffe losing his job weighed on Eli. "I'm sorry your career with the FBI is over because of me."

"I'm not. I'm as suitable for the FBI as fireworks and confetti are for a funeral."

Zeke patted Cedro's shoulder. "At least Cedro's got some good news."

"Yeah?" Eli said. "What, you're nailing it at school?"

"I am. But that's not my news." Cedro sat straighter like he'd been preparing what he had to say for some time. "The thing is, I've been born again."

Eli's gaze wandered away from Cedro. The subject of being born again and miracles confused him. Like when Doc Leena shared about God bringing her husband back to life. And when Lindsey shared her being filled with the Holy Spirit.

"That's a Christian thing, right?" Sutcliffe asked.

Cedro ran his finger around the rim of his Mountain Dew. "Yes. The day Eli found me at Clancy's, I was broken. So broken a maniac like Commodore convinced me he could give my life purpose." Cedro reached over the table and touched Eli's forearm. "Then you took me to Zeke's diner, and Zeke brought me to live with the Andersons at their farm. Mr. Bob and Miss Carol showed me my life was filled with regret and sin." Cedro's tone turned sober. "And they showed me what love really looks like. He raised his bright eyes and looked at Eli, then Sutcliffe. "So, a couple of Sundays ago, when the preacher at church asked if anyone wanted to repent of their sins and give their life to God, I walked up to the altar and prayed that Jesus would forgive me for all the bad stuff I'd done."

"So you got religion?" Sutcliffe said.

"I don't know...maybe." Cedro rubbed his scalp. "What I

do know is that I started feeling better...you know...inside. So good, I got baptized last Sunday."

"That's my man," Zeke said.

Eli's heart slipped into a familiar crisis, resisting a strange sense of urgency to embrace God. How could God forgive him for not saving Aziz in Afghanistan? Despite saving Tara, those nightmares raged on. Was he broken like Cedro had been? "What's changed?"

"Me," Cedro said. "Once I accepted Jesus, the heavy weight I'd been carrying disappeared. Mr. Bob calls it repentance. He says it's surrendering my life and letting God control everything."

"I'm happy for you, Cedro," Eli said.

"What about you, Mr. Eli?" Cedro asked. "I know Miss Lindsey's is born again. She told me when she talked to me in Solace." Cedro's gaze got dead serious. Piercing. "Are you born again?"

How could Eli be born again if he struggled to understand the concept? Repentance? Forgiveness? Weights lifted? He glanced up the road to avoid answering Cedro's question.

Thankfully, Julia Colt's RAV4 hugged the bend on the road leading to the lot. Julia, Tara's mom, was driving, and Tara sat in the passenger seat.

Lindsey's Civic followed close behind.

"This is a surprise," Sutcliffe said.

"Not really." Cedro waved. "I texted Miss Lindsey when we got here."

Eli didn't realize Cedro and Lindsey continued to communicate after they'd talked at the Anderson's farm.

"She wanted me to meet Tara." Cedro stood and stepped toward the car. "We have something in common."

Of course. *Leviathan*.

Tara and Julia exited the RAV4, but Lindsey stayed in her car, her phone at her ear.

Eli hadn't seen Julia since he'd brought Tara home the night, he, Sutcliffe, and Lindsey rescued her from Commodore. The same night he'd learned Julia had sent her boyfriend Rick packing.

Julia looked years younger. The tight lines around her eyes and creases on her forehead had faded. "Thought we'd come check out your new digs," she said. "Nice." Her tone wasn't convincing.

"Julia, this is Dakota Sutcliffe. He was with us— "

"Tara told me." Julia hugged Sutcliffe. "Thank you for saving my little girl."

A goofy smile spread across Sutcliffe's flushed cheeks.

Julia turned her attention to Cedro. "And you must be Cedro. Lindsey has told me so much about you." Julia placed her hand on Tara's shoulder. "This is my daughter Tara. I think y'all have much to talk about."

Lindsey got out of her Civic and waved her phone. "Manny's been trying to reach you."

"My phone's in the Jeep," Eli said. "We've been setting up the camper for the past hour."

Her stride was eager and had purpose. "He says NOPD is getting dozens of calls asking how to contact you." Her voice brimmed with enthusiasm.

"Contact me?" Eli said. "Why?"

"To get your help to find kids who've gone missing," Lindsey's eye's radiated enthusiasm.

A jolt of energy prickled Eli's skin. "How many calls?"

"Dozens, according to Manny." Lindsey's voice trembled with a delicate quiver. "He wants to know if you'll help."

Sutcliffe's brow quirked with curiosity. "Who are these kids?"

"Some are open missing persons files. Others have never been reported," Lindsey said.

"I certainly have the time," Eli said with a long exhale. "But I'll need help."

"Here's an idea." Sutcliffe's voice carried a steady cadence. "My father is on the board of a handful of non-profits that raise millions to fund art centers, hospitals, and natural conservatories." Sutcliffe ran his eyes from Tara to Cedro. "What cause could be more vital than rescuing kids in harm's way?"

"What are you suggesting?" Eli asked.

"That you and I establish an organization whose mission statement is to find or rescue these missing kids."

A light shiver rolled in Eli's gut. He and Sutcliffe had made a good team. They proved that rescuing Tara from *Leviathan*. But a non-profit? How did that work?

Julia's eyes gushed with glee. "And I'll help. God knows I understand how critical that mission is."

Tara bounced on her toes. "Me too."

Eli's stomach now churned. After years of being estranged from his family, he felt hopeful—hopeful that with the help of those around him, he could make a real difference in the lives of children and maybe, just maybe—cancel his debt for the Afghan boy, Aziz. "I'm not sure I'd know how to set this up." Eli glanced at Lindsey for assurance.

Lindsey's eyes sparkled. She clasped her hands together. "I know people. Good people. Donors who give faithfully to Safe Harbor. They'd be happy to help get you started."

Cedro cleared his throat. "I know what it's like to be one of those missing kids. I think you should do it."

With eyes glistening like wet lacquer, Lindsey stepped close to Eli. "Don't worry. God's got this. His plan is wonderful, and His wisdom magnificent." She slid an arm around his waist and leaned her head against his shoulder. "And I'll help you where I can."

Eli rubbed his hands together as he shifted his weight.

"But where do we start?" The words were staggered in hesitant bursts.

Lindsey's expression showed unwavering confidence. "It will be an exciting journey of faith, patience, and determination." An unmistakable air of confidence shined in her eyes. "Look, I don't have all the answers, and you'll make mistakes along the way." She placed her hand on Eli's chest. "But you can learn from God's Word and be led by His Holy Spirit. Through prayer and alignment with Jesus, and with the help of the people He's given you, you can do any job God gives you. I'm a living testimony."

A resolute smile played on Lindsey's lips as if she'd just seen a tiny light at the end of a long dark tunnel. "Eli, you've found your purpose. Now go for it."

Eli wasn't sure about what Lindsey was saying, but he couldn't deny the tugging in his heart. Seeing Lindsey's faith and confidence, he felt a surge of courage that emboldened him to step out.

He took a deep breath and exhaled slowly. "You're right," he said with growing conviction. "Let's do this."

FIFTY-ONE

Andre Badeau lounged in a beach chair surrounded by sand, under the shade of lush palm trees. He sipped a sugary Monkey La La from a tall glass and the Caribbean breeze from Roatan Island's West Bay soothed his warm, sun-bronzed skin. He was looking more indigenous to Honduras than to South Louisiana.

Although he was living like royalty on the Central American resort island, he missed his high-end riverfront condo, his busy schedule, his organization that managed an inventory of girls. But more than anything, he missed New Orleans.

He loved this island—for a vacation. But he was not the sort to spend his time idle. He'd acquired skills that required hard work. And possessed something critical to his return in New Orleans—a library of video recordings of men and women in powerful positions doing horrible things to kids. With that, he would rule New Orleans like his mentor, Javier, once did.

His nephew Freddy loved Roatan Island, sleeping late every day and getting high with tourist girls every night.

Badeau was setting a bad example. They needed to get out of this nirvana-like prison, get home, and get back to work.

The news from New Orleans was encouraging. Eli Colt had somehow rescued Tara from Commodore, something Badeau had to admit was impressive. But he'd learned from his informant at NOPD, Colt was no longer a police officer and had no power or authority. Something about jilting the daughter of a small-town mayor in Mississippi.

Javier had died last month, and the punk Marsh assumed control of what was rightfully Badeau's—Javier's empire. Marsh was over his head trying to deal with degenerate johns, cops, and politicians who had lusts for underage boys and girls. It was time for Badeau to get back in the game.

Freddy, finally awake from a long night of drug and drink, his eyes red and puffy, his hair disheveled like an old mop, plopped into the adjacent chair. "What's up for today, Unc?"

"Same thing as yesterday," Badeau said. "But don't get too comfortable. We're going home real soon."

PLEASE LEAVE A REVIEW

If you have enjoyed this book, it would be a tremendous help if your could leave a review.

Reviews help me gain visibility and bring my books to the attention of other readers who may enjoy them. You can leave a review on My Book page.

Get Exclusive Will Marler Material

Building a relationship with my readers is the best thing about writing. Join my Legacy Readers Club for more information on new books and deals plus:

A free copy of Eli Colt's adventure in Helmand Province, Afghanistan—"The Silver Star."

You can get your content for free by signing up on my website at www.willmarler.com.

About the Author

Will Marler is an emerging author of Christian crime thrillers. He grew up in New Orleans, Louisiana and now lives on the Gulf Coast of Mississippi with his wife, Wendie, and their 100-pound Rottweiler, Bear. This is Will's debut novel.

For more information:
www.willmarler.com
will@willmarler.com

www.ingramcontent.com/pod-product-compliance
Lightning Source LLC
Chambersburg PA
CBHW020652110726
47901CB00001B/164